BLAINE L. PARDOE

CONFEDERACY OF FEAR

BOOK THREE IN THE BLUE DAWN SERIES

D1600105

DEFIANCE PRESS
& PUBLISHING

ISBN-13: 978-1-955937-58-0 (Paperback)
ISBN-13: 978-1-955937-57-3 (eBook)

Published by Defiance Press and Publishing, LLC

Bulk orders of this book may be obtained by contacting Defiance Press and Publishing, LLC at: www.defiancepress.com.

Public Relations Dept. – Defiance Press & Publishing, LLC
281-581-9300
pr@defiancepress.com

Defiance Press & Publishing, LLC
281-581-9300
info@defiancepress.com

"The secret of freedom lies in educating people, whereas the secret of tyranny is in keeping them ignorant."
Maximilien Robespierre

ACKNOWLEDGEMENTS

I began this book just before the evacuation from Afghanistan as I was finishing *A Most Uncivil War*. We faced a humiliating and unnecessarily costly withdrawal from that country that was one of the worst planned military operations since Custer at Little Bighorn. Out of that debacle, a character was born in this novel, Su-Hui. Everything has repercussions, and I knew that what happened in Afghanistan could possibly impact other parts of the world. I hope the fate of Taiwan in the real world is better than what I fictionally portray. If my perspectives upset anyone in the communist Chinese government, I make zero apologies.

This is a novel about friendships and people fighting for ideals above ideas. Conflicting ideals and views about the future of our nation are merely the backdrop for these stories. An underlying theme in this novel is the love of daughters and sisters—Maddie, Maria, and Ya-ting and what we do to protect the ones we love. As this new fictional American Civil War broadens, so does the violence and brutality in my novels about the subject.

My thanks to the real-life Jack for his suggestions on the Supermax and the challenges it presents. Also to my loving wife who listened to me plan a prison break for weeks at a time. While I may end up on a do-not-fly list for this, it was probably worth it.

DEDICATION

To my aunts, Christine Miller and Marlene Pardoe. When my mother struggled during her war with ovarian cancer, both of these strong-willed women were incredible help both physically and emotionally. We went through a lot together—much like the characters in this novel. Strong women make for great characters, and even better relatives. I think of both of you often, so enjoy.

THE KEY CHARACTERS

Alex – Short for Alexandria (no last name given). Former Congresswoman from New York, she sits on the Ruling Council and commands the National Security Force (NSF) as its Secretary. She removed her opposition and folded the Social Enforcers into the NSF. She is the Newmerica Vice President-Elect.

Randy Birdsell. Leader of the Sons of Liberty (SOL) in New Hampshire.

Trudy Ford. Member of the Sons of Liberty (SOL) from the Upper Peninsula of Michigan.

Andy Forest. Andy's father was a member of the Sons of Liberty (SOL) and Andy was instrumental in recovering the original copy of the Constitution and Declaration of Independence.

Frank Campbell. Private investigator in Virginia.

Rebecca (Becky) Clarke. The Director of the Truth Reconciliation Committee (TRC) and member of the Ruling Council. Was instrumental in seizing control of Congress during the Liberation.

Travis Cullen. Former Navy SEAL, now a covert operative supporting the American administration.

Jack Desmond. Former Director of the Secret Service and now the American President's Chief of Staff. Jack was instrumental in bringing the former American Vice President to power and for years was the clandestine leader of the Sons of Liberty (SOL).

General James J. Donaldson. Commanding General, Newmerican Army.

Dominic Gant. NSF Operative.

General Hank Griffiths. Commanding General of the New Hampshire National Guard.

Deja Jordan. A Social Enforcer from Minneapolis.

Charli Kazinski. Current Director of the American Secret Service. For years she lived as an NSF officer named Angel Frisosky to avoid detection. She was with the last President when he died.

Caylee Leatrom. Former NSF Operative, she has flipped sides and now offers her skills to the Americans. She killed Alex's mother and brother.

Senator Earl Taft Lewis. One of the few surviving Senators after the Liberation.

Maria Lopez. Sister of Raul Lopez.

Raul Lopez. Former member of the Youth Corps, his murder of a man led to riots in Detroit. As a member of the Sons of Liberty (SOL), he liberated the Social Enforcement Camp at Valley Forge.

Rosa Lopez. Mother of Raul Lopez.

Captain Judy Mercury. Officer in the Texas National Guard and the American Army.

Daniel Porter. Former Chairman of the Ruling Council, and the President-Elect of Newmerica. Daniel orchestrated the overthrow of the government during the Liberation/Fall.

General Trip Reager. Renowned and scorned for his actions in San Antonio several year back, Reager is a Texan who is loyal to the American cause and is the Commanding General of the American Army.

David Steele. Maddie's younger brother.

Grayson Steele. Former conservative member of the Virginia House of Delegates and Maddie's and David's father.

Ted (no last name given). Former Texas Senator held prisoner by Newmerica.

Valerie Turner. Former New York City police commissioner, leader of a Sons of Liberty (SOL) cell from New York.

Rita Zhang. NSF Operative.

Hachi Zhou. Wife of Su-Hui, she is an active
member in the Sons of Liberty (SOL).

Su-Hui Zhou. Refugee from Taiwan. He is a
leader in the Sons of Liberty (SOL).

Ya-ting Zhou. Daughter of Hachi and Su-Hui.

Acronyms:

ADMAX – Administrative Maximum Facility – the
Supermax Prison's official designation.

ANTIFA – Acronym for Anti-Fascists. These radicals
violently rioted during the summer of 2020 in an effort to
influence the presidential election. They evolve into the
roles of Social Enforcers in the Newmerican nation.

ATF – Bureau of Alcohol, Tobacco, and Firearms. With the formation
of the NSF, this agency is now part of that new organization.

CHOP – Capitol Hill Occupied Protest. The occupation
of Seattle by protesters in 2020.

Fedgov – The Newmerican rebranding of the federal government.

FOIA – Freedom of Information Act

IWB – the Immigrant Welcoming Bureau formerly Immigration
and Customs Enforcement prior to the Fall.

JCS – The military Joint Chiefs of Staff.

NSF – National Security Force. This is combination of
all federal and local law enforcement agencies.

SAC – Special Agent in Charge.

SE – Social Enforcement. Groups supporting the
Newmerican government that operate beyond the law,
inflicting their own 'social justice' as they see fit.

SOL – Sons of Liberty. These groups of patriots
partisans fight for the restoration of America.

TRC – Truth Reconciliation Committee. Working with Big Tech and the mainstream media, the TRC determines what truth is and what is misinformation. It clears all official stories and either censors or blocks those that would be considered dangerous.

UP – Upper Peninsula of Michigan

UVA – the University of Virginia

PROLOGUE

*"Most people who use the word
'freedom' mean the opposite."*

Five Years Earlier ...
Arlington, Virginia, the Pentagon

Colonel James J. Donaldson stood rigid at attention in front of the Joint Chiefs of Staff (JCS). He had been summoned down three minutes earlier, and when he entered the room, he could feel the tension in the air as if it were static electricity. Part of the reason was the alert that the Pentagon was under. The rioters in the city had fired some sort of projectiles at the building, prompting an emergency sheltering for several tense minutes. It was a grim hint of the chaos that was unfolding across the Potomac in Washington DC. The riots had been expected, but these were different; they were morphing into something much larger, more planned. "Reporting as ordered," he said.

The Chairman looked up at him. "Colonel, as you no doubt realize, we have a dynamic situation unfolding right now. Do you know General Cooper?"

Brigadier General Harold Cooper was an old friend of the Colonel's his, all of the way back to their days at West Point. "Yes sir."

The Army Chief of Staff joined in, "Colonel, General Cooper has been given orders by the President ... illegal orders under the Constitution as we see it. He is organizing a force to go to the White House. Given that these are invalid and unethical orders, I am ordering you to take your security team and apprehend him and stop this rescue mission. No relief is to be sent against the civilian matter unfolding in DC. Understood?" The Army Chief of Staff nodded as well, giving his unspoken consent.

"Yes sir," he said. *Jesus, Harry, what have you gotten yourself into to piss off the JCS?* He thought.

The Chairman took over the conversation. "Under no circumstance is he or the people he's trying to assemble to leave this building. You and your people are authorized to use whatever force you see fit to prevent that. Now go … dismissed." The Chairman's words seared into his brain. *Whatever force you see fit …*

As he left the room, he heard a rumble in the distance. On a normal night, he might think that it was an approaching thunderstorm. This was not a normal night, not by a long shot. Rioters, tens of thousands of them if you believed the press, were swarming Washington DC. The White House was under attack and there were reports that the Capitol had been taken over. Several mortar rounds had landed in the parking lot at the Pentagon where he worked, setting cars ablaze and putting the entire building on alert.

He grabbed the attention of two security officers as he moved through the outer ring corridor, "Secure the exits," he ordered. Full lockdown. General Cooper nor any other force is to leave this building. Order up the ready response team. Send one squad to meet me at General Cooper's office; the others are to move to reinforce the exits. No one is in or out. Got it?"

They confirmed the orders and took off running down the hall. Donaldson took the elevator up to the third floor and went to his office. In his desk was his SIG Sauer M17. He put in a magazine and chambered a round. *The old man said whatever force … let's hope I don't have to use this.*

General Cooper's office was half-way around the ring on the same floor. After strapping on his holster and several spare clips, he began to run down the hallway. He was winded by the time he reached his old friend's office, a nagging reminder that he needed to step up his gym routine. Pausing at the door, he was unsure if he should knock or simply step in. Donaldson opted for a moment of surprise and opened the door.

There, behind his desk, was Brigadier General Harry Cooper, fumbling to strap on his tactical vest. He looked up and saw Donaldson as he entered. The General's eyes were transfixed on the weapon that was aimed at him.

Cooper stopped adjusting his vest strap and glared at him squarely with his light blue eyes. "Colonel, lower that weapon."

"Sir, I have been ordered to bring you into custody," he said, closing the door behind him.

"I am operating on orders from the President of the United States, your Commander in Chief," Harry replied.

"I have been told that those orders are invalid sir."

"They are not," Harry said. "The White House is under attack for Christ's sake! I am going to pull together whatever I can and get over there to provide security for them. I've already got a team of SEALs prepping their gear."

Things in DC are as bad as I thought. For Donaldson, this had been coming since the President had been sworn in, almost four years earlier. *He's pushed the American people too far, and they are finally pushing back. Good!* Many senior officers had disliked the man. There had been many a secret meeting in the Pentagon—some of which he had been part of—that talked about removing the President from office. The Chairman had hinted that he wouldn't follow orders he deemed inappropriate from the traitor in the White House. *Now it's finally happening! The people are standing up to his pompous bullshit.* It wasn't just that he had dodged the draft; half of the senior citizens in Washington DC had done that. It was his arrogance and his dismantling of social programs within the armed forces. *He has no right to try and undo the natural order of things. Harry, you are backing the wrong person.* "The Chairman and the Army Chief of Staff themselves ordered me to have you stand down, General."

"My orders supersede yours," he barked. "We don't have time for this stupid-ass debate. They are swarming the White House as we speak." There was something in his voice, a passion. Donaldson wanted to shake his head. *You were always so damned conservative Harry, and that's your downfall.*

"General, we go way back," he said calmly. "You are backing the wrong horse."

"How can you say that James? We have a chain of command. The President is at the top of it."

"He's unfit for the office," Colonel Donaldson replied coldly. "His stand against transgenders and gays is fucked up. Everyone in the senior command ranks knows it. It's outdated and prejudicial thinking. On top of that, he is trying to pull us out of the Middle East. We have had people fighting and dying there for decades, and he wants to cut and run. Men and women we went through the academy with died there, and that arrogant ass wants us to just pack up and leave? He needs to step down. The people know it; that is why they are rising up across the Potomac. What are you going to do, go out there and start shooting up a bunch of college kids protesting?"

"They aren't protesting," the General said. "They shelled this building a few minutes ago. They are trying to overthrow the government. And I won't use deadly force unless I have to. But I sure as hell am not going to let them overthrow the President of the United States in some third-world coup. I swore an oath!"

"They aren't trying to overthrow the government; they're trying to overthrow *him*," he replied. "He's a petty dictator. The people have spoken. He was voted out of office."

"He's called for new elections," snapped Cooper. "That's all."

The situation had been brewing for weeks. With the death of the President-Elect from an alleged aneurism and the assassination of the VP Elect, the nation had been struggling with a constitutional crisis. Donaldson saw it for what it was—a power grab by the tyrant in the White House. "He should hand it over to the Speaker of the House. That's what he's supposed to do."

"That's not what the Supreme Court said," Cooper snarled. "He's still the President, at least until the 20th of January. And I have a sworn duty to his office and the Constitution—as do you. We have a chain of command, and he's at the top, like it or not." He took a step to come from around the desk, but Cooper angled the gun at him a bit more menacingly.

"Hold it right there Harry," he said, dropping his old friend's rank. "You aren't going anywhere."

"Goddamn it James," the General replied. "Every minute we stand here, the situation gets worse. Step aside and let me follow my orders. Let me do my damned job!" He took another step, but Colonel Donaldson moved to block him.

"General … Harry … don't make me do this. Think about what side of history you want to be remembered for."

"That's one of the reasons you never got bumped upstairs James. You spent all of your time worrying about how things looked, rather than simply doing what was right and what was necessary. I'm not making you do a thing. Now, one last time, step aside, *Colonel.*"

The verbal salvo from the General hit home hard. Donaldson didn't waver. He held his ground. It hit him in that moment that the fate of the country hung with his next actions. *If I do what he wants, then the President is saved and we are forced to endure another four years of his Tweets and rants against the media. I am all that is between that and new leadership.* His blood pressure soared, and his temples pounded with each beat of his heart.

The General attempted to walk past him, taking that final step. Donaldson turned on him and squeezed the trigger. The bullet hit his left cheek, blowing out the back of his skull and spraying it on the flag hanging off to the right of his desk. General Cooper's dead body fell forward, right at him, hitting his knees on the way down.

Colonel Donaldson stood there for a moment, trembling slightly, tasting the gunpowder in his nose and on the back of his tongue. He had never fired a weapon in battle—his combat duties had left him deskbound for most of his career. Now he had killed a man, a fellow warrior. Tonight though, he had fired the most important shot in history. Carefully he holstered his sidearm, still shaking slightly from the excitement.

A bit of blood had splattered his left hand. He rubbed it, further smearing the crimson gore. He continued to rub it, rolling the tiny film of blood to where it wasn't visible. *There, it's gone.*

Everything will change because of me ...

Four Years Earlier ...
The Pacific Ocean East of Taiwan
Su-Hui Zhou remembered glancing over his shoulder back to his homeland of Taiwan and seeing the swirls of smoke rising from far too many places on the tiny island. The sight of it getting smaller in the distance made him weep, if only for a few minutes. His nation, his cultural identity, his job, his friends—everything has gone. He had saved most of his family, but they were far from safety, and his enemies were known to be ruthless.

Su-Hui had been a midlevel executive at Formosa Plastics Corporation when the initial attack had begun last week. Taiwan's fate had always been precarious on the world stage. It was the last bastion of true capitalism, and China resented their freedom and prosperity. The People's Republic, a name that on its own was a contradiction of words, had always claimed they were a 'breakaway republic'. That phrase was both a reminder and a threat to the Taiwanese people. "We still see you as part of us … and one day, you will be again." For generations, they had lived with the knowledge that across the Straits, a looming monster, 'the red dragon,' as his mother had called the threat, eyed them hungrily, waiting for the right moment to absorb them back into their communist fold.

There were things that had held China in check, namely the United States of America and its pledge to protect Taiwan. With the so-called Liberation, America had morphed overnight into something else—Newmerica. Just thinking about the rebranded nation made him angry. When China began being aggressive, with dangerous penetrations of his country's air space, and their deployment of aircraft carriers to the region, Newmerica was called upon to do what it had done before—rattle its saber. This time, it was different. The new quasi-socialists of Newmerica did something they had never done before when his people asked for protection.

They said *no*.

Their response was far from blunt. Flowery language about 'self-determination,' and 'China's historic claims to Formosa,' had been like pouring gasoline onto a bonfire. Everyone knew what it meant—Newmerica's vast military would not risk itself if China pushed to seize the island. A pending sense of doom seemed to smother his people. *We knew what was coming, and now there was nothing to prevent the inevitable.*

It was not a complete surprise. Almost as soon as the Ruling Council had come into power three years ago, they had knee-jerked the US military out of Afghanistan under the pretense of, "We accomplished our mission there." The Afghan government collapsed, and the Taliban took over, only to be replaced by more extremists and terrorists, including a resurging ISIS. The Newmerican press didn't cover the debacle, but international media sources did. Over a hundred thousand Afghan refugees flooded into the United States as their former nation plunged into utter chaos. Afghanistan had devolved into partisan tribal conflicts and a terrorist safe haven. The botched withdrawal was a signal to the allies of the former United States. All bets were off. *Even the North Koreans have begun firing missiles again ... they all know that Newmerica has no will to fight a war overseas.*

The Chinese read the tea leaves, eyeing Taiwan like a hungry tiger stares at fresh prey. The fighting started three weeks ago—the air battle over the island was spectacular, and it was terrifying to watch unfold. China had the numbers on its side, and slowly the Republic of China Air Force made the mainland Chinese suffer, even managing to counter-attack and sink one of their aircraft carriers. It was a fleeting moment of national pride that evaporated quickly. In the end though, the numbers of the enemy prevailed.

The communist Chinese navy forced landings in the Straits and with air superiority secured, the defenders were slaughtered. Helicopter forces deployed in New Taipei City on the north end of the island with devastating results. The surge of the communist Army was relentless. *They didn't care what they destroyed or how many men it took to secure victory.*

Su-Hui owned a small sailboat that he used for short trips on the weekends out of Taitung. Once the invasion began, he evacuated his family, loading the boat down with supplies and everything of value that they owned, and fled. Now, days later, there were times he felt like he could almost hear the wails of his homeland as it fell; the wails were carried skyward from the fighting in plumes of fires.

The journey thus far had not been easy. His mother was in perpetual fear and trembling, and she was somewhat confused by everything that had happened. She talked constantly about going home. Su-Hui's daughter was seasick on day two and had not reached the edge of the boat in time to throw up. Vomit and sea spray had been impossible to clean up. The food they ate was cold out of the cans; there was no means for heating it. His face sported the ragged start of a beard ... he didn't want to waste water on something like shaving. Sunburn seared the back of his neck and legs, but he ignored it.

His sailboat was not alone. Over a hundred boats of every kind were fleeing Taiwan. They stayed close to each other in case one of them ran into problems. One motor launch lost its engine, but was being towed by a larger sailing ship at this point. Another sunk with some of the passengers rescued by those boats that could get there in time.

They were sailing east because there were rumors of the Chinese navy sinking similar flotillas of refugees that were heading south. There was no leadership in the people that were fleeing; they huddled together almost on an instinctive level … a tribal sense of safety in numbers.

On day three of their flight, the wind died down, and the small flotilla slowed on the seas. A Chinese fighter jet roared low over them at one point nearly panicking his elderly mother who was in the cabin of the boat. The constant bombing during the invasion had terrorized her and his youngest child. Clearly the fighter must have seen them, but it did not launch an attack. The flyover was a reminder for all of them that they were not safe.

Four days into their sojourn, they saw a military ship on the western horizon closing with the tiny fleet of refugees. Su-Hui watched as it grew larger, using binoculars to finally spy the Newmerican flag on the ship, black with an up-thrust white fist. Word was passed over the radio and by simple shouts to other vessels. The ship, the *USS John S. McCain* swung wide of the group, then came in parallel to the ship.

Orders were barked out, both in English and Mandarin, telling the ships to slow, that they were there to help. That only made Su-Hui angrier. *If you wished to help, you should have joined us to defend our nation.* The large gray destroyer pulled alongside several ships, using cranes and baskets to lift the refugees aboard. It was a slow process in the churning seas. He was tenth in line with his sailboat, and carefully tacked his way into position, bumping hard on the hull of the destroyer in the process.

Three at a time, his family was lifted off, each carrying a suitcase or two containing what was left of their worldly possessions. The naval officer who came down in the first basket, finally loaded him and his son into the basket.

"What about my boat?" Su-Hui asked in his best English.

The sailor shook his head. "Sorry," he said. "We are only taking people at this point." As the basket was winched up, he looked at his ship, now starting to drift away. It had taken him two years to save the down payment on the vessel, and now it was simply cast adrift in the vastness of the Pacific. He watched sadly as it bobbed about like a child's toy in a bathtub. *I worked so hard to save for it ... and now it is thrown aside like garbage.* He then felt a wave of guilt wash over him. *My people have lost their nation ... their hopes ... their dreams. What is a sailboat against that?*

While the navy crew was kind, helping them aboard, checking them for medical issues, Su-Hui fumed. *None of this would have been necessary if Newmerica had answered Taiwan's plea for help.* A part of him understood it far too well; Newmerica was socialist without using that word. The entire world knew it. They called it 'progressivism,' 'neo-collectivism' or 'enlightened capitalism,' but he knew they supported China over a free Taiwan. *Their twist on economics has turned me from being a successful business person to being a refugee.*

Someone was going to pay for this. He promised himself that much. *These events will not define my existence. I won't allow that to happen. I will rebuild my life, and when I do, I will find the people responsible for the loss of my homeland and make them pay.*

CHAPTER 1

*"Your personal freedoms are nothing
compared to the greater good."*

*Newmerica Penitentiary, Administrative Maximum Facility
Florence, Colorado*

Raul Lopez felt as if the walls were closing in on him. The isolation cell they kept him in was cramped under the best of conditions, but when he sat there, alone, with nothing to do, the walls seemed to creep in tighter. It was psychological. He knew that was part of what they hoped he would feel, that in some weird way it might make him crack. *I won't give them the satisfaction.* That thought alone made him crack a thin smile. Glancing up at the camera in the corner ceiling mount, he made a point of nodding to it. *I know you are watching me. I won't give you what you're looking for.*

His interrogators, led by the woman that kidnapped him, had tried a lot of things to get him to talk. The furious threats of death had come so often that they had ceased to have meaning. For several days they had tried keeping him awake by blaring loud music in his cell. Not sleeping made his skin itchy, and it felt at times like he had slammed a beer back on an empty stomach. His motions seemed sluggish, and he struggled to form words. As much as they pounded on the table, slapped him, and even punched him, it had little influence.

There had been enough pummeling by his interrogators that he had made a game of counting the times he had been beaten. Sixteen was the current count. His bruises had bruises in some places. The injuries made it hard to find a position in his bed where he didn't hurt, but Raul prevailed. The frustration that his captors showed was what he drew some of his strength from.

The rest of his resolve came from the fact that Caylee was out there, and he knew that she would come for him. *I know her. She won't let me sit here. She will come.*

"Step back," came the order from the door, and Raul stood and moved to the rear of the cell. Then came the sound of the metallic click and snap of the lock. Two large guards entered. "Turn around," they said and as he did, he put his hand behind him, anticipating the click of the handcuffs. They came quickly, and the guards took him out.

Time was a blur for him in the cell. For 23 hours a day, he was either in his cell or in an interrogation room. His food was brought to his cell. For the one hour he was allowed out, he was taken to a freezing cold courtyard where there was a cage that he could walk around in. There was no direct sunlight even there. He would pace around there and stretch. Raul practiced some of the moves and exercises that Caylee had taught him. *There will be a time when they may be useful.* Besides, doing them made him remember the time they had spent together … it gave him a bit of focus. If nothing else, the sessions broke up the monotony. When the guards showed up, he assumed it was to take him to another interrogation session.

They led him down a series of twisting corridors. The interrogation room was a right, a left, a long corridor, and another left. This was not that path. *They are taking me somewhere else.* That made him more nervous than the thought of another intimidation session. He remembered the woman telling him that they were going to put him before a People's Tribunal. *Are they taking me to that?*

The Tribunals were the Social Enforcers' version of justice. When he had seen a few on television as a child, he didn't think much of them. A lot of people yelling, a guilty person being verbally blasted. Now though, he saw them for what they were—a farce—an illusion of justice. There were no rules, no laws, no real justice. To Raul it was a group of people bullying others, then shipping them off for whatever punishment they saw fit. *If this is a Tribunal, they will sentence me to death. I can make no defense that would convince them otherwise. They presume guilt to start, and things get worse from there.*

The guards jerked him down a different path. Mentally he kept track of the turns, right, right, downstairs two flights, left—through a door, through a checkpoint, then into a large cavernous bay. For four stories, along all of the walls were guardrails and cells. Above him were skylights, tinted an opaque white so that even if you looked up, you couldn't see the sky. The cells were like his, only painted a dull yellow color that made his orange Crocs look even more ridiculous in contrast. The difference he spotted was that the openings on the cell doors were larger, more open, with bars. In some of the cells, he saw faces staring out at him. Since he had been in the prison, he had not seen a single other prisoner. *I am not alone here.* He was led up a staircase to the top floor, then to a new cell.

"What is this place?" he asked as the guards removed his handcuffs.

"This is Unit J," the guard said. "Political prisoners."

"Is that what I am?" he asked.

"We don't know," the second guard said. "We had orders to bring you here."

This is a change, and with these people, a change might not be good. "I don't understand."

"You don't have to understand," the first guard said with a low sneer. "Stand back." He slammed the door, and the echo bounced around outside.

Raul moved to the tiny window on the door. It wasn't much, but it was better than the slab of a door he had earlier. He savored the moment, standing at the door, being able to look out. After a minute or two, he checked himself. *They did not bring me here for anything good.* That wasn't how the NSF or SEs operated. *Don't relax your guard ...* that's what Caylee would tell him if she was there.

"Hey," came a voice from the cell next to his. It was a more mature male voice, somehow familiar, though he could not put a face to it. Leaning hard to the right, he tried to get a view of the portal where the voice came from the cell next to him, but he couldn't.

"Hey," he echoed back.

"Welcome to Unit J," the other prisoner said. "I'm Ted." He sounded downright personable. That didn't mean anything. As far as Raul knew, it was an SE trying to lure him into saying something. Caution cloaked what he said.

"I'm Raul."

"Nice to meet you," he said. "What did they arrest you for?"

It felt fantastic to talk to someone that wasn't attempting to get him to confess or reveal names or places. It was strangely refreshing to hear that someone didn't know who he was. His face and life had been plastered on the television during the hunt for him. *They don't let them get the news here ... that explains it.* It was in that moment that he realized that he had no idea what was happening in the world outside of the prison. The election ... *I wonder who won?* He suspected the Ruling Council. Otherwise, he would be free. Then another realization hit him. He wasn't sure where he was.

"They say I'm a terrorist," Raul said.

The voice came back quick, "They say that about anyone that doesn't follow their party line. We are conservatives, which makes us all terrorists."

"I'm not."

The voice let go a single chuckle. "It's okay kid. We're all innocent here," he said.

"What are you in for?" Raul asked.

"I'm a conservative, a Republican."

Raul understood all too well. After the Fall, conservatives were targets. "You must have been someone important. Otherwise you'd have been sent to Social Quarantine."

Another chuckle. "I like to think I was," Ted replied. "Now I'm just like you, waiting for them to parade me out for a show trial and execution." He seemed oddly comfortable with the words he spoke.

"Where am I? When they brought me in, I was not sure even what state I'm in."

"They didn't tell you? I guess I'm not surprised. Raul, you are in the Supermax in Colorado," Ted replied flatly. "You are locked up with the worst criminals that the United States had and now the ones targeted by Newmerica's merry band of thugs. There are serial killers here, drug lords, even the Unabomber. You are in with the worst of the worst."

Another voice, coming from the cell to his right, spoke up. "And you're in Unit J, the equivalent of death row," the new voice added. "Sooner or later they will come for us. Sooner or later we are going to be paraded out for the cameras and put on display. After that—well, we are of no use to them. Some folks are here a short time; others, like me, have been here for years."

Raul leaned back from the door. He could almost feel the cameras hitting him, trying to read his face, probably recording his words. *I won't give them the satisfaction of a show. Caylee is out there, and she will come for me. I know it.*

The Southern White House
Nashville, Tennessee

Colonel Trip Reager hated only one thing as much as the Newmerican government, and that was the media. The snaps and clicks of their cameras barraged him like digital shrapnel as he arrived at the Southern White House. "Colonel, why are you here?" one reporter yelled. He ignored them. As he reached the door, a female reporter called out, "Will you be shooting any more unarmed protesters while in town Colonel?" She yelled loud enough for her shrill voice to dominate the others.

Trip stopped, hand on the door, then retracted. The reference to Election Day in Chicago was so distorted, so twisted; he couldn't let it pass. Slowly he turned back to the cluster of reporters. "Who asked that?" he barked.

A female reporter raised her hand, "Pat Templeton, MSNBC," she said back crisply. "Do you have anything you want to say to the family members of the innocent, unarmed people you slaughtered when you denied people the right to vote, sir?"

Reager marched up to her, his chest straining under his dress uniform jacket. "Well Miss Templeton," he growled. "You are lying your ass off when you say they were protesters. They opened fire on us first. These were armed troops. I was there. My people were protecting themselves and the election workers!"

"How dare you assume I desire to be identified as a female!" she quipped back. "I should expect something like that from someone nicknamed *Bloodbath.* Your insensitivity to people is well known. Even your own daughter won't talk to you. Isn't that correct? You are a failed father who slaughtered innocent civilians, so why should people believe you are anything less than a brutal killer?" He could sense the cameras turning to catch more of the confrontation. The click and snap of the photographers intensified.

Common sense said he should ignore her and walk away. It had been three weeks since the Battle for Chicago where he had led Texas and Missouri National Guardsmen into Chicago to provide for a safe and secure election. *It was not a peaceful protest, not by a damned longshot.* They had opened fire on him with garage-shop Technicals, weapons stolen from National Guard armories, and NSF-provided gear. The Illinois National Guard had tried to pry his people out of Chicago under a hail of bullets. Only his quick and decisive thinking had prevented an even worse slaughter.

Bringing up his daughter—that went too far. He chose to turn the focus on the nickname instead, rather than give the reporter the satisfaction. "What did you just call me?" he asked, taking the last step between the two of them.

"Don't play deaf with me, Colonel," she said back defiantly. "I believe you heard me; you killed unarmed and innocent people in San Antonio and went into Chicago and did the same thing. You earned the name *Bloodbath.* You couldn't keep your family together, so why should anyone believe you can keep this upstart country together? Are you here in Tennessee to prepare for your next slaughter?"

Trip smirked for a moment. *The politicians have to put up with this shit. I don't.* He started to turn away, then wheeled, throwing a haymaker punch into the reporter's jaw. The blow was so hard, it lifted her off her feet for a moment, twisting the arrogant smirk on her face, as she flew backwards into the throng of reporters. She was shocked, lying on the sidewalk, clearly in pain and stunned into silence.

"Any of you have a follow-up question?" he said, his fists still balled, ready for a fight. The wall of reporters said nothing. Silence seemed to grip the scene for a moment. Trip's eyes swept each one of them and he saw the media for what it was, an irritating force. They don't care about the truth; they just want clicks on their websites; they want notoriety. *Well, Little Miss Pat of MSNBC got her wish.* His eyes shifted to the rest of the reporters who were almost as dazed as the MSNBC reporter on the ground. "Any other wise-ass inquiries?" he asked as his jaw set. What he got back was silence. "I didn't think so."

He turned and entered the Southern White House. After clearing the security checkpoint, he was escorted to a conference room on the third floor. He stood, despite the available seats. He wasn't sure why he had gotten the summons, but it caused an eerie feeling like he had been called to the principal's office in high school. After nearly 20 long minutes passed, the door opened and Jack Desmond, the President's Chief of Staff entered.

Everyone knew Desmond's face, his stern facial expression, from his countless TV interviews. The Chief extended his hand and Trip shook it. "Colonel, Jack Desmond. Thank you for coming."

"Thank you sir," he said. Jack gestured to a seat and Trip sat down, Jack sitting right next to him.

"From what I was told, you had quite an entrance," he said smiling.

How did he know about that already? Desmond was good ... as good as he had heard. "I'd apologize if that caused some PR problems, but frankly, I'm not sorry. Given the chance, I'd probably do it again."

"That reporter is probably going to sue you and press charges."

"The way people feel about the media, I'll take my chances with a jury trial," he smirked.

"I'm actually jealous," Jack conceded with a smile. "I've been wanting to punch a reporter or two since I got this job."

Trip grinned back. "I take it you didn't have me come here to deck an asshole, sir. So why am I here?"

Jack leaned toward him in the seat. "First and foremost, the President wanted me to pass on his thanks and congratulations. Given the number of dead in Chicago, the optics of him meeting with you personally would be a boon to the Ruling Council. As such, you have to get your thanks from me."

"No thanks necessary," Trip replied. "I did what I had to do."

"The President and I don't agree. As such, you will be pleased to know that you are being promoted to Brigadier General."

Trip said nothing for a moment. A part of him wanted to turn it down. *I shouldn't get a promotion for killing other Americans.* The throb from his knuckles reminded him that these were not Americans—they were Newmericans. They supported an illegal regime that had seized power in a *coup d'etat* five years earlier. They had killed innocent people and had interned others simply for not having the same beliefs. *The people that I fought in battle chose their side and they chose to stand with other criminals.* "It is not necessary, nor expected Mr. Desmond."

"Well it's happening," the older man assured him. "It comes with a string attached though."

"Which is?"

"We need your help in planning and executing our next military operation. The President has an initiative, code-named Razorback. It is a military response based on the assumption that the Newmericans wouldn't accept the results of the election."

"That was a safe bet," Trip said. "They spent four years before the Fall playing the 'resist' card, refusing to accept election results. If the last President had won the 2020 election; they would have done the same thing. They would have stormed the White House and killed him. Anyone that thinks differently is delusional." Saying it out loud had a sense of finality to it. *Even though they won, they still rioted ... still killed the President.*

"Razorback calls for us to utilize our military forces to take back the states and pockets where Newmerica refuses to capitulate or acknowledge the election results. He pulled up a map of the nation on the wall monitor, color coded red and blue, with yellow. "We're the red states. The blue are where the Newmericans won the votes. The yellow indicates states that we won in the election, but have refuted the tally or outright not agreed to come into the fold.

Trip eyed the map. Georgia stood out as being surrounded by loyal states. Tiny New Hampshire was the same way. Trapped behind enemy lines.

"We find ourselves in a situation unique in our history, and you have the proven ability to think and act on your feet. It's exactly the kind of leadership we want in the *American* Army." The stressing of the word 'American' stuck with Trip.

His own eyes narrowed. "What exactly is our situation?"

"Muddled," Desmond replied. "Officially, the formal federal military is staying on the sidelines. The reality of the situation is that there are individuals and in some case entire units that are defecting to both sides. The bulk of the military is sitting on the sidelines for now. We have some bases, as does the enemy. I have several other generals working to take this hodge-podge of people and restructure it into something we can use. In the meantime, the loyal states' National Guard units, like your own Texans, remain activated and federalized under our direction."

"Where do you need my help exactly?" Trip asked.

"We won the election," Jack said. "Dozens of communities in states we have sway over have openly refused the election results. St. Louis and Kansas City are two examples of cities that are refusing to acknowledge America still exists. On top of that, four of the states where we won the vote—the state governments or the Governors—have refused to validate us as the winners. Namely in New Mexico, Minnesota, Ohio, and Georgia.

"New Hampshire is a magnet for both sides right now with both sides sending in people and material to support them. The problem is that they are effectively surrounded. We have the Sons of Liberty (SOL) there in force, but we are unsure how to help them when the Newmericans come at them—and they will. There's a feeling that the state might be a lost cause. I'd hate to lose them, but we aren't sure how they can hold out."

Trip walked up to the monitor and stared at New Hampshire on the map, saying nothing for a few long moments. *If they chose to fight conventionally—they are doomed.*

"Georgia is a real sticking point for us. We had issues in Atlanta election night. Without boring you with details, essentially we tossed out their votes. There was so much fraud there; it was ridiculous. Atlanta and surrounding Fulton, DeKalb, Cobb and Douglas counties essentially have decided to side with Newmerica and once they did that, the Governor of Georgia declared the entire state to be hostile territory for us. The phrase he used was that they were a, 'Newmerica Autonomous Zone.'"

Trip took in the words. *They love to name things or change the names of things.* "That leaves you with a rebel state in the middle of your own territory?"

Desmond nodded. "Atlanta is the key. It is a major banking center with manufacturing and a massive airport."

"I assume Newmerica isn't going to make this easy," Trip said.

"No," Desmond shook his head, "they are not. They have been bringing in National Guard forces from their other states, attempting to shore up Georgia. Atlanta and the surrounding area is hunkering down. Our own aerial drone flights show them digging defensive positions along the highways surrounding the city. The state borders are defended by the NSF, SEs, and even some misguided good old boys. Every day that passes, they are entrenching."

Trip drank in the words carefully, mentally processing the situation. "What do you need from me, sir?"

"What are your thoughts about all of this?" Desmond asked.

Trip pointed to New Hampshire. "If New Hampshire tries and slugs it out conventionally, they will lose. The Newmerican forces can and will invade—it's a quick victory for them, too hard for them to pass it up. Our forces need to fight unconventionally—wage an insurgency. Guerilla warfare on the occupation force can tie up a lot of Newmerican troops. If you want to fight up there, you take it to the woods, the hills, the mountains. That's what I would recommend there."

"Clearly I found the right person to talk to," Jack Desmond said. "What can we do to help them?"

"They will need experienced troops, equipment, and munitions. We need to get small teams in there to train an insurgency on how to fight. Winter could be our best ally up there. The Sons of Liberty are going to be a key too—the more eyes and ears we have on the ground, the better." Trip drew a quick breath. *I served in the Middle East and fought insurgents.* He had hated fighting that kind of war. It was a battle of nerves, a test of resolve, and many casualties. *Now I am actually recommending that kind of war. ... Times have sure changed.*

Trip shifted his gaze to Georgia. "Georgia is going to be a tougher nut to crack. That requires a more conventional military solution. We need to invade, secure, and hold. It's not going to be easy. It is isolated from the rest of Newmerica, so we will need to first establish air superiority to prevent additional forces from being flown in to reinforce them. After that, we put the squeeze on the city."

"Sounds like you're the right man for the job, General."

Two thoughts hit him. *It's going to take me a while to get used to that new rank. Damn, they are handing this Razorback initiative to me.* He knew this was not going to be easy, but neither was holding the heart of downtown Chicago a few weeks earlier. "Mr. Desmond ... "

"Please call me Jack."

"Jack," Trip said. "Surely there are other officers better suited for this Razorback initiative? Hell, even as a Brigadier, I'm not of sufficient rank to lead an army."

"The President and I don't think so. Your rank on paper is a formality – you'll be in command across the board. You have demonstrated the capability to use force. You don't abuse it. Some of our officers have hesitated, even under fire. They are worried about being labeled as murderers."

"They already call me a butcher," Trip conceded.

"A reputation can be a weapon against the morale of an enemy as well," Jack said.

He wanted to argue against that, but realized the folly. *They want to intimidate any opposition I face.* "Jack, allow me to be blunt with you. This isn't going to be easy. Millions of civilians may be impacted by a thrust into Georgia. For me to do this, and do it right, some innocent folks may have to suffer. I will want full control and authority on how I use my people in the field. I don't need some armchair quarterback calling plays for me. Are you and the President prepared for that?"

Desmond lowered his head for a moment, staring down in deep thought. When he raised his head, he looked over at Trip intently. "We have been fighting a civil war for the last four and a half years and losing. Most of the country never even realized it. In the last few months, we have finally started a counterattack. No one wants innocent people to be killed or injured, but we also cannot have the nation remain split. This is the *United* States of America. That word still means something.

"There's more," Trip said. "Politicians have a knack for trying to help, and by help I mean interfering with military operations. If I'm to undertake this, I need your trust to let me do what I need to do. Poking and prodding from the White House will not help."

Jack nodded. "I understand. If you are in the field, you command the field. If things change though, we reserve the right to give you a new set of priorities."

"Seems reasonable."

"New Hampshire is at risk, and Georgia is standing in defiance of a legal election. We need to move quickly, especially up north. We don't want to hand the enemy a victory if we can avoid it. I'd like to put New Hampshire under your care as well." He paused for a moment, sweeping the map with his eyes. Then he turned back to Trip.

"Okay, but know this: Sometimes the best way to win is to simply not lose. New Hampshire is deep behind the lines, so we may need to get creative with what we do there."

"I understand. Atlanta is your priority for now. If Georgia is allowed to persist, it might inspire other such defiant acts. Newmerica is counting on us to not come at them in force. We have the state surrounded, and their control of railways and strategic highways is an economic bottleneck we can't allow to continue. So, yes, we are prepared for whatever may come—including civilian casualties."

There was candor in Jack Desmond's voice that Trip appreciated. "Jack," he began slowly. "I took a lot of history classes in college. You know your history too, I'm sure. The last time war came to Georgia, it was General Sherman's push to the sea. You remember what happened to Atlanta then?"

"I saw *Gone with the Wind* and remember my history. Yes. Atlanta burned."

"Do you know who was responsible for it?"

"The movie said the Confederates, but as I recall, it was Sherman's troops."

Trip nodded. "The optics are the key point. Because of the film, history got muddled. People are willing to believe whatever they are presented, whatever fits their narrative."

"So you are saying we need to be careful, that the Truth Reconciliation Committee (TRC) and others are going to spin our actions?"

Trip shook his head. "What I am saying is that in the end, Atlanta burned. It doesn't matter who did it. Innocent people will suffer. I'm already painted as a butcher, a war criminal. They will weave that into a story that makes sense for people, regardless of what really happens." Memories of the reporter confrontation stood in his mind.

"So you don't want the job? Is that what you're telling me?"

"No. I just want you to know what you are going to be facing. I have fairly broad shoulders, except when it comes to loudmouthed assholes in the media. If I go into Georgia, it will be a fight. Parts of it will be nasty and ugly. I need full discretion on how I fight this war. I need you to be ready to offer a better story to the public than the one the TRC is bound to serve up."

"We will," Jack assured him.

"Very well. As long as we both know what we are getting into. I need to see what forces I have at my disposal," Trip said firmly.

University of Virginia
Charlottesville, Virginia

Grayson Steele sat across from the Public Safety Director for the University of Virginia in his cramped office. His name was Dwight Clemmons and from where Grayson sat, he was fat, and not the kind of fat where you would say, "He's a few pounds overweight." No, this man had rolls of fat that pushed the buttons on his shirt to the near breaking point. His face reminded Grayson of Porky Pig from cartoons he had watched as a child. His fingers hitting the keyboard looked like links of sausages.

He had risked exposing his real identity because his daughter, Madison, was missing. She had not returned phone calls or emails and when he went to her room, her roommate said she had packed up her things and simply left. Pris said it had been a last minute thing. None of it made sense. Maddie was going to be graduating from law school soon, going on for her internship.

Grayson had been a member of Virginia's House of Delegates as a staunch conservative. When the Fall happened, he and his family saw the handwriting on the wall and changed their names. They had moved, and he had taken an entry-level lawyer position in a very small practice. The Steeles, as they became known, had hidden in plain sight—always looking over their shoulders for Social Enforcement. Grayson knew what they would do with them. Social Quarantine Camps.

The Public Safety Director squinted at the flat screen for a long moment. "Well Mr. Steele, your daughter and a number of other students apparently took off on some sort of trip. None of them returned from it. These sorts of things happen from time to time. Kids get it in their heads to take off and don't come back." His voice had a tone that Grayson hated. *It's like he's telling me that this is okay. It's not!*

"Maddie wouldn't have taken off anywhere. Finals were just a few weeks out. Law school was everything to her." *Family was everything to her.*

The rotund director flashed a grin. "College students take off. It happens more than you think. She wasn't the only one that went on this trip. We have nine students, including her, that took off and didn't come back."

"And that doesn't strike you as strange?" His tone was clear; he was getting angrier by the moment.

"Now calm down Mr. Steele. We contacted the NSF and filed the appropriate reports. None of the kids have turned up. The NSF had the same thought we did. These kids have gone off on a little vacation of sorts."

"Vacation?" he fumed. "We met with her a week or so before she left. She never mentioned a vacation."

"Well now, sometimes these kids take off, you know, run away. Was there any family problem that might have triggered her to take off?"

Family troubles? *Hell yes!* They had been spotted by someone that knew them. Their cover had been blown and Grayson was in the middle of arranging for the family to move and assume new identities. Not Maddie though. They had insisted that she complete school, and she had agreed with that. "Nothing that would cause my daughter to run away. And she wouldn't have taken off with a group like that."

"I'm not sure what to say here," he replied.

Grayson focused in. "Listen, you have nine missing kids over a weekend, and you don't seem overly concerned about it."

"Sir, I am concerned," he said in a less-than-convincing tone. "I wish I could help you more," he said. "Our office handles matters here on campus. Once these kids leave here, it falls on the NSF. Now I know you have filed a missing person's report with them. You need to let them run their investigation and see what they turn up."

"I've met with them," Grayson said flatly. "They were almost as helpful as you've been." It was an understatement. The NSF detective he had met with Detective Schrank who said this happened at UVA (University of Virginia) from time to time, small groups of students turning up missing. They didn't think it was a serial killer or anything like that. To the NSF, this was a bunch of kids playing some sort of prank on their parents and officials. "Besides, if they had run into foul play, we would have bodies or other evidence," they said. To Grayson's ears, it sounded like that was the depth of the investigation—waiting for Maddie's body to turn up. He doubted that the director had even caught that slight dig in his words.

"Mr. Grayson, kids sometimes do things to get attention from their parents. Sometimes they change their lifestyle or want to sow their wild oats. At this age, being on a diverse campus, they meet a lot of people, get new ideas, and want to explore. Your Maddie is probably just fine. I'm sure she will show up at some point."

Grayson was far less convinced. "Maddie is not out sowing her wild oats," he said, rising from his chair. "Can you provide me a list of the other students you indicated that have up and disappeared?"

That flustered the portly director for a moment. "Well, I can't think of any reason not to," he said, turning on his printer and fumbling with the keyboard, stabbing at keys one at a time with his sausage pointer fingers. A moment later the printer hummed to life and a single sheet came out. He handed it to Grayson.

"If you hear anything, I want to know," Maddie's father demanded.

The director rose and extended his hand for a shake. "I will do that Mr. Grayson. In the meantime you need to relax. I'm sure she'll turn up sooner or later."

Grayson knew in the pit of his stomach that the odds of that diminished with each sweep of a second hand on a clock. Something had happened to his little girl, and he intended to learn the truth. Ignoring the man's extended hand, he turned and stormed out of the office, more determined than ever to find his daughter.

The District

The Secretary of the NSF sat in her office with two of her aides holding up different outfits. One, a dark blue, the other a stark white. She stared at both. It was an important decision, since these were the outfits she intended to wear at her swearing in as Vice President.

The store had sent her a bright red dress, but she had that one discarded. She knew she would look stunning in it, but ordered it taken away immediately. *There is no way that I would be caught wearing a color that is associated with the enemy.* Since she had taken control of the TRC, she had recommended that subtle change. The only time red highline banners appeared on the Internet or newscasts was to highlight atrocities and criminal acts associated with the rebel American government.

The problems she faced, however, were daunting. The Americans had crippled the Internet outside of DC, which had a ripple effect up and down the East Coast. The attack had left the TRC unable to do one of its primary missions—clearing and editing all digital media posted in the nation. As a result the Internet had been flooded with stories, articles, and email traffic about the Newmerican government, none of which was positive. For the first time in years, people had access to a wealth of non-cleared information. It was like a variant of COVID, the way it spread and developed a life of its own. Worse yet, it included the material that Caylee Leatrom had posted about the operative program and less-than-favorable activities of the NSF.

Her solution was bold: Relocate the bulk of the staff of the TRC from the District to the West Coast. There had been complaints, even a protest by the union representing FedGov employees, but she had ignored all of that. Having unfiltered information about the government in the public domain was far too dangerous. Slowly, but progressively, the inflammatory posts and sites were being taken down or labeled as fake news with the TRC banner. Assigning NSF resources to protect strategic Internet hub sites was a drain on the resources of her other agency.

There had been the botched assassination attempt of the President in Nashville. The press coverage out of Tennessee about that had been damning. Her people had crafted a story that it was nothing more than a false flag attack staged by the President to generate sympathy. It played well with many citizens, but she found herself questioning their feedback. *Are they so afraid that they are telling us what we want to hear?* Her new staff convinced her that was not the case, but it was a nagging feeling that she could not suppress.

Worse yet, the failed assassination attempt had made the NSF look weak. Part of the federalization of the police force had been to standardize operations and root out systemic racism prevalent in the police forces.

Another aspect of the formation of the NSF was never discussed—it was to impose confidence in the form of fear in the minds of the people. The NSF had been a well-oiled machine for years. The way the TRC covered them, they were unable to fail. Few people wanted to cross the NSF. Now, one of their top people had failed on a national stage for all to see. *We can't afford for people to think that we are less than infallible.*

The images of Julius Bernstein being arraigned on charges on television and the Internet had been disturbing. *He is a loose end that will have to be dealt with sooner rather than later.*

She knew her enemies would have to pay for what they did. *We are still struggling to keep the Internet up on the East Coast. They knew exactly how to hit us. People are daring to question what the Ruling Council has done. Daniel and I can't be sworn in soon enough.*

Tess Ditka arrived at her door precisely on schedule. One thing she had to admit: Her processor, Rebecca Clarke was good at picking top people. People like Tess had made her transition into the role of managing the TRC relatively smooth. "Madam Secretary," she said with a slight bow

"Tess, it is good to see you," the Secretary said nodding for the staff holding the outfits to leave them. "I trust that you have the set design ready?"

"Of course," she said, tapping her iPad furiously. The image appeared on the large screen that dominated the far wall of her office in the TRC.

She savored it for a moment. The flags of Newmerica, all sixteen of them so far, were draped in front of where the Tribunal would sit in judgment of Senator Lewis. Her office changed the flag often to ensure that every partisan group that made up the nation got its day in the sun. The previous flags of her nation had been retired, but she had insisted that they all be on display for this event. The visual effect was just what she desired. *It looks as if the whole nation is putting him on trial.*

The green bunting that highlighted the room had no hint of the old corrupt colors of the nation. It was in the room where the Senator would be tried for treason. The seat where he would be poised would be lower than that of the Tribunal. Tess had come up with that idea. 'It creates the illusion that no one is above the state.'

The Secretary knew that Lewis was an innocent man—at least

innocent of the charges of treason that had been leveled at him. Lewis had been planning to roast her publicly because of the documents that Leatrom had shot onto the Internet months earlier. The NSF was an elite organization that in her opinion did not need oversight to be effective. Lewis disagreed, and his hearings were going to be nothing but a witch hunt targeting the Secretary. So she had taken care of it. A team of her people had forged a wide ranging conspiracy with Lewis as a lynchpin. The hearings were forgotten now as Lewis was facing a death sentence.

"We should position his security attachment below the podium where the defendant stands," she said. "I want him shackled, but there is no reason to have that appear on the air."

"Good idea ma'am," Tess said, making notes.

"About the windows," she said. "Let's put curtains in front of them."

"I'd recommend something semi-transparent," she said. "The windows are behind the Tribunal members. I would like to have some light coming in there; it gives them a silhouette effect." She changed the image on the screen for a stand-in of a Tribunal member. "We will still be able to see their faces, but it gives them a bit of a glow that I want to exploit."

"Agreed," she said. "Do we want that carpeting? It reminds me of the Senate hearing chambers."

"It will be expensive to change that out and it will take some time. We could go with something more utilitarian ... perhaps a concrete surface?"

"Yes. It tells people that this defendant is not worthy of comfort. It makes us look like we are not doing something special for him. I want it to have a more utilitarian feel, industrial jail-like." Of course it would cost more money, and that was the opposite of the message being sent, but the effect was important to foster the proper illusion for the watchers.

"I will have them start work on it right away," Tess said.

"Excellent. Now about the broadcast. I've been thinking. We have a one-minute delay. Is that going to be enough? The Senator is bound to make a lot of wild accusations. Those things cannot be broadcast." She expected Lewis to be defiant, to try to throw her under the bus. *He won't get the satisfaction.*

"We can buffer it for two or more minutes. We will have a team standing by to do the on-the-fly editing. We have loaded the initial questions with things he will willingly say *yes* to. That way later, when he says *no,* we can replace his response with a *yes.*" As such, any additional time we give them will ensure that the presentation of the trial is more seamless."

"Then make it five minutes," she said. "I want the people to think that Lewis is nothing more than a defunct Senator, bitter about the government. We want him portrayed as the traitor that he is. That way when the Tribunal rules, everyone watching will believe that the sentence is just."

"I understand. My people will appreciate the extra time," she said.

"That will be all Tess," she said, dismissing her. As the door to her office closed, she paused to reflect on the coming events. *We need to divert the public's attention away from the return of a President and his claim that he won the election.* It was bad enough that people learned that he had not died as the Ruling Council had maintained. *That was the first crack in their confidence about us.* Then it was followed by the liberation of several Social Quarantine camps. Most people have had no reason to doubt what the TRC and the Ruling Council told them. *Now we have tripped up over several indiscretions.*

The trial would divert their attention, refocusing them on what was important. *This trial will be the first. If it has the desired effect, we have a number of people who will face justice. Each death will solidify our hold on the people. They will see that defiance against our authority has extreme consequences. Each execution will make us stronger.*

Better yet, our enemies will see the price of facing us and failing ...

CHAPTER 2

*"There is only one true justice—the one
defined by the government."*

The District

Major General James Donaldson stood at ease before Newmerica President-Elect Daniel Porter. Work outside—repairing the damage of the bombing attack on the Capitol—continued with the bang and clang of workers furiously attempting to finish before the swearing in ceremony. Porter had been interviewed after he declared himself a winner in the election saying that the repair of the damage was a sign that the nation was moving forward. Donaldson had been downright emotional during the speech. *It is what we all needed to hear, to bury the past and move forward to a brighter future.*

He had been summoned personally to meet with the chairman of the Ruling Council, now the President-Elect…an honor to say the least. His career had been meteoric after the night of the Liberation. By preventing any cohesive military response from the Pentagon the night that the government fell, he had been promoted and honored with several key positions. He had hated the Traitor President, so siding against him and his people had been an easy decision. *The man was morally weak and pathetic. Hearing that his death meant he suffered is beyond satisfying.*

The sudden reappearance of the former Vice President and his claim that he was the legitimate successor had caused political ripples in the Pentagon that were still echoing down the corridors. The military had stood down when called to defend the White House, defying the direct orders of the then-President. In the eyes of many, that made them complicit in the events that had unfolded. The JCS felt that they had elevated the military beyond the reach of the politicians. In reality, by choosing to do nothing, they had sided with the Newmericans

Now there was a self-proclaimed President, causing a quandary with many commanders outside of the District. They felt their oaths as officers and warriors compelled them to follow the President in Tennessee instead of the President-Elect seated in front of him. The Joint Chiefs couldn't simply flip sides. They were unsure who would eventually come out on top. A few senior officers ignored orders from their superiors and fled south to join the President. Entire bases flipped in some cases. Where the Pentagon had managed to keep the military out of the affairs of the Ruling Council, at least in his mind, now troops were refusing to stand on the sidelines. Some had sided with the Newmerican forces as well, further muddying the situation. *We've never faced something like this— the fragmenting of the military into three groups. The neutral forces, and those that side with one of the political governments.*

For General Donaldson, it was a situation ripe to be taken advantage of.

For most of his military career, he had felt as if he were in the wrong place at the wrong time. He graduated in the lower 25 percent of his class at West Point, a statistic that he sought to keep buried. While other graduates were given combat postings, he had ended up in logistics, then staff planning. It wasn't that he didn't want to get into battle; it just seemed like the prime opportunities went to others. He had chalked it up to bad timing and politics.

Things changed with the Liberation. Donaldson began to play the political game and proved adept at it. The death of his former classmate General Harry Cooper was something that he felt bad about, but not quite guilty. After all, he had only been following orders. *What happened to Harry was his fault, not mine. He suffered from idealism, and loyalty to a man that never should have held the office of President. I gave Harry every chance to stand down. It's not my fault that Cooper was too damned pig-headed.* Donaldson knew he had leverage on his superiors, and they had the same on him. *We share a secret with guilt on both sides.*

His first field command had been over the Arkansas National Guard four years earlier. It was supposed to be an NSF operation, but had gone horribly wrong with a lot of deaths by the time he had gotten there. *I organized things quickly and dealt with the problem as expeditiously as possible.* For a short time he worried that the press might label him the way they had Bloodbath Reager, but thankfully the TRC made him out to be a hero who saved lives. He savored the commendation he received for his efforts. *It was proof of what I was capable of.* And now he had been summoned to meet with the President-Elect. Everything was falling into place.

"Reporting as ordered sir," he said crisply.

"You may relax General," Porter said, gesturing to a chair opposite the Resolute Desk that he was now using as his own. It was one of the few artifacts saved before fires had devoured the White House during the Liberation. "The Chairman of the JCS said that he wanted you for an operation we are planning, I wanted to make sure you were the right person for the job."

Recommended by the Chairman ... he strained to suppress a smile. "Sir, I live to serve sir."

"This assignment should be easy. New Hampshire has refused to acknowledge our rightful government. They've mobilized their National Guard, thrown up roadblocks in the state. They are openly defying us."

"They are surrounded sir. Taking them out should be a cakewalk."

"That's what we were thinking. It's not enough to just go in there; we need to find the instigators of this defiance and make sure they are brought to justice. New Hampshire needs to be made an example for the rest of the country. We can use overwhelming force to intimidate their compliance. The message needs to be clear. If you stand against us, you will be punished or killed." There was a sternness in the President-Elect's voice that Donaldson enjoyed. "I assure you sir, I can make New Hampshire a symbol of what happens when people stand up against us."

"Excellent," he said. "That still leaves us with a challenge in Georgia. The belief is that the American forces will make a drive on Atlanta. They won't be able to allow us to have a state behind their lines any more than we can tolerate New Hampshire."

Donaldson had been following the election results and the fallout. The heart of Georgia, around Atlanta, was behind the Newmerican government. They had been proclaimed a Newmerica Autonomous Zone, which he liked the sound of. There was a peaceful sound to it that resonated with him. The rest of the state was a bunch of redneck supporters of the American President as far as he was concerned. He also was aware that loyal troops were being assembled and shuttled into Atlanta preparing for the defense of the city. "Any attempt to seize Atlanta will be very costly to the enemy sir. It is a dense urban environment, and we are moving in trained national guardsmen, many with combat experience. If the enemy tries to pry it from us, it's going to be costly ... *very* costly."

"What I need," the President began, "is a loyal field commander, someone that understands the nuances of this kind of combat. You showed that in the whole Arkansas fiasco with that terrorist cell. I need someone who can execute our strategy. Someone who is willing to make the tough calls that are going to be necessary. Your actions in Arkansas demonstrated a loyalty to what we are trying to do here in remaking the old nation. Most importantly, we need a quick victory—something that we can exploit in the press that makes us look good. We believe New Hampshire is just that."

"Are you offering me that job sir?"

The President-Elect nodded. "Loyalty to the cause is paramount. We believe that operations in New Hampshire will only take a matter of weeks. Based on your results there, you will assume command of forces in Georgia to fend off the attack we are sure is coming." He rose to his feet and extended his hand. Donaldson took a firm grasp of it and shook it hard back.

"I won't let you down sir," he said.

"Good," Daniel Porter replied. "We have already suffered contested election results, an assassination attempt, and treason in our ranks. I am counting on the military to deliver us some good news, something that the people can rally behind."

General James Donaldson left with a broad grin on his face. *Finally I will be able to prove to everyone that I am a good field combat commander. New Hampshire will be quick and easy—a decisive victory. My name will be known to the whole world.*

Los Angeles, California
Charli Kasinski pulled the electric-powered Ford van up in front

of Nadler International Airport's arriving flight lanes. The statue of the penguin-shaped Nadler was on the drive leading in, and she was amazed at how the sculptors had trimmed so much of his weight. The wave of renaming that had taken place after the Fall; John Wayne's name had been purged from the airport. Like so many locations, it now bore a new name, one of a liberal politician. *No one noticed or cared about the name of this place until some social justice warriors got their panties in a knot.*

She patiently waited in the queue for Andy to arrive. As she looked around, checking for any abnormal behaviors from security, she saw a trio of homeless people accosting passengers searching for rides. Out of the corner of her eye, she spotted a digital display sign that flickered on, "Being green is everyone's responsibility. Cut your electricity use." Shaking her head, she remembered now why she hated California as much as she did. *It is the land of contradictions. You can only drive electric vehicles ... they use digital signs to push their propaganda—all of which is powered by fossil fuel power plants. The people are so pompous about their extreme socialism that they ignore all of the problems associated with their bad decisions.*

To Charli, California was the poster child for everything wrong about Newmerica. Homelessness was rampant in the state. Renaming the homeless as, 'Housing Dispossessed,' or 'Permanent Residence Estranged,' did nothing to solve their plight. Their solution was to throw money to the impacted people who in turn spent it on alcohol and drugs. The result was to attract more homeless people to the state and to deny why they were there.

During her time hiding there, California's Governor loved to experiment with social programs. He tried construction of free tiny houses for the homeless, but as it happened, they turned them into slum neighborhoods in a matter of months. He 'reallocated' food for them, which left many grocery store shelves empty. Then there was the Housing Diversity Act—choosing where people could live based on 'diversity quotients'. Add the rolling brownouts in the summer, the release of prisoners to be used for fire prevention brigades, and food rationing to promote good health, and it was a toxic mix of things she did not miss.

After the death of the President, Charli had eventually gone into hiding as Angel Frisosky, a member of the NSF. She had lived south of

San Francisco and had loathed her life. Law enforcement in California was like walking around in leg shackles. Most crimes didn't even warrant a report; the prosecutors chose to prosecute only the most severe ones or those associated with guns. It was a convenient way to manipulate your crime statistics. Drug crimes were rampant, but the state had ruled that actually charging people with those crimes was usually racist, so it was an automatic discouragement. The criminals had more rights than the victims under the Newmerica regime.

The icing on the cake wasn't the myriad of failed acts and botched social programs. It was that most Californians were weirdly comfortable with their state's failures. *It's as if these people embrace disasters and fiascos.* For Charli, she had nothing but contempt for the citizens. *I would have led a revolution years ago before putting up with this craziness.*

Andy appeared and nodded to her as he approached the vehicle. He tossed his bag in the back of the van as he slid in, giving her a welcomed kiss. "Great to see you."

"Any problems with the flight?" she asked as she wheeled out of the pickup lane and merged into the slow crawl of traffic.

"They were obsessed with paperwork here," he said. "My FedGov ID, vaccination card, travel authorization approval? It's almost like they don't want people to come in."

"They are more paranoid than ever," she said as she exited the airport terminal area and moved onto a real road. "With our President being sworn in soon and the Ruling Council declaring the election a win for them, they are worried about this leading to war."

"At least the weather is great," Andy said, looking out at the palm trees they passed. "I came here a few times in my last job. I loved the climate, hated the human feces on the sidewalks and the drug needles thrown everywhere."

"You don't have to tell me. I was hiding in the NSF here," she said changing lanes abruptly. "I saw good officers regularly taken down by the SEs. All it took was someone claiming you made a racist remark, and you were off for a Tribunal or simply taken out of the precinct for an ass-beating in the parking lot. You were constantly looking over your shoulder as a cop."

"How'd you deal with it?" Andy asked.

She paused for a moment, drawing a deep breath. Charli had shared a lot with Andy since they met. He knew there were dark aspects to her personality. A part of her feared that when she shared the truth with him, he might balk and not want to date her any more. Charli weighed that against her desire that they not have secrets between them. "Truth?"

"Of course."

"There were some nights I went out and delivered justice on my own. If the SEs took out a good cop, I took out the SEs." She didn't have to define 'took out' to Andy; she saw understanding in his eyes.

"You did what you had to do," he assured her, which was a relief. "It's not much different than what we are doing here now. Sometimes people have to take things into their own hands."

"Thanks for understanding," she said. "Caylee has us set up at the Four Seasons. Travis should be arriving tonight."

"The Four Seasons?" Andy grinned. "I expected some seedy no-tell-motel."

"She said that they have good security. Besides, Jack is footing the bill. There's no reason for us to plan a kidnapping in a dump."

"Any luck in locating Rosa?"

"Not yet." Rosa Lopez was Raul Lopez's mother. During their planning meetings in Nashville, they had decided that rescuing him was not enough. His mother and sister were being held by the Newmericans, presumably at the Los Angeles's Century Regional Correctional Facility. Caylee had been blunt. 'It doesn't help us to just rescue Raul if they are holding his family hostage. We need to get them out first, and then we go and get Raul.' "I've got a false ID that I'm going to use tomorrow to get on the NSFCloud. Once we can confirm where they are, we can form a plan to get them out."

"What are the thoughts on that?"

"Travis wants to use explosives," Charli replied. "That seems to be his answer to most things. Truth be told, prisons are tough to penetrate. They do have weaknesses though. I've seen that over the years working in law enforcement. The biggest weakness is that they are built to keep prisoners from going out. Most are not constructed with the thought of anyone attempting to break in. That is the premise we are counting on."

"So it's a break-in?"

"Not necessarily. We need to find Mrs. Lopez first. Then we can get into the nuts and bolts of how to get her and her daughter out, assuming they kept them together. We also have to pin down where Raul is located."

They arrived 40 minutes later at the Four Seasons. As they parked and entered, Charli noted that the security staff were armed with assault weapons. There was a distinct split between the haves and have-nots in California. The poor were in constant strife. Rioting was not out of the ordinary. Crime was commonplace, and the NSF did what it could to stay out of the rougher neighborhoods. The wealthy, however, flaunted their security. *Everyone is about banning guns, except for the hired people that are protecting the wealthy.*

When they arrived at the room, Charli called Caylee first, letting the phone ring twice before she used the card-key to enter. Caylee motioned for them to come in and thanked Andy for coming. Caylee usually wore pants, but she was in shorts for the first time that Charli could remember. *It's hard to think of her having a relaxed side to her personality.*

Once everyone entered, Travis gave Andy a beer, and the four of them relaxed on the sofa and easy chairs. "While you were out, I picked up the rest of the uniforms," Caylee said.

"We are wearing uniforms?" Andy asked.

"*We* are," Charli said, nodding over to Caylee. "You and Travis are backup."

Eleven Hours Later ...

It had been a long time since Charli had worn an NSF uniform and just putting it on came with a feeling of dread. She had a fake NSF ID and badge. Caylee had her own. Anyone doing an in-depth check of their ID might spot the tiny flaws, but it was doubtful they would even check. Both Caylee and I were NSF at one point or another. *As long as we act confidently and behave like we belong there, no one is going to question us.*

There was no stealth. They walked into the glass covered lobby of the Los Angeles NSF North Hollywood Community Security Center as if they had worked there their entire careers. The desk officer looked up, but didn't even bother to challenge them. Once they were in the back, it was a matter of finding an empty office with a PC. Charli sat at the workstation and used her phone to pull up the ID and passwords that Jack had provided them. Caylee kept watch on the door.

The first time she botched the password; she realized it the moment she hit *Enter*. The second time she was slower, more careful. An NSF logo appeared with a swirling circle around it. *If this doesn't work, we will need to somehow get someone else's ID and password.*

The NSFCloud flickered on the screen in front of her. "Bingo." Caylee gave her a supportive nod, but said nothing as Charli went to work. She started with the list of current prisoners in Los Angeles's Century Regional Correctional Facility, but found no sign of Rosa or Maria Lopez.

"Anything?" Caylee asked.

"They're not there," she said, her fingers stabbing furiously fast at the keyboard.

"Look for their records. They must have transferred them."

"On it," she said slowly as she worked. It took a full minute of searching, Lopez being such a common name, but she found them. "Well, that's an unexpected twist," Charli said ruefully.

"Did you find them?"

"Yes. NSF transferred them right after Raul was captured."

"To where?"

"They handed them over to Social Enforcement."

"Crap," Caylee said. Charli understood her feelings. The NSF was organized. It had structure, so it could be navigated easily. The SE organization was a jumble of groups, some more sophisticated and structured than others.

"They went to Social Quarantine ... " Charli said reading the screen. "Some place called Santa Susana Pass Park. The camp's name is Grinder. Does that have any meaning to you?"

Caylee shook her head. "The clock is ticking. See if you can find Raul," she prodded.

Charli worked fast on the keyboard. Raul Lopez's file was listed as NS—National Security. Fortunately the IDs that Jack had scrounged for them were high enough to get access. It took another four minutes to finally determine where Raul was. *Holy shitballs! That's the worst place possible.*

She stared at the screen in silence, then inserted her flash drive, dumping all of the open windows down to the drive for storage. That process took another two minutes.

"You found him," Caylee stated.

"Yeah, I did," she said solemnly. "It's the worst possible place though."

"Where?"

"The Supermax in Colorado," she said, pulling the flash drive as the download completed. She logged off and wiped down the keyboard.

"Damn," was all that Caylee said. Charli understood all too well. The Supermax was a fortress in every respect. Where most prisons were designed to keep people in, the Supermax was designed to also keep people out. It was a daunting prospect. As she stood and moved to the door, Caylee peered through to make sure that the coast was clear.

As they walked toward the door, Caylee muttered just loud enough for her to hear, "Well that sucks."

"It's a damned fort," she replied in a low tone. "That doesn't mean it's impossible."

"We need to focus on getting Mama Lopez and Raul's sister," Caylee said, clearly attempting to compartmentalize the new information. "We do this one step at a time."

Charli nodded as they exited the building. *This mission just got infinitely more complicated ...*

Canaan, Vermont

Su-Hui Zhou sat behind the seat of his Subaru hybrid sedan with his wife Hachi next to him in the passenger seat. As they approached the New Hampshire border from Vermont, they pulled into the border checkpoint. The checkpoint looked more like some old fashioned gas station, a building with an extended roof that you parked under. Just beyond it was the Connecticut River and the state of New Hampshire. There was no line of vehicles. They simply pulled in, and a young man wearing the uniform of the NSF border guards approached the driver's side.

"Good day folks," he said. "Identification please."

Su-Hui handed them over. "You are from Indiana? Why are you

going to New Hampshire?"

Su-Hui nodded. "We wanted to get in some skiing. In our homeland snow is rare. We heard that the Canadian ski slopes were very good."

"Well I don't know about that," the guard said, surveying their passports casually. "We have some good ones in Vermont."

"You've picked a tricky time to travel. We are limiting traffic to New Hampshire. You mind popping open your trunk?"

He feigned disappointment. "We are no national security threat." Reaching down with a millisecond of hesitation, he activated the trunk hatch. The border guard walked to the rear of the vehicle for a few seconds, then slammed the trunk shut. Su-Hui suppressed a sigh of relief as the guard came up on the driver's side.

"You sure packed a lot."

"Cold weather clothing takes up a lot of space. My wife," he nodded to Hachi at his side, "she tends to bring everything with us. She even packed a swimsuit. Can you believe that?"

The young border guard grinned back. He looked convinced, but there was always a chance that he had not been. "Where are your skis?" he asked.

"We rent them. As I said, we have not seen much snow before. I fell quite a bit, even with the lessons," he said with a grin. "I'm glad I didn't spend a lot buying skis."

The young guard eyed him with a smile, handing back the passports. "You folks might want to reconsider going over there. New Hampshire has thrown in with the Americans. There's a lot of tension right now. I can't stop you from going over there; you seem innocent enough, but there's no guarantee that they will let you in." He nodded across the bridge to a checkpoint of concrete barriers that forced cars to zig zag for inspection by police on the other side. "You might be better off staying here in Vermont and skiing here."

His wife frowned beside him. "I really wanted to see New Hampshire. With all of this election business, you never know when we will get another chance."

The guard bent down to see her. "Like I said, you can go across. There's no assurance that they will let you in or out." The guard handed the passports back.

Su-Hui nodded to him; handed the passports to his wife, and they slowly turned onto the road and crossed the bridge. Snow started to fall, melting on their windshield as he reached the checkpoint on the other side.

The guard in New Hampshire was accompanied by a trooper from the National Guard. He was not wearing the NSF insignia, though Su-Hui could see where the patches had been sewn on by the slight fade to the coat. "Good day," the older guard said. "What can I do for you?"

He handed the guard his passports, and then bent down slowly and reached under his seat. He pulled out two small plastic cards and presented them slowly to the guard. The two officers reviewed the two sets of ID; then the older trooper turned and started talking into his walkie talkie. The conversation seemed to go on for several minutes. He walked in front of their Subaru and read the license plate number. After another few tense moments, he walked back over to the driver's side of the vehicle and returned the ID.

"Mr. Zhou, your liaison is at the Hope Baptist Church. Drive straight ahead to where the road ends. Hang a left. It is on the right."

"Thank you."

"No sir, thank you and God Bless America," the trooper said.

The directions were easy to follow and Su-Hui pulled into the parking lot of the church. It was an old, stately structure, stark white with a steep sloped roof and tall steeple. They got out, and the cold wind stung him. Twilight was coming, and off to the west, over Newmerican territory, the sun was setting behind the tree line. Pulling his wife close to him, he made his way to the front door of the church.

The warmth inside was welcome. As he stepped inside, a hulking man in a red flannel shirt came over. "They told us you were coming," he said. "You must be Su-Hui. I'm Randy … Randy Birdsell." He extended his massive, calloused hand and squeezed Su-Hui's so tight that it almost hurt.

Randy handed the plastic ID cards to the trooper guard who surveyed them. "Welcome to New Hampshire," he said. Gesturing into the church, Su-Hui saw many people milling about. Tables lined the walls, and several of the pews had been removed. Weapons were laid out along with crates of ammunition and a wide variety of implements of destruction.

Most of the people wore green camouflage and covered a wide range of ages—some with silver or white hair to younger men that were clearly wearing uniforms from recent military service. "I take it you had no trouble getting here," Randy said.

"None. We brought what we were asked to. Three boxes of remote detonators, a box of dynamite, detonating caps, det cord, and a few other surprises. It's in our car in the parking lot, the blue Subaru."

Randy put his fingers to his lips and whistled loudly. "Derrick and Jane. Go on out to the blue Subaru and bring in what these two fine folks brought us." Two of the younger people in the church started for the door while Randy escorted the Zou's further in. "We have some fresh coffee brewing if you'd like a cup."

"Thank you," his wife said, heading off in the direction that Randy had pointed. "I'm glad you got through. Word is they might be sealing the border off pretty soon. If that happens, you might be stuck with us for a while."

"That was always the plan," Su-Hui said. *After what happened to my daughter. Newmerica has to be made to pay.* He remembered his struggles as a refugee when he first came to the nation. It had not helped that he had come into California, a cesspool of socialism if there ever was one. Newmerica had stripped him of far more than all of his money. It had cost him his daughter.

After they moved from California, he had stumbled onto the Sons of Liberty almost by chance. They had reached out to him, not pushing ideology, but helping him get on his feet once he managed to get free from California. Where Newmerica taunted its values of diversity and inclusiveness, they were often little more than words. His new neighbors who were in the SOL had actually embraced his family as equals and had helped them get on their feet.

The swearing in of the American President in New York had been jaw dropping. It galvanized Su-Hui. He immediately went to his friends in the Sons of Liberty and pledged his support—whatever that entailed. *After what they allowed to happen to Ya-ting, I need to fight against these people.* When they had asked him to smuggle much needed equipment into New Hampshire, he did not hesitate, despite the long and dull drive through Canada in the winter.

Newmerica cost me my homeland, and for that, they must be held accountable. America never would have abandoned us in our time of need. Hachi did not just understand; she wholeheartedly agreed with him. As his wife had said, "The things in life we cherish are the things we must struggle to obtain." When he had suggested going alone on the trip, she had simply packed her bags silently and put them in the car. He had rarely been so proud of her.

Randy introduced him to several other members. They were not from New Hampshire alone. He met two brothers from Texas and a tall, black youth from Arizona who wore a massive .44 magnum automatic on his hip. Two tough looking women from South Carolina were cleaning weapons on a church pew and greeted him warmly. After the introductions, Randy turned to him. "Some folks here in town have a spare bedroom and they will take care of you tonight. After that we are going to have you go to Stratford and from there, Lisbon. That's going to be your home for the time being. We have a few checkpoints along the way, but we can tell you how all of that works tomorrow."

"I expected more National Guard," he said candidly.

Randy chuckled. "Oh, they are around. We have no intention of fighting these assholes the way they want. Our guys are hunkered down and hidden. If they try and push across that bridge, well, there'll be blood flowing in the street."

Clearly there is a level of organization I am not seeing. It was strangely reassuring. Randy continued, "My wife would kick my ass for not being more hospitable. Are you folks hungry?"

Hachi joined him, cradling a hot cup of coffee, speaking before he could raise the subject. "Famished."

"Well, you passed the Spa Restaurant on the way in. You give them the code letters, and dinner is on the owner, Rachel. They are patriots just like the rest of us."

"What is the code?"

Randy flashed a wide grin, causing both of his chins to ripple. "GBA"

God Bless America. Su-Hui smiled. "I think we can remember that."

CHAPTER 3

"The loss of some petty freedom is nothing
compared to what is gained."

Newmerica Penitentiary, Administrative Maximum Facility
Florence, Colorado

Deja Jordan hated being in Colorado during the winter. Coming from Minnesota, she was used to the biting cold, but the air was a little thinner in Colorado. The cold seemed to penetrate her body a little more than back home. Even inside the massive prison complex, it took several minutes for her feet to start to warm up. While the thermostat said it was 68 degrees, to her it felt like 40.

She had requested returning to her home in Minneapolis, but had been turned down. "You know this Raul Lopez best. We want you to get what you can out of him before his Tribunal." That was the excuse she had been given. NSF headquarters in the District had sent her two experts on interrogation. They had coached her, taught her techniques that she didn't know existed, helped her craft her questions to convince her prisoner to talk. So far it had been to little avail.

Almost every day she spent hours with Lopez, attempting to pry from him the names of the people that had assisted him along the way, details about the Order of the Bell, and the name of the mysterious woman that had helped him cross the Ohio River with such stunning and deadly efficiency. She really wanted to know how a kid who had been in the Youth Corps had somehow become a domestic terrorist. *If we don't get that answer, there could be others out there that flip against the cause.*

It wasn't that Raul stood mute. He just never gave her what she was looking for. She had the guards hold him while she beat him savagely, asking him about the Sons of Liberty between each punch, but he only looked up at her and grinned through the pain and blood. They waterboarded him twice, but both times the guards had botched it and had left him half-drowned and passed out, and he had to receive mouth-to-mouth. They had starved him for a few days, but it never shook his resolve.

Deja had always found abuse effective in getting people to talk, but Raul refused to capitulate. She slowed those sessions, not so much out of respect for Raul, but because they were stirring bad memories. Before her father left, he had been a beater. He would demand answers for things from her mother, and if she didn't give him the ones he wanted, he would backhand her, hard. One time, she remembered her mother spitting out a tooth. Deja had jumped her father, attacking him, only to be kicked hard herself and sent painfully into a wall, cracking the wallboard in a few places. *One thing I inherited from Momma was the ability to take a hit.*

During one interrogation session with Raul, she saw a thin spray of blood hit the white cinderblock walls of the room from one of the guard's punches. The splatter pattern reminded her of a similar image from her childhood involving their living room wall. That was when she ordered the guards to stop. She felt futility in the effort, and wondered if it was because of her father.

She knew remarkably little about her father, Jamar Jordon, beyond the rage he couldn't control. He had gotten her mother pregnant with Deja when she was only seventeen. They had married long enough for her to get his name, but she didn't even have a picture of him. Her memories were that he was gone more than he was there; and when he was there, he brought the fight with him. Her father was a drinker, though she only realized that in her later years. She had fading impressions of him coming home in the middle of the night, that aroma of alcohol … she didn't make the connection until she was a lot older. Her mother had kicked him out; at least that was what she had told her young daughter. Deja always wondered if he had just given up and moved on. If they divorced, she didn't know about it, and was wise enough not to bring it up with her mom.

Patience was the key with Raul. She would sit and talk with him about anything. She wanted him to open up, but he wasn't about to do that between punches or kicks. Deja spoke about her childhood, her friends, joining Social Enforcement, whatever she felt like. Most of the time Raul sat quiet, but bit by bit, he was starting to open up to her. He would add to the things she was talking about with his own life experiences. *He's breaking down without even realizing it.*

The problem was that her patience was wearing thin. She woke up at night in cold sweats, terrified of his words from one of their first interview sessions. Deja had pressed him for the name of his female accomplice, the one that had devastated her team in Ohio. Raul had replied, "She's the person that is going to kill you before this is over." Then he roared with laughter. That line and the laugh tore at her sleep, made her wake up and jerk upright, her heart pounding. *That woman murdered most of the SE team. I was almost taken out by Lopez with a shotgun. Who was she? Where did she develop those skills?* Raul's confidence that she was still out there, that she would kill her, was a feeling that Deja could not shake. It whittled away at her sleep like a rat nibbling on cheese. The deadly possibilities that lurked in the shadows of her mind were punctuated with the thought that Raul's accomplice was going to come for her.

No. It wasn't possible. This was the Supermax prison. No way in, no way out. As she made her way through the three security checkpoints, she entered the conference room off of Unit J. She had him moved there since isolation didn't seem to faze him. The prisoners in J were forgotten dredges, leftovers from the Liberation. Some had been politicians; others had been alt-right radicals that had opposed the Ruling Council. The FedGov liked to spread out such events, use them to help keep the population in line with an occasional dose of fear. Deja appreciated the strategy because it worked.

There were two forms of justice in Newmerica. The law was a slow and ponderous process full of loopholes, technicalities and inequities. The law was the realm of the police and lawyers. The guilty sometimes got away with crimes because they had wealth or a good lawyer or both. The law lacked equity to her, despite what the politicians promised. Social justice was the tool of the SEs. Tribunals were not burdened with laws or rules. Social justice was administered by a simple majority rule—the voice of the people. It was administered quickly and effectively. As a Social Enforcer, she enjoyed the rush of social justice, the righteousness of a Tribunal done right. That was what awaited Raul, eventually.

In the meantime she had him transferred into Unit J so that he would start to let down his guard. Confinement there was far less rigid than in the rest of the Supermax. There were cameras everywhere, and microphones picked up everything he said. With a hint of freedom in his new surroundings, he might let slip some facts or details about his associates that she could use.

She hung her coat up and stood before the man who was chained to the table. He raised his head to make eye contact with her and then looked down as if he were unimpressed that she was there. She dragged the chair across the gray epoxied floor, making an annoying metallic scraping sound as she turned the chair around and straddled it backwards. Two guards stood behind Raul, outside of his field of vision. It was deliberate on her part. They were a constant threat that he couldn't see until they acted.

"If you're here to question me, you might want to skip ahead to the beating," Raul said slowly.

"I'm not in the mood to beat the shit out of you," she replied. "But I do want to spend time talking."

"I've got nothing but time on my hands, Deja. Of course, you could change that."

She had told him her name during one session, a 'good cop' approach that had failed utterly. She hated hearing it come out of his lips. *Best to ignore it ... time to put the twist to this little spic.* "Been making friends?"

Raul shrugged.

"I saw the video of you talking with Ted. That old fuck can't help you. The only reason he's still breathing is that your buddies down in Nashville didn't know that he was alive to begin with. What possible good would it do to kill someone that everyone assumes is already dead."

"He seems harmless enough," Raul said. "Then again, your type seems to like beating up on kids and senior citizens."

"What does that mean? 'My type'?" She felt her right fist ball up. *Go ahead, say black ... say female ... give me a reason.*

"An Enforcer," he said, as if he sensed her rage. "You decide what is right and what is wrong. Anyone disagrees with you—you inflict what you call *justice*."

"Your new friend is going to grow old and die in here," she said, refusing to take the verbal bait. "If he's lucky."

"The same may happen to you."

"It won't. I pissed off you and your bosses. You've already told me that I'm going to be judged by one of your Tribunals. I already have a death sentence. Isn't that how this works? You assign guilt; then do the trial?"

When he put it that way, it sounded bad. Deja plowed past his comment. "That might not happen," she offered. It was a lie, but she didn't care. "You see that arrangements can be made. Ted has lasted here for five years. If you cooperate, give me some information. You might get the same sort of arrangement he has. It's better than the death that awaits you."

Raul looked at her with eyes that did not betray his thoughts, dark orbs that offered nothing back. "What you want, I can't give you," he said. "You want names of my friends. You want a confession."

He's particularly chatty today. His time in J is softening him. "You keep protecting them, and I would respect that if they weren't a bunch of criminals. Your buddies in the Sons of Liberty—we're already on their trail. It's just a matter of time before we round them up. If you could give us a name or two, that would be nice. Your buddy Paco, he folded quick. That's how we found out about Father Ryan."

A hint of pink rose in Raul's cheeks as her word hit home. "You aren't worthy to speak his name," he said slowly.

"It's too bad that he died before I got my hands on him," Deja pressed. "Those old pedophile priests are a lot of fun beating."

Raul said nothing for a moment, regaining his composure. "I barely remember my real father," he said in a voice that was on the verge of trembling with emotion. "When we came across the border, he had already left us. You never met Father Ryan. You know nothing of the man other than the lies you say. For a short time, he was like the father I never had." Raul paused. "What is your relationship with you father?"

Deja was prepared for many things, but not that. Anger flared in her, a rage she couldn't fully define. It was a mix of wondering if he actually knew about her father, to 'how dare he?'

She said, "We aren't here to talk about my father. Let's talk about

Ryan. Tell me Raul, did you resist him fondling you, or did you like it?"

Lopez simply chuckled at her, which only added to her indignation. "He's a big threat to you," Raul said. "Even though he's dead, he represents some sort of threat to you."

"And how's that?" she demanded.

"He taught me your true nature. He showed me just how corrupt Newmerica was. He taught me what hope was. You can beat me. You can kill me, but I have shown the world the truth of what you people are. Those people I saved at Valley Forge—they were living examples of your evil. You can throw me in front of a Tribunal, put me in front of a firing squad, but you can't make the world unsee what I have shown them." He then put on a thin smile.

Deja glared at him. She nodded to one of the guards standing in the corner. She had not planned on having him beaten, but there was no other appropriate response in her mind. As the guard threw the first punch, she rose from her seat and left the room in silence. Only the moans and sounds of hits on Raul filled her ears.

Manchester, New Hampshire

General Reager stepped off of the C-17 Globemaster aircraft and straight into a snow-filled gust of wind. He had been in cold weather before, but not this cold. He came down to the steps and was greeted by a small contingent of officers who flashed quick salutes. "General Griffiths is inside sir," a lieutenant of the New Hampshire National Guard said. They escorted him into the terminal, and from there to the small United Club lounge that they had apparently commandeered.

He peeled off his winter coat and his uniform hat and was quickly saluted by General Hank Griffiths. He was a wiry man, short, a lean face that was nothing but skin and muscle tissue. Trip had read his profile before flying in and knew not to judge him by his size. *Three tours in the Middle East, four Purple Hearts, two silver stars. Griffiths is a scrapper.* "Pleasure to have you here General Reager," he said.

"Pleasure's all mine, though this weather is a bit much."

"You're one of the last flights in or out. I was a little surprised you came personally." Newmerica had issued a warning that after midnight, no aircraft would be allowed to fly in or out of New Hampshire airspace.

Trip knew it was a prelude to military action, and insisted he be on one of the last flights of supplies to come in. "We don't transmit much. The old NSA is part of the NSF right now and are likely listening to everything we broadcast. They have the same kind of hardware we do, so it's not like they are going up against some foreign government."

The lieutenant handed him a hot cup of coffee and Griffiths ushered him into a small meeting room. "I take it you didn't come up here for a pep talk."

"No," Trip said, taking a seat and then a sip of the hot, black coffee. "On paper, you report up to me, and since I proposed this strategy, I thought it might be good for us to meet face to face."

Griffiths wasted no time. Nor did he have a PowerPoint slide show. "We have mobilized our forces and organized our forces into what I call, *Harasser Teams*. Fast, mobile, able to hit and run. I agree with the strategy; in a straight-up battle, we could be overrun by sheer numbers. We have already planted IEDs at key junctures, places where we can bottle them up. The SOL is helping in the upper part of the state and are positioned inside of Lebanon and Nashua. They are going to let any initial force in, and then use IEDs and hit and run tactics on the supply lines once they get in here."

"The supply lines are the key," Trip said.

There was an old axiom in the military that applied. "Amateurs talk about tactics, professionals talk about logistics."

Trip continued. "They can subsist for a short time off of the local population, but if we pinch their supply lines long enough, it will leave them in an impaired state."

General Griffiths nodded. "For the last week or so, we have diverted gasoline tankers to hidden locations so we can use them. Same with incoming food shipments. The locals aren't happy about it, but they are more pissed at the thought of Newmerica invading New Hampshire."

"Local support for this effort is key. Once they see armed units patrolling their streets, it will drive up your supporters in the community. I assure you."

"Agreed. We've formed some Home Guard units, recruits from the VFW—all with combat experience. They are hankering for a good fight! The State Police are coordinating with us as well. When the invaders cross the border, the police are going to fade away to wage guerilla operations. They have a shitload of riot equipment, armored vehicles, M1117s for SWAT; you name it."

Trip drank in the information and was so far impressed by General Griffiths. "The key is to let them in. Then put the squeeze on them."

"The Sons of Liberty are going to operate out of the forests and mountain regions to the north and west of the state. A lot of our people are good skiers and can get into areas they won't be able to enter for the next three months or so. In a lot of areas, if they try and pursue us, they are going to find themselves in a world of hurt."

"Good," Trip said, taking another sip of the coffee. "The planes I flew in with have an Avenger short-range mobile defense missile system. I also have brought crates of old Stingers, some Carl Gustafs, and some Javelins. Once you start the squeeze, they will resort to flying in supplies. You start taking out their aircraft, and it will frustrate the hell out of them."

"Excellent. Sir, I need to know, am I permitted to execute operations in the surrounding state?"

The question intrigued Trip. "What do you have in mind?"

"They are going to be utilizing ANG forces out of the surrounding states. In anticipation of that, we relocated the majority of our Air National Guard equipment to private airfields, places they wouldn't expect to look. Our equipment is going to be hidden fairly well, an advantage of a lot of snowfall. I'm harboring my aircraft during the winter. Those little fields get buried pretty fast anyway. Come spring, however, we will be able to escalate with an air offensive. I'd like to hit their air bases when I get the chance."

"I can't foresee a problem with that. If those states are mounting operations against you, that makes them riders in this rodeo."

"If necessary," Griffiths said cautiously. "I'd like to be able to send some of my Harassers into those states as well. Our Governor feels strongly that if they are coming here and waging war, that makes their states active participants in this invasion. I think they need to feel a little of the heat themselves, if you catch my drift."

It makes sense. Hit the supply lines before they ever reach New Hampshire. "Not a bad idea General. As long as your targets are military, I don't see a problem. In fact, you might want to leverage the Sons of

Liberty for those kinds of missions. They blend in with the locals better than uniformed troops."

"I've already started on the plans and target lists."

Trip was impressed. "When they come, the ground commander will likely want to seize the local TV and radio stations so that only their side of the story gets out. The TRC is going to try to convince the locals that this is for their own good; that they are liberators; that no one should provide your troops assistance."

Griffiths nodded. "They are barking up the wrong tree with that thinking. The people of this state are damned independent. They are not fond of any government, let alone one that comes with an army. Truth be told, I hadn't thought about the media much. We can probably mobilize them, have them broadcast remotely using some of our equipment and the gear they have in their own mobile news units."

"I would recommend rounding up any known Social Enforcers you have in the state. Put them in quarantine or in jail. They are likely to get might uppity once Newmerica tanks and troops roll in." He realized for a moment just how much of his Texas drawl had crept into his voice and mentally brought it into check.

"Already on it. The State Police have been monitoring them, and the plan is to apprehend them all in the next few hours."

The mention of the State Police triggered another thought in Trip. "During the Fall, Newmerica targeted the families of law enforcement. It was one of the ways they got them to stand down during the coup. You might want to pass the word to law enforcement that their families need to go into hiding."

"Colonel Raymond of the State Police is a loyal American and started that process a few days ago. Nobody is going to be putting the squeeze on them."

"Good." His mind quickly shifted back to military matters. "Our intelligence says they are mostly massing on the Massachusetts border," Trip said. "I have my G2 pumping the latest to your people."

"I saw. They have units coming in from Connecticut, New York, Maryland, and some air support from Michigan," Griffiths said. "Vermont has a convoy in Woodstock, no doubt to make a move on Lebanon, and beyond."

"It's a hodgepodge of National Guard units, which might work to your advantage."

"There's always the risk that they will surge—send in a lot more forces to try and smother our efforts." There was a hint of caution in his voice, the kind that came from an experienced combat commander.

"I know. Don't worry about that. I intend to give them a different priority down south," Trip said, allowing himself to smile slightly. His move on Georgia was being staged already. *I'm counting on them not being able to handle two things at once.*

"Very good," General Griffiths replied. "If you'd like sir, I can arrange a quick inspection of our forces here at the airport."

Trip waved his hand. "We can skip the formalities if you don't mind. Your people have a lot to do and a narrowing window of time to get it done. The last thing they or you need right now is some top brass interrupting their work."

"That's most appreciated sir."

"And that's another thing. My job as your commanding officer is to support you. While I love the formality of the military, we can drop rank when it's the two of us. Call me Trip."

That brought a smile to the face of General Griffiths. "Call me Hank," he said extending his hand. Trip gripped it firmly and shook it.

"Alright then," he said standing up. "Get me a list of anything else you need. With this air embargo they are going to push, I can't guarantee I can get it in via the airport, but there are other ways to get it to you. Give me your list, and I will do what I can to make it happen."

"I'll have it before your plane is refueled," Hank replied.

Trip locked gazes with the man's light blue, almost gray eyes. "You grab them and hold them here. Drag it out. Bleed them. I will give them something else to worry about. Together, we can make both of them regret stealing our nation from us."

Springfield, Illinois

The Vice President-Elect of Newmerica had deliberately chosen the Abraham Lincoln Presidential Library and Museum for the meeting. The facility had been closed for three years, but was still maintained. Lincoln had fallen out of favor with the Newmerica government right after the Liberation. He was a white male that had long been credited with freeing the slaves. That version of events, preached in schools for over a century, didn't fit the narrative that Newmerica desired. It was important for people of color to believe they had controlled their own destiny. Lincoln's involvement, especially as a Republican, was awkward. Where some politicians had been simply erased from discussion, he had been recast as a minor player in the freeing of the slaves.

Lincoln's statues were taken down, and while the library was left standing, it was well understood by citizens that they should not be seen visiting it. Everyone assumed correctly that the visitors were being monitored. It made things easier for Social Enforcers to identify individuals that needed their special kind of persuasive visitation.

Her NSF bodyguard detail had increased since the assassination attempt at the Capitol weeks ago. They were stationed on the roof and all around the building. She didn't fear a real assassination attempt by the American President. *He's bold, but he worries about how we look in the eyes of the rest of the world. Daniel and I are not burdened by those concerns.*

The assassination attempt was so large and daring that the majority of people never saw it for what it really was—a false flag attack. She had orchestrated it perfectly, the ultimate lever for her to purge the last bits of political opposition in the government and simultaneously generate pity for her and Daniel. She had played up the event afterwards. For two weeks she had kept one arm in a sling, knowing that it would garner sympathy from many. The fact that the entire attack had been staged was a secret that she alone possessed. *I followed the prime rule of assassinations—kill the assassins.*

Alex was extremely proud of what she pulled off. She had only wished her mother was still alive to have seen her as the next Vice President. *I would never have told her what I had done of course … she would have been proud of our victory.* The Vice President-Elect was denied the chance to tell her mother of her great victory. A rouge operative, Caylee Leatrom, had viciously murdered her mother and brother. *When she is finally caught, I will see her scream in agony for what she took from me.*

A knock at the door came from one of her security detail, and he opened it to usher in the delegates. She walked over to them and extended her hand. "I thank you for coming," she said with a smile that was only partially fake.

The trio of men was led by a tall man whose leathery skin was dark and wrinkled. He shook her hand. "Booker Hickox," he said. "General of the Free Texas Movement." Gesturing to his two compatriots, he introduced them. "Salem Marshall and Miley Hines," he said. Where Hickox seemed at ease, she could sense the fear in Hines and Marshall. She liked it when people feared her. It was an advantage that she savored.

They took seats and she said nothing until her security detail closed the door. "I'm pleased that you agreed to travel up here for a meeting," she said.

"You can imagine my surprise at the invitation, Madam Secretary," Hickox said with a heavy Texas drawl.

"Vice President-Elect," she quickly corrected him.

"Of course," he said with a single nod. "As I was saying, your NSF folks spent a lot of time searching for us over the last few years."

"A free Texas was not something that we were comfortable with at the time," she said. "Times have changed."

She couldn't take credit for the idea; that went to Daniel Porter the President-Elect. "Texas has long been a thorn in our side because of being part of Newmerica."

The dishwater-blonde-haired woman, Miley Hines, interrupted her. "We never saw ourselves as part of Newmerica," she said proudly.

"I am aware of that," Alex replied, shifting in her seat. "For us, you and your people were an annoyance. Now that there is someone out of Tennessee claiming to be President, our view is that we have a mutual enemy." Texas had always resisted the Great Reformation. When Social Enforcement tried to destroy the Alamo, they had been slaughtered. Texas had only tolerated the Newmerica government because there was no alternative. Booker Hickox and his people had offered an option. They had been pushing for Texas to leave Newmerica and be its own nation. The movement had a lot of backers over the years. Now that Texas had thrown in with the American President, the situation was muddied.

"You've been hounding us for some time," the gray-haired Salem Marshall said. "Now you want to kiss and make up? A lot of our people got sent to prison and Social Quarantine for standing up against you."

There was anger in his words, a resentment that she couldn't ignore.

"What I am proposing is a truce of sorts. As a gesture of good will, your people in our custody will be released. We will provide you with what you need for your movement to expand. We know your people can't be happy with Texas being part of a fragmented United States. You will never have a better opportunity than now to stage a revolt."

They glanced at each other, clearly having broached the topic before. "We have plenty of financial support," Hickox said.

"Yes. The Russians and Chinese have been funneling you money, especially in the last month or so."

"How do you know about that?" Marshall demanded.

She smiled slightly. "Please Mr. Marshall. The National Security Agency rolls up under the NSF. Did you really think we wouldn't notice foreign governments transferring your little organization that kind of money?"

Booker Hickox blushed, if ever so slightly. "We have backing. I'll admit that. What can you offer that money can't buy?"

"Money is worthless against tanks and armored vehicles. I can arrange for your people to get, shall I say, a deterrent against them. We have access to a lot of National Guard armories and the kinds of weapons that can help you. I can get you communications equipment that isn't easily tracked. Munitions. You name it."

"And all we have to do is take Texas from America," Hickox said.

"That's all we want. You get a free nation and we both give America a kick in the nuts," she said.

The trio looked at each other with Marshall leading the nod to accept the bargain. "I have to admit, I feel like I'm crawling in bed with the enemy," Hickox replied.

"Our mutual enemy makes us allies, whether you want to embrace that or not," she replied. The tall Texan nodded once and extended his hand. She shook it, her tiny hand nearly engulfed by his calloused one. She held back a smile but was overjoyed. *America will be able to do little against us if they are fighting a civil war in their own backyard …*

CHAPTER 4

"Data is the cement of our nation's foundation."

Santa Susana Pass Park, California

Caylee Leatrom drove the late model Jeep they had rented down the ravine, using it for cover. She stopped and put it in park, checking the GPS on the dash. Satisfied she was in the right place, she walked some 80 yards farther down and used some washed out tree roots to pull herself up and out.

She had a hard time imagining anyone coming to Santa Susana Pass Park for relaxation. It was dry, desert-like conditions. Sagebrush dotted the rocky outcroppings along the steep hills. In many respects, it reminded her of Death Valley. It was so desolate. She continued to hike up the hill and finally came across the road. She crouched low, following the roadway back parallel to the ravine below where the dust-covered Jeep was parked. It was slow going, but she knew not to rush it. She had already shot one rattlesnake an hour ago and she was close to her objective.

She had been on several dozen operations, starting with her time in the Army and then as a contract employee with the CIA, and finally as an operative for the NSF. The Secretary herself had betrayed her, set her up to be killed. That had set in motion a series of events, including her turning on Newmerica and killing the Secretary's family.

There had been one op she had done that she remembered fondly, and that was getting Raul Lopez out of Pennsylvania to what they both thought was safety in Tennessee. Newmerica wanted Raul badly, bad enough to insert a team that managed to extract him. She had grown fond of Raul; she trained him on how to fight and helped him through his struggles as the NSF tried to put the squeeze on him. *I made one mistake. I let myself get too close to him.* Caylee didn't regret it, but knew she had to acknowledge the fact.

It wasn't a romantic thing. She liked his raw innocence. He was a good listener in a world that spent most of its time talking or broadcasting. Most people his age were hooked on social media as if it were a drug, not Raul. To him, what mattered the most was personal interaction. He was a victim of Newmerica. Their SEs came at him, and when he defended himself, it led to riots. He found the Sons of Liberty and helped them save the lives of dozens of people he liberated from the Social Quarantine camp at Valley Forge. *When they finally found him, they crafted him into their worst criminal, a domestic terrorist. They lit up the entire nation searching for him, and when they found him, they kidnapped him.*

It infuriated her that they had stolen Raul back. Caylee was not the kind of person that dealt with defeat well. First, it was rare. While she made mistakes, especially early in her career, she always managed to learn from them and grow. This was different because it was personal. No one was asking her to bring back Raul; she was doing this because it was the right thing to do. *And the first step is to take away their leverage—his mother and sister.*

As she climbed along the dirt roadway, she spotted the camp in the distance. It was located on a dusty hillside, stripped of brush. It was larger than expected, with several factory-like buildings at the far end of the camp, past the rows of barracks. There were six guard towers, each manned with one or two guards, from what she could see with her binoculars. There was a large cinder block structure, single-story, painted gray. *That has to be their headquarters or administration.* The factory structures were puzzling. *I have seen a few Social Quarantine camps. I've never seen these kinds of structures.*

As her eyes swept the camp, she pulled the camera that hung on her neck and snapped several photos. Prisoners were clearly visible. She doubted she would see Raul's mother or sister, but wanted to see as much of the defenses of the camp as possible. They had solar panels on the roofs of the structures, and she saw the power lines going in. There were no landline telephone wires. Just power. *They are dependent on cell service. That might be useful.*

The sign over the entrance was weathered badly, the effects of wind and dust. "Santa Susana Camp 201," told a story as to how many Social Quarantine camps there were. When she had been working as an operative for the NSF, she never gave them a thought. People didn't talk much about the camps other than to acknowledge that undesirable elements of society were sent there. *I was like so many people, as long as they didn't impact my life, I never gave them a second thought.*

She counted the barracks—*fifty-four*. That's a lot of people—*more than any camp I've ever seen. Why so large?* Los Angeles was nearby and was huge, but this was not the only quarantine camp outside of the city. Size mattered for the mission of extracting Raul's mother and sister. The bigger the camp, the longer it would take to locate them and get them out safely.

The smokestacks of the factory began to release white smoke, and she surveyed them carefully with her binoculars. *Something isn't adding up.*

The camp had a massive parking lot with at least two dozen old, yellow school buses parked there. *They are moving a lot of people ... but to where ... and why?* The more she looked, the more confusing the situation appeared. Two buses roared up the road near her position, kicking up a fine dust that covered her as she ducked low. They entered the camp, and the prisoners were slowly marched out toward the barracks. *There is more going on here than meets the eye.*

An unmarked semi-trailer lumbered out of the camp, taking several minutes to get past the main gate. It was a commercial hauler. The vehicle started out of the camp, taking the road down toward her location. She slid behind a large boulder to avoid being seen. Dust swirled around her as the lumbering semi blew past her. Rising just enough to look at the back, she jotted down the license plate number. *It must be associated with those large factory structures.*

She climbed down the hillside slowly, making her way back to the Jeep. She needed to get images from another vantage point, and the sun was already starting to set. Every little bit of information she could gather was potentially useful. As she started the Jeep and turned it around in the dry ravine, she thought once more of Raul. *Hold on kid ... I'm coming ... first things first though.*

Nashua, New Hampshire

General James J. Donaldson couldn't feel the bottom of his feet in his boots as his Bradley fighting vehicle rumbled north out of Nashua toward Manchester. He stomped them several times quickly, but it did little to shake the cold. The warmest thought that he could muster was that he didn't plan to be in New Hampshire long. *Their pitiful little National Guard force is outnumbered and outgunned. If all goes well, I'm only in this cold place long enough to accept their surrender.*

Donaldson was riding into New Hampshire with the Connecticut National Guard. The New York NG units were advancing out of Brattleboro, Vermont from the western edge of the state. He had taken two hours to deploy in Nashua, eating up precious daylight, but for the General it was time well spent. An NBC news team along with their TRC handlers had filmed him at the Welcome to Nashua sign, where he praised his troops for a successful first phase of their suppression of the rebel state. "Nashua is just the beginning of bringing New Hampshire back into the Newmerica family." Playing to the press was vital. *The people need reassurance that this defiance is not tolerated and is being handled.* He liked having the press follow him. *I need to be the face of this victory.*

Per the TRC reps' suggestion, they had taken down the racist stars and stripes flag of America and in its place had hoisted the latest Newmerica flag. It whipped in the brisk wind and the TRC crew put searchlights on it for the shot so that it was fully illuminated. He was proud, not so much of the flag, but that they had gotten the perfect shot.

The initial thrust into the rebel state had been easy. Roadblocks took some time to remove, but thus far there had been little in the way of resistance. His Vermont Air National Guard forces out of Burlington reported that what little force the New Hampshire Air National Guard had was not visible. In fact, it looked as if their lone airport had been abandoned. While that had been a surprise, it was not a staggering one. *For all of their bluster, apparently they don't have the desire to fight. I can't blame them given the weather.*

The State Police had disappeared as soon as the column of tanks came into view—no doubt out of fear. They broke ranks with the NSF, and none of them wanted to be captured and subjected to whatever the Social Enforcers had in mind. The loyal SEs had been rounded up two weeks earlier, no doubt out of fear that they might provide Donaldson's force with assistance. *It doesn't matter. Once we have the state in our control, we can free them from jail.*

As they moved north on the Everett Turnpike, he heard a rumble of an explosion up ahead. The Bradley lurched to a halt, shaking the occupants in the back. "What is going on?" he demanded, getting to his feet.

"Problem ahead sir," was all the vehicle commander would offer. "The column has halted."

He popped the rear hatch and was blasted with a gust of snow-filled air that made his eyes water. Donaldson started up the turnpike passing three more vehicles of his column to where he could barely make out the rising smoke against the darkness of the encroaching winter night. Passing six other vehicles, he immediately saw the issue. The bridge ahead over a body of water was gone. One Humvee was hanging over the hole where the bridge had been. Smoke rolled from under the vehicle where it had apparently been damaged when the bridge in front of it had exploded.

A squad of troops were clamoring along the water's edge, attempting to pull two men from the frigid pond that bisected the road. Another team was running a line out on what little remained of the bridge, hooking it up to the rear bumper of the damaged Humvee.

The General moved to the Humvee that was now the lead vehicle and patted it. The commander, a sergeant, rose up. "What in the hell happened?"

"The bridge blew up with three of our vehicles on it," he said. "It just disappeared."

Three vehicles—damn! All of the column was loaded with troops, which meant he may have lost upwards of twenty men. The air was already in the single digits meaning that anyone hitting the water only had a few moments of possible survival before succumbing to hyperthermia and death. The sign at the end of the bridge said Bowers Pond. The four lanes of the road that led north ran out some 15 yards, then disappeared.

Where the low bridge had been was now simply a broken hole in the ice. Support pillars in the middle of the pond still held up a small bit of the bridge, but the rest was now gone—along with any vehicles that had been on it.

Anger rose quickly. *I should have ordered the bridges checked.* There was another road, somewhat smaller off to the east that skirted the body of water, but now it would mean backtracking the column. *I need to get orders out. Chances are they have rigged other bridges with explosives.*

As he stood next to the vehicle, he heard a series of cracks from the far side of the pond. Two of the troops on the rescue detail dropped, one screaming in pain. The sergeant next to him jerked back in the turret, blood spraying onto the snow that covered the top. The sergeant's body slumped limp as he bled out. His hot blood seemed to leave a momentary wisp of steam in the frigid winter air.

As the General poked his head up, he saw three or four flashes from the far side of the pond in the dense copse of pines. *They staged this. It is an ambush. They could have easily killed me!*

General Donaldson immediately dove for cover behind the Humvee. Two shots hit the Bradley that was behind him, pinging in the twilight. "I want suppression fire!" he ordered. Then it hit him that no one was there to listen to him. Darting back to the Bradley, he grabbed the radio. "This is Hawk One; lay down suppression fire on those flashes on the far side of the pond," he ordered.

The turret above him began a series of bangs as the cannon opened up. Donaldson left the vehicle, grabbing his walkie-talkie this time. Machine guns from the Humvees of the column dumped bursts of fire across Bowers Pond into the tree line of pines on the far side. Tracers, now brilliant, flashed across the icy waters, peppering the area where flashes had been seen. Explosions from the Bradley tanks in the formation shook the snow off of the bows of the tall pines on the far side. Two of the trees took direct hits and exploded, one collapsing onto the frozen waters of the pond not far from where the bridge had ended until a few moments earlier. No more flashes came from the trees, a sign that fighters had been killed or were in retreat. "Cease fire," he ordered. It took a second for all of the units to respond, the last machine gun spraying a lonely burst into the dark trees before going silent.

The General moved down to the bank of the pond. One of the men pulled from the water was wrapped in blankets and being led up. He saw Donaldson and paused, quivering with cold. "We never saw it. The bridge just disappeared," he explained as he was led past him. Down by the water's edge, one man lay dead in the snow, and another was wounded. The headlights from the road above were bright enough to illuminate the blood on the stark white snow where his comrades were attempting to wrap his wounded arm.

General Donaldson helped them lead the injured man up the shallow embankment to the road. When he reached the road, he returned to his Bradley, mentally processing what had happened. *They aim to fight a guerilla war. Why not do it in Nashua?* His training had always told him that such warfare favored built-up urban areas. There was a temptation to order his forces to shift over to the side road immediately, but night was setting in. *They may have blown this bridge to get us to take that other road. I could be ordering my men into another ambush.* Hesitancy ate at his thinking. Many of his colleagues had been stationed in the Middle East before the Newmerica withdrawal. They had fought insurgencies before. For James Donaldson, it was a new kind of war. *We know a great deal about how to wage this kind of war.*

The wind outside picked up; he could hear it whistling somewhere in the vehicle, no doubt a hatch that was not secured. We need to return to Nashua for the night, regroup. Manchester isn't going anywhere. He grabbed the walkie-talkie. "This is Hawk One. We are going to regroup in Nashua and start again in the morning." His own Bradley turned around but didn't start back down the road; there were simply too many vehicles that would have to go before it. Where he *had* been near the front of the column, he was now at the rear.

Paranoia surfaced. Maybe that was what they anticipated—us turning around, exposing our rear flank. Did we kill the people on the far bank, or simply drive them back temporarily. Bowers Pond was big, but that didn't mean that they were safe from fire coming across the river. "Hawk One to the units near the pond. Redeploy to act as a rear guard in case they are going to fire at us from the far side." The Bradley once more turned, facing its original direction, moving slightly off the side of the road.

Pausing for a moment, he tried to gather his thoughts. *They planned this all along. That's why the State Police disappeared at the border. They let me come in. They knew we would be driving on Manchester.* Slowly, he mustered his resolve. *Their leaders will regret thinking that I will tolerate this kind of war.*

Covington, Virginia

Grayson Steele sat in The Rail Bar and Grille with his wife and son, eyeing the door every time it opened. He was waiting for an old friend to enter. Frank Campbell was a private investigator. Grayson had used him many times before becoming a member of the House of Delegates to perform investigative inquires for his law firm. When he became frustrated with the NSF's response to his pleas about finding his daughter Maddie, he decided to risk exposing his identity by calling Campbell for help. While he trusted the man, there was always a chance that Social Enforcement might burst into the small restaurant and grab all of them.

He had wanted to come alone, but his wife and son insisted on coming. David, Maddie's younger brother, had changed after her disappearance. He had become silent, withdrawn. There was a rage in him; Grayson could see it, but getting David to open up about it was proving impossible.

The family had moved to West Virginia after they were spotted by a friend. He was still working on getting their names discreetly changed, but was facing hurdles with that. Covington was right across the border between the two states, and seemed to be a good place to meet. The only hiccup with the trip was that there were security crossings on the state line. It was no longer the border between two states. It was the border between two nations—Newmerica and America. Armed troops stood facing each other 200 yards apart. For Grayson, it was a reminder of how tense things were becoming. *We have been at war for a long time, and my family has been in the crossfire of it, but now it is more open.*

He was a little relieved when Campbell entered the grille alone. Frank Campbell was a short, black man, skinny, wearing a frumpy, fleece-lined jean jacket coat that made him look more like a day laborer than a private investigator. He waved his hand to his old acquaintance and came over and sat next to David. The waitress brought him a glass of water, and the detective settled into his seat. "It has been a long time," he said, taking off his coat.

"Thank you for coming," Grayson said.

"I did a little poking around with my contacts at the NSF," Campbell said. "Your hunch was right; they are not really actively working the case. They are in wait mode, waiting for someone to come forward with a tip or something tangible."

A long sigh came from Grayson. Before he could respond, his wife did. "Will you be able to find her?"

Campbell looked his wife squarely in the eyes; then he looked over to Grayson. "In my business, you don't make promises you don't know if you can keep. I will dig, more than what the police have been doing. I don't want to get your hopes up though. To me, this doesn't add up. Your daughter just doesn't come across as the kind of person that would run away."

David spoke up. "She didn't. Somebody did something to her."

Grayson was surprised that his son had weighed in. "She isn't alone. A number of kids disappeared that weekend." He slid the list over to the investigator.

Campbell looked at the list. "They all mysteriously disappeared?"

He nodded. "It doesn't make any sense."

The waitress arrived to take their order. Campbell ordered nothing other than a black coffee. He watched her leave and only spoke again when she was out of earshot. "I got hired two years ago by a family down at Virginia Tech. Same sort of thing—their son goes missing along with another few kids."

"Did you find him?" Mrs. Steele asked.

"It turns out the group was lured off campus and killed. It was a student SE group that was behind it. It never made the press because it was treated as SE activity. Social Enforcers are able to operate at will, as you already know. The school never wants to get involved because it's a no win situation for them, and the NSF turns a blind eye to this kind of stuff since Newmerica came into being."

His words seemed to suck the energy from the table. Grayson saw his wife's jaw sag, then quiver slightly. David stared at the man next to him, mute, brooding. It made sense in some sort of dark twisted way.

Campbell seemed to sense the impact of his words and tried to recover slightly. "It doesn't mean that's what happened to Maddie," he said. "I believe in being honest with my clients though—even more with my friends."

His wife nodded, suppressing a sob. "I understand."

Campbell folded the list and slid it into his jean shirt pocket. The waitress arrived with the coffee, and he waited for a long few minutes before taking a sip. "I have a young guy I work with. I will have him do some checking on the names on the list—see if we can find any connections with these kids and your daughter or in any other way. In the meantime, I'm going to check with car rental places to see if any vehicles have turned up missing. If they left campus, they had to have had transportation." He paused for a moment. "I know you don't want to hear this, but it is going to take some times—a few weeks at least."

Grayson nodded. "How much is this going to cost?"

Campbell waved his hand as if to cut him off. "You sent me a lot of business over the years before the shitstorm came down. I'm only charging you expenses. The rest is my sweat equity."

"I can't let you do that."

Campbell shook his head. "You really don't get a choice Grayson. I have a daughter the same age as your Maddie," he said glancing at Grayson's wife for a moment. "I know how I'd feel if she just up and disappeared.

"These Newmerica thugs operate with impunity. If these campus SEs are involved, they need to be brought to account and answer for what they did. I will look for your daughter and hopefully find some answers, even if they aren't the ones you want."

Grayson nodded. "Okay Frank. Thank you."

"God bless you," his wife added.

"God bless America," Frank Campbell added, hoisting his coffee and taking another long sip.

Stratford, New Hampshire

The Daniel Webster Highway was a two-lane affair that snaked through the dense forests of New Hampshire. The heavy snows had made it a narrow corridor where the blowers and plows had tossed the snow out of the roadway. Anyone driving down the highway would have felt as if they were driving in a tunnel with no top; the snow on the sides of the road was almost five feet deep.

As Su-Hui watched the approaching convoy of military vehicles, he cursed the stinging cold. *I thought I knew what winter was like in Indiana, but I had no idea what it was really like until I came here.* The locals had made sure that the brother and sisters that had joined New Hampshire's cause were properly outfitted. Despite the new boots and thick coat, he could not shake the cold.

They had been preparing for long days and nights for the inevitable invasion. Newmerica had broadcast it as if it were a television series. The mainstream media had interviewed guardsmen who told stories of how proud they were to move into the 'treasonous state' to help 'liberate' the people trapped there. They even had special music and graphics that came up when discussing the suppression that was about to come to New Hampshire. The resistance was being packaged for the viewing public to consume.

For Su-Hui and the other members of the Sons of Liberty that had sneaked across the border to help fight for the state, the hype on the television and radio only motivated them more. The talking heads of the media made it sound like New Hampshire was filled with terrible people, corrupt in their thinking. That had not been Su-Hui's experience. Everyone he met was incredibly friendly and thankful for the outside assistance. His wife Hachi had stayed at one of the SOLs many hidden operating centers where she was helping organize the meals and a makeshift hospital.

Su-Hui had been joined by a number of others from the Sons of Liberty. One had come from New York City, a feisty black woman that had been an official in the police department there before the Fall. She led a resistance group, NYF—New York's Finest—and was not the kind of person that you had a lot of chit chat with. Valerie Turner was all business and had been helpful in setting up their surprise for the convoy.

As he lay there, he reached down to the chain he wore around his neck. He touched the three brass bullet casings that hung there and thought of his daughter, Ya-ting. The bullets were important to him, a reminder of why he was in this fight to begin with. The bitter memories that clung to them came with a glimmer of hope. Somehow knowing they were there was reassuring to Su-Hui.

As the long line of green camouflage vehicles drove up the road, Su-Hui got anxious. "Now?" he asked, his hands holding the detonator.

Valerie lay next to him in the snowbank on the hill that overlooked the road; she shook her head. "Not yet."

"They are on top of the surprise," he reminded her.

Valerie was less than swayed. "Do you want me to hold the detonator?"

Su-Hui shook his head. *I need to be patient.* "I was in the Army for two years—my training would have had me set it off already. Apologies."

"No apologies are necessary." Turner continued in a low tone, as she angled her sniper rifle slightly, ruffling the white sheet that camouflaged their position on the hilltop. "We want some of them to get farther past. We'll break up their formation that way. We'll trap some in the middle, unable to move. Shooting fish in a fucking barrel."

As he watched, four more vehicles passed the point where the det cord had been wrapped around the big pine trees. "Alright," Turner said slowly. "You are good to go with setting off number one."

He turned the switch to the first of the triggers on the detonator and threw the switch. The det cord went off along the bases of the trees, raining splinters in every direction and shaking off massive amounts of snow. Four of the large pines fell from both sides of the road, crashing down on a Humvee that bore the New York National Guard logo on the side. The falling tree crushed the hood of the vehicle, blowing out one tire and raining snow from the bows all over it.

The column stopped. With the snow embankments, turning around would be difficult, even for the tracked armored vehicles. "Alright, you can set off number two now," she said. Su-Hui grinned and switched to the second switch. A half a mile back down the road, another series of detonations went off. The trees came down, thudding against a M113 armored personnel carrier as they now cut the column of vehicles into three parts. The ones in the middle were the real targets; they were trapped with trees cutting them off on both ends of the highway.

Soldiers got out, weapons at the ready. Most were wearing winter camouflage and seemed to be concerned they had been ambushed. *They have no idea what is happening ... it is just as Randy and Valerie had said.*

Switching to the last of the triggers on the detonator, his fingers hovered over the buttons that would set the charges off.

"Wait a minute. Let them come out and try clearing the trees," she said.

"I was planning on that," he replied.

They did exactly what she said they would. Two squads of troops were out, trying to figure the best way to deal with the lead blockage. Su-Hui assumed they were having the same problem at the rear end of the ambush as well. He could hear someone barking out orders. Chains were pulled out and vehicles ahead of the sudden roadblock were trying to jockey for position in order to pull the trees out of the way.

Valerie took careful aim with the big sniper rifle. "Wait for it," she said, her breathing sounding shallower as she aimed. She squeezed the trigger and the gun kicked. "Now!" she said mid-recoil.

Su-Hui hit the detonator on the third trigger. Four IEDs went off. These were artillery shells rigged with detonators that had been buried in the snowbank along the trapped section of vehicles. Snow flew into the air. A ball of fire billowed skyward, rolling in on itself, contorting with a cloud of black smoke; then came the concussion of the explosion and the sound of the ka-blams that filled the brilliant blue sky. Another Humvee was thrown sideways into the snow embankment, and it caught on fire just a few seconds later. The boxy M113s were badly damaged from what he could see as the snow stopped falling.

Valerie Turner did not seem shaken. She coolly aimed and fired another shot, though Su-Hui could not see if she hit her target. She squeezed off another two shots, then slid back under the cover of the sheet that hung like a low tent over the hole they had dug out on the hilltop. "I think I've shared enough ammo with the enemy for the day. We've had our fun, time to move out." As if to accentuate her point, he heard gunfire from below, nervous soldiers shooting in random directions.

Su-Hui gathered up the detonator and the wire roll and followed her down the back side of the hill to where their snowmobiles waited. Turner moved casually as did he. The National Guardsmen could not hope to find them or come up the hill in time to stop them. As he bungie-corded the gear down, he watched her strap the massive sniper rifle to the side of the seat. "You've done this before," he said, marveling at her calm.

"No," Valerie said. "It has been a long time coming though. This isn't a war of lightning strikes. It is attrition, slow and deliberate. We wear them down over time. That's the key to winning."

Su-Hui turned on his snowmobile and tightened the scarf that covered his face. A part of him struggled with what he had just done. *I have killed men and women, and it is wrong to feel good about it.* His mind went back to the memories of fleeing Taiwan when it fell to the Chinese. *Newmerica deserves this punishment. They doomed my nation and made us unwelcome visitors in this nation. Now they will pay the price for what has been lost.*

CHAPTER 5

"The American dream is a corrupt racist myth."

Newmerica Penitentiary, Administrative Maximum Facility
Florence, Colorado

Raul sat at the steel table with his tray of food, eyeing it with disgust. He appreciated the fact that he was now able to see and communicate with others, but the food they were given was the same swill they served when he was in solitary confinement. The beans were only slightly warmed, and their sauce was watered down and runny. What passed for a hamburger was a gray patty on a stale bun that looked as if it had been sat on. Covering it with ketchup helped camouflage the taste.

He was still sore from the most recent beating he had received. The swelling in his jaw had gone down, but it still felt tender. He didn't remember a hit on his upper arm, but there was a fist-sized purple bruise that was starting to fade to a jaundiced yellow color. It had been worth it. His interrogator, Deja Jordan, had lost her temper. *It isn't much of a victory, but it is a good start.*

Ted sat down across from him as he did every morning. The other prisoners tended to keep to themselves. One man would pick at his food, eat a little, then rock on the small bench until he was taken back to his cell. Another prisoner spoke to him several times, wanting to know what was happening in the outside world. For several nights, Raul felt popular, telling them about the swearing in of the President and the relief of Valley Forge.

Ted was the only one that did not become disinterested in him. The older man had shoulder-length, silvery-gray hair with a streak or two of black that defied his age. He had a full beard and a mustache that had a little more black hair in it. When Ted finally saw his face, he remembered who the man was—a prominent politician from his home state. Ted smelled like an old man, a strange sweaty aroma that he associated with one of his high school teachers. Raul had presumed that Ted had died during the Fall, but here he was, alive and as much a prisoner as himself. *I always thought he was taller when I saw him on TV.*

Ted took a bite from his burger and chewed it heavily. "I've had worse," he said as he swallowed it.

"The food is terrible," Raul said, nibbling on his burger apprehensively. He knew he had to eat, regardless of the taste. Most of his day was spent either working out in his tiny cell or contemplating the limited options of his future. "They are likely trying to starve us."

Ted paused for a moment, then looked around the common space in the corners of the ceiling. "You have to always remember they are watching and listening to everything we say. If you complain too much, they just amplify the thing you are bitching about."

Raul glanced around and saw at least two cameras. There were two in his cell as well. Even his bowel movements were being documented. The thought of Deja having to watch him shit made him at least a little happy. "Thank you for reminding me."

"You also should assume that everyone in here could be a mole."

"A mole?"

"A plant … an agent of the NSF or SEs or whatever damned acronym they are using now. They will put them in with the prisoners like us in hopes that we will open up with them. There was one in here a year or so ago. One guy spilled his beans about where his family was hiding and then they got visited by the SEs."

"What about you?" *Do I dare trust Ted?* He was a politician, which meant that Raul had a little suspicion about him to begin with. *Ted was powerful before the Fall. Maybe he has survived by turning on the others?*

Ted chuckled. "My advice stands. Don't trust anyone, including me. You shouldn't trust anyone in life who tells you that you can trust them. That's my general rule."

There was something oddly reassuring in the way he laughed at the question Raul had posed. *I need a friend, not to share secrets with, but someone to talk to.* Memories of being in isolation made him fidgety. There was no form of real entertainment for the prisoners other than conversation, and some were already quiet and distrustful. The television they had only spit out TRC propaganda, and now that he saw the programming for what it was, it was boring. Ted had a calm about him, one that told him that he had somehow come to cope with being locked up—a thing that Raul needed to master. He eyed the older man and dared to ask a question that had been nagging him. "I have been meaning to ask," Raul said, poking at his beans. "How did you end up here?"

Ted shook his head. "I was at a fundraiser back home when they seized power. I went up to my ranch, a private little getaway. I made the mistake of contacting the Pentagon to try and get an assessment as to what was going on. Someone there turned me over to the authorities. Damned FBI HRT team came in and arrested me. Of course by then, half of the House and Senate were already dead, and they were telling us that the President was in custody."

"I would have thought they'd put you on trial."

"No. I'm sure that bitch in charge of the NSF wanted to, but the thought of me mounting a defense probably stopped her in her tracks. Hell, they had already killed most of my colleagues. I think they were holding me for some sort of leverage. I never really found out. My own theory is that they just plain forgot they had me in custody. They probably hope I will up and die of old age, but I'm not quite willing to go, not yet at least."

"I will go to trial soon," Raul said. "They want to make an example of me. The woman that oversees my beatings has told me as much."

"Does it frighten you?" Ted asked.

Raul nodded. "Good," Ted said. "If you are frightened, you are alive still. We all have fear in this place, Raul. There were times when I used to wonder if the legal system was broken. It was never meant to have the flaws that it did. As a politician, I believed we should fix them. What this Ruling Council has built in its place is designed to be unjust. The concept of a fair trial is gone. To them, fear is what keeps people in line as opposed to the rule of law. It started with COVID; then the Fall …

they used fear as a lever to get us to do what they wanted. They have dehumanized people, made us a commodity. This woman you've told me about, the one that interrogates you, she doesn't see you as a person. You are a number—a threat.

"Well, if you have fear, that means you are human still. So despite everything she's tried on you, she's failed."

There was something in the way that Ted said it, with a flash of a smile under his beard and mustache that made Raul feel good. "There are times when I feel like I should talk … that it might stop the questions."

"But you don't."

Caylee wouldn't want me to. Raul would never say that out loud, but that was the source of his resolve. There were times when his resistance was strained, when he was near the breaking point, but memories of Caylee always gave him something to mentally cling to. "If you were me, what would you do?"

Ted chuckled, stroking his silvery beard in thought. "Raul, you need to make your own decisions. From what you've told me, you have done a pretty good job so far. You don't need my opinion. I'm just a forgotten politician, locked away until I give them the satisfaction of dying in my sleep. But if you want to know, I would keep my mouth shut, just like you've been doing." The older, shaggy man paused for a moment. "Are you religious Raul?"

He nodded. "Catholic."

Do you remember Psalm 69?"

He felt a moment of embarrassment at not knowing it. "I don't."

"It's helped me in here. I don't remember the exact verse, but that's not important. It goes something like, 'The Lord hears the needy and does not despise his own people who are prisoners.' If you are a good Christian, it doesn't matter what these people think about you; you're still loved by God."

Those words made Raul feel good. Ted had been an important man before the Fall. He wasn't trying to pry information out of him; instead he was giving him an important message—trust your faith. Faith was more than just the Bible though. Faith was a trust in others. Raul had a person he had faith in, Caylee. *I know her. She will eventually come for me.*

"Do you have family out there?" Raul said, nodding off at the wall.

Ted nodded. "I did. At one point an interrogator told me they were dead … I guess that was to break my spirit. Another a few months later said they were in Social Quarantine. I don't know where they are really. I like to think that they managed to get away. Otherwise they would have used them more to get me to break. What about you?"

"They have my madre and sister. I saw my mother on television." The thought of his family angered him for a moment. *They used her to try and lure me in. She was nothing but bait to them.*

Ted seemed to understand; his knowing nod said more than words. "They would want you to be strong Raul. These people will use them against you, but remember, they raised you to be better than the people who are beating you."

That helps … my madre would *want me to be strong.* Ted leaned in closer to him, speaking in a whisper. "They can't take everything away from you in here. They can't take hope." He winked at Raul, almost playfully. Suddenly Raul felt something on his shoulder, a beefy hand. "Finish up; you have 2 minutes until afternoon lockdown," the large guard said.

As Raul forced down the rest of his burger and a few now-cold spoonfuls of beans, he found a new determination to resist his jailers and the interrogations of Deja Jordan. *Caylee will come. It may take time, but she will come. I need to always be prepared and when she breaks me out, I will take Ted and the others I can with me.*

Blytheville, Arkansas

General Trip Reager looked at the convoy of vehicles that were staged on and around I-55 in Blytheville, Arkansas. The flat plains on both sides of the highway were a virtual parking lot of Humvees, armored personnel carriers, and a few tanks. There were only a few trees, and those had long ago shed their leaves for the winter chill. Unlike New Hampshire, there was no snow on the ground here, just a brisk wind.

He had chosen this location for the force to enter Missouri because it was open and exposed. He wanted the media to film the force, at least from a distance. More importantly, he wanted the military commanders of the Newmerica forces to see this as a threat.

St. Louis was one of the Newmerica Autonomous Zones, just like Atlanta. They harkened back to the CHOP (Capitol Hill Occupied Protest) in Seattle prior to the Fall. It was a few hours travel north on I-55. It stood in defiance of the election and of the rest of the state, a hotbed of Newmerica loyalists. In that respect, it was very similar to Atlanta.

His enemy expected a reaction from the American forces, and Trip was going to provide it. The venture into Missouri, however, was not the real thrust. His objective was Atlanta. This push was a diversion, something to draw the attention of the Newmericans while the real operation kicked off on the Georgia border, heading for Atlanta.

Trip knew he was a magnet for the media. Punching out the MSNBC reporter had only fueled the ire of the left-wing media. CBS ran a segment on their evening news about Trip, highlighting the 'slaughter' he led in San Antonio and wrapping up with images of dead bodies in the streets of Chicago. The last part irked him slightly. He had been there, on the ground, when the Newmerica forces had attacked his people. The stack of dead bodies was a piece of fiction, actors or some other staged clip. It was all designed to make him look far worse than he was.

All of the media channels that were certified by the TRC replayed his punch for days. Trip would never admit it out loud, but he still laughed each time he saw the footage. The reporter had it coming, as did the CBS producer that had crafted the hit piece on him. *I will gladly apologize once they start practicing actual journalism.*

That was why he was in Blytheville: to draw in the media and attention. His role as ground commander of the loyal American Army implied he would be leading the next operation. While they all focused on his presence there, the real operation would launch into Georgia. There would be plenty of time for him to join the real task force.

As he walked around the green and brown camouflaged Humvee, a huddle of reporters saw him and moved up to him quickly. A flurry of calls of 'General,' and jumbles of questions barraged him worse than any physical barrage he had ever found himself under. *This is why I'm here, to distract them.* It was hard not to smile at that thought.

One voice found a gap and rose above the others, "Don Voigt, ABC News. General is that invasion of Missouri a prelude to further aggression against the Newmerican government?"

"Last I checked, Missouri is part of the United States of *America*," he said firmly, almost as he had rehearsed it. "And this isn't an invasion. We are simply moving on St. Louis to restore order there."

"But St. Louis is a free, autonomous zone," another reporter said. "Sending in military troops is simply going to result in innocent people being killed."

"The Governor of Missouri asked that we address it as a rebellious seizure of the heart of St. Louis. Our forces aren't going up there to cause trouble. This autonomous zone is in defiance of the legal authority and government there and cannot be permitted to remain." Those words had been prepared by Jack Desmond's people at the Southern White House, and he did his best to stick to them. His Texas drawl was his only personal contribution.

"Isn't the legitimacy claim of the American President the same of that of Daniel Porter and the Newmerica government?" another reporter asked in a follow-up question.

He knew it was a verbal trap, but he ignored the risks. Much of that was his military training. When faced with an ambush, you either avoid it, or plow through it and into the ambushers. "Like most true Americans, I believe that these Newmerica thugs got into power in a coup d'etat. You want to talk brutality, ask what happened to the majority of the House and Senate. They tried to kill the President now, twice. Once when he was Vice President and once just a few weeks ago. Newmerica is a fallacy, a lie perpetuated by a bunch of opportunist politicians and ANTIFA thugs. So don't waste my time asking me about legitimacy."

His words caused the younger, inquiring, female reporter to blush, both with embarrassment and anger. "At least they didn't blow up the Capitol," she added.

"And neither did our side," Trip slashed back. "You are accepting their lie as the truth. The President has told the people he had nothing to do with the assassination attempt on the Ruling Council. So far none of the alleged conspirators have come to trial. Why don't you go on back to the people holding your leash and do your damn job!" He turned back to his Humvee and started to get inside. "Oh, this press conference is over," he said, slamming the side door behind him.

Out of their view he chuckled. The lieutenant next to him made eye contact. "I don't think they are used to people talking back to them."

"They are lapdogs," Trip said. "They want sound bites, click-bait. The truth doesn't mean a damn thing to them."

The lieutenant nodded. "We got a short message from General Griffiths sir," he said, handing him the scribbled note he had taken. Trip eyed it carefully.

"Operations progressing as planned. Enemy forces are in Manchester. Taking the fight to them per plans. Griffiths"

It was clear that the Newmerican offensive was way off of its timetable. Manchester should have been taken on the first day, not four days later. From the field reports he had been getting daily from Griffiths, the insurgency had made the enemy commander nervous, overly cautious. Of course that was aided by the Sons of Liberty and their guerilla attacks, by the locals, some imported militias, and the National Guard. Losses to the Griffiths' forces had been four so far, the result of an inexperienced team wiring an IED improperly.

Newmerica wasn't reporting their losses, but the estimates were at least a dozen destroyed vehicles, half that number damaged. Dead troops were thought to be around forty troopers so far. The body count was in their favor, but this was a war that was more than statistics and body counts. This was about defiance to the Newmerican authority. This was about whittling away at the enemies will to fight. *I learned in Iraq that insurgencies wage war not just on the personnel, but on the will to fight. We need to keep the pressure up on these invaders; make them afraid to leave their base; hem them in. If we do this, eventually, we will shatter their morale and crush their willingness to stay.*

He folded the message in quarters and tucked it in his jacket breast pocket. "Alright Lieutenant, let's send the go code and have General Morgan start the advance." The lieutenant sent the coded phrase, "Kids in the Hall." Outside, the APCs and other vehicles roared and rumbled to life and began to advance, both on the highway, and on either side of it heading north.

They were not going fast. They didn't have to as a distraction and General Gerald Morgan knew that. Their job was to look bigger and more threatening than they were. Many of the armored personnel carriers were carrying token crews. The media would be allowed to trail the convoy, but not come into the encampments out of fear that they might expose the ruse. Morgan would lead his 'assault force' north to St. Louis, but would stop at Bloomsdale, Missouri. There they would take a defensive posture, as if they were preparing for reinforcements and the inevitable assault.

St. Louis will fall, but not right now. He patted the driver on the shoulder. "Alright, peel off and get me to the airfield," he said. The Humvee started to move, making a tight turn, sloshing the occupants to the right side of the vehicle as it accelerated. Trip needed to get to Auburn, Alabama where the real war was prepared for their drive on Atlanta. There was a bit of worry that the media would expose his ploy. That was offset by the fact that it only had to work a few days, just enough for him to get the real attack group on the move. *There's an advantage with the press not doing their job well, and I fully intend to exploit it.* That thought alone made him smile.

The District

Deja was led down the hallway to the last door. The Secretary's assistant opened the door to the outer office where a staff of three worked. She led Deja to the double, cherry wood doors, and opened them with a button on the wall. She gestured to Deja who stepped in.

Deja had never been to the District before. The limo that picked her up at the airport in Virginia drove her past the monuments of note. She particularly enjoyed the ruins of the White House, now a few charred white walls, the tombstone-like markers for the martyrs that died during the assault to take down the Traitor. The Ruling Council had sworn that it would not be rebuilt, that it was a monument to a way of life that was gone, erased. When she saw the memorial on the grounds, she fully understood. *We had to destroy it. We had to tear down the old system. They left us no other choice.*

The Secretary's—no, she was the Vice President-Elect now—her office was remarkably pristine. The shelves on the wall behind the desk were lined with medals and awards that she had received, along with what Deja assumed were family photos. One wall had a shadow box with a burned piece of what might have once been the old American flag, obviously some sort of souvenir. The Vice President-Elect sat behind a massive desk, clear of paperwork, with a pair of monitors linked to the laptop. When she saw Deja she rose and extended her hand. "You must be Deja Jordan, our latest hero."

Deja was embarrassed as she shook her hand. The Vice President-Elect gestured to one of the padded leather seats opposite her desk and she slid into the chair, noticing how uncomfortable it felt. As she looked at the Vice President-Elect, she was impressed. Her suit was perfectly tailored, her long, black hair, pristine. More than that, she had an aura of authority about her. She was a presence. Where Deja's fingernails were simply cut, the woman she faced clearly had a professional manicure. *I am in the room with a woman of true power ... the kind of power that I have always known existed, but never saw.*

"I'm no hero ma'am."

"Never sell yourself short Deja," she said. *She's using my first name!* It was enough that she had been summoned to The District on a private jet. At first she had thought there was trouble, but on the plane she found several outfits laid out for her to choose from. All she was told by the lone flight attendant was that the Secretary of the NSF wanted to congratulate her. "What you did by bringing in Raul Lopez was a brilliant piece of detective work."

"I had a lot of help."

"Of course you did," she said as her assistant brought in a tray with tea for the two of them. Deja normally didn't drink tea, but she did not want to look ungrateful in front of the leader of the SEs. She nervously took a saucer and added a lump of sugar. "We all have help, but you demonstrated real leadership out in the field. Lopez was public enemy number one—a domestic terrorist of the highest order. A true threat to national security."

Deja was basking in the compliments, but felt a tug of hesitancy. She had spent a lot of time with Raul Lopez. He was many things, but she didn't see him as a threat to national security. Even as a terrorist, from what she had seen in his file, his direct involvement in the Detroit riots was murky at best. Yes, he had been the impetus for the shooting at the Youth Corps, but the rioting had been the work of the local SEs. It was true that he had been part of an SOL team that had freed prisoners from a Social Quarantine Camp, but there was little to indicate that he was the mastermind behind that attack. In fact, in the time she had spent with Raul, she saw him more as a kid that may have been in the wrong place at the wrong time. The only difference in her mind was the incident on the Ohio River. There he had shown daring, bravado, and cunning. Even so, it was his unnamed accomplice that had done the most damage.

As she sat there, watching the Vice President-Elect sipping tea for a moment, Deja realized that she didn't feel at all like a hero. "I did what was necessary."

"And that makes you a hero. You'd be surprised how few people are willing to do what is necessary. All we have to do now is shape that story a little and put some polish on it. You will be an inspiration to young women everywhere" she said with a grin. Deja was taken aback for a moment. *Me ... an inspiration?* Those were thoughts that never occurred to her. It was impossible to deny the excitement in that.

Before she could speak, there was a short knock at the door and her admin ushered in a photographer. The Vice President-Elect rose to her feet and Deja did the same. "Ah good, let's document this formality."

Deja was momentarily confused as her host turned and pulled out a small box with a medal. She moved next to her, and the photographer came and adjusted Deja's position, her shoulders, etc. He then moved a few yards away and gave a thumbs up. "On the behalf of a grateful nation, I present to you the Justice Star. ... " She held out the medal, a shimmering golden star on a blue ribbon. ". . . The highest honor in the NSF and SE. The people of Newmerica thank you for your exemplary service." She stepped forward and pinned the medal on her chest while the photographer clicked several photos. Then the Vice President paused, posing for the camera, extending her hand as Deja numbly shook it.

The photographer was ushered out as quickly as he came in. "I have been shepherding the TRC recently. While you're in town, my people have arranged for Time to do a cover piece on you. It is always a positive thing when one of our people succeeds the way you do and we want it on the news. *The Today Show* wants an interview as well as *Good Morning America*. Good safe TRC certified journalists."

"I—I've never been on television," she said in dismay. *I have no idea what to do or how to do it.*

"Don't worry," the Vice President-Elect assured her. "My people provided them with the questions, and you'll have copies of those and the answers we crafted for you. They are only guides of course; the important thing is that you be you ... answer honestly. The TRC will clear the reporters, and we will make sure there are no curveballs. These little interviews won't take any time at all. Then when you're done, what you need to do: You can have your choice of assignments in the NSF. You will find that the Newmerican government can be rewarding for those that are loyal to the cause."

Choice of assignments ... that was something she had never considered. Deja had been so buried in her work, the thought of doing something else had never occurred to her. She thought for a moment about Raul Lopez and felt a wave of guilt. *I haven't finished my work with him.* The nightmares still plagued her sleep, Raul taunting her that the mysterious woman with him would kill her. *I need to know who that person is and take care of her before she does the same to me.*

"I haven't had much luck in breaking Lopez, not yet. Before I move on to something else, I need to finish what I have started. I need to break him."

The Vice President-Elect nodded slightly, seeming to take in her words. "You are obsessed with him, aren't you?"

Deja felt a blush rise to her cheeks. "Yes. He had an accomplice, one that nearly wiped out an SE team. I need to know who that person is. Whoever she is, she's a threat to anyone that crosses her. I *have* to find out who she is."

"I know how you feel," the Vice President-Elect responded. From the lower tone in her voice, Deja knew they were not empty words.

She took a sip of her tea, then continued. "I have come to believe that a good obsession gives a person purpose and focus. I understand that emotion all too well. My mother and brother were murdered, and I too have had a bit of obsession about seeing the guilty party brought to justice." Pausing, the Vice President-Elect seemed, if only for an instant, to struggle with a wave of emotion that hit her. *Someone hurt her ... badly. She and I are not that different.*

She quickly returned to her stern, business-like expression. "I believe we can accommodate your request Deja. My people say you have been doing a great job. You are a quick learner and you listen to their advice. There's no need to reassign you at this point. You're motivated to get the information out of him, and that will help you in the end."

She paused for a moment, clearly considering the options. "We can use this to build on your story. It wasn't enough for you to capture him. You needed to see that justice was done … that kind of thing. Besides, once you do break him, there will be a Tribunal and justice will prevail. We will make you the face of all of that—an 'avenging angel' of sorts who strove hard to track your prey and saw it all of the way through to resolution. You, Deja Jordan, are going to be an inspiration for young people everywhere, proof of the need for Social Enforcement. Validation that the SEs are a vital part of our society.

"There's more of course. I think that these kinds of ceremonies are important, not just for the people but for those in the ranks of Social Enforcement. I know that a few of them are struggling with their absorption into the NSF. Seeing one of their own honored will go a long way toward easing their concerns." *She sounds genuinely concerned for the SEs which is a good thing.* The Vice President-Elect sat down and Deja followed suit.

"Thank you for this," she said, looking down at the medal for the first time. Light from the window glanced off of it with a shimmer. The SEs didn't have medals … *this was another change.*

"Since you mentioned it," Deja said, pausing for a sip of her tea. "A number of my friends have voiced some worries about the organization. There is a belief that a number of senior leaders of the SE organization have disappeared or died rather mysteriously."

"Really?" the Vice President-Elect asked. "Deja, I've learned quite a bit in this job as you can imagine. Every time there is a reorganization of department as large as the NSF and SE, there are these kinds of dangerous rumors. Let me assure you; nothing untoward happened. People were merely reassigned to new roles, in some cases even promoted. The NSF has seen nothing but value in having Social Enforcement as part of their ranks now." Her words were so light and casual that they felt entirely genuine.

Maybe Trey was wrong? Maybe I was? Trey Phillips in the Philadelphia SE group Righteous Liberty had planted the thought in her head that a number of senior SE leaders had died or disappeared. *Is it possible that someone is doing something without the knowledge of the Secretary?* As Deja looked at her, she doubted it. *She was on top of things—organized.* "Tell me Deja, where did you hear these rumors? I would like to get in front of them … talk to the person, alleviate their fears."

Suddenly things had changed, and Deja felt a wash of apprehension come over her. She had not anticipated being asked to name names. "It was simply casual talk ma'am. I don't think any sort of follow-up is needed."

The Vice President-Elect sipped her tea slowly, setting the fine china cup on the saucer. "Deja, I just want to make sure that all of your comrades in Social Enforcement know that I care about them and will remove any concerns they have. Such rumors can hurt morale, and with our nation at war with America, we can't afford to have such distractions. I'm sure you agree."

"Of course," she said, the words flowing without thought. *Am I betraying Trey's trust? No, she's just going to call him, explain things.* "I'm sure it is nothing, I shouldn't have even mentioned it."

"Please, I insist."

Deja paused and drew a long, deep breath. "It was Trey Phillips with Righteous Liberty. It was just a passing comment. I'm sure he didn't mean anything." The moment she spoke his name she felt a pang of regret, a desire to take back Trey's name. She had no tangible reason to feel that way, but could not suppress the emotion.

The Vice President-Elect must have sensed it too. She reached out and touched her hand in an assuring gesture. "Deja, I'm just going to talk to him, answer some of his questions, put this little rumor to bed."

"Thank you," she said fumbling for the right words.

"It's the least that I can do for the new hero of the nation. Your life is going to change, at least for the short term. When those images make the news sites and the story of what you accomplished is published, people are going to look up to you in a new way. From what I've heard, you are more than up to the burdens that being an inspiration can carry."

An inspiration? She didn't think of herself in that way, but as she glanced back at the medal on her chest, she realized that things had changed. *My mother will see the article; see me with the Vice President; she's going to be damned proud.* She stopped thinking about Trey and allowed herself to grin broadly with pride. *A few weeks ago I was just a digger hunting down some punk kid; now people are going to look up to me.*

"I am up to it," Deja assured her. "I will make you proud."

"These are trying times. We are going to have to ask everyone to step up in the fight against the tyranny that America represents. No sane person wants to go back to the way things were during the Traitor President's time. I know you will step up to the tasks that are to come. I know you will make everyone see the SE organization for what it really is, a unifying force in our nation," the Vice President-Elect said, taking her last sip of tea.

CHAPTER 6

"You are a winner if you believe you are a winner."

Santa Susana Camp 201, Santa Susana Pass Park, California

Charli had been the one to come up with the plan. It was not one of brute force, like the one Travis had suggested. *He likes explosives far too much.* Charli had lived in California under Newmerican rule; she understood their Social Enforcers there and the laissez faire approach to authority. She knew how to deal with these people, or so she hoped. Caylee had sat silent during her presentation of the idea, making her wonder if she approved. At the end Caylee simply had said, "This will work." That was the best kind of endorsement Charli could have hoped for from Caylee.

They drove up to the gate in their rented electric Jeep-Zazz with the appropriate ID and paperwork that Caylee had prepared for them. The guards at the gate examined their paperwork and IDs, made a call, then told them where to park. Charli eyed the perimeter guard towers out of the corner of her eye and saw no unexpected movements.

Both she and Caylee had taken efforts to disguise themselves. Caylee had put on a false, dimpled chin, and had elongated her nose. Her experience in tradecraft was impressive, even surpassing what Charli possessed. Charli's disguise had been focused on raising her chin structure and altering her eyebrows, almost connecting them into a unibrow. *I feel stupid doing this, but why give the NSF anything they might be able to use against us?*

As Charli angled the Jeep-Zazz into what she assumed to be a visitor parking space, opposite the sea of old school busses, a man approached her and Caylee. He wore pants that were so wide they barely clung to his hips. His gray guard shirt was unbuttoned, exposing a barely white wife-beater undershirt. "Yo—I'm Todd Parsons. I'm the day lead for this camp," he said extending his hand. Charli shook it, then Caylee. "I'm Laura and this is Christine," she said gesturing to Caylee. "We are here for a prisoner transfer to our camp in Utah." Charli handed him the falsified orders.

Todd looked at the papers with a wrinkle on his nose, as if they smelled offensive, "Transfer to Utah, eh?"

Caylee nodded. "Canyonlands, Camp 312."

"We don't get a lot of transfers," Todd said, looking at the second page of the orders. "I need to call this in, you know, verify." There was a hint of suspicion in his voice.

"Of course," Charli said. "I'd do the same thing if I were you." She knew she had two weapons on her, and Caylee had at least that many. *Hell, Caylee is a weapon all by herself. If this goes south, we are going to have to shoot our way through it.*

He pulled out his cell phone, scrolling through his contacts. Lifting the phone to his ear, Todd must have connected. "Yo, Roger. This is Parsons out at Camp 201. I've got some ladies here that want to transfer two prisoners."

Charli drew a shallow but deliberate breath. *This had better work ...*

Crown Castle Cell Tower 6781, Santa Susana Pass, California

Travis stood at the base of the tower with his laptop hardwired into the main controller. "You're up Andy," he said, stabbing his finger at the spacebar.

The phone receiver he held to his ear crackled for a moment; then he heard the voice. "Yo, Roger. This is Parsons out at Camp 201. I've got some ladies here that want to transfer two prisoners."

Andy Forrest was nervous, but mentally committed to doing this and doing it right. *This covert stuff is Charli's world, not mine.* He had insisted on coming along because of Charli. The thought of her going out on some dangerous mission would have left Andy a ball of nerves for weeks, if not longer. It made more sense to go with her, even though he was not trained for this kind of work. Charli had been the center of his world since they had helped with the swearing in of the President in New York. They had been through a lot together and, in a weird way, being with Charli had made coping with his father's death easier, even though they rarely talked about it. She was the center of his world, and being able to help her gave him the mental clarity to tackle the assignment.

They had monitored the calls coming into and out of the camp for several days, checking names and comparing voices. Roger Martin was a regional camp director for Social Enforcement and spoke at least once a day with the camp director. He sounded like a punk-ass kid to Andy, with a fake swagger and a street tone to his voice that sounded more stupid than effective. Despite his age, he had been given sway over three camps—at least those were the ones that Travis and Caylee had been able to confirm. Andy had rehearsed his voice, which seemed remarkably easy.

"Yo," he said in a rough, almost gravelly voice. "Yeah. They are there to pick up two hot politicals you have."

"So we're cool in turning them over to these folks?"

"Yeah," Andy replied with remarkable calm. "They are just some low priority folks. National wants them in Utah, something about some big splash they have planned with the media. You know—big time TV coverage."

"Alright," Todd replied. "You want me to give these folks the grand tour?"

Andy looked over at Travis, unsure for a millisecond how to answer. Travis nodded and Andy shrugged. "Sure man. Thanks."

The line went dead. He paused and took the phone from his ear, then wiped the sweat from his brow. "You did great," Travis said. "I cranked up the static on this end. I doubt he suspected a thing."

Andy flashed a grin. "Thanks. I don't know how you people do this for a living."

Travis continued to monitor the cell tower traffic. "It's not like we have a lot of choice Andy. We have to play the cards we've been dealt."

Andy grabbed his bottle of water and took a deep gulp. *He's right about that.* His thoughts turned to Charli. *Come on—get the mother and daughter and get out of there ...*

Santa Susana Camp 201, Santa Susana Pass Park, California

Caylee followed Todd Parsons as they walked through the camp, with Charli walking behind her. Andy must have done a good job because the camp lead insisted on a tour. He had called over one of the guards and had shown him the paperwork, directing him to find the Lopez family members. In the meantime, he insisted on a tour.

Her eyes constantly checked her surroundings, looking for anything that might be a threat. It was an old habit, always planning for a way to escape if the situation turned sour. Her mind raced with scenarios that involved Parsons as a hostage. Taking out the guard towers was the trick, but it was doable. Travis could cut the power at the cell tower with a single keystroke. *Always have a plan to kill everyone and get away ...* the mantra of operatives.

"What's with the buses?" Charli asked, gesturing at them.

Todd nodded at them. "New program started a few months ago. They take our inmates out to the fields to do manual labor. We get them out there at sunrise, and they work until it is dark."

"What fields?" Charli pressed.

"Poppy," he said. "Best stuff too. I was told that in the next few months, the Governor is rolling out a new program to control crime. We're growing poppies to harvest them for the opium that will be processed into heroin."

"How is that crime control?" Caylee asked, almost dreading to hear what the response was going to be.

He winced and cocked his eyebrow at her, as if her question was stupid. "A lot of the crime we have is druggies robbing people to fund their habit. The gov is going to give out free heroin—meth too. Word is that there is a quarantine camp down in Death Valley that is a massive meth lab. Nasty-ass conditions, worse than here, but it is producing huge quantities. Giving this shit out is supposed to stop the other crimes. Drug users won't have to be stealin' or robbing any more to support their habits. Pretty wild shit, eh?"

"Yeah," Caylee responded. It started with making marijuana legal, which eventually led to an increase in meth and heroin use. While it might solve some crime problems, it was bound to create an increase in drug use. *Typical government program ... chock full of unintended consequences. Only in California do they reduce crimes by simply not calling them crimes.*

They walked down a white limestone path to one of the large buildings. "This is our solar panel assembly building," he said opening the door. Despite it being winter, the building felt like a sauna as she approached the doorway and entered. It was not well lit, but there were easily 200 prisoners working the floor, each wearing dull tan uniform shirts that were filthy. The air stung of chemicals, almost to the point of making her momentarily light headed. "So you're using the inmates to do what? Assemble the panels?" she asked as he handed them masks.

Parson's nodded. "Let's get up to the office; this stuff is pretty nasty in terms of what it will do to you," he said, leading them up an industrial staircase to an office on the second floor. Inside, the air was purified and air conditioned. Three of the camp guards were up there, lazily looking down on the floor of the factory from the windows. The three of them took off their masks and Caylee quickly noticed that none of the people working below were wearing them.

"So the state is making solar panels?" Charli asked.

"For two different companies," Parsons said with a glint of pride in his voice. "It helps them keep the cost down to have our people do the work."

"The chemicals really reek," Caylee stated.

"It's the coating sealer. If they were making these in a regular factory, they couldn't do it without a lot of expensive equipment for ventilation and safety. Seriously, you get a drop of that stuff on you and it burns. On top of that, the shit causes cancer and COPD like you wouldn't believe. OSHA ain't here in the camps. We don't have to worry about those regulations with these people. That's the only way to produce this stuff so that it is cost effective. Nobody cares what happens to these people."

'These people' ... are still people. Caylee used to think the way that Parsons did. As an operative, she did her job and never allowed herself to think of the people impacted by her work as anything other than targets. It was necessary in her line of work to dehumanize people. There was a buzzing in the office, some sort of alarm. One of the guards moved to the window and grabbed the microphone on the ledge under it. "Pickup on line two," he barked, his voice echoing out on the shop floor. There was

a flurry of movement in the far corner of the factory floor.

"What is that?" Caylee asked.

"Oh, we just had someone drop on the line. Sucking in those fumes will do it to you eventually. The old or people with conditions—they don't last long down there."

"Does that happen often?" Charli asked.

Parson's nodded quickly. "Sure. We used to do medical treatment, you know, but with the new directives out of the District, we just work 'em until they drop. At least the state is getting something for putting them up and feeding them, right?"

Caylee understood. *They are working these people to the death. This isn't a solar panel factory; it is a death factory.* She refused to display shock. "How many prisoners die a day here?"

Parsons paused in thought for a moment. "Last time I checked, we were running seven or eight a day—between this and the poppy fields. The new orders out of the District cut their food allowance and most of them are only here a few months before dropping."

"That's about what we have at our camp," she said, not displaying any emotion. She cast a quick glance at Charli whose eyes showed that she was keeping her rage in check. "You must be bringing in new inmates here at a pretty high rate."

"Every Friday the replacements come in, like clockwork," Parsons said. "For a long time we were just housing them here, but the District and the Governor have changed our state's camps, using the inmates for manual labor until they drop dead."

"What do you do with the bodies?" Charli asked.

"We have a processor that takes them. Their bones are apparently ground up for some sort of fertilizer. I talked to the guy in charge of transporting them. He said that they are used in the vineyards mostly, some in the fruit nurseries. A good use of traitors, don't ya think?" Parson's smile grew as he spoke.

"It certainly solves a problem," she said with no emotion in her words. *These have ceased to be prisons. They are death camps. Jack needs to know about this. The world needs to know what they are doing to their political opposition.* In that profound moment, she realized that the grapes for California wines were fertilized with dead human remains.

"It is impressive," Charli said with the same flat tone in her voice. *She's good. She's keeping her emotions in check too.*

"If the other camps are doing what we are, in a few years, we won't need Social Quarantine anymore," he replied with a sense of pride that made Caylee wish she could kill him where he stood. He was wrong, and she knew it. *Newmerica was built on the concept of having enemies that needed punishment and now extermination. Once the old enemies were gone, they would have to find new ones. That is the way of tyrants.* The thought of the good citizens of California drinking wine whose grapes were fertilized with dead people made Caylee swear off of wine from that point forward.

In the factory, she saw four of the inmates carrying a limp form of a man to a small office-like building within the factory floor, only a single story tall, with no windows. The other workers didn't pause in their work on the assembly room floor, either out of fear or out of the routine nature of the death. *They didn't even try to save that person.* Caylee watched the horror unfold below her. People were tormented and died in Social Quarantine; that was known, though few discussed it openly. *This ... this was different.* This was deliberate, where the other deaths were accidental or unintentional.

Parsons was like her in her old life, another cog in a machine. As much as she found herself despising him, she understood how he ended up where he was and thinking the way he did. *Newmerica is training people to not think, to not question anything. The FedGov does all of that for them. People are expected to do what they are told to do. Compliance is everything.*

Someone entered the air conditioned office where they stood and walked up to Parsons, whispering in his ear. His face winced slightly as the other guard spoke, then turned and walked away. "Problem?" Caylee asked.

"'fraid so," he replied. "You came for a Rosa and Maria Lopez, right?"

Caylee's stomach knotted because of the way he asked the question. *Something is wrong.* "Yeah, that's who we needed to pick up."

Parsons shook his head. "Sorry for the bad news, but one of them is dead ... "

Concord, New Hampshire

General Donaldson looked at the twisted remains of the armored Humvee that had been blasted into the thick bank of snow along I-93 just north of the Merrimack River. It lay some five feet down the embankment, sunken into the plowed snow, leaving black smears on the stark white powder. Boot prints littered the deep snow where rescuers had tried to extract any survivors. From the look of the mangled vehicle and the crater on the highway, Donaldson knew that it had been a vain gesture. There were no survivors.

New Hampshire was supposed to be an easy victory, but resistance groups, traitors to the cause, had been savaging his convoys and patrols at will. While the major cities were under his control at this point, the countryside was not. That was where the terrorists lived and thrived.

New Hampshire was not his only problem. An invasion group had come into southern Missouri, clearly heading for St. Louis. Donaldson had flown in to personally manage the defense of the free autonomous zone. The American assault group had driven north, then had stopped, forming their own defensive position. It was confusing as all hell to him, a blown opportunity. St. Louis had some military defenses, elements of the Missouri National Guard that had remained loyal to Newmerica, but other than that, their defenses had been sparse. The slow pace of the aggressors had allowed him to shuttle in additional troops from Minnesota via the airport, and now St. Louis was prepared for a fight. For James Donaldson, his swift response had been a matter of pride. *I have made it difficult for them to consider moving on St. Louis, which is a victory in itself.* The snide officers at the Pentagon that whispered behind his back that he lacked practical experience on the ground would be eating crow for some time.

The General understood that in the public's eyes, and those in the Pentagon as well as the fragmented Newmerica Army structure, all saw him fighting a defensive campaign and reacting to the American efforts. Deep down, he was determined to change that image. He had issued orders mobilizing the Illinois National Guard to mount an offensive into Iowa. Illinois troops had suffered a significant losses on election day in Chicago and were clamoring for a chance to redeem themselves. Seizing a big piece of the farming state would be a setback that America deserved. *Everyone will see me for what I am, a great field commander.*

Satisfied that he had blunted the thrust in Missouri, at least for the time being, he turned his eyes back to frigid New Hampshire. The insurgents were inflicting real damage. Every day there was another attack. Even in the cities that his troops held, foot patrols found themselves targets for snipers that would shoot, then disappear. Only once had the New Hampshire National Guard showed itself for a fight, and that proved to be a quick skirmish at Keene. Donaldson had pulled in the Vermont Air National Guard which had used antiquated A-10 Thunderbolts to blow up a handful of APCs and fighting vehicles. It had driven the enemy off the open fields and into the dense woods around Keene, making pursuit and engagement much more complicated and risky.

As General Donaldson studied the destroyed Humvee, he considered his situation carefully. The reason that the Sons of Liberty and the locals were able to fight their guerilla war at all was because the citizens were supporting them. It was an age-old story. Such insurgencies died on the vine once the locals stopped their support.

What I need is a way to turn the locals against the resistance. If I come down too heavy-handed, I might end up helping the enemy. Major Dawes, his G2 officer, sidled up beside him. "General, they also hit a patrol in Gorham. Captain Farley's Maine unit. Initial reports are we lost three vehicles and have eight dead, seventeen wounded."

"Let me guess. The enemy has faded into the hills," he said glumly, the mist from his words seeming to hang in the air in front of him as if it were a visible memory of what he had said.

"They were on skis. Some were armed with Javelins and clearly knew how to use them. When the vehicles tried to scatter off the road, they triggered IEDs. Our forces spotted them on infrared, but pursuit proved too difficult. The deep snows and their familiarity with the terrain allowed them to get away. We had to fly choppers in from Maine to get the wounded and dead out of there," Dawes replied, his arms crossed over his chest in an effort to stay warm.

Donaldson's mind danced over options. "How small is Gorham?"

The major shifted his feet slightly. "A few thousand, not much more than three thousand."

He remembered the town, not far from the Maine border. *I need to squeeze these people, make them turn on these traitors.* "I have to believe that Captain Farley wants a bit of revenge on the people that tore into his people."

"General, that would be an understatement."

They are using the winter against us. Perhaps there is a way to get the weather to fight for us. "Have the Captain move into Gorham and secure it. Then send in some engineers. I want them to cut off the electricity to Gorham and the surrounding counties."

"Sir?"

"You heard me. Nothing permanent mind you. I will broadcast to the people and give them an hour warning or so, but after that the lights go off. We will keep them off for three days or so. The citizens of Gorham need to understand that if they are giving support to our enemies, they will suffer for it. A few nights of bitter cold should be enough to get their attention."

Major Dawes continued to shift from foot to foot to try and shake the cold, but to little avail. "Sir, it gets cold up there, even colder than here. You take out the electricity, and we may end up with some folks freezing to death."

Donaldson's eyes narrowed as he looked at him. "Major, we are at war. In war, people suffer and in some cases die. I will give them fair warning and an explanation as to why this is happening. They need to understand the consequences of making bad decisions and supporting these insurgents. Most of them probably have fireplaces or backup generators; and those that don't can go stay with neighbors who do. These people need to understand the implications of backing the wrong side in this conflict. A bit of winter cold for a few days and nights will serve as a warning to everyone in the state about the price of their freedom."

The Major nodded. "Yes sir. I'll get a team of engineers working on it right away." He left quickly, heading down the road. Donaldson ignored the dissipating squeaking sounds of the major's boots on the crisp snow, and returned to looking at the blasted Humvee.

This is measured and non-violent. I'll get the TRC to position it with the rest of the state. *People will refuse to help the rebels if it means them or their family members suffering a night of bitter cold.* He forced a smile to his face, pleased with the solution he had arrived at. *I owe it to our dead to do this. And if they don't respond, well, there are plenty more cold nights ahead …*

Lisbon, New Hampshire

Lisbon, New Hampshire was a small town with a single row of buildings to form the center of town, half of which had been boarded up in the economic downturn that Newmerica claimed never happened. It was on the border with Vermont—Newmerican territory. There was a Dollar General up the street, which served as the only remaining grocery store for the community. The abandoned three-story structures of the downtown had been loaned to the resistance movement by the local that owned them.

The upper floors were converted to bedrooms and barracks for the resistance fighters that had come in from other states. There were plenty of them. Some from New York, Vermont, and even a family from Maine that had arrived with enough firepower for a platoon of infantry. Randy Birdsell had done an outstanding job of organizing them, keeping the groups aligned and focused. Local families cooked meals for the resistance, did their laundry, helped in every way possible. Very few seemed content with the brute military invasion of New Hampshire.

Su-Hui Zhou had to admit that he was getting used to the cold weather. He had been on three missions so far, trudging through the deep snow, striking at the Newmerican military in places where they never would expect it. The missions were exhilarating, he had to admit that. Deep down, every time he pulled the trigger to detonate an explosion, it was as if he were striking back for what happened to Taiwan. Memories of the loss of his nation to the Chinese still burned in his soul. *We waited for our ally to come to our aid, but Newmerica refused. Instead they picked us up, labeled us as 'boat-people' and 'refugees'. They demeaned us when they should have come and shed blood to defend our people.* That was part of what had motivated him to eventually join the Sons of Liberty movement.

He and his wife Hachi kept busy when not out striking at the enemy. They sat at a folding table, filling magazines with ammunition. Hachi had been Su-Hui's source of determination. Never once had she complained since he had proposed coming to New Hampshire to help fight the invaders. It was beyond being a dutiful wife, he knew that. *We have lost more than our home coming here. Our family has been destroyed.* Glancing to his side to where she sat, she offered him a smile, saying nothing. She didn't have to. He saw the love in her face ... love, and a sense of duty.

It was tedious work and at times his hand and wrist ached, but Su-Hui did not complain. *How could I, sitting next to my wife who never expresses her displeasure?* In that way, she gave him strength to continue. Besides until the next assignment there was little else to do. Watching the news was to watch propaganda. General Donaldson had been on the night before, talking about the punishment of the people of Gorham for supporting the SOL. Su-Hui wondered if it would have the General's desired effect. *They are like the Chinese. They have only brute force and oppression as their tools. They work on the short term if applied correctly. No matter what, they always create more resistance than they crush.*

Randy appeared in his yellow and black flannel shirt that was unbuttoned enough to show his thermal underwear. Birdsell paused at the table, planted his big fists on his hips and smiled looking down on them. "How are you holding up?"

"We are well," Hachi answered before Su-Hui could. "Though I worry for the people of Gorham."

Birdsell nodded. "As do I. Which is why I want to borrow your husband."

Su-Hui rose to his feet and Hachi gave him an approving nod. He followed Randy downstairs to what had been a laundromat on the main floor. The washing machines and dryers had been removed when the business closed, but the flexible ductwork hung down along the walls, covered with cobwebs. On the main floor, there were nearly two dozen members of the SOL from half a dozen different states, milling about, sitting on folding chairs, all wearing many layers of clothing. The main windows were covered with plywood but showed signs of frost in the corners, a testimony to the weather outside. As he came off the stairs, he spotted Valerie Turner talking with a group of people. The moment their eyes made contact, she gave him a single nod of acknowledgement which he returned.

There was something near the back of the big room, near the double doors to the outside, covered by a tarp. It had not been there the last time Su-Hui had been downstairs just a few hours ago. *It must be some new equipment or ammunition.* He shuffled into the crowd as Randy stepped away from him, moving to the center of the room.

Randy pulled up a battered old chair and stood on it. "If I can have your attention please," he called out, and a ripple of silence went across the room as all eyes fell on him. "I'm sure you all have seen the news and heard about Gorham. Going after civilians is an escalation on the part of the invaders. The time has come for our next op, and this one is a bit of a doozie. We need to show the outside world that we are different than the Newmericans. We don't target innocent people. We also need to demonstrate to these outsiders who have come into our state that they have to pay a price for coming here to impose their will." His words brought about numerous nods and murmurs of support from the group.

Randy cleared his throat slightly, then continued. "We've all heard the jets overhead … A-10s, Warthogs. They are running ground support missions for the Newmericans. Those jets can tear up any vehicle on the ground. I've spoken with the other groups, and they have been suffering every time those things get a bead on them.

"The Vermont National Guard has been flying them out of Burlington. I've spoken with General Griffiths, and he wants us to mount what he calls a *harasser* group. Our mission is to cross the border into Vermont and attack the Air National Guard base in Burlington."

"Randy," a young, dark-skinned man spoke up. "That's like what? A hundred miles? Vermont isn't exactly friendly to us."

"Eighty-six," he replied.

"In this weather?" a chunky grim man named Herb Fletcher asked. Herb was a persistent dissenting voice regardless of who was speaking or what was said. There were times when Su-Hui wondered why he had come to New Hampshire in the first place. *Some people wallow in negativity, and that is Herb's story.*

Randy held his hands up as if to push back the questions, ignoring Herb entirely. "Calm down. I know it sounds like a long way into enemy territory, but we have a plan." He pointed to a man near the back of the room who stood next to the tarp-covered object. The stocky man pulled the covering off revealing a snowmobile. This snowmobile was different than others Su-Hui had seen. The rear seat was elevated and welded bars rose up between the passenger and the elevated seat. On top of the mounting brackets was a machine gun. Every eye in the room fell on the modified snowmobile.

"We've outfitted five of these rigs," Randy said. "They allow us to make the trip cross-country, off of the main roads at least."

"What about fuel," a man asked with a New England accent. "My snowmobile back home couldn't make the round trip to Burlington and back."

Randy grinned slightly. "We are going to send in a truck with fuel for a rendezvous, so that the teams going will be able to get back."

"That base isn't likely to be undefended," a large, blonde-haired Captain of the New Hampshire National Guard said with confidence ringing in his assurance. His nametag read Trautman. "And those fighters might spot us on approach."

Randy pointed to a stocky person that Su-Hui assumed was female, but couldn't be entirely sure. She was built more like a man in terms of her stature and attire, but her hair and face seemed to be that of a woman. She hoisted an olive drab tube in the air for everyone to see. "That is a Stinger anti-aircraft missile. We have those and a couple of Javelin anti-tank missiles and some Carl Gustaf's as well. Add in the machine guns and the element of surprise; we should be able to catch them off guard."

Su-Hui looked at the missile and then back down to the modified snowmobile. There was something exciting about the prospects. Hitting the Vermonters was full of risk, but at the same time, it would rattle the resolve of the people of that state. *They are less likely to want to send their National Guard here if we are able to strike them there.* From a strategic sense, it seemed more than viable to Zhou.

"Now, many of you have never handled machine guns or these missiles—so there is going to be some training. Even if you have driven a snowmobile, doing it with a gunner behind you is going to throw off your center of gravity, so you'll need some time practice too. We need to move quick. The General wants us to deliver a blow to them before everyone forgets what is happening in Gorham. We want the Newmericans to link what they have done with our response."

As Randy climbed down, many people began to talk at once and inspect the snowmobile. Birdsell walked over to Su-Hui and said, "Listen, I'd like you to be one of the gunners that goes on this raid," and Birdsell put his hand on Su-Hui's shoulder.

It was a distinction to be singled out and Su-Hui felt himself blush. "I am most honored Randy," he said. "I haven't fired a machine gun since I was in the Army, and certainly not one of these."

"You're smart. You'll learn it quick," he assured him. "This isn't going to be easy," he confided in a lower tone of voice so others in the room would hear their private conversation. "It's a long way to go, horrible weather, on unfamiliar ground."

"My expectations are set," Su-Hui said. "I am pleased you selected me."

Randy cracked a smile. "Don't let it go to your head. This is a long way to go and weight is a factor."

That caught Su-Hui off guard. "You are picking me for my size?"

"Not just that," Randy said. "But I won't lie to you. It moves you pretty high on the list. We have a lot of vets in our ranks, but you are different. You listen carefully … you're thoughtful. A lot of them are trying to work through the problems of the last war they were in. That, and you do something that a number of these folks struggle with."

"What is that?"

He leaned in closer. "You follow orders. The Sons are full of independent-minded folk. Right down to the person, they like doing things their way. Coordinating these patriots is exhausting. On the other hand, you seem to understand. You don't question everything I ask for. You just do it. Other people ask to work under you. If we are going to win this thing, people need to be more like you."

The compliment was important to Su-Hui. His hand unconsciously drifted to the three brass bullet casings that hung on the necklace he always wore. Touching them was a reminder of why he was there—and it was a commitment—a promise. "I thank you. I came here during the exodus from my homeland. America … the old nation … never would have let my people down. Since I came here, I have been looking for that country that pledged itself to defend Taiwan. With all that has happened to my family, the Sons of Liberty offered a glimmer of hope that America might be brought back. I've never ridden a snowmobile or fired a machine gun, but I will learn. I won't let you down." His word was a commitment, one that Randy seemed to understand.

"I know you won't. Besides, I had to pick you for this," he said, leaning back. "Weight is a consideration and you're fairly small."

Su-Hui's mouth fell open as Randy cracked a smile. "I'm kidding Su-Hui," he said with a wink. "Well ... mostly ... "

CHAPTER 7

"People who question authority are plotting against us all. Call 1-888-EXTREME and report risks to your nation. It is your duty!"

London, Kentucky

Frank Campbell came up beside Grayson Steele's car and rapped on the window. The short, black man always managed to look to Grayson as if he had slept in his clothing. He didn't care how he looked, as long as he got results. The call he made two days ago had gotten results.

London, Kentucky was a stately town. The tall, white pillars in front of the Laurel County Courthouse conveyed that sense. The oak and hickory trees were devoid of leaves, but were thick and old, standing like soldiers along the streets.

When he and his family had driven through the town, there were still the digital signs and billboards put up by the TRC, but they had been shut down. They passed a burned out church, a Methodist structure, on the street corner—red brick with a tower. It had been burned, a gutted shell, no doubt from the rioting around the time of the Fall. Churches were often targets of Newmerica's rise to power. The black scarring from the flames marked the sides of the crumbling brick tower. Yet there, in bright red, spray painted over the charring, was GBA! The paint was relatively fresh, defiant. He had nodded when he saw it. *Yes, God Bless America.*

They had come to the Hampton Inn on Campbell's word that he had news. Grayson rolled down the window despite the spittle of a light misting rain. "Hello Frank."

Campbell leaned in on the half-rolled-down window. "I got lucky," he said. "The NSF had information about Maddie and her classmates that went missing in a Yellow Case File. I managed to pry a copy and get some names."

"What is a Yellow Case File?" his wife Langley asked, leaning over so that she could lock eyes with Frank.

"The NSF has a pretty hands-off policy when it comes to Social Enforcement. There's no point in arresting SEs that break the law when the prosecutors refuse to press charges. Things are even worse now that they have merged the SEs into the NSF. A Yellow Case File means that they don't do real investigation. Tips go into the file, but they don't put boots on the ground unless it is deemed necessary."

"So you got the names of the other missing students?" Grayson pressed.

Frank nodded. "Better than that, I *found* one of them. Her name is Clarice Timoroso. She's in room 121."

"Does she know where Maddie is?" David blurted from the back seat.

Frank's face stiffened for a moment, and Grayson knew in his heart that was bad news. "She does. I hate telling you this, but Clarice is one of three students that survived what happened."

His words hung in the air, and a chill came over Grayson. The family had come to terms with the fact that Madison was likely not alive, but hearing confirmation still hit him hard. For a few seconds, he couldn't speak. Frank seemed to sense that, and continued. "I'm sorry I had to be the one to tell you. I didn't want you breaking down in front of her. The kid is scared enough as it is. She's got answers for you, but remember, she's been through a lot herself."

Langley sobbed once, then regained her composure and wiped the tears from her face. "Alright," Grayson said, opening the car door. The misting rain hit his face, but he ignored it. "We need to know what happened."

Later, he wouldn't remember going into the Hampton Inn at all; he was so numb. His family followed Grayson and Frank who unlocked the door, and they entered. A young woman sat on the edge of the bed. She was wearing a Dunkin Donuts uniform, though the name badge said "Trixie" not Clarice. Her face was red and she was clearly nervous.

Frank stood between them. "Clarice, this is the Steeles, Maddie's folks."

Before Grayson could utter a word, Langley moved past him. The moment she got close, Clarice began to cry. Langley said noting, but cried along with her, hugging her tightly in the way that only a mother can. Grayson sat on the other bed while his son David stood, arms crossed, silent … anxiously waiting for his mother to stop so he could hear the words.

"I'm so sorry," Clarice sobbed as Langley slowly let her go. "We were afraid. We split up and went into hiding. We knew they would come for us if we didn't." There was terror in her voice, but she continued to speak, somehow holding the fear in check.

"Clarice," Grayson said, leaning toward her slightly. "I'm Maddie's dad. This is her mom and brother. We have no idea what happened to her. Can you tell us?"

She nodded rapidly, wiping the tears from her cheeks. "I got approached by some people on campus. They said they knew I was conservative. They told me that Social Enforcers on campus, knew too and wanted to hurt us. They told me—told us—that they helped students like me. They were going to get us out of there, take us someplace safe up near Front Royal. I met Maddie at the Rotunda. She had a bag too. They must have told her the same thing." Clarice paused and used a tissue to wipe her nose. Each word she spoke was clearer, more in control.

"We got in vans and left campus. I thought that they were helping us, but they weren't. We pulled off along the road. They said it was so we could stretch our legs. I went in the bushes to go to the bathroom. When I got back, they pulled out guns." For a moment, her voice seemed to drop slightly, both in volume and tone. She paused, nervously taking a breath. Grayson felt as if he were in a dream of some sort. The rest of the room was a blur. He hung on every word that Clarice spoke.

"They had done it before there. They said the bodies were in a ditch nearby. Nobody was going to find our bodies, not out there. They started shooting, but Maddie, well, she had a pistol. She killed two of them. There was blood everywhere! We rushed the third one. He kept firing. Then those of us that were left got him. He struggled with us. Someone got Maddie's gun. He tried to run, but we shot him over and over and over."

Langley turned away from Clarice who was crying while David rocked nervously on his feet, his face going beet red. Grayson wanted to cry too, but a part of him was relieved. He knew what had happened to his little girl. She went down fighting; and that was something that made him feel both horribly sad and tremendously proud. He reached out and rested his hand on Clarice's shoulder. He wished deeply that he could have spoken those words to Maddie. "It's okay. Everything is going to be fine." It was the kind of lie that only a parent could say.

Clarice nodded again. "We took the bodies over to the creek where the others were. We didn't want the police to see them out there in the field and come after us. We couldn't take the time to bury them—I'm so sorry! We had to get out of there, we weren't sure if they would come back. We split up, used their vans to get away. We contacted our parents. I have a cousin here, so my family sent me to live with her, to hide."

The thought of his little girl rotting along some creek bed tore at Grayson Steele, but he had to remain strong. "Clarice, do you think you can tell us where to find our little girl?"

Frank spoke up, and for the first time in two minutes, Grayson realized he was still in the room. "She's drawn me a map," he said as the girl continued to nod.

"Who were the students that did this?" David said, his voice cutting through the air like a dagger.

She turned to his son slowly. "One was Tina Bee; she was the one that brought me in. There was a guy named Brad, and I never learned the name of the other one, the one we killed. They said they were with the Grays. They are an SE group on campus. We didn't know that until the end. They were gloating about it—how they did it every year with students like us."

He wanted to talk, but we couldn't form the right words. Clarice continued. "I would be dead if it wasn't for Maddie. If she hadn't had that gun, the few of us that got out would be dead right now. She saved my life. I barely knew her, but she stepped up and saved us."

As he tried to gather his thoughts, he slowly closed his eyes, mentally picturing the scene. Maddie was a hero, but in the end, it wasn't enough. *She gave her life to save others.* Pride came with the agony of loss. *I tried to warn her to be careful, that bad players were out there. Her death isn't her fault. I bear some of the blame.*

Grayson's sorrow shifted slowly to anger, but somehow he kept it in check. "I'm so sorry," he managed to say. Langley moved forward and once more hugged a wobbly Clarice who rose to her feet. Both of them cried. Grayson felt both rage and a numbness at finally knowing that Madison was dead. The family had talked about it; they knew that after all of this time the odds of her being alive were almost zero, but *almost* was still something to cling to.

Rising to his feet, he looked over at David, but it was clear his son didn't want a hug, He was full of rage, his arms crossed so tight that every muscle seemed to flex. Grayson turned to Frank. "What do we do now?" he was almost whispering.

"The few kids that survived are all in hiding; it was a fluke that I found her," he replied in the same tone. "None of them will ever testify. They know if they go public with what they saw, the SEs will come for them."

"There are other bodies out there, other families that have lost their kids to these murderers," Grayson said. His composure was slowly returning. "They need the answers we have. They deserve closure, even if it is the worst possible news."

Frank nodded. "I have her map, but I haven't been out there," he said, handing an envelope to Grayson. "If you send it to the NSF, they will sweep it under the rug—they don't have much choice since the SEs are part of their organization now."

"They have to act, especially if there are other bodies out there."

"You need to be there when they look. Tell them you got an anonymous tip. Don't tell them the story, but lead them to the bodies. If nothing else, the NSF will hopefully identify the victims and let the other families know what happened. If you try and make this a big deal in the press, your cover identity is going to be blown, and you'll end up in Social Quarantine yourself."

He's right ... I still have to protect my family. It's not enough though. These Grays ... something has to be done with them. The lawyer in him screamed madly—not only for retribution but for justice. In that moment, in the Hampton Inn, Grayson Steele knew what he had to do. *This is not just about Maddie. It's about her and the other kids they have taken out and killed. If the NSF won't act, I will.*

"Frank," he said. "I owe you for this," he said as his wife and Clarice chatted behind him.

"No you don't," Campbell said. "I can't take a penny from you, not after what they did to your little girl."

"I insist."

Campbell shook his head almost angrily. "It's not happening Grayson. Remember who you are talking to. I'm a black man. I know what a lynching is. I know what it is like to have your family hauled off and killed just because of who they are. I never experienced it, but it is part of who I am as a person; it's in my DNA. My dad would say that it's good that you are experiencing this. It's payback, so you could see how we have had to feel for generations.

"I'm not my dad." Frank paused for a moment.

"I have a little girl of my own, younger than yours, but I can't imagine what it feels like, what your family went through. They did your family wrong. I couldn't look myself in the mirror knowing that I didn't help you. I think the good Lord sent you to me to help you get closure. It would be a sin for me to take your money."

"I need to see this through," Grayson confided to him.

The stocky private eye nodded. "I know. I still have some people that might be able to help you. It goes without saying: Be careful. It's not enough that everyone is out to get you. Revenge is like cancer; it can eat you alive and by the time you get the symptoms, it can be too late. Having said that, I have a daughter too. I know what I'd do if I got this news," With that he patted the mostly concealed pistol on his hip.

Fairburn, Georgia

General Trip Reager was pleased so far with the speed of his advance. The Newmerican forces had taken the bait with his decoy operation in Missouri, even taking several companies of Georgia National Guard to St. Louis. Now, one day in, he had led a lightning fast attack into the Peach State.

Trip commanded from the back of a modified Bradley fighting vehicle. They called it the porcupine because of the number of antennae that stabbed skyward. The Alabama National Guard provided air cover and a constant feed on the positions of the enemy troops. There had been one quick aerial combat when a Georgia Air National Guard flight had strafed his northern task force, only to be pounced on by the Alabama fighters. Both sides had lost an aircraft, but the Georgia forces had not returned to Atlanta having flown northward, probably heading for Virginia, the nearest Newmerican state.

He had dubbed the operation Red Glare, a nod to the "Star Spangled Banner." One task force, Twilight, had split off and had reached Douglasville. Their mission was to swing around the northern part of the city, cutting off all access to the north. Another task force, Gleaming, under Colonel Chester Kendrick of the North Carolina National Guard, just reported being in Stockbridge, south of Atlanta. They were to swing around Stone Mountain heading northward, also blocking roadways. Those two task forces were to unite just north of Alpharetta, completing the investment of the city. Trip would personally go in with the third task force, Brave, whose mission was to hit the south of the city and to seize control of Atlanta Hartsfield-Jackson Airport. In just over two days following their kickoff from Auburn, Atlanta would be cut off from Newmerica and the rest of the world.

There had been some resistance, but most of it came from NSF police attempting to blockade the fast moving troops. Opening fire on armored vehicles had proven to be a valiant act of stupidity. The few units of the Georgia National Guard that did show themselves fell back into the safer confines of the city.

Trip understood the thinking. Urban battlefields favored the defender. You could make the attacker bleed heavily to take a city block. Snipers could take cover in buildings, and when the buildings were blasted, the rubble was just as good. Blowing up a tank or other vehicle could clog a road. Moreover, to take a block, you might kill a lot of civilians, which would be a public relations disaster.

Typical military doctrine would be to surround the city and slowly tighten the noose, taking a block or neighborhood at a time. It would be messy, vicious, and would cost him men and women that he could not afford to lose. Red Glare was going to take on a more traditional siege approach. Rather than try to pry the Newmerican defenders out, he would cut off their food supplies, and kill their electricity and drinkable water. Alpharetta was key. Holding it cut off Lake Lanier, Atlanta's primary source of fresh water. Rivers wound through the city, but they were far from drinkable, even with boiling.

The enemy would be given one way out, Memorial Drive to the east, through Stone Mountain. Trip would offer the hospitals immediate evacuation. Civilians that wanted to leave would be allowed to use this road to leave. *I won't have to destroy Atlanta and kill thousands this way. The autonomous zone will eventually be deserted.*

The military forces in the city would be forced to leave eventually as well, and there would only be one way out, a path that Trip's forces fully intended to defend. *I won't allow them to fade out into the countryside and wage a guerrilla war for Georgia. Hopefully they will just surrender. If they opt to fight, then a fight is what I will give them.*

There was a loud trio of raps on his Bradley's rear door, and his aide de camp opened it. Newly promoted Captain Judy Mercury stood at the ramp as it lowered, letting in the early evening sunlight. "General, there's someone here you may want to meet."

Grabbing his helmet he put it on and followed her out as she spoke. "I've been working with the Sons of Liberty teams, going over their assignments, etc. I've got a new one that showed up, and well, I have some concerns with them."

If Judy has concerns, they must be serious. He followed her over past an Abrams tank that was in the middle of refueling. Beyond them was a group of twenty to twenty-five men, all wearing green camo. They looked more like a paintball team than a military unit; some were so overweight that their camouflage was straining to hold in their beer bellies. There was one female, or Trip assumed it was a female, who was more rugged looking than most of the men. Trip followed her over to them and one stepped forward. The man standing at their front was the antithesis of most of his men. He was slender, tall, with slick-backed blonde hair. In his late thirties, and his face was gaunt with high cheekbones and sunken jowls. His light sideburns led down to a pointed goatee.

"Prentis Beauregard," the man said extending his hand. Trip shook it as Captain Mercury stood beside him.

"General Reager," he replied.

Beauregard beamed slightly. "I'm well aware of who you are. Your reputation proceeds you."

There it was, that constant shadow of his past actions. For a long time it was whispers of San Antonio, but now Chicago was spoken in conjunction with this name. Slowly, Trip was coming to grips with the thoughts that those battles were defining who he was. *I'm not nearly the butcher that people think I am.*

Beauregard continued, "I'm in command of the Aryan Knights. We've come to fight alongside you boys." He spoke with a ring of pride in his voice.

Aryan Knights … *white nationalists. I can't think of anything prefaced by the word 'Aryan' that is good.* Trip glanced over to Mercury who gave him an almost undetectable nod. *Now I get it.* "Well Mr. Beauregard, we will not be needing you and your men in this effort. I suggest that you boys go home and leave this matter to the American Army."

His words clearly puzzled the man who stroked his light blonde goatee. "Word is that you've got Sons of Liberty chapters attached to you. We are no different than them," Beauregard said with his Georgia drawl ringing proudly in the air.

"Actually, you *are* different," Trip said, defiantly planting his fists on his hips. "The SOL is not a racist organization. I'm willing to bet that you folks are." Trip's own Texas drawl was unleashed in full rebuttal.

"We ain't the racists," one of the less chunky members of the Aryan Knights said. "The racists are the ones in Washington DC."

Beauregard interrupted his comrade. "What Jacob is trying to say is that we have the same enemies that you do—the Newmerican scum hunkering down in Atlanta. We want to be part of the liberation, just like the Sons of Liberty."

"Your kind never understands. You call them racists while you run around and do racist things. You're almost as bad as the Newmericans. Worse. You feed into their whole narrative. Every time you get involved in something, a protest, an attack, whatever—you only validate what the TRC and the damned progressives in the District say about all of us. You do more damage to your own cause than good. You taint the actions of real patriots. The best thing that you can do right now is to get in your pickup trucks and ride on home."

"We will not," the stocky woman said. "We have a right to take part in this." Beauregard nodded in agreement. We are going to go into the city and fight whether you like it or not."

"No," Trip said flatly, letting the word hang in the air for a long moment before continuing. In that moment, he made eye contact with Mercury and tapped two fingers onto the side of his helmet. She gave a nod, meaning she understood the signal, and passed it on discreetly to the MPs in the security detail near the mobile HQ.

Trip sighed hard, loud enough for them to hear his consternation toward them. "I can't afford my military operation to be associated with some good old boys that hate black people, or Jews, or whoever it is you hate this month. The SOL is going in, coordinated with us. They are fighting for the restoration of America, not the Confederate States. You would play into the TRCs view that we are all a bunch of racists. So no, you don't get to go in."

"We have a common enemy," Beauregard said proudly. "That makes us allies."

"That is a logical fallacy," Trip countered. "The enemy of my enemy isn't necessarily my friend. And in this case, we are not friends, allies, comrades, or any other label you want to toss on our relationship. We are nothing to each other, unless you get in our way."

Beauregard's eyes narrowed; his bushy eyebrows slanted, and his jaw shifted out slightly as he glared at Trip. "Well then, we will go in to Atlanta on our own accord." His voice was filled with pride and defiance—two things Trip wanted to make sure he squashed.

"Sir, I have been courteous up to this point. Now allow me to be respectfully blunt. One, if you go in there, we will consider you enemy combatants, and you will be dealt with per our rules of engagement. Two, if you think you can just run off into Atlanta, burning some crosses, beating up innocent civilians, then you will do it without your weapons." He turned to Captain Mercury who clicked her fingers and pulled her own sidearm. All around the Aryan Knights, soldiers lifted and aimed their assault weapons.

The Knights clearly understood their situation quickly, and Trip exploited their shock. "Lower your weapons slowly, and place them on the ground." He drew his own weapon and aimed it at Beauregard.

For a millisecond a part of Trip hoped they would react, that he would have an excuse to kill them. It wasn't that he wanted to; he had plenty of blood already on his hands. What he wanted was for them to be gone, erased. *If we are ever going to move forward as a nation, these idiots need to stop their goofy-ass shit.*

The Aryan Knights understood their plight and slowly, angrily, they lowered their weapons. Captain Mercury ordered one of the troopers to grab the civilian assault weapons and take them away. Only then did the soldiers lower their weapons. Mercury held her hand up to stop the action from proceeding.

"You sir, are a mangy dog, turning on your own people like this," Beauregard said bitterly to him as Trip holstered his weapon.

"Mr. Beauregard, this is a civil war. Every time I order a unit into action, I am turning on my own people. You're pissed off at me, and I may have earned that. The reality is, I don't care. When we win this war, and I believe in my heart we will, we need to have a reckoning with folks like you and your Knights. In the meantime, I have little time for this bullshit."

He turned and stormed back to his mobile HQ. *I'm fighting this civil war. Those assholes are busy fighting the last one.*

Newmerica Penitentiary, Administrative Maximum Facility Florence, Colorado

Raul entered the room and saw Deja Jordan waiting for him; he noted that she was wearing more professional attire than he had ever seen. She was also wearing a hint of makeup, which was new for her. She stood opposite the small table where they usually met, gesturing to the chair, as if he had a choice. The guards handcuffed him to the table as he settled in, trying to glean whatever he could from his captor.

"You have a new look," he said.

Deja's face didn't betray any emotion. "I had some time in the District in the last two weeks," she said, putting a magazine on the table as she took her seat. It was *Time*, and on the cover was her, as well as a small inset box with his arrest photo. "Takedown—Public Enemy Number One is Arrested." His booking photo was clear, but his then-bald head had a thin, black stubble starting to come in. They doctored up the image to cover his facial bruises; that much he noticed. His gaze was one of confusion. *They changed the picture, so it wouldn't show how much they hit me. Like everything with Newmerica, it's a fraud.* Raul looked at it for a moment, drinking in every little detail, then turned his eyes back to hers. "You must be pretty popular now," he finally said.

"I've made the rounds on the talk shows, thanks to you."

"Is that supposed to impress me?"

She offered a light shrug in response. "I don't care how you feel Raul. I only showed that to you so that you understand the gravity of your situation. You are big news. You are never going to get out of here. At some point, we will have a People's Tribunal, and justice will be applied. That's how the system works."

He leaned back and grinned slightly. "If you think that intimidates me, you're wrong. You've made a mistake, and you don't even know it." Her photo caught his eye again.

"How's that?" Deja asked.

"No one knew who I was until my picture showed up on that video that the Order of the Bell put out. When no one knows who you are, you can't be hunted. There's no pursuit. My life was not great until that moment, but I was learning to deal with it. I had friends. I was in hiding, but things were not bad.

"You got your name and image out there. For you, that seems like a good thing. You got some publicity for what you did. From the look of it, you got some medal." He nodded at the *Time* magazine cover with her photo. "The problem is, when you did that, you exposed yourself. Now the people out there that are my friends know who you are. They know your face, your background, all very useful things. You no longer can hide, just like me." He smirked at the end of what he said. *Caylee will see her and come at her—it's going to happen.* Clinging onto that thought was his best way of facing their sessions.

For a second, Deja said nothing, an indication that his words had hit home with her. Her face muscles flexed as she tried to control her anger. For Raul, it was as good as if he had punched her. In his current situation, it was the best result that he could have hoped for. "Tell me about your friends Raul. You seem to think they can get me. I think I deserve to know who is coming at me."

There it was—her attempt to pry Caylee's name from him. "You don't."

"Don't what?"

"Don't deserve to know her name. All you need to know is that she is out there. She will be looking for me and for you. And you have given the whole world your name and face."

Her eyes narrowed to slits for a moment, and then she grinned. It was the kind of smile that was not bravado, but confidence. *If she's smiling, that means it is nothing good for me.* "You are so smug, so arrogant," she said. "You act as if it's your right to be that way, that somehow you are entitled to that."

Raul didn't respond. He didn't feel arrogant at all. He was confident, not so much in himself, but he was confident in Caylee. Leaning back in his seat, he wanted to cross his arms, but the handcuffs prevented that. Deja pulled out a large, brown envelope and put it on the desk. "I had hoped it wouldn't come to this. I've tried to convince you of my sincerity. I wanted you to understand that my people will stop at nothing to get the answers from you that I asked for. You refused to play along. I tried to tell you that it was important to respond to me, but you chose arrogance instead. Now you will see what the price of that attitude was."

She pulled a large photograph from the envelope and slid it out in front of him. He couldn't tell at first what it was; then he saw it was a female, lying on what appeared to be some sort of table. Reaching out, he turned the table slightly. Then he saw the face.

Madre! It was his mother. She had lost a lot of weight, to the point where he barely recognized her. She was dressed in a plain tan outfit and looked as if she were asleep. It wasn't sleep though, he could see that. *They have killed her!*

Tears ran down his cheeks as he slid the photo back to her side of the table. Raul looked away from Deja. *She died because of me. They murdered her because I refused to talk.* He refused to sob, refused to give his captor the satisfaction of his agony. With his hands shackled, he couldn't even wipe the tears from his face as he turned back to face her.

"Raul, I tried to tell you that there were consequences for your keeping quiet."

"You killed her."

"No. You did. If you had talked, confessed your crimes, cooperated in any way, this might have been avoided."

Raul felt the guilt swell in him, but only for a moment. Slowly he got on top of that emotion, and pushed it back into the dark recesses of his mind. *This was not my fault, no matter how much they try and lay this at my feet.* "Nice try," he said through gritted teeth. "I didn't kill her. Her blood is on your hands."

Deja shook her head. "I had nothing to do with this. Your mother and sister were in a quarantine camp. I never said a word about her; I merely tracked how she was doing. I didn't order her death, but the camps … well … they can be rough on the old and the young. Your mother just couldn't handle life there. She wouldn't have been there in the first place if you had simply confessed and given me the names I wanted."

"Your people killed an innocent woman."

"She wasn't innocent," Deja countered quickly. "She was your mother."

"That isn't a crime."

"Isn't it? You're a terrorist. She's the one that brought you into this world. She certainly failed in raising you, letting you turn against your own people like you did. That makes her guilty in my eyes and those of the rest of the country."

She's trying to twist this, to make me responsible for her death. "You captured me. All you had to do was order her release. She was no longer of use to you. That makes this your responsibility."

Deja shook her head. "I don't think you understand the game you are playing Raul. I play to win, and sometimes to win, you have to cheat. Your mother was leverage to get you to talk. You refused, and because of that, she died. It really is that simple.

"Consider this. We have your sister too. She's still alive the last time I checked. But like I said, the camps can be rough places. I've heard stories of prisoners raping each other, killing one another. With your mother gone, no one can protect Maria. I would hate to see her end up like your mom, or worse."

Raul felt the rush of anger but held it back. He feared for his sister, but knew that unless he gave Deja everything she wanted, Maria would be held prisoner. *What would Caylee say to that?* He knew that answer. *She would say that I can't trust anything they say. Deja won't release Maria ever. They can't allow someone out there that might want revenge.*

"If she dies, you lose your leverage," Raul said firmly. "I doubt you will ever set her free."

Deja shrugged. "Give me something Raul. Let's start with the name of that woman that was with you. You do that, and I will make sure she's taken out of the general population in the camp. Your cooperation means she gets a chance at survival. All it takes is a name, even a first name. You do that, and you have my word, your sister will be taken care of."

It was tempting; that was hard to deny. Raul resisted it though. *I won't betray Caylee.* He sat upright in the chair, and he stared intently into her eyes. "You murdered an innocent woman. You can tell yourself that it wasn't your fault, but it was. What is more important, I know it. And when my friend comes for me, you will die."

Deja slid the photo back in front of him. "You keep that," she said. "Take it back to your cell with you. Look at it Raul, study it long and hard. Think about what you could have done to save her. Go to sleep at night knowing that you could have prevented her dying like that, far from home, alone."

CHAPTER 8

*"The only trust that matters is between
you and the government."*

Baker, California

The small jet kicked up a lot of dust on the flat tarmac of the Baker, California airport. The engines throttled back to an idle, then stopped as the ground crew moved in to begin refueling. The dry air was good for her sinuses as she drank in the bleakness of the area surrounding the isolated airstrip. Caylee Leatrom shielded her eyes from the dust that had been stirred into the air; then she looked down at Maria Lopez.

Getting her out of the Social Quarantine Camp had been easy, almost too easy. The SEs running the camp had been downright helpful in finding her toiling in the poppy fields. They had her shower and get a fresh set of clothes, probably the first fresh uniform she had worn in weeks from the look of it. While she had been cleaned up, her hair was a tangled mess that Charli had helped her with.

There had been a debate prior to leaving the Los Angeles area, namely around the other people trapped in the camp. Andy had argued that they could not just leave them there. "They are working them to death. If we only take Maria, many others will die."

Travis said that it was easy to take down the camp, but it was Charli who had pointed out the painful truth. "Even if we get them out, we don't have the means to move them; we have no way of getting them to some place safe. If we turn them loose, they will be rounded up again and probably shot as escapees." It had quelled Andy's passions.

For Caylee, however, it was a reminder of Raul all over again. *He had help at Valley Forge, a plan, support. We lack all of those things.* She had ended the debate with a simple sentiment. "We can't help them today, but we will come back. We are better than our enemies. We don't leave people behind. That's why we are going to rescue Raul, and why we will eventually get those people to freedom."

"This is your ride," Caylee said. "These people are friends. They are going to take you to safety."

Maria moved closer to her, holding her hard. Caylee could feel the fear in her grip. While Maria was around thirteen years old, her time in the camp had aged her. It was visible in the wrinkles on her face. Charli and Andy had gotten her something to wear. Not her prison guards. Charli and Andy had gotten her food; the kid had been practically starved. Even with her new clothing, Caylee could see her ribs. Travis warned them not to let her gorge; it would actually hurt her—despite her protests. While they had explained to Maria that they were friends of Raul's, Caylee wasn't sure she fully understood. Just mentioning his name made Maria look around, as if he were there. There was a vacancy in her eyes, almost as if she were looking past them when they talked. *What they did to you was wrong, another item on a long list of crimes.* She was quite sure if they had not arrived when they did, she would have perished in a matter of weeks.

The information on the camps themselves was of interest to Jack Desmond. They had contacted him with a burner phone purchased at a 7-Eleven. Everyone knew people died in the camps, but what was happening in California was a 'war crime,' according to Jack. No one argued any differently with his assessment.

"I want to stay with you," she said just loud enough for Caylee to hear.

"Where we are going isn't safe."

"I want to stay with you," Maria said.

Caylee looked down at her, into the dark pools of her eyes and saw a glimmer of Raul looking back at her. It tore at her emotions in ways she had not expected. Seeing Maria reminded her of Raul. Even though she had known him for only a short time, she felt a crushing obligation to bring him back. It wasn't about America's rebirth or striking a blow against Newmerica—it was about friendship and the obligations that came with that.

She knelt down to look Maria eye-to-eye. "Maria, we are going in to find your brother. Where we are going isn't a place for someone your age. It's dangerous."

"I don't want to be alone again." It was not a request. It was a plea.

Charli knelt down next to Caylee to try and help. "Honey, you won't be alone. Our friends are going to take care of you."

Caylee leaned a little closer to Maria. "You want your brother back, don't you?"

The girl nodded.

"Well, we need to go where he is and get him out. He's going to want to see you when he is free. I need you to be a brave girl and go on this plane. It will take you where you are safe. And when we get your brother, we will bring him to you. I promise." The last sentence was not hollow words simply aimed at calming a frightened child, but they were a commitment.

Travis led over the pilot, a man with a shaved head and a mustache which had a twist on each end. "This is Rutger," he said to the small group as Andy moved in with them. "Ex-SEAL. We served together. He's going to take you to safety," he assured Maria. The young girl heard the words, but looked to Caylee for assurance. Maria received a confident nod. "If Travis trusts him, I trust him."

"We need to get moving," Rutger said, extending his hand to Maria. "NSF will have tracked me by now and will be heading this way. They'll be expecting drug smugglers in case you run into them."

Maria nervously took the stock man's hand and looked back at Caylee. The grizzled former operative gave her a short wave, and Rutger led her to the jet's stairs. "We need to roll," she said calmly as the stairs were folded up and the hatch on the plane closed.

"She'll be fine," Charli said.

"I know. She reminds me of her brother, that's all," Caylee responded.

As the jet taxied and then rose into the sky, they got inside their new rental car and sped off on I-15 heading toward Nevada. The flat arid terrain offered little. "They'll have a checkpoint in Nevada," Travis said from behind the wheel.

Caylee nodded, and Charli, who sat beside her, locked gazes with her. "You alright?"

"What do you mean?"

"You are always, well, frosty … crisp. Ever since we got Maria out of that camp, you've been more emotional than usual."

Emotional? At first it felt like an insult, but she knew Charli and knew it wasn't. "We didn't get Raul's mother," she said. She died before they arrived.

"Through no fault of ours," Charli reminded her.

"I wanted to get both of them."

Charli shook her head. "You are the most pragmatic person I've ever met. Everything is binary with you. Black and white. This mission was full of unknowns. We were lucky. We saved Maria without having to go in there guns a'blazing. Mrs. Lopez was dead before we got to her. That doesn't make the mission a failure."

Caylee heard the words but struggled to shake the feeling that she could have done more. Charli was right, but it would be hard to explain to Raul. *I've always been this way; it is hard to shake.* "You're right Charli. I need to focus on getting Raul out of the Supermax. Thank you."

From the driver's seat, Travis spoke up. "I've been giving that some thought. The information we have on that prison has shown me that it was well named. They don't use contractors like other prisons. The guards are tough ex-law enforcement or military. The prison has multiple layers of defenses—both outdoors and indoors. The guards could defend that place against a platoon of Special Forces if they had to."

"You're not cheering me up Travis," Caylee replied.

"I wasn't trying to," he said. "I was offering a realistic assessment of what we are up against."

"So how do we do it?" Andy asked from the front passenger seat. "There's always a way."

Travis nodded. "There is. If you want to extract a prisoner out of a place like that, there's only one way to do it."

Charli weighed in. "From the inside out."

"Bingo," Travis said with a smile.

"How do we do that?" Andy asked.

Caylee drew a long breath. "We do it by being the sneakiest bastards on the planet," she said with a surge of raw energy that invaded her. "They're smart, but we need to be smarter. We'll need some identities, airtight ones, the kind that opens doors for us. And once we get inside, we get Raul out."

Concord, New Hampshire

General Donaldson sat in the Crazy Goat restaurant with several of his staff officers expecting to enjoy the rare taste of real food. Things had been chaotic over the last few days. He had finally ordered the power restored in Gorham, not so much out of generosity on his part, but because of the fact that the Southern White House and the Pretender had spoken about it publicly. The Vice President-Elect had reached out to him personally to say that in the interest of public relations, the power should be restored. Apparently the images that made it onto the Internet showing old women and children nearly freezing to death wasn't playing well with the citizens, despite the spin by the TRC that they had harbored insurgents.

As if that weren't bad enough, the surprise drive on central Georgia had only added to his public relations woes. General Bloodbath Reager had managed to surround Atlanta and the loyalist counties by the time he got word about it. Donaldson had responded quickly, flying in two companies of Army troops that had defected to the Newmerica cause. They had arrived on one of the last flights into the city. Now the airport runway was cratered by American artillery.

He had not been caught entirely with his pants down, despite the complaints that had come directly from the President-Elect. For several weeks he had Georgia and Virginia National Guard in the city, preparing for its defense. Bridges were wired with explosives for when Reager decided to assault the city—as he was likely to do. Trenches and defensive gun placement had been put into place by Army engineers, making Atlanta a difficult nut to crack. He was sure that General Reager would come. *I've studied him ... he's aggressive. Poke him enough and he always responds with brute force. When that happens, he will bleed in the streets of Atlanta. We will turn it into a modern Stalingrad if we have to.* He was looking forward to handing Reager a humiliating defeat, despite being caught off guard at the moment.

The waiter brought their main courses out, a thick bed of ravioli for him that made his mouth water. One of his officers, Marine Captain Robert Farley, had a rib eye steak and baked potato placed in front of him. He locked eyes with Donaldson before touching his utensils. "Sir, do we have any new information on that New York SOL team?"

He's anxious for some revenge, and I don't blame him. The Marines had been attacked with a hit-and-run assault by the Sons of Liberty out of New York. They had killed one of them, but the others had fled on cross-country skis. Farley had four wounded and two dead as the result of their ambush. "Sorry Captain, but they disappeared into the forests. Our dogs were able to track them for a while, but they put cayenne pepper powder down on their tracks. Once the dogs got some of that in their snouts, well, the hunt was off."

Farley grimaced at the news, and Captain Don Frost spoke up, "Our air ops did destroy a probable group operating in Laconia."

"Probable?" Farley asked.

"It was a group that appeared to be setting a roadside bomb. Rather than risk engaging and losing them, we called in an air strike. Splashed all four of them. There didn't seem much point in trying to confirm what they were doing after the fact." There was a sense of pride in Don's voice that Donaldson embraced. His journey in life had not been easy, but he had watched it with interest. *I remember when she joined the Army four years ago.* Donna Frost had been one of many warriors that had undergone sex change surgery while in the service. When Newmerica called for volunteers, many of them answered out of fear that the Pretender President would roll back the freedoms they had embraced. The TRC ran warnings all during the election, and the general had no doubt that they were well deserved.

"Sir," Major Beardsley of the New York National Guard spoke up from the far end of the table as the waiters finished putting the meal on the table. "What is the situation in Atlanta looking like? They aren't covering it much on the news."

With good reason, no doubt. Some of it was security, to prevent a panic on the part of civilians. Even if the TRC wasn't doing it, Donaldson would have demanded. It was an embarrassment, the invasion of Georgia. People would want to lay it at his feet, but it was more a failure of intelligence. Trying to implicate the NSF was a dead end. No one wants to cross swords with the Secretary of the NSF, especially with her now being the Vice President-Elect. "Despite the rumor mill, things are relatively under control. Yes, the Americans have surrounded Atlanta, but we have crack troops in there, not to mention a lot of local support. Once Bloodbath Reager tries to take the city, he's going to realize that it comes with a pretty hefty price tag."

Donaldson took the linen napkin out and polished his silverware, an old habit. Eyeing the ravioli, his mouth began to water. Out of the corner of his eyes, he saw the wait staff. As if on cue, they all stepped out of the dining area and back to the kitchen. It was an odd gesture, something not registering right with Donaldson. *Where are they going?*

Outside there was a glare of light, car headlights shining in. There was no headlong parking in the front. *This is all wrong!* "Clear the room!" he barked, almost falling backwards as he shot to his feet.

The front window of the Crazy Goat shattered in an explosion of sound and bits of glass shrapnel as bullets sprayed the interior. Donaldson felt a small tug on his left thigh and wood and glassware shattered under automatic fire. Major Dawes tried to dive for cover, but his head exploded, spraying gray matter and gore all over Donaldson's uniform. As he tried to dive for cover, his left leg buckled and rather than jump, he fell hard. As he dropped, he heard the whiz of a bullet cut the air near his head.

There was a squeal of tires outside, and a car roared off as gunfire popped and crackled on the street. Donaldson looked down at his leg in horror. His green uniform pants had a growing stain of crimson seeping from underneath. *I've been shot!* He nervously fidgeted with his belt, fumbling with it clumsily before getting it off. He didn't feel the wound until he saw it, and then it burned hot. He manhandled the belt around his thigh and pulled it tight as a tourniquet to stem the flow of his blood. Pulling the belt secure hurt like hell, but he knew it was better than bleeding to death.

"Sir, are you alright?" Captain Farley asked. Donaldson saw a cut on his face, no doubt from shattered glass or a plate during the attack.

"Yes—yes," he stammered. His entire body was trembling. "Contact perimeter security. I want those bastards caught," he said. Blood coated his fingers crimson and sticky, but he held the tourniquet tight. Around him he saw several of his command staff stand up, but a few like Dawes remained on the floor. Outside, rifle fire snapped and popped in the distance, and a bitter wind blew in from the now obliterated window, stinging at his nostrils. Adrenaline surged through his body, and his ears felt hot. Looking down at his wound, he saw the shattered plate of ravioli lying next to him.

Looking toward the window and the billowing curtains, he saw the limp form of his G2 Officer Major Dawes. Half of his head was gone, and the sight of his exposed brains, and the vacant stare in his dead eyes made Donaldson gag, fighting back the urge to vomit. *They came for me ... personally. This was not just a random attack, they came at me and my command staff. These savages will need to pay for what they've done.*

He had been under fire before, but nothing like this had ever hit. He remembered the standoff in Kirbyville, Arkansas four years earlier in that flash of memory. *This is going to require a similar response. It's the only thing these terrorists understand. Brute force.*

Burlington, Vermont

Of the nine armed snowmobiles that had set out for the Vermont Air National Guard Base in Burlington, only eight had arrived. One of them broke a belt on the long winding journey through the hilly countryside and had to be abandoned. Su-Hui Zhou had been paired with a member of a Michigan Sons of Liberty cell, a female lumberjack named Trudy Ford. She had handled the snowmobile as if it were an extension of her body, even with him on the back with the machine gun. They had taken up a position outside of the perimeter of the air base's chain-link security fence, hidden under the boughs of a thicket of pines whose lower limbs were weighed down with ice and snow. They had dug into the two feet of snow, forming a small shelter of sorts. The snowmobiles of their harasser force were concealed a few yards away, under other pines.

The journey had taken a lot of time. The raiders had used the roads, but only for short distances. Once in Vermont their biggest worry was not Newmerica military forces, but locals that might phone them in. As such, much of the trip was done cross-country. The gray skies overhead indicated a coming snowstorm, but that wasn't Su-Hui's biggest concern. He was more worried about making the attack and getting out. They had hoped to use the moon to allow them to attack at night, but the cloud cover had spoiled that chance. Now they faced the daunting thought of a daylight attack. Trying to flee in snowmobiles, in the dark with their lights off, there was far too much risk of running into a tree or terrain that would cripple their vehicles.

The air strip was plowed, and the arched hangers were lined up and covered with snow from what he had seen, peering off in the distance. A few sentries were on patrol, but for the most part, they were huddled in the warmth of their guard shack, something that Su-Hui was slightly jealous of. His toes were so cold in his boots that he had stabbing pains every now and then that forced him to stand and walk around to increase the blood flow.

Captain Brace Trautman of the National Guard was in command of the raiders. He came to their hole several times, making sure they were okay and refining the plan. His youth made Su-Hui a little concerned, but his knowledge of military tactics and details seemed to erode that concern. The raider's intent was to take out the guard shack with the bulk of their force. Two of the snowmobiles including Su-Hui's would enter the air base through holes that would be cut in the fence a few minutes prior to the battle. One team was in charge of destroying the aviation fuel the pumping station used to refuel the jets that had been bombing them. One unit would plant explosives on the munition bunkers at the far end of the air field while the others would take out the aircraft on the ground. The key was speed. Barracks were filled with airmen and ground crews once the shooting started. Keeping them at bay was Trudy and Su-Hui's mission. Trautman used the snowbank as an ad hoc map, dragging his gloved hand in the snow to show them where she wanted them to go. Sui-Hui pointed out some possible avenues for attack, which Trautman incorporated into the plan. Sui-Hui thanked him for his observations. The go-time was in another hour, which would give them an hour or so before darkness fell, enough time to put distance between the harassers and the base.

Trudy used a plastic chemical hand warmer and tossed one to Su-Hui which he thanked her for. "What motivated you to come here and fight?"

134

he asked as she broke the chemicals in the bag, massaging it to start their reaction.

Trudy frowned. "I was working in the UP, my family's little logging company. Business was good before the Fall, even with the virus. Everyone wanted lumber, and we had trees and sweat, as my dad liked to say."

"What is the UP?"

"Upper Peninsula, that chunk of land north of Michigan." She held up her mitten-gloved hand and gestured with her other hand over the other hand as if it were a map. Su-Hui nodded and Tracy continued.

"They overthrew the government, and things went to shit. The government showed up and said they were going to limit the number of trees we could take down. Some bullshit about it being bad for the environment. My dad told them to fuck off. He said that if we didn't cut down the trees, the Chinese or Canadians would cut down their trees. Him not cutting logs wasn't going to solve their little made-up environmental BS. So he refused to comply."

Trudy shook her head slightly at the memory. "They came for him at night, a bunch of Social-Fucking-Enforcers. Hauled him off for two years of Social Quarantine. They smashed our equipment. Said it was their form of 'due process'.

"I've been on welfare, god damned reparations because I have Chippewa blood in me, but it was wrong. Cutting trees was in my blood. Dad wasn't the same after being in the camp. My two brothers headed south looking for jobs.

"I'm here because they broke us. Those bastards in DC broke us. We were a family business; we were together. It wasn't easy work, but it was honest. They took that from us. My dad is a shell of the man he was because they took from him one of his children—his business. I'm here for some payback.

"What about you?"

Su-Hui shoved the warming plastic bag into his right hand mitten and the relief came a moment later. "I guess I'm here for payback too." He thought about the trio of bullet casings that hung around his neck and what they represented to him.

Four Years Earlier ...
Los Angeles, California

The Immigrant Welcoming Bureau (IWB), formerly ICE, was situated in an old office building in downtown Los Angeles. The walls had scuff marks and dings from mistreatment, and the lobby had a musky smell to it, not quite like mold, but a touch musty. The digital lighting was new, an obnoxious whiteness that only served to point out the run down conditions of the office.

Su-Hui and Hachi sat in their seats with a rigidity about them. He understood bureaucracies and the people that ran them, but his limited experience with the Newmerica government, as well as the State of California, was testing his patience. Ever since they had arrived in Los Angeles, his family had been shuttled about, from shelter to shelter, while they waited for approval to settle. He had met with one family from Honduras who had crossed the border illegally, but were being treated far better than his family. There were refugees from Afghanistan and the disastrous pull-out by Newmerica. Refugees were processed in a matter of two days. One man in the shelter had told him he would be better off going to Mexico and crossing the border there, but Su-Hui knew the risks with the cartels and coyotes. *We will do this legally and in the end, it will all be alright.*

The woman behind the desk was overweight to the point where her buttons were straining to hold in her bulk. The jacket she wore was old and hadn't fit her in years. Her black-rimmed glasses had dandruff on them; he could see the reflection of the flakes from the dirty window of the office. She said nothing to them as she looked at their file and checked her computer.

"Well then, Mr. and Mrs. Zhou, your application for green card status is still under review."

I knew that coming in here. "What seems to be the problem? We have met others that have come in and gotten approval in a day or two. We have been here for weeks."

She offered a fake smile; it was so obvious that he took it as an insult. "Mr. Zhou, I understand your frustration. Our nation was ill-prepared for the influx of people fleeing your nation. Given some of the diplomatic tensions between Newmerica and China at the moment, it is slowing down the process. I am sure you understand."

He *did* understand but held his thoughts in check. *I know that Newmerica abandoned my people to their fate. They deserted us, went back on their commitments. Because of that, Taiwan is now part of China again and I and my family are adrift.* "I assure you," he said holding his anger in check, "I am more versed in the political state than you at the moment. That does not change the fact that my family is being shuttled between shelters. While I attended a year of college here on an exchange program, the rest of my family is in a strange land. I have my assets still, transferred from before the fall of my home. Can we at least move somewhere safer than the shelters?" His wife, Hachi, nodded at his side, not betraying how much English she understood.

The large woman shifted in her seat which squeaked slightly under the strain. "I could initiate a housing request with the State of California on your behalf. That way when you are fully processed by the IWB, you will be eligible to purchase or rent a home immediately."

She was helping more than others he had met with, so Su-Hui accepted. "That would be deeply appreciated."

Stabbing at her keyboard, she raised her glasses to read the details on the screen better. "It looks like there are openings in several neighborhoods, and I can get you on the list. Downey has several homes and apartments that would be good, as does Bellflower, Compton, and El Monte. If you don't like it here in LA, I know of some openings up in San Jose south of San Francisco where they need people of your ethnic background to help balance their community."

"I do not understand," he said. "I thought that we would go out and find a neighborhood and residence we were comfortable with."

She smiled and shook her head. "Mr. Zhou, it doesn't work that way in California. We have a Housing Diversity law that was passed last year. Each neighborhood has a ratio of acceptable cultural backgrounds that are allowed to live there. You being Chinese—"

"Taiwanese," he snapped, cutting her off. No one was going to accuse him of being Chinese, not after what they had done.

"Well yes ... of course," she stammered, "Regardless, given your cultural heritage, you can't move into any community you happen to like. Diversity is a strength. As such, California requires a balance of cultures in a community."

"There are relatives of mine already here," he said curbing his anger again. "I was hoping to live near them, so they can assist us with this transition."

"See, that's where the problems come in. While that seems good for you, it is bad for the overall culture of the city. When you allow that kind of thinking, you end up with Italian or Latino neighborhoods. This system prevents that kind of geo-cultural clustering."

"What is wrong with living around those that can help you?" his wife Hachi said, speaking up for the first time.

The woman chuckled slightly at the question. "Everyone knows that having a diverse community is better."

"How?" he pressed.

"What do you mean, how?"

"How is it better? Have there been scientific studies into this? What backs up such a claim?"

Clearly the woman was not used to being challenged. "I'm sure there are," she said. "It's just well-known that diversity and inclusiveness make everything better."

For a long moment, he and his wife said nothing. *They are making claims that have no basis in fact.* Finally he tried another approach. "When I came to America, I was told people were free. People I met were free to choose what they did and where they did it. All I am asking for is a choice as to where we live."

She nodded and grinned. "And you have it. You are free to choose from these communities where you can live." She responded as if she were granting a wish or doing him a favor … oblivious to the reality.

In that moment, his hate for Newmerica rose to another level.

Burlington, Vermont

Trudy Ford listened to his story and asked no questions, hanging on every word. Only when he stopped did she respond. "So that is what drove you to the Sons?"

He shook his head. "It was another stepping stone on that journey. We played their game; we got our status and moved to San Jose. What happened there is what eventually turned me to the Sons of Liberty."

He was about to tell her more when their radio crackled. "All teams, the holes in the fence are cut, time to mount up," came the stern voice of Captain Brace Trautman of the New Hampshire National Guard. It's show time." Su-Hui and Trudy grabbed their gear and exited their makeshift snow bunker. The sting of the Vermont winter slashed at the exposed parts of his face above his scarf as he climbed into his slightly elevated seat behind her. He dusted the snow off of the M249 machine gun that was mounted there. It had been modified for belt feed, and he had spent several hours training on the weapon. This was different though ... this was not shooting at targets; this was war, up close and personal.

For a moment, he wondered if the snowmobile would start; it seemed to protest the weather, and then it purred to life under him. "You ready?" Trudy called from the driver's seat, turning enough to face him.

He gave her a thumbs up with his mitten.

She didn't gun the snowmobile, but accelerated smoothly as they rose over the hill. The other snowmobiles of the harasser force were converging on the base as they aimed for the hole in the fence line off to their left. As they approached, he saw that whoever had cut it had not cut it quite high enough for him to clear it. Su-Hui leaned back as far as he dared while Trudy threaded the snowmobile through the hole like a piece of thread in a needle. One little barb of the chain link fence snagged the arm on his coat and tore it open, spilling out some of the white insulation.

Leaning back and up, he heard gunfire from the guard shack. There was a loud whomp in the air, and he saw a fireball rise from what had to be one of the snowmobiles. A spray of machine gun fire followed.

Trudy aimed for their target, which was far past the hangers. Through one partially opened door, he saw the menacing form of an A-10's Warthogs, with a fiendish grin painted on the side of the fuselage. He had seen the jets before, from a distance, firing down at the resistance groups and National Guardsmen. Seeing one so close made him cringe slightly at the raw power they represented.

When they reached the barracks, Trudy wheeled the snowmobile to an angle toward the door some 25 yards from the structure. "You're up!" she called, and he swung the gun toward the doorway. "Make her sing!"

A flash of light came from the inside as the door opened, and two men spilled out. Su-Hui didn't hesitate at all; he fired in fast bursts, catching them before they got more than two yards. Blood splattered behind him as they fell. He then aimed at the door itself and fired two bursts into it, a warning to anyone else that might come out.

He had been on several missions with the SOL and the National Guard. He had killed before, but always from a distance—with explosives. This ... this was different. It was close and personal. Su-Hui knew he should be feeling some sorrow, some remorse for his actions, but he couldn't. His mind went to his daughter three years earlier and the horrors his family had endured. In that millisecond, what he felt was a sense of release ... if not outright joy.

A crash of broken glass came from a window at the far end of the barracks to his right. Three fast pops from a pistol barked from the hole. He angled the shots and destroyed what was left of the window and the surrounding opening, chewing up the wood exterior with bullets. They must be discouraged ... he swung along the eight windows facing them, spraying each window with a burst.

At the far end of the taxiway, another snowmobile parked near the munitions bunker, and he could see the white-clothed figure of the driver get out with bolt cutters and explosives in hand. From the hangers, he heard the doors open. The cacophony of sounds was punctuated every so often by gun fire, some from machine guns, others the deeper popping noises from pistols or other guns. This black smoke rolled from in front of the guard post in the distance, no doubt from one of the harassers' snowmobiles that was ablaze.

From the far end of the barracks, he heard the crack of gun fire. Someone was behind the corner of the building, shooting back. He aimed at the corner and fired a sustained burst through the building, stitching the wood with holes and throwing bits of siding into the air. He wasn't sure if he had hit the shooter, but if nothing else, he had driven him back. He checked his belt and saw he still had some rounds to go before he had to reload.

He turned back toward the door that was still ajar and saw a flash. There was a hard tug, almost like a punch, that hit him hard, almost knocking him from his seat. His left arm felt like it was on fire. *I've been shot!* Ignoring the hot pain there, he aimed for the doorway and unleashed a long burst all around the doorway.

"I'm hit!" he called out to Trudy. Glancing over he saw little blood, but did see the hole in his forearm near where the pain was throbbing. He knew he had to reload, but it felt as if every movement of the left arm or hand was only making matters worse, with more ripples of agony rushing into his body. Su-Hui focused, struggling furiously to load a new belt of ammunition. Gone was the frigid cold; his body was wet with sweat and he felt his vision waver for a moment as he finally reloaded. Trudy must have sensed it. She moved the snowmobile some 20 yards down, angling back slightly. If nothing else, their movement would make them a harder target to hit. As he finished reloading, he could hear the cracking of gunfire all around him mingled with an occasional explosion, muffled by the snow on the ground.

Swinging the M249 around, he unleashed a long burst, spraying the side of the barracks from end to end. His vision blurred as he finished the gunfire; the weapon barrel steamed as bits of snow landed on it. He leaned on the shoulder rest of the machine gun to prop himself up, but even that action made his arm ache.

His vision narrowed, tunneling. He wanted to call out for Trudy, to say something to her, but he could not form his words. Su-Hui thought about Hachi in that last second of consciousness; his daughter Ya-ting in the hospital; his mother; of Taiwan burning as he fled. The last thing he remembered before passing out was the rumble of a massive explosion in the distance.

CHAPTER 9

"Justice is subject to perspective."

The District

The Newmerican President-Elect, Daniel Porter sat next to her, surveying the proceedings with a well-rehearsed grimace on his face. She sat next to him, mustering her efforts to avoid grinning. All she offered the cameras was a look of stern resolve. While the Tribunal was being filmed on a delay and many of the shots had been carefully orchestrated, the Vice President-Elect knew that she would not afford to look as if she were gloating over Senator Lewis's plight. *It is important that this Tribunal look fair, but more important that it appear just. Our enemies are watching and will exploit even the most minute facial expression.*

She had chosen the Social Enforcers personally for the Tribunal. Treason and attempting assassination were serious charges and required individuals who could appear sincere and open on the camera. The Vice President-Elect knew the truth, and the charges and evidence were complete fabrications. As the Secretary of the NSF, she had her best people create the evidence and even set off the bomb. It had been necessary. Senator Lewis was a rarity in the District, a politician that had not been deeply corrupted by power. He had no mistresses, no young boys on the side, no evidence of graft. He had been preparing a Congressional investigation of the NSF, something she could not stand for. *Who does he think he is, investigating me?*

The public whispered rumors about NSF operatives, but their

existence had never been confirmed or denied. Caylee Leatrom had changed that when she had dumped hundreds of pages about the program onto the Internet. For many, it confirmed their suspicions that such people were being used by the NSF to enforce policy. Senator Lewis was more interested in the details that Leatrom had released—murders, sabotage, and other skullduggery that were outside the law. His hearings posed a risk to the NSF, one that she could not stand for.

I tried to reason with him. I offered him ample opportunity to not pursue his investigation. He has brought this on himself. She was not a person given to half-measures. There were others in the Newmerican administration that had either posed a threat to her, or were rivals to power. So she had tied them in with the false narrative of being part of a grand conspiracy. *Those that had the audacity to cross me will face the same Tribunal, and share in the fate of the Senator.* She couldn't wait to see the former Director of the TRC, Becky Clarke, when she was forced to endure the power of the organization that had been built. The irony was delightful to the Vice President-Elect.

There were other reasons for her to be happy on this day. Word had come that her Texas rebellion was almost ready to erupt. They were asking for more sophisticated military hardware, a sign that they were preparing to make their stand. She didn't doubt that the Americans would respond brutally to such a rebellion; the fate of the people she supported was of little consequence to her. What mattered more was the angst and public relations nightmare that an uprising in Texas might bring.

As the Senator was led into the chamber, she could see that he had been cleaned up. He wore a suit, but no tie. His shirt had press marks showing that it was not his usual attire, but one ripped from a fresh package and not ironed. There was a look of anger on his face as the two Social Enforcers that led him in made him stand at the podium. They chained his hands to the top of it, forcing him to face the members of the Tribunal.

"Earl Taft Lewis," the Tribunal leader said in a deep voice. "You stand before this People's Tribunal to determine your guilt in plotting and executing an assassination attempt of the Ruling Council and whether you are in league with the Pretender President's administration in committing treason."

Lewis was still defiant. A part of her admired that; another part knew that he didn't realize yet the full gravity of the forces that were against him. "I'm innocent," he said proudly. "Furthermore, I demand a legal trial, not this kangaroo court. I want a lawyer. I have rights."

The Tribunal leader shook his head. "Rights? You don't have rights here. In this room, only the people have rights—not the accused. Denied. And your innocence is not what we will be discussing, but your guilt."

Crimson rose on the older man's face. He turned and glared at Daniel, then at her. She offered him nothing but an icy stare. "This isn't a legal proceeding," he countered. "Social Enforcement has no backing under the law to try individuals or dispense justice."

Another member of the Tribunal, Dorothy Rae, a large black woman spoke up. "Shut up or we will shut you up. You will talk when we tell you to talk," she yelled pounding her fist on the elevated judges' bench where the Tribunal sat.

Lewis shuffled slightly at her angry words but remained quiet. On a large television screen, facing him and the Tribunal, images appeared showing the explosion at the Capitol—the heart of the assassination attempt. The Vice President-Elect's operatives had set and triggered the blast, but that was a secret they took to their graves. Her team at the TRC had crafted the images of the explosion from several angles, throwing in security camera footage of the effects of the blast inside of the building.

After multiple views of the blast, the images shifted to the injured being taken from the building, including her, holding her arm. Daniel had blood on the collar of his shirt and a dazed look as he came through the settling dust and smoke—coughing. A few lower staff members came out, blood gushing from wounds, filthy from pulverized stone dust.

The images continued for nearly 30 minutes before the screen went blank. During the entire time she watched Lewis, who did little more than shake his head at the images of carnage. When the screen went black, the Senator turned to the Tribunal leader. "What possible good is served showing those images? They have nothing to do with determining my guilt. We all saw those videos on the news. You are simply attempting to inflame the people viewing them," he pronounced.

Ever the fighter ... good. When he's sentenced, it will make his downfall even more enjoyable. A large woman, almost goth in appearance, who sat on the Tribunal, responded with angry indignation. "The accused is warned once more to keep his mouth shut. We will determine what is introduced into evidence and what isn't."

"With all due respect, I'm entitled to defend—"

"You are entitled to what we tell you that you are entitled to!" snapped the Tribunal leader.

Lewis refused. He turned to face her. "This was all your doing," he called out from the podium. "You staged all of this to implicate me in crimes I didn't commit. You were so worried about my hearings into the NSF that you framed me! It won't work Madame Secretary. I won't stand here and be a fall person for something that you fabricated."

She savored his emotional outburst, and immediately opted to play to it. Rather than speak, she rose to her feet. Every eye in the room and the cameras fell on her as she dipped her gaze downward and shook her head in mock sadness. Reaching into her small, blue Birkin bag, she pulled out a tissue and dabbed her eyes, as if his words had hit her hard.

The Tribunal leader called out ordering the guard to action, "Gag the accused!" and two SEs moved on the Senator. He struggled, but his hands were chained to the podium. There was little that he could do. Guards produced a ball gag and strapped it to his head. Rage, fear, and embarrassment washed across the face of the old Senator as he tried to resist but couldn't.

The Vice President-Elect watched; then she turned to Daniel Porter. "Now," she whispered. He rose to his feet and the two of them slowly walked out of the Tribunal room. As they exited the chamber, the Tribunal leader called for the first witness.

Once out of view of the cameras and attendees, Daniel looked over at her. "Are you sure that it is a good idea for us to *not* be there?"

She tucked the tissue back in her purse, nodding to him as the members of their Secret Service detail moved in beside them. "Walking out the way we did will make the Senator look indifferent to the victims' treatment. Our presence was there strictly to lend legitimacy for the Tribunal after all. We will need to be there at the end when they sentence him, but otherwise it will be boring.

"Besides, we have a lot to do. Inauguration is approaching," she said offering a thin smile. "We have a great deal to plan."

Daniel nodded and the two of them started down the long hallway. *A few days of this Tribunal and then we can move to the rest of my enemies.*

Alpharetta, Georgia

Alpharetta had been a sleepy city outside of Atlanta until a major consulting company announced that it was a perfect place for big tech companies to establish a foothold in the south. Almost overnight, Alpharetta exploded with massive office building complexes, housing developments, and schools. For a while, everyone went there, robbing each other's talent in a desperate effort to dominate the emerging market.

Like so many such communities, it grew faster than the infrastructure could keep up. Roads got clogged, and ultimately the promise of the community being a competitive edge evaporated. It had become just another small city that had been consumed by large companies. Prices for cheap homes soared when demand peaked. With the arrival of COVID, office space was abandoned as businesses learned employees could work effectively at home. Some of the businesses simply consolidated their work elsewhere. What was left was a hollow shell of empty office buildings, a shadow of the promise that city once was said to possess.

It was in one of those abandoned offices that General Reager had set up his command. The space had a bit of a musty odor, but he ignored it. Aroma could be coped with. What mattered to him was victory.

The encirclement of Atlanta had been far from error free. The Georgia National Guard that had dug into the city was well equipped and willing to attempt to test General Reager's defenses. Controlling the major roadways prevented large troop movements into the besieged city, but the grip on the city felt like Swiss cheese to him. There were over a thousand little ways to sneak in or out, and while his forces were tightening their grip, it often brought them into contact with the city's defenders.

He had overseen the destruction of the runways of Atlanta Hartsfield-Jackson Airport. One errant rocket had hit a 757, turning it into a flaming wreck on the runway. The locals attempted twice to repair the damage, but his artillery made such efforts pure folly. Several regular Army units that had defected to Newmerica had been intercepted trying to get into the city, resulting in brisk firefights. The city's declaration of being an autonomous zone had little meaning to Reager. He was slowly tightening the noose around the city, reducing the number of avenues that could be penetrated.

Captain Mercury entered his office through the open door. "Sir, our 'guests' have arrived."

Trip smiled, brushing his crew cut back with a sweep of his hand. "Escort them in and stay with them."

She paused for a moment. "Sir, the map?" she asked and nodded at the map that was held up with magnets on the rolling whiteboard that dominated his office.

Trip understood her query. Normally, he would have the map taken down, or turned around. He thought: *I want them to see it.* "It's fine," he assured her.

A minute later, she escorted in the two visitors. One was a short, black woman with a hair style clearly done to play to any cameras that might be present and wearing a pristine blue dress. He had learned long ago how to tell a good hair dye job from a drug store box job, thanks to his ex-wife. The visitor's was expensive. She stomped in, clearly defiant and angry. The face of the mayor of Atlanta was known to him, as was her reputation for forcing conflict with authority.

The other visitor was a male, big all of the way around both in height and around his midsection. He wore a long-sleeved, black hoodie and black jeans with a thick leather biker's belt. An empty holster hung on his left hip—*a cross body draw if he's right handed.* He surveyed the room as he entered. Captain Mercury closed the door and stood at parade rest.

Best to start this as cordial as possible. "Good day, I am—"

The angry female cut him off. "We know who you are General," she said. "You have a hell of a lot of nerve cutting off electricity and water to the noncombatants of the city."

Well, that didn't last long. "Mayor Longfelt," he said. "I would be more than happy to restore services to the good people of Atlanta as soon as you accept the results of the election and dismantle this so-called autonomous zone and turn in your arms."

"That isn't going to happen," the big man next to her said before the mayor could respond.

"And you are?"

"Geraldo Vasquez," he said proudly. "I am in command of the People's Free Autonomous Zone of Atlanta. We don't recognize your authority in our state; nor do we accept your invasion." Trip eyed him with his almost pasty-white skin. He's the whitest guy with that last name on the planet. The general understood instantly; *he probably identifies with being Hispanic.* Under normal circumstances, he would have chuckled, but these were far from normal circumstances.

"Mr. Vasquez, you can ignore our presence all you wish, but we are here."

"You're an invading Army in defiance of the Newmerican election," the mayor weighed in.

"Georgia is part of the United States. My orders come from the President of the United States. I can't invade something that I represent. *Your* actions are in defiance of the election results."

"You'll never take Atlanta," Vasquez said angrily. "Send your troops in, and we will show you."

Trip grinned. "I don't have to invade. If I were going to rush in at you, I'm quite sure you would have staged ambush points, IEDs, and a whole array of nasty little surprises. I don't have to invade. This is a siege ... you may want to Google that while you're here, since you have no cell service inside the city. It is my intent to withhold power, water, and food until you capitulate."

"That's barbaric," Mayor Longfelt snapped. "You're a monster. You'll be starving hundreds of thousands of innocent people. Everything I've heard about you is correct."

He drew a deep breath and let out an audible sigh. "We can spend a lot of time calling each other names and making baseless accusations. I allowed you to come out and meet with me to try and avoid unnecessary loss of life."

"Withdraw," Vasquez said in a growling tone.

"You are proceeding under the assumption that you have some sort of authority here, Mr. Vasquez. Let me assure you. You have none." He kept his tone in check so that it was factual, not emotional.

His words sent a splotched red color rushing to the cheeks of Vasquez. The mayor ignored it and turned to him. "We have hospitals and nursing homes in the city."

Trip nodded. "I understand. Route 10, out of the city—Memorial Drive—is an open corridor. You can evacuate people on that roadway. Folks needing medical care will be taken to hospitals or facilities that will take care of them. We will be temporarily interning folks to make sure you are not trying to sneak out combatants."

"Many of my constituents won't want to leave. Atlanta is their home."

"That is their choice. Until you decide to capitulate, those are the rules we will define." Out of the corner of his eye, he saw that Geraldo Vasquez was taking in every detail he could from the map in his office.

"We have children in the city, families, old people," the mayor stated. "Cutting off their food and water is cruel punishment. People will panic when they figure it out. There is already hoarding, and the looting and riots are bound to follow. You are a war criminal!"

I have been called that ever since San Antonio. The words no longer bothered him as much as they used to. Hitting that reporter that called him "Bloodbath" had purged a lot of his hate for the labels that the opposition threw at him. "Name calling won't resolve your situation. As I stated, Madam Mayor, anyone is free to leave the city. If they choose to live under those conditions, so be it. If they choose to remain in the city, it is because you won't let them leave, or they opt to be there."

"What about the fire department? If we have a fire, they won't be able to fight it," she needled.

Trip shrugged slightly. "You have illegally declared your city independent of the United States of America. If you are concerned about fires downtown, looting, or anything else, then kick out these autonomous zone people and accept the election results."

"We won't go!" boomed Vasquez. "We have every right to be there … in defiance of your oppression of the citizens of the city."

He did not suppress the chuckle, and let it go a little longer than he probably should have. "Did I say something funny, General?" Vasquez demanded.

"My apologies. I have found that many people are brave and full of bravado when their stomachs are full and they are warm. This is winter and even Atlanta gets cold at night. I think your bluster is cute. As to your right to be there, I tend to agree—but not in defiance of the American President."

"We will fight you," he said boldly, even angrier at the laugh that had been delivered.

"Okay," he said, standing a bit more erect and putting his fists on his hips. "Bring it on, Mr. Vasquez. But know this: We will not be playing fair or showing restraint. You are acting in rebellion of the legal authority of America."

"America doesn't exist anymore," Vasquez said proudly. "The only authority I answer to is Newmerica. I will defend her to the death."

"Offer accepted," Trip snapped, shedding his pervious humor instantly. "When we come, and eventually we will, this isn't going to be like those peaceful protests six years ago. We will not be using rubber bullets or firing tear gas. I didn't bring the state police with me. I brought an Army. We have tanks, fighting vehicles, artillery and a lot of guns. I won't tolerate the people under my command coming under attacks of any sort. If you throw a brick in my direction, I'm sending back a 120 millimeter high explosive enema in response."

Geraldo Vasquez was furious, but his jaw hanging open meant that he understood the rules of engagement. Trip turned back to the mayor. "I'm a reasonable person, to a point. We will provide you instructions for getting your people out of the city safely. If you are reasonable and respectful, this does not have to end in misery or bloodshed."

Pausing for a moment, he leaned slightly in her direction. "You know my reputation, overinflated though it may be. If that's the case, then you know I will not hesitate. I will take care of those under my command. I will win this conflict because that's what I do."

She glared at him as if he were the devil himself standing before her. Her lower lip was quivering, not in fear, but rage. She spun on her heels and stormed for the door. Vasquez followed, taking the time to glance once more at the map on the whiteboard.

Captain Mercury waited until the door closed, then stepped over to him. "I think they got the message. But that Vasquez fella—he got a good view of the map. It has our troop placements on it."

"Does it?" he asked, nodding at the map. Mercury went over to it and swept it. "This doesn't show our disposition. We don't have troops in many of these locations."

"I know, Captain," Trip replied. "He thinks he has gotten some useful intelligence. His type lacks practical combat experience though. He will look at the map and think we are weakest along the exit road, Memorial Drive. He'll see weak points in our lines that aren't there. If he has half a brain, and I think that's all he's got, he'll pass on the word."

"You fooled him."

Trip shook his head. "I let him think he fooled me. In the meantime, the mayor will evacuate the infirmed and hospital patients. We will be accommodating, courteous, and do everything we can to help them. We will broadcast information to the citizens on how to extricate themselves from the city, if they desire that. I will have helicopters drop pamphlets on neighborhoods with instructions should any of them desire to depart. Our portable drone jammers will prevent the TRC getting messages in to counter ours.

"They are cut off from the outside world. For a few days, it is fine. When they start running low on toilet paper, food, and water, they will consider our offer. A chance of getting a shower and a hot meal can be appealing to civilians who are denied that."

Captain Mercury nodded. "They are bound to try and force a military victory and breakout. What happens when they mount their counterattack?"

"Mr. Vasquez saw the map. If he's got the brains God gave a sand flea, he will pass on what he saw. They will sense weakness and we are going to let them feel it. I want them to come; I want them out of the city and fighting on ground of our choosing rather than where they would have the advantage." Trip walked over to the whiteboard and tore down the false map.

"Warfare is more than bullets and bombs; it is getting in the head of your enemy and controlling their thoughts and reactions."

"Sun Tzu," Mercury offered.

"Damned straight," he replied, wadding up the big map and stuffing it into his wastebasket.

Newmerica Penitentiary, Administrative Maximum Facility
Florence, Colorado

Raul finished his pushups in his cell. He no longer counted them; he found the counting served as a reminder of the passage of time and he hated that. Instead he did the push-ups and sit-ups until it hurt so much he could do no more. The working out was paying off. In his small, polished stainless steel mirror, he could see that he had never been as muscular as he was now.

Some of the political prisoners in Unit J didn't work out. No doubt, they didn't see any reason to. Raul had a reason, a fragment of reality that he clung to. *Caylee will come for me, and I need to be fit and ready when she does.*

The guards opened his door for the evening community time. Every night they brought the prisoners out and let them have an hour of socializing on the unit common space. That was a rarity in the prison; most prisoners were simply put in cages where they could walk, ten paces at a time, back and forth for freedom. Unit J was different than the rest of the Supermax.

They put on the television, always locked onto CNN with no means of changing it. The TRC logo in the bottom told him everything he needed to know about the news ... that it was twisted and positioned to tell the Newmerican point of view. He watched it with a jaded eye.

As he settled on the steel bench, he saw the lead story was out of New Hampshire. The banner read, "White Supremacists Wage War of Terror on Innocents." The image showed a building burning and people running away, protected by soldiers. The smoldering hulk of some sort of tank morphed into the image. *Why would they be fighting in New Hampshire?* The reporter referred to the fighters as, 'The Defiance,' which made them seem ominous yet intriguing to Raul. *I wonder how long they spent coming up with that name for the resistance.*

Ted came over. His shoulder-length hair had been recently cut shorter, though it was still hanging past his ears. His white and black beard was trimmed. Prisoners were given scissors to use for grooming, and they were all but worthless—plastic and duller than the scissors they gave children in elementary school. Still, the older man looked less ferocious than usual. "Do you mind if I join you?"

Raul nodded. Ted was always fun during community time. After the death of Raul's mother, Ted had been supportive. "She would not want you to feel guilt Raul; you know that." Raul wanted to believe him, but the guilt still followed along.

One of Ted's strengths was that he seemed to have a knack for interpreting the truth out of what they were showing on the news. Of course there was no way to verify what he said, but his version was always one that came with a tinge of hope tied to it. In the Supermax prison, hope was a precious commodity.

"What do you make of all this New Hampshire news?" Raul asked.

Ted grinned under his mustache and glanced at the television. "They are trying to spin the story that these are domestic terrorists. I've been to New Hampshire. The folks up there are independent thinkers for the most part. From what I can piece together, they didn't accept the lie about the election results that the TRC is peddling and those folks are fighting back."

"Won't they just send in the Army?" Raul asked.

Ted chuckled. "The military is in a quandary I bet. When the previous President ordered them to help defend the White House, they turned their backs on him, and hung him out to dry. The man had his faults, hell, I dreaded every time he got on camera, but he was right about a lot of things. He warned every one of the 'deep state,' but the media mocked him. It turns out that the deep state not only existed, but had corrupted the military.

"They disobeyed their Commander in Chief. That's treason. They allowed a coup to take place, and that is sedition on their part. Now the new President has declared himself the winner of the election, as has that asshat Daniel Porter. The Constitution requires them to follow the President, but two people are claiming that title. They are afraid of the legitimate President coming into power because they might be held to account for their actions. At the same time, they know they are bound to the rule of law. So they will straddle the fence rather than commit to one side or the other."

Ted had a great way of taking complicated matters and making them easy for Raul to understand. "What of that trial?"

"I knew Earl Lewis back in the day. He's a straight arrow. I half-expected him to step down after the Fall. The thought that he was involved in a conspiracy to kill the Ruling Council is ludicrous. And this trial, it's not about justice. His guilt has already been assigned. This trial is a show … it's about pushing more fear into the people."

That was Raul's take on it as well. *Every time the man tries to defend himself, they shut him down.* "They'll probably send him here when they are through with him."

Ted shook his head for several moments. "I'm afraid not Raul. He's a traitor, or at least that's what they are saying he is. This trial is to demonstrate their power. They will kill him. Knowing these people, they will make it a public event. It's a damned shame too. Lewis was one of the few good guys on the other side."

"There are no good guys in Newmerica," he said flatly. "Only different shades of bad."

Ted leaned back and there was a gleam in his eyes, one that Raul had not seen often. "There are good people there; they are just feeding a corrupt system and don't know it yet.

"I like to believe that everyone has some good in them. Of course, that was our mistake … *my* mistake." He looked up past the television that hung from the ceiling as if he were looking through the walls of the prison.

"What do you mean?"

"Some of my colleagues were not working in good faith. They said all of the right words to my face and to the media, but in the end, they were plotting the scheming to bring down the country. While I wasted my time trying to find some common ground for both parties, they were planning to have me murdered along with the rest of my party. I underestimated some of them, especially the Secretary of the NSF. I knew she was smarter than she projected, but I never realized the depths she would go to."

Raul understood. She was behind Deja coming after him. "When did it all go wrong?"

"I've had a lot of time to think that over," he said, returning his gaze to Raul. "I think it was when COVID hit. The opposition learned something people in power never should—that their constituents were willing to surrender freedoms for a false sense of security and safety. Once it hit them that they could control large parts of the population with the fear of something that had a 99 percent survival rate, well, they couldn't stop. So they ratcheted up the fear of every variant. They shut down entire sectors of the economy, and no one batted an eye. Anyone that questioned their so-called science was blocked on social media or labeled a crazed conspiracy nut. And just when people started to think things were going to go back to normal, they whipped up the hype for a new, more deadly variant. People got used to fear; it was all around them, every day. They came to expect it; they needed it, and they needed the government to tell them what to do. You know, there are still people who won't go out in public without a mask ... who won't leave their house out of fear?

"All of that was smoke and mirrors for what they were really doing. They called them, 'social reforms,' but they were really altering the very foundation of our democracy. The average person was just happy to get checks. They were encouraged to turn in their neighbors for the slightest infraction. Their Army of Social Enforcers didn't have to play by any rules."

Raul absorbed every word that Ted said and saw the underlying logic. "I never saw it; no one I know did. We just went along with things because we were told to. It was easier to comply than to speak up. In that way, I was part of the problem."

Ted put his hand on Raul's shoulder and squeezed it slightly. For an instant, he remembered Caylee doing the exact thing with him. "When they overran the White House and Capitol, very few people did anything to stop them. Those that did were killed, or sent to places like this," he said looking up and around the unit. "It was never your fault. It was *our* fault."

Raul looked at Ted who offered him a smile, but he could not shake his guilt about the affairs that had engulfed the country. *Caylee was right; until bad things happened to me, I was ignorant of what was happening. How much of the country is the same way right now?* Ted seemed to sense his feelings and continued to speak. "The part I am concerned about are our enemies abroad. The Chinese have profited from all of this. Russia has seen us focus on internal enemies, allowing them to advance in the Middle East and Europe. Ask Taiwan and the Ukraine what the impacts of all this have been. They laugh at what we've become. We are now no better than the people we once stood against."

"These people have much to answer for," Raul said bitterly.

"Indeed they do."

"When I am free, I am going to make sure they pay," he said. Memories of the photo of his mother that Deja had shown him several days before his death came rushing to the forefront of his mind. *She was innocent of anything other than being my mother. They killed her because of me.* Ted's words gave him focus and direction ... vengeance.

"To do anything you'll have to be out of here," Ted said. "And no one gets out of here."

"I will," Raul assured him.

"How?"

"I don't know yet. I just know that my story doesn't end here."

INTERLUDE

"Being afraid is being vigilant."

Four years earlier ...
San Jose, California

Su-Hui Zhou was proud of what he had built since arriving in Newmerica a year earlier. Despite the onerous regulations and red tape, he had been able to open a carry-out restaurant in San Jose called the Taste of Taiwan. He had never envisioned himself being a restauranteur, but he felt that owning his own business was the best way to build financial security.

It was an uphill struggle from the start. He had been forced to open the restaurant some 15 miles from his home. Regulators told him he couldn't open it closer to home because there were already too many Chinese restaurants in the area. It was a mark of non-diversity. He tried to point out that his was Taiwanese, not Chinese, but Newmerica and the State of California did not see the difference any longer.

The taxes and fees they had to pay were staggering. It was as if they didn't want him to open a business. For all of the taxes he paid, he could not see what benefit came from them. There was a huge homeless problem in the city and the suburbs. When he called to get one man removed from his doorstep, a social worker came and chided him for not being sensitive to the man's plight. As he glanced at the doorway, he remembered the confrontation all too well. *I was sensitive, but he was blocking my door.* For over two hours, the social worker berated him for not helping the man, not giving him a good meal. 'Don't you know what these people have been through?' she had snapped at him. "I lost my homeland and came here with the clothing on my back. I too was homeless. So, I can probably identify with his plight better than you," Su-Hui had snapped back. That had infuriated the woman enough to leave, escorting the filthy, homeless man away.

It was not easy operating under the weight of California's oversight, but his experience in bureaucracy from his previous career helped Su-Hui navigate the hurdles thrown in front of him. *I had always believed that America's foundation was small business. Newmerica seems bent on preventing small businesses from forming.*

His mother and wife worked as cooks. Su-Hui's son, Akio, was his delivery person, and his daughter, Ya-ting, took orders at the counter. There was no seating in Taste of Taiwan. The constant surfacing of variants of COVID would have made investing money on such space a waste. The latest was the Upsilon variant, or UV as the media called it. Every time a new variant emerged, it was hyped as being more deadly or spreading faster than all others, and California reacted by locking down businesses. By only doing pickup and delivery, he had been able to weather the risk of shutdowns.

While he never had considered owning a restaurant, Su-Hui had come to love his little business. It kept his family close, and after the fall of Taiwan, he felt an indescribable urge to keep his loved ones close to him. Even as he flipped the door sign to open, he drank in the heady aroma of the pork cooking in the kitchen. Mingling with the spices he had consumed from his youth, just standing there, in the small lobby area, it was easy to remember his lost homeland.

He was about to go in the back to prepare his food order for the week when he heard the chime of the front door. Three men strolled in— two white and one Hispanic—each wearing a black jean vest over their weathered T-shirts. They looked around the small space of the ordering foyer and Su-Hui could sense that something was wrong. They weren't picking up menus or even looking at the board showing the items being offered. Ya-ting appeared at the ordering window and asked if she could help them, but they ignored her. Instead, the tallest one walked over to where Su-Hui stood.

"You're the owner?"

"Yes. May I help you?"

"I am Beckett. We are Social Enforcement for this neighborhood. We go by the Regulators," he said with a hint of pride.

To Su-Hui, it was little more than a gang name. He knew what they were. More importantly, he knew what they represented. Social Enforcers were bullies that operated beyond the law. Just hearing who they were made him nervous. *There is likely nothing 'social' about this visit.* "I can recommend the port with Ma-Po-Tofu? It is our daily special."

"We didn't come for food," Beckett replied, shooting a long glance at Ya-ting at the ordering window. "We came because there's a problem."

His mask of innocence was sincere and calm. The last thing he wanted to do was escalate a situation with the three men. "What kind of problem?"

"Three days ago, you interviewed a woman of color, Trina Darbin."

He remembered the young woman well. She had come in and demanded a job. Out of courtesy, he had given her an interview. "I do remember talking with her. Unfortunately, it did not work out."

"Why is that?" another of the young men asked angrily. "You have something against people with different skin color?"

He ignored the tainted question and focused on the taller leader. "She had never worked in the restaurant business before. She said that she could only work three hours a day and wanted more money than I am able to pay, more than what I pay my own children. As such, I did not offer her a position here."

"You see," Beckett replied. "That's the problem. California has diversity and inclusiveness requirements when it comes to hiring. We've done some digging into your little restaurant here. You only have Chinese working here. That's against the established social requirements."

"We are not Chinese," he said. "We are from Taiwan."

"That is China," the third man said.

"No, it is not. Maybe on a map, but Taiwan will always be separate to me and my people," he said with pride. "You are correct. I only employ Taiwanese because so far, I have only hired members of my family. I had no job openings at the time. I offered Miss Darbin an interview strictly as a courtesy."

Beckett shook his head. "You see, that's a problem."

"I do not know how I could be a problem at all. I had no job openings.

It is my business. If I was hiring, I would hire only qualified people. For now, I have only employed members of my family because they know the food, the ingredients, and can speak with the others from our homeland when they call in … all of which are requirements to be able to work here."

"You should have hired Trina," said one of the men behind Beckett.

"Even if I were hiring, I would not hire her. You cannot run a business where the employees say when they will work and demand more pay than others that have worked here much longer. It would be a foolish decision."

Beckett glared once more at Ya-ting for a long moment, and then turned back to him. "I don't think you understand. You need to have a diverse workforce. It makes a better product."

Diversity again! It had forced him to move to a neighborhood in San Jose that he would have never considered moving to. He had a neighbor that came from Guatemala and another who was a refugee from Afghanistan. They were good people, but not necessarily the kind of people he would have voluntarily moved next to. Worse was the disparity of their situations. The family from Guatemala had come across the southern border illegally, and had already been granted citizenship. At the same time, he was a year into the process to legally become a citizen and felt like he was nowhere closer to finishing that legal ordeal. *The inconsistencies of this so-called diversity are frustrating.*

"You say that diversity makes a better product, but I do not see it. Miss Darbin does not know how to cook, let alone how to cook *our* dishes. She has never worked a cash register or dealt with the public. My family members all have this experience. How would hiring her make things better?"

Su-Hui's logic peppered Beckett, but only seemed to make his brow wrinkle slightly. "Everyone knows that diversity and inclusiveness make things better. You would have to teach her."

"But I do not have to teach my family members."

"Are you some sort of racist?" asked Beckett.

It was Su-Hui's turn to get angry. He balled his fists and took a step closer to the taller man. "I am many things Mr. Beckett, but I am not a racist. You know nothing about who I am."

"You need to have a diverse workforce," he snapped back. "I suggest that you reconsider hiring Trina. She's a good kid. She will learn fast enough for you."

"That may be, but I do not have any openings. My time with her was a courtesy."

"Maybe you can have your daughter over there go out and get another job," one of the other men said, nodding toward the ordering window. Ya-ting heard his words and left, not wanting to be dragged into the discussion.

Su-Hui knew it was wiser to diffuse the situation. The easy course of action was to comply. The problem was not one of Trina Darbin's race— but of principle. *Ever since I came to this country I have been forced to do one thing or another. I have bent to every request in hopes that it might be the last, and yet more keep coming. I do not need additional help. Hiring her would be paying some sort of extortion to these thugs. Worse, Ya-ting would have to find a job. And who would suffer, other than my daughter? The customers—that's who.*

This was something where he could not concede. In the back of his mind, he knew it was a stupid issue to take a stand on, but he had reached the end of his patience. "I will not be firing my daughter to hire someone who is unqualified for the job." His jaw slid forward as he spoke.

"You might want to think that over Mr. Zhou," Beckett warned. "We aren't some regulators coming in here from the state. We are Social Enforcers. We are not tied up with the rules that others have to play by."

"Are you threatening me?" he asked through clenched teeth. He already knew that answer, but he wanted to see if Beckett would stand behind his words.

"You can take it any way you want," the man said, his eyes narrowing as he looked down at Su-Hui. "I suggest that you call Trina back and hire her. If you don't … well … shit happens." Before Su-Hui could reply, Beckett whipped around and headed for the door, followed by his comrades.

His wife, Hachi, came from the kitchen area and moved by his side. "I heard what they said."

"And what do you think?"

"I saw that girl, Trina. She was lazy and arrogant. You built this business to take care of your family. No one should come in and tell you what to do or who to hire. This is ours." There was a ring of defiance in her voice.

"Agreed. These people are unaccustomed to being told 'no'. We have not heard the last of them."

His wife took his hand and squeezed it hard, letting him know that she stood beside him both physically and emotionally. He smiled because it was all he needed.

Kirbyville, Arkansas

Colonel James Donaldson got out of the Blackhawk helicopter just after it touched today, clutching at his beret as he ducked and trotted off the makeshift helipad. Rolling forested hills with leaves turning to their brilliant autumn colors surrounded the clearing where the Army had established its forward base. Squinting to avoid the dust that was kicked up by his landing, he was greeted by a Warrant Officer who escorted him through the maze of parked vehicles and tents to a hunting lodge flanked by vehicles that still bore the FBI and ATF logos.

Of course the FBI and ATF were gone—recently absorbed into the newly formed National Security Force. The Ruling Council had pushed to merge all of the nation's diverse police forces into a single entity. It made sense to him. Individual departments had already demonstrated that many of them were filled with racist and corrupt officers. Bringing them under a single federal umbrella would streamline efforts to identify the unethical and dangerous officers and purge them.

As he entered the hewn-log lodge, he took off his hat and coat and surveyed the room. What had been the seating area had been converted to some sort of a makeshift headquarters. A number of federal agents, one park ranger, and local law enforcement were gathered around the table. As he approached, all eyes fell on him … and for a moment, he savored it. *That's right, I'm now the one in charge.*

This had all begun over guns. The Ruling Council had passed the Newmerican Safety Act, but implementing it was proving to be a challenge. As part of the new law, a 'buyback program,' owners of any guns deemed to be assault weapons were to turn them into law enforcement for reparation points that could be converted to money.

Likewise, no person was allowed to own more than fifty rounds of ammunition. Anyone that refused to do so would be classified as a potential terroristic threat.

Many had outright refused to comply. The Colonel thought of them as ignorant fools. Gun violence had been a documented problem for decades in the old nation. Removing the guns would eliminate the deaths. It was so simple. Just outlawing guns was not enough; they had to be rounded up; otherwise there would always be holdouts that refused to comply. He understood the Constitution full well and knew that the vast majority of people were not part of a militia. *People have no just cause for the kinds of firepower they have at their disposal.*

Standoffs were popping up like a cancer. It made identification easier for the people that were against the Great Reformation that founded Newmerica. A part of him wondered if that wasn't one of the motivators in pushing for the Safety Act—to force the hands of those that disliked what they called, 'The Fall.' *These arrogant fools wrap themselves in an obsolete flag and call themselves patriots.* Donaldson did not feel sorry for the people that started such standoffs. *They flaunt laws over common sense ... and that will cost them.*

Most of the standoffs ended with gunfire, though a few had enough brains to surrender. In a few cases, Social Enforcers had taken family members into Social Quarantine as leverage against the gun-lovers— an effective way to get them to stand down. That technique had failed in Kirbyville, with several families that proclaimed themselves as gun collectors banding together for protection and refusing to comply with the new law. Four families covertly began to fortify positions in the wooded hills of Kirbyville, stockpiling everything they needed for a long siege, if it became necessary.

This standoff was triggered by a confrontation on the main street, Margaret Avenue, when the ATF had tried to pull off a roll-up arrest of the leaders of the group. Almost immediately it had gone haywire, with gunfire erupting in the streets. Then the 'gun nuts' as Donaldson thought of them had gone up in the rugged hills and had defiantly dug in. They had expected a confrontation at some point and were well prepared. Local law enforcement, now part of the NSF, had warned that going up there to force them out was going to be costly, but the ATF and FBI agents felt differently. As the standoff dragged out for four weeks, it was clear that the people holed up in the cabins had no intention of coming out on their own. They had tried an assault, which had resulted in the deaths of six agents with many more wounded.

The call had come for the National Guard to go in, but the Ruling Council had pointed out that these were now terrorists—domestic—but still terrorists. They wanted overwhelming force. They wanted to make an example out of these good old Arkansas boys, and the best way to do that was to have the military fully commit.

When the mission had come up, Donaldson had quickly volunteered. There were few opportunities in peacetime to garner the kind of attention that might lead to a promotion. He knew that many of his peers saw him as a desk jockey, not a field commander. And while this was far from being a true military operation, it would gain attention in the media, and that would help position him for advancement and the chance to lead a full-blown military mission someday.

The Army Chief of Staff had been more than willing to grant his request, especially when he reminded him that he had been the one that had prevented a Pentagon response to help save the Traitor President. It had been an ugly affair, one that he was proud of. He knew that the Joint Chiefs didn't entirely like what they had done that night, especially the Marine Corps Commandant who had resigned over what had gone down the night of the Liberation. Donaldson was not ignorant of the reason they may have given him the assignment. *They may hope that I fail, or get killed. That would allow them to sweep their own decisions under the rug that night.* He was determined to come through this operation alive and well. *They will have little choice but to promote me.*

"Good people," he said so as to avoid any hint to sexism, "I'm Colonel Donaldson. Effective immediately, I am in command of this operation, per orders from the Army Chief of Staff and the Ruling Council."

"Daniel Evers, Special Agent in-Charge, ATF," a tall man at the map said. "We received word you were coming sir."

"How about a run-down on the situation?" Donaldson asked.

Another man with golden blonde, cropped hair moved beside him. "Akron Bonner, SAC, FBI," he said; then he turned to the map on the large table. "We estimate that there are at least a dozen men and women with an array of illegal weapons dug into a small hunting camp on top of this hill," he said and stabbed his finger down. "They have set bear traps and other little booby traps around the camp, making approach complicated. They've dug foxholes, lined the exterior of the cabins with sandbags—so they are preparing to hold out. Estimates also say that there are at least three children up there, and two of the men's wives."

"I know about the assault," he said grimly. "Why did it fail?"

A man wearing a sheriff's uniform with a newly-stitched-on NSF patch spoke up. "I know these men and women Colonel. They are not crazy folks. Hell, I am in the VFW with the Aton Fedorov. He is a gun collector, not some whack-job gun nut. This whole thing got out of hand when the ATF and FBI tried to apprehend them on our main street. Surrounding their property just made matters worse. Give me some time and I think I can talk them out of there."

"It seems that the time for talk has come and gone. They have killed a number of federal officers who were trying to enforce the law," Donaldson said. *I did not come here to talk them out. People are going to want justice, and justice means we are going to have to pry them out of there.*

Outside there was a rumble of arriving tracked vehicles. Donaldson had brought with him elements of the 10th Mountain Division and on the way in, he had seen their convoy on the winding road leading up to the lodge from his seat on the Blackhawk. The sound of the vehicles approaching outside was identifiable by everyone in the room. They all glanced outside and then back at him. "That would be our reinforcements," he said proudly.

Walking over to the door, he opened it and was followed by the officers in the room. The Bradley armored fighting vehicles and M1117s moved into lines extending out from the lodge. The smell of diesel from the vehicles wafted in the autumn breeze. Painted in a woodland camouflage digital pattern, they churned up the grass on the hillside as they lined up.

"Colonel," the ATF commander spoke up. "You've got enough firepower here to wipe out the entire county."

"Yes, I do," he said. "No offense Agent Evers, but you had a chance to bring these people in, and it has resulted in law enforcement in coffins.

I'm not here to do anything other than end this standoff."

"That will end it," Agent Bonner of the FBI said as his eyes followed the deploying armored force. "The problem is that if you go up there and blast them out, you'll be martyring them. These fanatics that are holding out with guns have a lot of people supporting them. I remember watching a documentary on Ruby Ridge and regardless of their guilt, you are going to be turning them into heroes for some people."

Donaldson frowned at the words. That's the problem with law enforcement. They always rely on half-measures to get things done. "The Ruling Council thinks that this has dragged out long enough," he said, staring at Agent Bonner. "Do you know what these standoffs do? They convince others to do the same, especially when they drag out like this one. The TRC has limited the amount of media coverage these people have gotten, but this is seen as an affront to the authority of the FedGov. If they are allowed to continue this, others will see it as a model to follow. It 'inspires' them to resist our authority. It creates lawlessness.

"On the other hand, if we go up there and force them to surrender, people will get the message loud and clear that the mandates issued out of the District will be followed. I don't care how much of a gun fanatic you are, once they see tanks rolling in, they will not even consider trying such a standoff."

The sheriff didn't seem impressed with his perspective. "There are kids up there and women. You kill or injure them during this little venture of yours, and you'll be giving a cause to everyone still holding a weapon. I learned a long time ago that passionate people with a mission are the most dangerous."

The almost folksy way that the sheriff spoke did resonate with him. *Promotion will be harder with the blood of children on my hands. I need for it to at least appear that I tried to get these people to surrender peacefully.* "Alright Sheriff, we can try it once your way. But this is the last time for talk. If they don't comply, then I will go through them like shit through a goose."

Three hours later he marched up to the forward observation post, a sandbagged bunker that was perched on a small knoll opposite the cabins. During that time he had reviewed where law enforcement had dug in and devised approaches for his troops. The enemy was surrounded, on a heavily wooded hilltop. *They may know the ground, but we have the firepower on our side.*

The Colonel kept low as he stepped into the bunker, looking through the firing slits that had been created, and he could barely make out the roofs of the cabins through the brilliantly colored leaves. At initial glance, it didn't look like much of a defensible position. Then he spotted the foxholes and the crudely made *cheval-de-frise* barricades that limited personnel movement. Several trenches were dug around two of the four log cabins. Sandbags around the structures and lining the defensive positions only added to the obstacles. *They are dug in there like ticks. No wonder the FBI's frontal assault failed.*

In the pit of his stomach, he knew that trying to talk to these terrorists would not work. They had already been talked to, and they refused to respond. This time things might be different. Along the side of the knoll, several Bradley fighting vehicles rumbled forward. Their engines were easily loud enough for the people in the camp to hear. He waited. *Let them see what they are going to be facing; maybe that will convince them to be reasonable.*

He was handed a bullhorn and rose up just enough to broadcast clearly. "Attention. This is Colonel James Donaldson, United States Army. You already know you are surrounded, but what you need to know now is that I have brought a company of armored fighting vehicles with me. By order of the Ruling Council, you are to lay down your arms and surrender."

There was a short pause. Then a voice came back over the hollow that separated the two hills. "Go fuck yourself you damned traitor!"

He had expected that from them … but it still made him angry. Especially the word 'traitor'. *I risked everything the night of the Liberation, and no one outside of the Pentagon knows about what I did. I saved the nation from the greatest traitor to ever sit in the Oval Office. Traitor? I am a hero to the cause!* He drew a long breath and reined in his temper. "You have women and children there. When we come, and we will, they may be injured or killed. Will you at least consider sending them out?"

There was a long pause, one that dragged on for at least 3 minutes. He tried to put himself in the mind of his opponents. *By now they have seen the vehicles; they know we are not pussyfooting around anymore. It's one thing to be a martyr. It's another when you are sentencing your kids to their deaths. They can't defeat the armored vehicles, so perhaps common sense will kick in. Maybe this will get them to do the right thing.*

Looking down, he noticed that he was rubbing his left hand with his right. Once he noticed the gesture, he stopped, confused as to why he had been doing it in the first place.

CHAPTER 10

"Oppression is the bedrock old-America was built on."

Broadway, Virginia

Grayson Steele stopped the car alongside the field near the culvert where the creek flowed under Highway 11. Glancing down at the map that Clarice had drawn for him, it seemed to be the right place—just a short trip north of the 7-Eleven. Climbing out of the car, he noted the stubble of corn stalks poked up with a dusting of white frost on them. He walked out into the field for a moment, looking around, trying to mentally picture the scene as Clarice had described it to him.

There was a temptation to simply pass on the map to the NSF and let them do their jobs, but part of him wondered if they would even bother to try. Frank had summed it up well; when it came to Social Enforcement, the NSF tended to look the other way. Grayson had to know the truth. He needed to find his daughter. There would be plenty of time to call in the police if he was successful.

His wife and son had wanted to come with him, but he knew the condition they were likely to be in when he found them. *His wife and son had been through enough emotionally without seeing what might be found.* A part of him wondered if he was going to be prepared for what he might see, but the need to find his little girl smothered those fears.

The ground crunched slightly under his feet as he walked out into the field. The ground was frozen enough from the night that it was like walking on uneven concrete. He almost tripped over one of the corn stalk stubs that jutted skyward like little tree stumps. The long motte of trees along the bank of the creek were his ultimate destination, but he first walked out in the field. *This had to be where it happened—where Maddie had fought, died and saved the lives of the others.* Grayson's eyes took in the frozen ground around him, spying a glimmer of brass. Bending over, he picked it up—a spent bullet casing. *She was here, right here.* It was cold in his fingertips as he scraped off a small piece of dirt that clung to the cartridge. Clarice's story was holding true, as much as he hated that.

Grayson turned to the trees. It was there that she claimed they had dragged the bodies. She had told him other bones were there, the remains of other victims of the students that had planned to kill her. He was walking, but almost unconsciously closer to the creek, as if his legs had a will of their own.

The embankment dropped off sharply for three feet; then leveled out for about 3 yards; then dropped off to the icy waters of the creek. The trees clung to the first dip, massive oaks and hickories that somehow defied erosion. Tall, dead brown grasses surrounded them, along with small briar bushes. As he got closer, he could hear the sound of the creek's rippling water.

Reaching the edge of the embankment, he forced himself to look down. At first, he saw nothing out of order, but as he glanced upstream, he saw colors—bits of clothing. There was something else, something white.

Half-climbing, half-falling down the first embankment, he headed upstream where the brown grasses were matted down, crushed by animals or possibly a flood of the small creek. As he got closer, he saw the white objects for what they were, bones. The clothing was torn in some spots, no doubt by animals that had been trying to get at the bodies underneath. Other than the clothing, it was hard to picture the jumble of clothing and bones having been bodies. Some bones were scattered even on the opposing back of the creek and as he glanced down, he saw one near where he stood, some 40 feet away. A few of the limbs he saw were not fully decomposed; a sickening layer of skin, blackened and leathery, clung to them.

The lawyer in him screamed to back away. This was a crime scene. The father in him made him walk forward, careful to avoid stepping on potential evidence. He got within 10 feet of the dump site and stared silently at the remains. A backpack lay at the water's edge … a shirt was caught in the briars near the rise in the embankment. The bones were everywhere. Two skulls drew his attention, their jaws missing; it was as if they were staring at him. For a moment he looked at them, wondering if one of them was his beloved little girl.

Out of the corner of his stare, he spotted a gray hoodie bearing the emblem of the University of Virginia. Maddie owned one of those. He took a step toward it but stopped. There were bones atop of it, a splatter of orange Virginia clay. In his heart, he knew it was hers. *I found her!*

Grief, held in check for weeks, overcame him like a tidal wave. Grayson dropped to his knees; they crunched on the frozen ground. Tears came, followed by a horrible powerless feeling. This was his worst nightmare, his little girl unceremoniously dumped in a ravine. The bones, all of them—covered with a dusting of frost—seemed to scream at him. His mouth opened and he screamed as he never had before, a guttural cry of anger, rage, and hate for the people that did this to Maddie and the others. His breath hung in the air in front of him as he had a moment of hyperventilation. His tears were cold rivulets on his cheeks.

Slowly he managed to get control of his anger and grief. *How many other kids are here? How could the school have allowed so many to disappear, and they never raised a flag?* He rose to his feet; his knees were wet where they had melted the frost on the grass. Grayson's body was numb as he stared at the heap of long dead bodies. He spied another skull, half buried in the embankment, only a few feet away. Somehow he had missed it. The bones were less white; these were yellowed slightly, and the dirt was slowly burying the evidence.

Grayson backed away, and then climbed out of the creek embankment. He walked almost zombie-like, stumbling around the corn field toward his car. When he got to it, he leaned against it as if it could prop up the weight of emotions he felt. He pulled out his phone and fumbled to find the number for Detective Schrank of the NSF.

Within 3 hours the field had changed. The NSF had come, one vehicle at first, to confirm what he had found. Now there were at least ten. Two large, black crime scene investigation vans were poised on the road leading back toward the 7-Eleven. NSF officers were in the field with metal detectors, and a large portion of the creek was marked off with yellow and black police caution tape. White clad investigators knelt almost out of view in the embankment, marking the ground with little flags. Bags tagged as evidence came out, a trickle at first, then a stream of them. Clothing, bags, bones, and other personal effects were brought out.

He had called his wife and told her one simple line, "I found our little girl." He had broken down crying after that as he watched the police trudge out across the field toward the creek. She wept as well; then she said she wanted to join him. "No. You don't want to see this. You don't need to see it honey." While he wished she were there to support him, he knew the sight of bones coming out would devastate her.

The salt-and-pepper-haired Detective Schrank had interviewed him, but Grayson refused to say who had given him the map. He wasn't going to betray Clarice the way that she and Maddie had been betrayed. Schrank had not been supportive when he had first met with him. Now, with bodies being found, he was obligated to do his job. Grayson suppressed his contempt for the man because he hoped he might get him closer to the people that had done this.

Schrank brought him a cup of 7-Elevan coffee, which Grayson only sipped. "That's a hell of a scene over there," the detective said, nodding at the body recovery site. "Are you going to be okay? I can call in a social worker, a counselor, if you need it."

Will I ever be okay? "You should have looked—you should have done your job," he growled.

"I told you before," the detective said. "Even if I could pin this on some Social Enforcers, the prosecutors won't file charges. The SEs operate outside of the legal system. It's been that way ever since the Liberation."

"This isn't about the law," he said. The coffee's warmth penetrated his fingers. "This is about what is right and what is wrong."

His words hit the detective hard; he could see that ... he also was glad they had. "Look, Mr. Steele, without the support of prosecutors, there's no point in pushing such investigations. The campus authorities won't help. If anything, they encourage this kind of activity."

It was hard to argue that. He remembered meeting with the rotund Public Safety Director for the University of Virginia who had blown him off. *They have created this culture, one where students can kill other students without repercussions. They let students like Maddie get abused for years on campus and never protected them.* To Grayson, there were a lot of people that were guilty for the death of his little girl. A lot of them need to pay for what they did.

"So what happens now Detective?" he asked with an icy stare.

"My superiors can't ignore this," he said. "Missing students are one thing. A mass body dumping sight is another. I intend to be honest with you, as I have all along. We will identify the victims first. We will launch an investigation. That will be for the press and the public. We will interview a lot of students, all of whom are going to deny they know anything about what happened. We'll haul in these Grays that you told us about, but realistically we need to have some physical evidence to link them to this in order to proceed with charges. Even then, the prosecutors are likely to allow them to plea bargain down to little crimes—if it even gets to that point. No one wants to risk what follows when it comes to prosecuting progressives for crimes against conservatives. Add in that if these bodies date back, it makes the NSF look incompetent."

I don't care how you look! "So nothing happens because everyone is afraid of looking bad?"

Schrank paused for a moment. "Look, I have a little girl of my own, just a few years younger than your Maddie. I feel for you. I really do. As a father, I'd be furious if I were you. But I'm a detective. I will push this as far as I can, but I have to think about my job as well."

As frustrated as he was with Detective Schrank, the man had been painfully honest with him. *This is all for nothing. They will create the illusion of an investigation, but in the end, nothing will come of it. Maddie's killers will snicker about getting away with it, and worse, they may be emboldened to do it again.*

Grayson had embraced a resolve to find out what had happened to his daughter. That had been fulfilled. Now a new doggedness filled him. *If the system can't function ... if it can't provide justice, then I will. The people responsible for her death need to pay.* He would be the instrument of justice for Maddie.

A news van, emblazoned with Channel 7, on the side, wheeled into the long line of police cars. Detective Schrank saw them and shook his head. "I suggest you get out of here Mr. Steele. The press can be pretty insensitive, and they are going to want to talk to you as the person that found this place."

Grayson looked at the detective and the camera crew. They were busy getting their equipment out of the back of the van. Schrank was probably right; the smart thing to do was to leave before they could talk to him. In that moment, he didn't *want* to do the smart thing. *These Grays, the students that organized these murders, all think they have gotten away with it. They need to feel some of the fear that they put in my daughter and these other kids.*

A few minutes later the correspondent from Channel 7 found him. "Sir, I understand that you found these bodies. How did that unfold?"

Grayson looked at her, then straight into the camera. "My daughter was one of the victims. She was killed by a group of students at UVA. I came out here looking for her—and I found them all."

"How do you know it was a student group?" she asked.

"That doesn't matter," Grayson said. "What matters is this. They will face justice for the murders they have committed. If the prosecutors and investigators won't do their job, I will. Justice will be done … one way or another. My daughter's killers are going to pay for their crimes. It would be best for them to turn themselves in and confess, because I am not looking for their absolution—I want payback!" Before she could follow up, he stormed over to his car and got in.

It was the wrong thing to do; he knew that. At the same time, it felt wonderful. *Let them start fearing retribution. Let them start to worry.*

Newmerica Penitentiary, Administrative Maximum Facility
Florence, Colorado

"What do you mean you transferred Maria Lopez?" Deja asked Todd Parsons over the phone. Her voice was so loud in the tiny prison office that it almost caused feedback on the phone.

"Well, yeah," he said far too casually. "We got a transfer request to some camp in Utah."

Deja's rage filled her ears. She had checked. Maria had not been transferred anywhere—there was no record of it with Social Enforcement. While they were far from perfect with their record keeping, often downright sloppy, they were fairly good at keeping track of people in Social Quarantine camps.

"Damn it!" she spat. "You guys turned a prisoner over to people without doing the necessary checking."

It was Parson's turn to get angry back. "Hey, you can chill the fuck out. I cleared it with my boss before we let her go. I'm not a moron."

"I spoke to your boss," she said. "He never authorized you to do shit with Lopez."

For a moment there was silence. "I don't understand," he stammered. "I spoke with him."

In that moment Deja realized the full scope of what she was facing. Whoever it was somehow faked the call with him. Parsons was duped, fooled, but not by amateurs. *This is the work of professionals.*

"Do you have videos of the people that came into the camp?"

"We have cameras," he said. "I'm not sure if we've recorded over that stuff or not."

"Pull everything you've got," Deja commanded. "I need to see who it was. Shoot it over to my account in the NSFCloud immediately."

"I will. I'm sorry. I thought this was legitimate," Parsons replied with a dejected tone.

"Just get me the video," she said, and then hung up. A part of her wanted to throw the phone into the cinderblock wall and smash it, but she knew that would not help her situation. The day had begun with a simple idea: Get Maria Lopez recorded pleading with her brother Raul to cooperate. Raul was tough, Deja knew, but with only his sister alive as family, and secure in the wrong hands, he might crumble. Of course now that would never work. *Someone took her out of there ... they stole my leverage.*

It had to be someone from the American government ... that was the only group that would be willing to take such action. People were not broken out of Social Quarantine other than the series of raids that Raul was part of. *They didn't come for the whole camp like Valley Forge. They came for one person.* That thought was disturbing on its own. They came for her because of Raul. *Someone knew that I was using them to try and coerce him; it's the only thing that makes sense. That was her only real value, as leverage.*

She leaned back in her Herman Miller chair and stared at the monitor for the PC she was using. *Why not just rescue Raul? Why waste time on his sister when we still have him?* That answer was in her own designs for Maria. *They know we would use her as a hostage.* Taking her back meant one thing to Deja. They were going to be coming for Raul. It wasn't enough to have him; they had to remove any threat to his usefulness.

On the surface, the thought that they would come for Raul at the Supermax seemed to be a fool's errand. Then her mind raced to the mysterious woman that was with Raul, the one that had massacred an SE team. *She will come for him. He believes that.* Raul said that she was going to kill Deja, and now she wondered if she really was capable of doing that.

The files appeared almost an hour later in her folder. She opened them and looked at the two women. The image was grainy; the Social Quarantine camps tended to use cheap surveillance cameras. One figure she didn't recognize at all. The other looked eerily like the blurred memory of the fight on the Ohio River. *It could be her. The nose looks a little different, as does her chin, but that could be a disguise.* She highlighted the face and tried to enhance it, but it had only a marginal impact. Best to leave this to the experts. She sent the entire video clip to the NSA team that supported criminal investigations in the NSF. *I need a name—an identity. If I know who she is, it is the first step on the road to beating her.*

The loss of Maria Raul posed a problem. It had been Deja's hope to use Maria to get her brother to speak. With her gone, and with Rosa his mother dead, what she held over Raul was nonexistent. His resilience had impressed even the team assisting her with the interrogations. Blackmailing him with threats against his family was seen as the best way to coerce his cooperation.

One of the things she wanted was for Raul to reveal who his allies were—those in the Order of the Bell, in the American government, and the mystery woman that had nearly gotten her killed. *The only real advantage I have is that Raul doesn't know that Maria has been rescued. As far as he's concerned, she's still in Social Quarantine. If I don't say anything to him, I can still use her as leverage.* It wasn't a great deal of satisfaction, but it was a start.

She fidgeted while waiting for a response to her video identification and checked her social media and email. *The New Yorker* wanted an interview; the author had been pre-cleared by the TRC. Her local newspaper, the *Star Tribune*, wanted to do a joint interview with her and her mother. That had the most appeal of the two offers. Her mother had been enjoying Deja's new celebrity status. The fact that she was so proud made Deja happy. *We have had some rough years together in my youth; now all of that hard work is paying off.*

After several hours, her work email chirped and she saw a response from the NSF. The notes were long, clearly generated by some sort of AI. She scrolled through the results on her screen. Candidate one: A 41 percent match with Angel Frisosky, Corporal, NSF San Jose, California. Missing.

Candidate two: A 68 percent match with Caylee Leatrom, FILE BLACK LABELED, NSF DIRECTOR.

She glared at the name. *Caylee Leatrom—she was the alleged operative that put all of that information on the web! She claimed to be an operative, though the now-Vice President-Elect claimed that the operative program was a myth.* Deja ignored the first female. All that mattered was the second. She squinted at the image, enlarging it more. *She is the woman that I saw at the bridge. No wonder Raul got away. He was being helped by an operative.*

Leatrom's file was sealed, something called 'Black Labeled,' whatever that was. It would make sense if she was an operative. They wouldn't like anyone in the NSF reading about her. She was wanted, not like Raul. Lopez had been a public enemy. She was more than that; she was a risk to the state. The search for this Leatrom is under the radar but maybe even more important. *How did she get connected to Lopez?* Her mind was a-tingle with possibilities.

I need to confirm with Raul that this was the woman that helped him. That will be a gut punch to him. Holding that information back has been a matter of strength with him, personal pride. *Once he knows that I know who she is, that will hit him hard. Next I will need to make sure that we beef up security. Now that we know who we are looking for, it will make things easier.* Slowly she began to formulate a plan, pulling together the various elements.

If the Vice President-Elect sealed her file, she would want to know that Deja had spotted her. *Everyone was so happy that I captured Raul. I wonder how they will react when I bring Caylee Leatrom to justice? I'm a celebrity now. I will be even more so once she is in custody.*

I can't wait to share this with Lopez ... but first, I need to send my findings to the District.

Smyrna, Georgia

The rumble of mortar rounds off to the north and west of his position in Smyrna, Georgia was eagerly welcomed by General Trip Reager. The smoke rising from Sandy Springs was exactly what he had hoped for. He refused to suppress his grin as he stood in the open hatch of the Bradley and looked at where the fighting was starting. *They are finally taking the bait.*

Trip wanted them to try a breakout in Sandy Springs. He had created the illusion that it was a gap in the investment he had of Atlanta ... a way where the defenders might be able to make a breakout. When Geraldo Vasquez had been in his office, no doubt he had seen the false gap and had relayed the hole to the city's defenders. They were finally making their move.

The reality was that Sandy Springs was thinly defended, but just to the north, Roswell and Dunwoody had been converted into a strong line of trenches that were well manned, enough to blunt any attack led out of the city. *They just need to hold them in place long enough for the Hail Mary we deliver.*

For days the sick and elderly had filed out of Atlanta toward Stone Mountain. The hospital in Alpharetta was full, and a small tent city had sprung up on its grounds and in the parking lot to handle the overflow. The children and their families that were evacuated were taken to schools in the area where they were housed. In the last few days, that stream of refugees had dwindled to a trickle, a sign that the city was nearing the end of its evacuation.

There had been some skirmishes, mostly south, near the airport. Some National Guard units had tried to secure a wider perimeter near the airport, no doubt to allow them to get reinforcements in. The fighting had been short and brutal with the attackers driven back several times.

Trip had expected them to try that.

The defenders did have some successes. A trio of C-130s out of Langley in Virginia had come in low, under the radar, and had managed to parachute in some hardware. It had been a ballsy move—some real white-knuckle flying—and it had forced Trip to change his combat air patrols to account for low flying aircraft.

Trip's strategy for detail with Atlanta was to starve them out, rather than fight their way in. His forces were engaging constantly as the defenders probed the front lines, but they were not making a rush into the city like they wanted to. Charging into Atlanta was a move that would bleed him, so he simply refused to play the game they desired.

The booms in the distance told him they were finally making their thrust, an attempt to break the siege and fight outside of Atlanta. The mortars would fire five rounds, then redeploy so that they could not hit with counterbattery fire. They were dropping their shells where they presumed Trip's troops were, at least according to his forward observers. Trip wanted them to advance out and head north. His headphones crackled to life. "This is Colonel Hobbs," came a familiar voice from his ground commander in Roswell. "They are taking the bait, General. Their Technicals just collided with our defenses in Dunwoody, and we have a battle forming up here. I see M-117s coming up the road as well."

"Excellent. Keep their attention Colonel. We will kick off in ten," he said as they switched to his task force's tactical channel. "This is Reager to Task Force Twilight Two. The enemy is heading north. Our job is to surprise them and swing east and north and cut them off. We need to drive like hell, punch through their defensive lines, and cut them off. We do this, and we secure the northwest suburbs and trap their attack force outside of the city. Artillery batteries Alpha and Bravo, you may begin your bombardment. The rest of us start our advance in 9 minutes. Reager out."

The artillery barked to life, their shells racing skyward and dropping down on the defensive lines a half-mile ahead of where he and the Task Force Twilight Two were poised. The ground shook, not just from the outbound fire, but because of the explosions they were causing. He saw a ball of fire from some vehicle that had blown up and rolled skyward in front of his Bradley, black and orange and sickly.

He tried to picture the commander, who was in the heat of his own battle to the northeast. Would he hear the rumble of the bombardment? Would his local commanders warn him that they were being hit here in Smyrna? If they did, he might see the trap and try to respond to it. He waited, watching the smoke in the distance as the defensive positions straddling US-41 and I-285 were pounded and blasted. A part of him pitied the men and women that were assigned the position, but he tempered that feeling with the knowledge that they would think nothing of killing him and his people.

Trip checked his watch after several long thunderous minutes. *It's time!* He toggled his mic as the last of the artillery barrage roared downrange. "Twilight Two, let's roll!" The Bradley fighting vehicles kicked up the stink of diesel fumes, and the squadron of Abrams tanks seemed to growl as their turbine engines came on. His command Bradley lurched forward, pushing him hard against the back of the hatch ring as they started the race down the road.

The closer they got to the perimeter defenses, the more he saw the carnage his artillery had caused. The overpass of I-285 was mostly rubble. Gunfire began to fire from within the concrete debris, a testimony to the tenacity of the defenders that had survived the bombardment. One bullet pinged off of the Bradley turret, and Trip lowered himself inside, pulling the hatch shut.

The bang-bang-bang of the Bradley vehicles opened up from the vehicles that were flanking his own; then his own fired, the firing incredibly loud. He wished he could see what was happening outside, but he trusted his people knew their mission. *God knows we went over the plans enough times.*

He heard a pair of fast explosions outside. From his time in the Middle East, they sounded eerily like RPG fire. *I wonder where in the hell they got those from?* A larger explosion, the main gun of an Abrams tank responded—a sound like no other on the battlefield. A few milliseconds later, there was another explosion in front of his Bradley. The fighting vehicle lurched upward; he presumed they had reached the embankment of I-285; the turret reloaded and fired off a quick succession of rounds again, and then lurched downward. The firing seemed to drop off to a trickle as the task force raced through the blasted hole in the enemy lines.

Trip switched to the channel to get him the force to the north. "Colonel Hobbs, sit rep."

The sound of a battle came to his ears, more intense than the fighting where he was. "We are fully engaged here," Hobbs voice came over the headset, his voice strained and the staccato of machine gun fire pop-pop-popping nearby. "We're holding our own, but they seem to have brought a bit of an attitude with them."

"The ball is in play, and we are running it," Trip replied. "Let me know if they seem to notice."

"So far nothing," he said as Trip lurched in the Bradley from some sort of sharp turn. An explosion rang out over the headset. "Sir, I would sure appreciate it if you would finish tearing these guys a new asshole."

Trip smiled, steadying himself as the Bradley continued to lurch. The high-pitched pings of gunfire hitting the side of the fighting vehicle were a reminder that indeed they were in Indian Territory, as he liked to call it, behind the enemy lines. "I will let you know—Reager out."

The next hour and a half was a running battle, which Trip saw little of from the back of the Bradley. He had poked his head up once, only to have shots dance off of the Bradley near him. Most campaign commanders would have directed events from a command post, but that wasn't Reager's style. He wanted to be there in the heat of the fighting because that way he could make decisions on the spot, without any communications lag. The risk was that if his Bradley was blown up, command would pass to his subordinates. *Of course, in that scenario, I'm dead.*

When they reached the suburb of North Buckhead, the sweep was complete. The Newmerican forces realized what was happening, but far too late to stop it. They had tried to break off from Colonel Hobbs and head back south toward the city, only to slam into the tanks and vehicles of Trip's Twilight Two force.

One explosion went off next to the Bradley, rocking the 27 tons sideways so hard that he banged his helmet into the side of the interior hard enough to make his neck ache. It was like charging bronco at a rodeo hitting the clown in a barrel. Some of the Twilight force secured the roadways they had come in on, redrawing the siege lines for the city. The firefight that broke out was intense with the force trying to get back into the city. The ricochets of machine gun fire off of the hull were in quick bursts, each one loud and rattling when they hit. Smoke and ozone stung at his nostrils and seemed to stick on his tongue as he breathed. A nearby Abrams roared, firing its massive main armament over and over, each one making everything throb. Trip worked the communications system furiously, trying to get a feel for their positioning in relation to the enemy. Hobbs gave him a short video feed as the enemy tried to withdraw, only to have Hobbs' troops follow them.

A trio of explosions went off in the distance, loud and distinct. Trip risked opening the hatch to see what happened. One of his Bradley fighting vehicles was ablaze some 80 yards off to his right, churning oily black smoke skyward. Within just a few yards of it was the burning hulks of a pair of other Bradley tanks—these aimed at his force. The flaming Newmerican tanks sizzled and banged as ammunition cooked off inside. The hot splatter of melting metal sprayed upward each time. *They tried to bum-rush us—and paid the price. Then again, so did we.* He shook his head as he looked at his own mangled Bradley, silently muttering a prayer to God for the crew. Most of them stumbled out of the smoking green hulk—cut, battered, but alive. His instinct was to rush to their aid, but he had a battle to win … it was a matter of priorities.

The infantry support was moving up to a copse of tall pines off to his right and laying down suppression fire as they darted for cover. Smoke rolled everywhere around him, and the air stung at his nostrils, the smell of melting metal and diesel fumes were tinged with expended ammunition.

The enemy position was 100 yards in front of him where he saw the blasted shell of a Burger King that was half-engulfed with fire, and a small strip plaza that was more rubble than stores at this point. He looked forward and saw something stir from the Burger King's ruins, a rifle held up with a white pillowcase billowing in the cool breeze.

"This is Reager—hold your fire," he commanded into his throat microphone, and the gunfire started to break off. One Bradley continued to fire for a half-minute, clearly not having gotten the order. Its shells tore into the strip plaza, blowing apart the brick façade with 25mm explosions. Finally it stopped firing.

A trio of infantry emerged from the Burger King, holding the white flag skyward and walking toward the American task force. Trip pulled himself out of the hatch and disconnected his communications harness, so he could go and meet with them. He walked forward, meeting them near one of their destroyed Bradleys. The heat from the fire radiated outward enough for him to feel the warmth.

The Newmerican officer leading the delegation was a Colonel in Georgia National Guard urban combat fatigues. He was cut on his neck, not badly, but enough for blood to stain the gray and black digital pattern on his uniform. His name patch bore the name Johnston. "General," he said flatly as a Sergeant at his slide lowered the weapon that had served as their flag. "I would like to discuss the terms of a cease fire."

"The terms are simple," Trip said. "Unconditional surrender of your forces, or we finish off your little force once and for all."

"Sir," he said, shuffling his stance slightly, "those terms are most harsh. My people have fought, and you have us flanked, but we still have fight in us."

"No you don't. If you did, you wouldn't be here," Trip countered. "Surrender your forces Colonel, or we will blow the whistle and restart this game and you will lose."

"My personnel are mostly from Georgia," Colonel Johnston said. "They would like to return to their homes."

"They will be interned for the duration of this fight," Trip replied. *We have taken a bite out of Atlanta, but this campaign is still far from over.*

"You'd make us prisoners of war, sir?"

"I would," Trip replied as several small arms rounds in the nearby Bradley cooked off, bang-popping inside the flaming hulk. "I didn't ask for this war that you brought on yourselves by declaring the city an autonomous zone. If you want to play adult games, you get adult prizes."

The Newmerican Colonel nodded. "That was a damned sneaky move, driving into our rear."

"Thank you," he said, clearly surprising the Colonel with his response. The older man's eyebrows cocked with his words. "I'm here to bring Atlanta back into America, one way or another. I suggest your take this offer of unconditional surrender, lay down your arms, and come out."

"Damn you," the Colonel growled. "Alright. Damn it—you win."

Trip nodded. "Smart move. Go and tell your troops your decision; then go north and present yourselves to Colonel Hobbs." Trip, as the ranking field officer, normally would have been the person to surrender too, but he knew that Hobbs and his people had been badly battered in the fighting. *He deserves the honor of this victory far more than me.*

Trip watched the Colonel leave, a beaten man. We are far from taking the city, but we have shaken things up. *We've given them a loss, and that will hurt their morale. Add in the cold, thirst, and hunger, and they may be willing to capitulate. If not, I will pry this city from their grips ...*

CHAPTER 11

"The suffering of one is the suffering of all."

Concord, New Hampshire

General James Donaldson hated the cane he had been forced to use, hated his limp, and hated the resistance movement. Over a week earlier, he and his command staff were viciously ambushed during a dinner. One bullet had hit him in the left leg, the upper thigh. The bullet had torn through his muscle, missing the artery. While he was told that it would heal fine, he had been forced to use a cane, which he loathed. It reminded him of his grandfather, and he knew he was not old, nor should he have been so infirm at his age.

The last weeks had been filled with disappointments. A group of marauders had struck at his only forward air base in Vermont, killing several dozen and destroying the aircraft and facilities. Adding insult to injury, the Vermont Governor had called him while in the hospital and threatened to pull his National Guard forces from his forces in New Hampshire. *What did he expect would happen? That somehow they wouldn't strike back at his state?* The loss of air power from Vermont made him more dependent on New York and Connecticut, but their Governors were demanding to know what steps he was taking to ensure that they didn't suffer similar attacks. *Civilian leaders are an unnecessary burden. They whine and bitch and leave men like me to do the real work ... the dirty work.*

He entered the State House flanked by three soldiers that were his personal security detail, careful to watch his step on the icy walkway.

With the military occupation of the city, normal city services like clearing sidewalks had become less frequent or effective. The warmth of the interior of the massive structure was comforting. Outside of the State House was a platoon of infantry who were in their dress uniforms, along with the two prisoners. *They will need to wait until I have had my discussion with these so-called leaders.*

The New Hampshire Governor and Executive Council were housed there, and he was looking forward to facing them down. The Governor—in additional to refusing to ratify Daniel Porter as the winner of the election—had been defiant about the Newmerica military presence in the state. *This will convince them of our resolve. This defiance needs to come to an end.*

Since he had come to liberate the state, the Governor and his people had been placed under house arrest. Nominally, they were in charge of the civil matters in the state, but with an Army in place in every major city, their authority existed more on paper than anywhere else. He had been against treating them as well as he had been, but the Ruling Council wanted to keep up the appearance that some sort of civilian authority was still in place. *Their damned almighty daily guidelines as to how to fight this war are not helping. They are adding more confusion.*

Normally an attack on a military commander in the middle of an operation would have been a disaster in the media. Donaldson was fortunate that the TRC had full-sway with the press. They had made him out to be a hero, wounded bravely by cowardly terrorists. The General had taken the time to watch the final pieces, especially his interviews, and was confident that his public image had come through relatively intact.

While he had been recuperating, word of an offensive operation in Atlanta had come in. Colonel Johnston made a bold assault, but in the end he had surrendered nearly 25 percent of Atlanta's defenders to the Americans. *We drew some blood, which was good, but we can't afford such losses going forward.* The only part of the debacle that had been good, in his mind, was that he had been in the hospital when it happened, so very little of the blame fell on his shoulders. *Johnston saw an opportunity and got suckered into a trap. I never would have fallen for that.*

Slowly he made his way to the Senate Chamber. He had chosen that place for its size, grandeur, and historical significance. This afternoon, on Christmas Eve, he knew the leadership of the state would be pulled away from their families. *A small price to pay given they had sat back and let this rebellion fester. It nearly cost me my life.*

One of his detail opened the door for him, and he drank in the splendor of the room. The walls were filled with brilliant murals of old America's past. *Once we have pacified this state, those will need to be painted over*, he mentally noted as he walked in.

The Governor at least had the courtesy to rise to his feet while the rest of the executive council remained seated. Donaldson made his way to stand before them where they sat directly under the gold-covered dome that loomed far above his head. One of his men started to bring a chair, but the general waved him off. *I want to stand for this.*

"Good evening," he said coolly. "I appreciate you coming on such short notice."

Clearly from the sour expressions he got from the dozen attendees, they were far from pleased at being summoned. The Governor slid into his seat, brushing back his jet black hair. "General, I assume you have a reason for demanding a meeting on Christmas Eve."

Politicians are so arrogant. How dare he speak to me in such a manner? Donaldson mustered a small grin. "I thought that this might be a good time for us to discuss you recertifying the election and pledging your support to the Newmerican candidate, Daniel Porter."

The Lieutenant Governor, a red-haired female, spoke up. "Nothing has changed since you first demanded that of us—when your troops invaded our state."

"I disagree. A great deal has changed. We have established our presence throughout New Hampshire. You have been conquered, whether you have bothered to realize it or not. Newmerica controls your cities, your infrastructure, everything. The only reason you have not been replaced is that so far, it has proven to be a low priority—though that could be averted, with your cooperation."

"We've already certified the election," one of the members of the Council said.

Donaldson shrugged. "You can tell the press you found a flash drive with more votes on it, or that there was a ballot box filled with votes that somehow got overlooked. It doesn't matter. I can have the TRC craft something if you are struggling with a good excuse. But I do require your compliance."

The Governor stirred, "General, you are not as in control of the state as you claim. Not everywhere. There are resistance fighters out there now who are contesting your control. You yourself were wounded right here in Concord by one of them. Even you must admit that your control is tenuous at best. New Hampshire is the definition of defiance."

That word inflamed his anger slightly. The word 'defiance' had been the name of the resistance. Spray painted letter "D's" often tagged destroyed vehicles or buildings. "It's adorable that you feel that way," he said. "Oh, I admit, some of your citizens have caused minor problems. Those issues will go away once you recognize the reality of the situation that you are in."

"Our people voted, and they voted for the President of America, not your Newmerican candidate," the Secretary of State, a portly white-haired man barked. "We have no intention of reversing the decisions of the electorate in this matter."

There must be something in the water that makes the people of this state so defiant. "I can see that you are all set in your decision. Let me show you something that may persuade you about the folly of your position." He turned to one of his men and gave him a nod. A minute later the platoon of infantry entered along with two men dressed in civilian garb.

The prisoners' clothing was stained with perspiration and droplets of long-dried blood. One, the female, had a purple bruise on her right eye that stained her nose as well. The man, older, in his 50s, had several cuts on his chin and cheeks. All of the damage was from their apprehension and interrogation sessions. They had been locked up for a week with no change of clothing, no showers, and their body aroma hung in the air for everyone to experience.

"These two individuals were part of the resistance group that attacked me and my officers," he proclaimed. "We questioned them extensively, but much like all of you, they have an independent streak in them. They refuse to give up their comrades who tried to assassinate me and my command staff out of some misguided sense of patriotism.

A level of tension rose in the chamber with the arrival of the troops and their prisoners. A lone civilian, wearing a TRC jacket, came in with a camera to film the event. With a simple nod, the man and women were paraded past the table where the executive council themselves had sat; the man and woman were put at the far end of the room. The platoon lined up opposite of them, and the cameraman moved to where he could get a good angle. The prisoners, realizing their plight, stood erect, almost proud. *What a waste. They think their deaths in some way will change something. They are arrogant people who tried to kill me. They are little more than terrorists.*

Once more he looked to the Governor. The man's dark eyes glared back at him, and his face seemed to tense as the General locked gazes with him. "As guerillas … domestic terrorists, I had a great deal of latitude in trying these criminals. I opted for a military Tribunal. While they didn't confess, we had plenty of people identify them as being part of the attack. Anyone care to guess what the judgment was?" It was hard for him not to savor taunting the leadership of the rebellious state.

"General," the Governor said, standing. "This is not necessary. If you shoot them, you're no better than they are. You'll just be martyring them. Wouldn't it be better to simply lock them up?"

They tried to kill me! Holding his temper was not easy, but somehow Donaldson managed. "We can play semantics with the words we use and be tied to this situation all night long. This is Christmas Eve, and I want to spend some time with my troops. However, if you want to spare their lives, all you have to do is comply with my earlier request." The General set his cane on a nearby chair, standing on his own force of will.

Most of the executive council looked at the Governor whose cheeks reddened. "Their blood is not going to be on my hands General Donaldson. Before this is over, you will be held to account for what you are going to do."

Defiant prick. Donaldson didn't admire the man any more than he admired the two prisoners that had refused to talk. Refusing to comply with orders was not something to be admired. "Very well. They die."

The words seemed to send a minor jolt to the prisoners. The male rose fully upright, head tilted proudly. "Oh, say can you see. By the dawn's early—"His tone was horrible and off-key, but insolent as he sang. The other prisoner joined in on the second line of the now-banned anthem.

"Ready … aim," he said as the platoon swiftly complied. "Fire!" The gunshots indoors, almost perfectly in union, were so loud that the noise popped his left ear, leaving a ringing noise. Blood sprayed the wall mural of John Stark, hero of Bennington and Bunker Hill. The two terrorists dropped like marionettes whose strings were suddenly cut. The female landed on top of the man as their blood oozed onto the plush carpeting. The smell of expended gunpowder lingered in the air, mingling with the gasps of shock from the executive council.

For a half moment, he said nothing. He was about to reach for his cane, but noticed that he was rubbing his left hand with his right. It was a strange, unconscious gesture, one he didn't remember the origins of. Once he saw it, he stopped, vigorously scooping up his cane as if it were a sword in his avenging hand.

"Governor up until now I have demonstrated remarkable restraint with these attacks. I can see the error of that thinking. This is war, plain and simple, and I will treat it as such. I am declaring martial law in the state. Civilian authority is gone until this state capitulates and accepts the rightful authority of Newmerica."

Lisbon, New Hampshire

Su-Hui's arm was still in a sling. He didn't think he needed it, but Hachi insisted that he keep it there as the doctor had ordered. Having been married for 26 years, he knew it was far wiser and easier to do what his wife wanted.

He was not a Christian. He wasn't even a practicing Buddhist, though he never would have said that when his mother was alive. In his life, there had never been the need or the time for organized religion. Despite that, since coming to the United States, he found himself enjoying Christmas. The holiday had some religious trappings, but it seemed to be a time of year that forced families to come together. For both Hachi and him, it came this year with a feeling of loss because they couldn't be with their children. He had used a burner phone to call his son, Akio, back in Indiana. There was fear that the NSF would be monitoring cell phone traffic to try and find family members tied to resistance in New Hampshire. He was unsure of all the technical tweaking that had been done with the phones and the towers, but Randy had assured him that no one could trace their call.

On Christmas Eve, after dinner, he and Hachi had called Ya-ting. She did not respond, but the attendant assured them she had heard their voices and even cracked a smile. He wanted to believe that, but in the back of his mind, he seriously doubted it. That did not deter them from trying. *If nothing else, I wanted her to know that we were thinking of her.*

Su-Hui barely remembered the trip back from the raid in Vermont. Trudy had somehow lashed him to the mount for the machine gun with their scarfs and had managed to drive the snowmobile, in the dark, top-heavy with his dead weight tied on, through the snows. From what he had been told, the attack had been a spectacular success. Shaky video footage of the explosion of one of the munitions bunkers had been something he wished he had been conscious to see firsthand.

The harassers were something of heroes in the ranks of the resistance, and as one of those that was wounded in the attack, people seemed to look up to him. Initially, he was embarrassed by the attention. What changed it was when he was hugged by Valerie Turner. She was always so tough and rigid, but when she finally saw him, she hugged him tight. For her to feel so moved meant a great deal to him. Getting wounded for the cause, the so called Defiance, was a badge of honor for him.

The resistance groups in Lisbon had laid low after the raid in Vermont. There was genuine concern that their success might make them a bigger target, and Randy insisted that they take a short break from striking at the Newmericans. A few of the groups used the chance to send some of their people back home, especially those that were from adjoining states. Indiana was too far away for the Zhous to consider such a trip. Besides, he needed to heal from his wound.

One of the SOL teams prepared and served the Christmas dinner. It included turkey, cornbread, green bean casserole, and venison sausage. The heady aroma from the food was enough to make Su-Hui's mouth water. Wine was poured, and the sounds of joy and laughter filled the common space that they shared. It struck Su-Hui as strange to hear the mirth and laughing. So much of what the resistance did was serious. For a few minutes, people seemed to be relaxing, enjoying life. *Can we ever return to a state where this is the norm?*

A local preacher, a Methodist, led a short prayer and Su-Hui began to enjoy the meal. Valerie Turner sat across from him, wishing both him and Hachi a Merry Christmas, a sentiment that he returned. She asked about his wound, and he told her it was fine, casting a darting glance at Hachi as if to say to Valerie, "Let's not talk about this in front of her." To her credit, Valerie got the hint.

"How did you end up being in the Sons?" he asked her.

Valerie paused after she finished chewing, as if searching for the right words. "Before all of this, I was a police commissioner in the New York PD. When they rolled us into the NSF, I was against it. I spoke out about it. I always felt that law enforcement was best when it was local. Making us part of a bigger bureaucracy just didn't feel like the right answer. They fixed the problem by firing me, along with every other officer that felt the way I did."

"They had spent a lot of time and effort during the virus blaming the police for being the bad guys. It was hard to get a job. I did eventually, at half my previous pay, and I hated it. I was born to be a cop. And the NSF became more political than policing. I saw street gangs declare themselves Social Enforcers, just so they could operate beyond the law. So I assembled a group of officers who brought *real* law enforcement to the streets. We protected innocents from the SEs, and even from the NSF. It wasn't easy … we worked in the shadows. It gave me a sense of purpose, a reason to get out of bed."

Su-Hui nodded. "I heard a rumor that you were behind the swearing in of the President. Is that true?"

Valerie cracked a big smile. "You bet your ass."

He smiled as well. "That was incredible to watch."

Hachi weighed in. "We were so excited when that happened. It was the first thing on TV in years that was unexpected—not scripted—it was exciting. They had told us he was dead, and there he was taking the oath of office. We were so happy—so proud."

Valerie nodded. "We were lucky that day, that's for sure. There were a million things that could have gone wrong." She was about to continue when Randy pulled a chair to the middle of the room and stood up. All eyes went to Birdsell there, and the look on his face was dour, despite the levity all around him. "Folks—folks if I can have your attention," he said.

"We just got word on the radio that you all need to know," he said. "General Donaldson has declared martial law in the state. There's a strict 7 p.m. curfew from tonight on." He paused, as if trying to find the right words. "Donaldson ordered the execution of two of our brothers and sisters in Concord. The images are all over the TV, and they are horrible. I don't want any of you surprised when you see them."

The executions were not entirely a surprise to Su-Hui. The Newmerican forces were getting more frustrated all of the time by the resistance they faced. *Brute force is always the refuge of tyrants.*

Randy gathered himself and continued. "This is an escalation on their part, an act of desperation. The Army is no longer going to treat us civilly, but they are going to execute any prisoners. It means we are getting to them. We are wearing them down. I'd understand if any of you decided to go back home. No one will think less of you."

"Fuck 'em!" a voice called from the crowd.

"I say we hit them. Hit them hard," a female called from the corner. A roar of support rose from the Sons of Liberty in the room. Su-Hui felt it too. *I have no desire to go home, not after all we have done.*

Randy asked the preacher to lead them in a prayer for the people that were escalated, and Su-Hui and Hatchi bowed their heads as the preacher uttered his sorrow-filled words. When he finished, they turned back to their meal. Suddenly his appetite seemed to have evaporated. He picked at his turkey. His mind was not on Christmas, but on the war he was in.

"Will you go home?" Hatchi asked Valerie.

She shook her head. "My home is America. New Hampshire is my home. Every state is my home. If I turn my back now and go back to New York, I will always kick myself in the ass for doing it. The enemy is here, so I am here. I'm staying and fighting. What about you?"

Su-Hui nodded. He didn't even look at his wife; he knew her resolve. "I will not abandon these people the way that Newmerica abandoned our homeland."

Turner gave him a smile and held her glass up as if for a toast. He and Hachi lifted their wine glasses and tinked their glasses against hers. *We are all in this together …*

Las Vegas, Nevada

Andy Forrest was stuffed with food. They had traveled to Las Vegas and had gotten a room on the Strip and had ordered a Christmas dinner. It was filling and the room on the Strip was definitely not where he had planned on ever celebrating Christmas. Then again, his life had been one of turmoil mixed with moments of sheer terror and adventure since his father had died. He could have tried to leave the life, but there was a part of it that he thrived on. *I lost everything in my life, my father, my family, my job ... everything.*

A big piece of his sense of being was occupied by Charli. She had helped rescue him, and the two of them had become incredibly close. A part of him feared that she was drawn to him simply because he was available, but those thoughts faded more each day. Charli had led a life in hiding for years, posing as an NSF officer in San Jose and a number of other places. When Jack Desmond had found her and brought her into his Sons of Liberty, she had changed.

Charli had an edge to her. She shared her past with Andy. She had been behind the destruction of an NSF facility in Virginia, costing hundreds of lives. He should have been repulsed by that, but he understood why she had done that. The worst guilt she had was that, despite her efforts, she had failed to save the life of the President she had sworn to protect. Andy knew that she felt guilt for what she had done, and he did what he could to ease her inner pain.

We need each other. I need her so that I won't be alone, and she needs someone to help her cope with what she has done and endured. Some couples had love to bind them together. Andy and Charli helped each other deal with their emotional pain. There were times when he wondered what bond was stronger.

Charli, Travis, and Caylee had been assembling data on the Supermax prison where Raul Lopez was housed. Each had sources they tapped to gather intelligence on the facility. Andy felt a bit like a fifth wheel when it came to planning such things. *They all have experience in this kind of work. I was just a business consultant that shipped jobs overseas. This is their world, not mine.*

"I hate to ask this," he began, as he paced around the coffee table covered with paper, maps, and photographs. "But where are we on cracking this nut?"

Travis grinned. "It isn't that straight-forward, Andy," he said. "This place is a fortress."

Caylee leaned over the table. "We are talking a 37 acre facility. There are 490 prisoners, 350 staff, with steel-reinforced concrete perimeter barriers to prevent vehicles from approaching. Two razor-wire fences surround the prison with attack dogs on patrol between the fence lines. The perimeter has motion sensors and is fully camera covered. Lasers cover the outside and pressure sensors on the grounds as well, so the exterior approach is next to impossible. The guard towers have machine guns and allegedly have anti-aircraft missiles."

Travis took over the summary. "There are 1,400 remotely controlled doors—complete coverage of the interior by cameras and other sensors. You kill the power or if the control room is cut off, all doors automatically go into lockdown mode. The facility has backup generators, so killing the power is even more difficult."

Charli then spoke up. "The prisoners are kept in solitary 23 hours a day. Most of them don't know where they are in the prison. There are no maps, so they can't even plan to break out."

"Jesus," Andy said. "It's Fort Knox."

Charli nodded. "Guards can't even bring in their lunches; they eat what is warmed onsite to prevent anyone from smuggling food in. This is one of the few prisons that doesn't use contractor employees; they are all FedGov employees. Anyone coming into the facility undergoes pat downs, metal detectors, and the occasional strip search."

"What in the hell are they protecting?"

"The worst of the worst," Caylee said. "Terrorists, double-agent traitors, prisoners who have escaped from other maximum security facilities. These are the kinds of people you don't want out in the public."

Andy cringed at the thought of the kinds of people inside. "So this isn't at all like when we walked out with Raul's sister."

Charli shook her head. "No transfers without a lot of authorization and verification. I can't see that approach working."

"There's got to be a way to pull this off," he said.

Andy watched as Caylee studied the aerial photographs of the massive facility. There were images of multiple buildings or units, each one connected by long exposed walkways. Anyone walking between buildings would be in plain sight and would be covered by armed guards. *Hell, they have almost as many people overseeing the prisoners as they have prisoners.* Caylee's eyes narrowed as she surveyed the images. "If we had a tank, we could approach the facility and blast our way in, but we still wouldn't know where he is located. They could call for local support on top of their own defenses. We don't just have to get in and recover Raul; we have to get out of the state and back to safe ground."

Travis moved beside her. "That means a helicopter. Landing a plane there isn't practical given the sloping of the ground. Bringing in a chopper, we can land either inside or just outside of the perimeter."

"What about the anti-aircraft missiles?" Andy asked.

"The proper application of firepower can solve almost every problem," the former SEAL countered. "With a helicopter, we can fly out of the state—keep low, below radar."

"We still have to get him to the chopper," Charli said. "And that means we have to do this from the inside out."

Andy was caught off guard with her comment. "What do you mean?"

Caylee spoke up. "We talked about this before. We need one or two people on the inside of the prison. It's the only way for us to locate where Raul is. It also gives us the capability to negate some of the security measures to get him out."

Travis spoke up. "Our inside team will be outnumbered, and they have to get out as well. We can blast our way out of the cells."

"How are you going to get explosives in?" Andy pressed. One thing that was consistent about Travis Cullen was his desire to use explosives.

"Oh, I can get them in," he assured them. "We don't need to do it all at once. A little bit at a time is the way to go."

"We'll need a helicopter and a damned good pilot," Charli said. *One crazy enough to try this,* Andy thought.

Travis spoke up once more. "I know a guy who knows a guy," he said grinning. "He's wonky, but ex-military with combat experience."

"Getting people on the inside is going to be tricky too," Caylee said. "The background checks in that facility are likely to be over the top. The IDs that we craft are going to have to be airtight, top-notch trade craft."

"Jack should be able to help us on that front," Charli said.

Andy stared down at the data, then at the small cadre of people in the hotel room. He had to feel a bit proud. No one was suggesting that they stop, that the task was too big. *These kinds of people don't think that way.* It was something that he had been missing in his life. *When I was a consultant, people always threw up barriers and blocks to moving things forward. Charli and Caylee ... they see everything as a challenge that can be overcome if they think about it long enough. Travis, well, he can blow up anything that gets in the way.*

Andy saw Caylee pull up a copy of *Time* magazine for what had to be the twentieth time since she had seen it. On the cover was a proud, black woman, and a small image of Raul Lopez. The magazine's cover was starting to show wear from the number of times she studied it. "There's not anything about the prison in that piece," Andy said, having read it himself.

Caylee looked over at him. "There's a lot there. The woman on the cover is the one that captured Raul. She's going to be at the prison; she's heading up his interrogation according to the article. We crossed paths at the Ohio River. Tossed some lead at each other. We are not going to have to beat the prison; we have to beat the people there—and she is one of them." There was something in the way she said this that told Andy she might be looking forward to such a confrontation.

"You have something in mind?" Charli asked.

Caylee tossed the magazine onto the coffee table. "I'm working through a few ideas. They made a mistake putting the article out. It tells me a lot about her personal life and that is where she is weakest." There was a grim quality to her voice that told Andy he didn't want to know the details of what she was thinking. One thing he knew for sure. Caylee wasn't the kind of person you wanted to piss off.

Travis pulled out a stapled set of papers. "We have a list of the guards and their FedGov profiles. That will help us craft some cover IDs where we minimize exposing ourselves. We need to be inside that place for at least two weeks, if not more, to figure out where it is vulnerable."

"That assumes there are vulnerabilities," Andy said. "From what you've all said, this place is impenetrable."

Charli quipped, "Anything built by man can be overcome by man. Humans always introduce flaws; it's simply a matter of us finding them."

Her response garnered a big nod from Travis.

Andy then glanced around the room and could not help but chuckle. "Something funny Andy?" Charli asked as the others looked at him.

He paused, trying to wipe the smirk from his face. "It's just that we are here in Las Vegas planning a breakout from a facility with top-notch security that is thought to be unbreakable. I mean seriously; this is like a scene from *Ocean's Eleven*."

Even Caylee grinned as Charli spoke up. "We can do this. The biggest key to their defense is that no one is willing to even try to break a prisoner out. They are hiding behind their reputation. Even the name, 'Supermax,' is designed to intimidate. Its reputation is its best barrier to breakout attempts. We can pull this off because they never would expect us to try." Her words summoned a series of nods around the room.

We can pull this off. It's not about the planning—it's about being willing to try.

CHAPTER 12

"If you are not in fear, you are not aware."

East Lake, Georgia

General Reager moved into the long-abandoned store in the Strip plaza followed by Captain Harnessy, his G2 intelligence officer. On the outside of the boarded-up store, the bricks were charred where they protruded beyond the aged plywood. Red graffiti on the plywood was old, but still readable: *Black Lives Matter.* It was a sign that the business had been one of many victims of the riots during the virus summer, or in the post Liberation era. If not the rioting, the crashing of the economy that the progressives in the District had inflicted on the people. Outside was a mix of infantry and the civilian Sons of Liberty fighters, mingling and talking with each other, sharing cigarettes, and a few were even chuckling. As Trip entered, he could smell a mustiness, and a hint of smoke that oozed from the ruins. *How many businesses did we sacrifice on the altar of the Ruling Council's lies?*

As he stepped in, he heard the crack of distant rifle fire. It was common all along the front lines throughout the night. The sentries he had posted tended to shoot first, rather than risk getting shot themselves. The defenders mounted raids, often to steal food, water, or ammunition. Sometimes they were successful, but more often than not, they were identified and fired at … the advantage of having an abundance of night vision gear.

Trip had hoped that today there would be a reduction of gunfire between the lines. It was Christmas Day, and even in the most brutal of wars, both sides tended to use the day dedicated to peace. The fact that the Newmericans were firing didn't entirely surprise him; he knew they held religious holidays in contempt. *They haven't entirely outlawed it ... yet. They just renamed it the Winter Holiday out of fear of someone being offended.*

For Trip, the holiday with the troops meant he would celebrate the holiday. After his divorce, he had been alone during the season. When his family was together, Christmas had always been a joy. His wife cooked a meal they would feast on for days, and he always enjoyed watching his daughter open presents. Those days were gone though—little more than fading memories for him. At least today he could grab a late dinner with the men and women serving under him.

The fact that they tried to steal food and water was good news as far he was concerned. It meant that his stranglehold on Atlanta was starting to work. There had been riots in the city early on, which the TRC claimed was his fault. In reality, people were trying to grab all of the food they could before it ran out. Hoarding, while officially banned by the autonomous zone, was commonplace.

Inside was Mason Carter of the Sons of Liberty group, the Firebrands. Next to him was an attractive young female in full tactical gear. She wasn't wearing the cheap stuff he usually saw with the SOL; she was a professional. Under the grease paint smears on her high cheekbones, he associated a name with her face—Darcy Belle—commanding the 'Bama Deplorables'. He gave both of them a nod.

"To what do I owe the honor?" he said, taking his helmet off and tucking it under his left arm.

"We both just got back through the lines," Mason Carter said with a low drawl. "Damn near got shot by the sentries, despite having the password."

"That means they are doing their jobs," Trip replied. "What did you learn?"

Darcy Belle threw open a topographical map. "We've pinpointed their troop placements along the east side," she said. "They have gotten their hands on some land mines and have started to plant fields of them, mostly in parks, the kinds of places where you have larger fields of fire." Her slender finger stabbed at the map to show the locations as Trip leaned over to see.

"We don't use mines," Trip said flatly.

"I don't read Chinese," she said. "But the crates looked to have Asian markings on them."

This is what things have come to—purchasing inhumane weapons from our enemies. It was one more crime that the Ruling Council and the Pentagon would have to answer for at some point. Trip was counting on living to see that happen.

Carter spoke up, pointing to the north end of the airport. "In one of the hangers, I swear they are setting up some sort of forward air observation post. I saw the radar dish on the tarmac; it was new, not like the shit usually out there."

They are going to be bringing in air support. Damn. Thus far, his own air assets had flown CAP, combat air patrols, and had fended off attempts to fly ground support missions. *They wouldn't be setting up an observation post just for the grins of it. They are planning on escalating.* "It's good news that you spotted them; bad news they are setting it up."

"It's just out of range of our artillery," Carter added. "They have a shitload of sandbags around it too, not to mention gun positions of their own."

"Tell me about their troops placements," Captain Harnessy asked.

Belle traced her finger along six inches of the map. "These trenches are lightly manned, mostly decoys from what I saw. They have been pulling troops back, working on a new band of defenses closer to downtown. The indications I saw point to them compressing their defensive lines the next time we push them."

"It makes sense," Harnessy said, glancing over at Trip. "They can hold ground better with a tighter concentration of troops."

Trip nodded, his mind racing with options. "I don't want them falling back," he said firmly after several long seconds of silence. "If they make us fight in the city, it will get messy."

"What do you have in mind, General?" Belle asked.

Trip pointed to Stone Mountain on the map "The enemy needs to think they have a chance to fight us in relatively open ground. Stone Mountain has a lot of forests, lakes, and some good open fields … tank country. They need to have hope. If they don't have hope, they dig in like rats. If they think they can pull off a victory, beat us outside of the city, then we can crush them without laying waste to Atlanta."

"How do we do that?" Carter asked.

"Up until now, you've been sneaking in, wrecking a little havoc, and gathering intelligence. I'm suggesting a little change to that. We want you to pass your people off as the enemy. For this to work, you need to pose as Social Enforcers."

Carter winced at those words, but Belle didn't. "We'll need some names to drop, like the name of the SEs we are impersonating. We've already had to fake our way through the lines twice posing as Enforcers, so this isn't that big of a stretch."

The wrinkles on Carter's face seemed to fade the more she talked and the more he thought it over. "It might be possible. It would be best if we pose as infiltrators, that somehow we sneak through your lines to join them in the glorious defense of Atlanta," he said with a twist of sarcasm in his words.

Trip looked over at Harnessy, who gave him a single nod back. "That's not a bad idea," Reager replied. "Your mission can be summed up in one word: misinformation. Next time you are through the lines, we need you to spread rumors that the weakest point of our lines is along the line of Memorial Drive, where we have been letting the civilians out. I need your people to plant seeds with them that a breakout toward Stone Mountain is viable. In fact, it's a good move. I need you to be subtle though. If you come right out and tell them that, it will make them nervous. The best way for this to unfold is for them to think it is their idea. Your job is to say the right things to lure them out."

"They will test your defenses before making any move," Belle said.

"They will find what we want them to find," he replied.

"It's going to be tricky," Carter weighed in. "They will be suspicious of us if they catch us coming through the lines."

"Think of this as community theater," Trip said cracking a grin. "Being under siege messes with your thinking. People become paranoid, but they also are desperate for hope. If you give them hope that getting out toward Stone Mountain is a chance to deliver us a devastating blow, they are eventually going to try and run with it."

They spent several minutes going over the intelligence that the two SOL teams had gathered during their last penetrations of the front. The lack of food was starting to wear on the defenders, as was the general health conditions. They were boiling water from Lake Clara Meer just so they had enough for civilians to drink. The Newmerican morale was still strong, but was starting to show cracks.

When they finished with the briefing and making plans, Trip thanked both commanders. "I hope you will join us for Christmas dinner," he offered. "It's not great, but it is better than MREs. We've got ham and turkey. More importantly, we've got showers and laundry if your people want to clean up."

"That is most appreciated," Carter said.

"Thank you General," Belle added.

He and Harnessy led them back to the mess area. When he arrived there, he was greeted by laughter and the sounds of men and women doing something they didn't get much of a chance to do—relax. Reager made sure that he was at the rear of the chow line, behind the Sons of Liberty. It was more important that his people first get their meals. There was still plenty of everything as he made his way to a seat next to enlisted personnel with Darcy Belle taking a seat opposite of him.

As he sat down, he took a moment to savor this Christmas day. Trip Reager realized that it was the best one he had enjoyed in years.

The District

The Vice President-Elect hated this Christmas. It was the first one where her mother didn't get a chance to prepare a holiday meal. It was a Christmas without her brother Gabe. Caylee Leatrom had killed them both, a vengeance attack by a traitor. She had never had to plan what to do on Christmas, but this year she was alone. There had been thoughts on her part about putting up a tree, but there was no real point. It was rare that she had visitors to the apartment, and the tree would only serve as a reminder of what Caylee had taken away from her.

She had started the day at Arlington National Cemetery, visiting the monument to her mother. *If she were here, she would tell me to not be so bitter ... that I needed to smile more.* That was her mother's only weakness; she forgave people. The Vice President-Elect never felt that capability. When people crossed her, she remembered it and made them pay for their audacity. If you let people wrong you and do nothing about it, you only encourage more of that behavior. *My mother was far too generous with people. She chose to see the good in them. I have been forced to see many people for what they are, dangerous.*

She had hired a chef to prepare a private holiday dinner for her. It was excellent, the best the money could buy. There was far too much food. She kept the leftover dessert, a chocolate pie, but threw the rest of the uneaten food away. Leftovers was never something she enjoyed. It reminded her too much of the years of her life when she had been forced to stretch each meal out.

Sitting alone and watching holiday-themed shows was not on her agenda. There was someone she needed to visit ... Senator Earl Lewis. The Tribunal had found him guilty of treason the week before the holidays, live on TV. People were following the Tribunal almost to the extent that they had tracked the OJ Simpson trial decades before. The credit for that was something she took as her own. *I staged this like a reality TV show, with cliffhangers on some days, surprise witnesses, and evidence that shocked people.*

Her Secret Service detail arranged for her limo and went with her to the District Central Social Correction Facility, the old prison. One of her detail, her normal driver, had not come ... insisting that he had the day off and wanted to spend time with his family. She could appreciate that, but informed him that if he didn't come, he'd be without a job. *It is a shame he is making me fire him on Christmas. It's a bigger shame that he doesn't have the right priorities in life.*

She blew through the security; they had been told to expect her arrival in advance. She came to the room where Lewis was waiting. He wore a fading orange jumpsuit and was handcuffed to the table. When she entered, she dismissed the guards although her Secret Service detail would be watching from the two-way mirror that dominated the wall behind her. She ordered the microphone in the room disabled, assuring the agents that they could come in if they saw him get violent. *I don't want anyone to hear what I have to say to him.*

The Tribunal for the Senator had been a fantastic show. But the longer it went on, the more people began to sympathize with him. She didn't fully understand it. The manufactured evidence against the older man was solid. Her senior people in the TRC had been running polls and had come to the conclusion that a growing number of people were questioning his guilt. She had hoped that this meeting might reverse that.

The former Senator looked gaunt. He had started to grow a ragged gray beard. The bags under his eyes seemed to grow darker each day. As she sat opposite of him, she could see that he was still defiant, doing his best to hold his anger toward her in check. The fact that she had gotten to him emotionally gave her all she needed to smile at him.

"I thought we should have a little chat," she said calmly. "Since you have been found guilty and know what the punishment for treason is, I thought you might be open to a little dialogue."

Lewis said nothing for a long half-minute. "You bought and paid for this fiasco. We both know that I had nothing to do with that assassination attempt. Every bit of evidence you introduced was fake, just like I told the Tribunal."

"It's a pity those comments never made it to the public," she said, ratcheting up her grin. "All the people saw was you fuming and dejected after the videos and texts were presented."

"You may have fooled the nation," he snapped. "But we both know the truth. This wasn't a trial; nor was it a quest for justice. It is a political assassination on your part. I know my role in this; I'm to be the victim. You may paint me as a conniving killer, but we all know that is pure bullshit."

"I prefer to think of you as an example for others that might think about rising up against Daniel and myself."

"We have little to talk about," he countered, leaning back in his chair as far as he could given that his hands were shackled to the tabletop.

"That's not true," she countered. "Next week, with most of the country at home, you will be brought out, and the sentencing will be given. Your death, on the net and on TV, will be watched by everyone.

"I have it on good knowledge that the Tribunal will call for you to be hanged. From what I'm told, they are going to recommend that you be strung up with piano wire. I'm no expert on it, but from what I've been told, the wire will cut into your flesh while it slowly strangles you to death. It is an agonizing way to go, so I've been led to believe."

"I'm sure you'll enjoy it."

"This has never been about me, despite what you may think," she said, saying the lie with complete comfort. "This has been about your questioning how I run the NSF. When you die, anyone thinking of going up against me is going to think twice. They will remember your twitching body swinging by a wire, and they will purge those thoughts."

"That you believe that it will crush resistance is an error. You will only confirm what people think. Not only that, things may not play out the way you anticipate. Even if it does unfold the way you think the people will see you for what you are … how you *really* are. Conspiracies will haunt you for years after I am gone. And the best part—most will be right. You aren't doing away with a problem. You are creating thousands more."

"It is quaint that you think that," she said. "But I also control the TRC, which means that I control what the people think."

"Not everyone takes the media at their word. If you think that is the case, you are delusional."

People didn't talk back to her the way that Lewis did. They feared her. As much as she liked that, she did enjoy the fact that he was willing to resist her words … but only so far. "You give far too much credit to the masses. Most people don't want to think; they want someone to do it for them. One thing we have learned from COVID is that people will set aside common sense and want to do what they are told to do, even if it is against their best interests. They will turn on their neighbors for reparation points and a chance at recognition. They don't want to have to think things through, and we have been more than willing to do the thinking for them."

"How's that working for you?" he sneered at her. "The American President won the election. From what little news I get in here, I know that civil war is breaking out. Not everyone wants to drink your Kool Aid from the sounds of it."

"That is all moot," she said calmly, so that he could not see any impact from his words. He was stoking a bit of anger in her, but she didn't want him to have a glimmer of satisfaction from it. "What I came to do is offer you an option for the inevitable. I'm doing this because of your long service to the nation."

"What can you possibly offer me? I'm going to be strung up and hung."

"If you were to confess … admit that you were working in conjunction with the Pretender President's administration to assassinate us, I might be able to convince the Tribunal that hanging is too vicious. We could go with something like lethal injection, something where you won't feel the agony of your death. Surely that is something that would be of interest to you."

Earl Lewis leaned back for another long moment of silence. "You are asking me to lie."

"I'm offering you a chance to avoid suffering. Think of it this way: It would be an act of dignity, your last contribution to Newmerica."

The older man smiled back at her. "I don't think so."

She had expected him to be defiant, but she had also reasoned that when faced with death, he would choose a painless option. *Why would he want to endure pain and suffering?* "Are you sure Senator? This is not an open offer. I'm bringing it to you today, on Christmas, as a gesture of generosity. That generosity is a door that will close when I leave this room."

He laughed in response. It wasn't a mock laugh, or a chuckle that was forced. It was genuine. "You *need* me to implicate the enemy. This isn't about some gesture of good will; you must realize that some people out there know I am innocent and being railroaded. You don't do anything out of the kindness of your heart—you don't have that in you. You're desperate."

"I assure you, I've never been desperate."

"Well, I won't reconsider. We both know I am innocent."

"No one is innocent Senator," she quipped.

"I am. I never wanted you dead until they locked me up and accused me of the crime."

She tried to turn the conversation, to twist it hard back to her offer. "You are facing a painful death. Your family will be watching your last minutes suffering, choking for air."

Mentioning his family made him purse his lips for a moment. "My family knows I'm innocent as well. You want to threaten me with hanging? I say this—let me swing. You kill me, sooner or later, someone *will* come for you with the same intent. And it won't be some made-up assassination attempt. It will be real. And in your dying breath, I want you to picture me choking to death because of what you did."

Anger rose to her face like a campfire doused with gasoline. The Vice President-Elect rose to her feet and headed for the door. *I will see you swing, and twitch, and die ... and I will enjoy it!*

Newmerica Penitentiary, Administrative Maximum Facility Florence, Colorado

Raul had enjoyed his Christmas meal, despite the meat obviously coming from a can and the gravy being watered down. It was light colored, heavily salted—he presumed it had been a turkey at some point, though it didn't taste very much like any he had eaten before. He had eaten worse as a child in those years when his mother had struggled to get by. Back then, Spam was a regular choice for protein, and he even grew to like it when it was cut thin and grilled up. He ate his meal in his compact cell, alone. If it hadn't been for the guard telling him that it was Christmas, he wouldn't have even known. Time passed strangely in the Supermax prison.

This was his first Christmas without his mother, and that weighed heavily on him. He felt guilty for her death. *If it wasn't for me, they never would have taken her into custody.* While Raul knew he was not responsible for her death, he felt his actions had set her demise in motion. He was also burdened with the thought that his sister was a hostage of the Newmericans as well. *I can cope with being here. The fact that Maria was still a prisoner is only because of me.* He hated to think of what the guards might do to his younger sister.

The guards told him that he had a visitor after dinner. He was shackled and escorted out of Unit J, knowing full well who he was going to be facing: Deja Jordan. Outside visitors were not allowed for the prisoners in Unit J. *Only she would show up here, probably to rub it in that I am away from my family for Christmas.* Mentally, he braced himself more with each chained-step for their inevitable discussion.

They secured Raul to the table, and he shifted in the metal chair as she entered the room. Deja was wearing new clothing, an outfit he had not seen before. Since she had been in *Time*, Raul noted that her tastes had improved. Gone were the sweatpants she had worn when he had first arrived. She also had makeup on, more than usual. Her lips were bright red, shimmering as she pulled up the chair in front of him.

"Merry Christmas Raul," she said, strangely smiling. Out of everything he saw with her, the smile was the only thing that warned him of anything being wrong. *She would only smile if something bad had happened for me.*

Raul didn't respond as Deja continued. "I hope you enjoyed your dinner. I hear they scrounged up turkey for you and your comrades."

"Was that what the meat was?" he replied. "It was hard to be sure."

"I spent last night with my family in Minneapolis," she said, offering him a rare bit of personal information.

"That's nice for you."

"I bet you would like to see your sister," Deja prodded.

Ah, there it is—this is her angle—use Maria and the holiday to break me. Raul said nothing, but simply looked back at her, denying her any hint of emotion.

"Your sister is fine," Deja said. "She's in quarantine in California. She's quite upset with your mother's death. It means she has no family there in the camp. Maria's alone there now. Of course, you've been at one of the camps before. You know that things are not very structured. Things can happen there, outside of what the guards see. Maria is an attractive young girl, strong, but, like I said, bad things can happen. I'm sure you don't want anything to happen to her."

Raul felt the blood rush to his face as he shifted in his seat. It had been almost a year since he had seen Maria. Deja was right; she was strong—but she was also young. *She hasn't seen the things I have ... hasn't experienced what I have.* "You must be fairly desperate to try to get her to shake me."

"Oh, I don't need her to rattle your cage," Deja said. "You see, there's been a turn of events."

"What do you mean?"

She pulled a manila envelope onto the table and an 8" x 10" glossy photo of two women. One of them, Raul didn't recognize at all. The other looked strikingly like Caylee. He did what he could to hide his emotions and leaned back. "Who're they?"

"One, we don't know ... I'm hoping you can shed light on that. The other is your friend, Caylee Leatrom."

He shook his head. "Is that name supposed to mean something to me?"

Deja grinned even more. "You and I both know that this person, your mysterious partner, is the one you claim is going to kill me. Well, I know who she is now Raul ... everyone does. I know all about her and what she claims to be. She will not be coming for you; I have seen to that. If she shows up anywhere near this facility, she'll be shot on sight."

Silence followed the threats that Deja laid before him. Raul didn't flinch, but he knew she was studying his face, and he knew with each beat of his heart that he was confirming the truth of Caylee's identity to her. *I never gave her up* ... he was proud of that, and angered that Deja had figured out who she was. After over a minute, he spoke again. "If you know who she is, then you know just how much danger you are in."

"I'm not worried at all Raul," Deja replied. "Even if she figures out where you are, this place has never had an escape. You are locked up in the deepest, darkest hole Newmerica has, surrounded by a professional Army of guards and defenses that you can't imagine. She will never get anywhere near you, let alone get you out of here—so you may as well get thoughts of rescue out of your head."

Raul stared at her intently and forced a thin smile. "You clearly have no idea what you are up against." He leaned back and came to grips with the fact that this was the worst Christmas he had ever endured.

CHAPTER 13

"America was the product of its creators:
Pale, male, and stale."

Concord, New Hampshire

General Donaldson stood at attention as he adjusted the laptop screen so that the camera caught him clearly. The secured video link was boosted by the tiny satellite dish on the roof of the building. The office he had commandeered had been that of the Lieutenant Governor. She had been infuriated at his action which had resulted in her being escorted out of the State House. He had thrown her personal pictures and wall decorations and degrees in a box that sat in the corner. Politicians all did that; hung up their awards; plastered their offices with photographs of themselves with other dignitaries ... to him, it was all about their egos. He had cleared out her clutter and had made this a military office, one worthy of the conqueror of New Hampshire.

Daniel Porter, the President-Elect of Newmerica, faced him with an angry expression on his face. "General, the situation in Atlanta is no longer acceptable."

"Sir, the city is under siege, but the local field commander, General Kotter, has assured me that they can continue to hold out for at least another month, perhaps two. Yes, there has been some looting and violence, but I've been assured that the citizens are doing well, despite the hardships."

"The TRC is editing what comes out, but the people there are suffering. Every day more of them file out of the city. No power, no food, no water ... it's unacceptable. If that's allowed to continue, the only ones there will be your people and the SEs."

"The policy I have supported up to this point is to allow the civilians to leave," he said, hinting that it was not his idea, but one he approved of. "It allows us to stretch out our supplies for those that remain."

"It makes it look like the people don't support us. The Americans are getting footage out to non-aligned media showing how many people are leaving. While our allies in Big Tech are helping block a lot of that media, some of it is getting through. There is a sentiment that we are losing control of the situation there."

There's not a lot I can do about the media. The Truth Reconciliation Committee was good at crafting a message that the people of Atlanta were defiant, dug in, fighting alongside of his troops. Every civilian that remained was a hero according to the Newmerica press. It was inspiring, if not a stretch. "Are you proposing that we do not allow civilians to leave the city, sir?"

"I am not. The Ruling Council, as a whole, believes that the time has come to put an end to this flight. It's not sending the right message, and at this time, it is important that we appropriately stage this thought with the citizens."

"That will make things complicated sir. Some of the citizens are not likely to react well to being told they can't leave."

"I don't care about that. You have hundreds of Social Enforcers in the city—have them do their damned jobs. Anyone complaining is essentially aiding the enemy. Make an example out of a few of them, and the rest will fall into line. Tell them that for their own safety they have to shelter in place. It worked during COVID. They will do what they are told."

General Donaldson doubted it would be that easy. From his discussions with the military commanders in Atlanta, the locals were past irritated. This isn't at all like the COVID situation. "Many of these people already feel trapped here. We've had a few, shall I say, incidents here. Not outright riots yet, but rebellious activity. They all know friends and family that have evacuated the city. Telling them they can't is going to cause a lot of issues."

"I don't care how you position it. Tell them that the Americans are no longer allowing people to leave. Tell them they are shooting civilians.

What you tell them isn't as important as their compliance. It doesn't matter if you use threats or lies—get them to do what is needed to support the cause."

Donaldson nodded grimly as the President-Elect continued, "You need to find a way to reverse the military situation. It is bad enough that things in New Hampshire are bogged down with this damned Defiance. We can't afford to lose Atlanta. What are your plans for victory, General?"

He drew a long breath, using the moments to assemble his thoughts. "Sieges can be broken three ways. One is to wear down the resolve of the sieging forces to where they give up and go home. Two is to send a relief force to punch through the surrounding enemy and relieve the city. Third is to break out and fight on better ground.

"In this case, the enemy is refusing to suffer the losses of contracting their lines beyond what they did a few weeks ago. They show no signs of getting weary and going home. The second case, launching a relief force, is extremely problematic. Our nearest friendly forces are in Virginia, which would mean driving through two enemy states just to get to Georgia."

"So, what are your plans for a breakout?" Porter demanded.

"I have General Kotter looking at a number of options. We have to choose carefully. Our last attempt cost us a big chunk of the northwest suburbs because we misjudged the enemies' intentions." There was more to it, but Donaldson did not want to open that can of worms. *We got suckered into that thrust north. They had an attack force that swung in behind us because Colonel Hobbs failed to do enough reconnaissance.* One thing that Donaldson had done well was to hang that debacle on Hobbs.

"We need to do something," Porter said bitterly.

"I agree sir, but we need to do it right."

"Agreed … reluctantly," the President-Elect said. "How is the situation is New Hampshire?"

This was a front in the war that Donaldson could not pass off to someone else … this was his baby. "Our clamp-down on the insurgents continues sir. I have been assured that the executions we broadcast have lowered the morale of our opposing forces. We have seen very little activity in recent weeks."

"I still have the Governor of Vermont wanting to bring his troops home," Porter replied.

"Sir, that raid was a fluke, a lucky punch on their part. I have shifted more troops to the borders to ensure they can't pull the same stunt again."

"The fact that we still have insurgency activity at all is a problem."

Donaldson knew that all too well. The throbbing from his wound made sleep difficult for him. "You don't have to remind me sir. I was shot during one of their attacks."

"This can't go on indefinitely," Porter said.

"Our strategy is one of active patrolling. They have been using the winter weather as the means to cover their activities. Once the snow melts, they will lack the ability to move cross country without our pursuit. Most of their cover will disappear when the snow is gone."

"So we have to wait this out until spring?" Frustration was clear in his tone.

"We aren't waiting. We are keeping the pressure on, active patrol routes, using some of our aerial drones to monitor their movements when we do spot them. But honestly sir, until the weather starts to warm, it is going to be a drawn-out process."

"Our nation needs a win, General," Porter said. "I was told that you were the man that could deliver it. So far all we have seen is losses." The threat was clear in the President-Elect's voice.

"Sir, we have suffered losses, but in the end we will prevail. The issue we are facing with Atlanta, not being able to relieve or reinforce it, is exactly what the Americans are facing with the state of New Hampshire. Our strategies are sound—textbook in fact."

"General, just remember this: Your enemy has studied the same textbook." He continued a warning: "And if you don't hand me victories soon, you will find yourself guarding cargo containers on the West Coast," he snapped. He shut off the video feed before Donaldson could reply.

The General felt a blush cover his face as he stared at the blank screen. *I am doing all I can. If he thinks he can replace me with someone else who will do better, good luck to him.* As he stared at the monitor, he noticed that he was rubbing his left hand nervously, something he stopped the moment he saw it. The pressure for a fast victory was something he couldn't ignore or talk his way out of. *I need to deliver a blow on one of these fronts, something devastating, or I will be nothing more than a footnote in Newmerican history.*

Newmerica Penitentiary, Administrative Maximum Facility Florence, Colorado

Charli Kasinski had worked hard on immersing herself in her new persona, Dana Bartlett. When she had been in hiding after the death of the last President, she had adopted several identities and knew that the key to becoming another person was in the details. Dana Bartlett was ex-Army where she had served as a prison guard at Leavenworth military prison. They had chosen that qualifier since the bureaucracy of the FedGov ensured that the Bureau of Prisons would not be able to get her falsified records from the Army; she had made sure there were records there—just in case.

Dana was a bit of a loner. She had served in the NSF, but per her interview, she wanted to get back to her true love, being a prison guard. "I like the power, the control aspects of that job," she had said in her interview. The warden had been impressed enough to bring her in. It had helped that the warden was female as well. Dana had played off of that, "I hope one day to rise up to where you are, a warden." Dana/Charli had played to the warden's ego and desire to support other females; it was something that she had enjoyed leveraging.

Part of the character she played was the physical disguise. She wore a nose prosthetic that gave her what Caylee called, 'a Roman nose,' big to the point of being obnoxious. Her hair had gone to a darker color and was worn much shorter than she preferred. A fake mole on her left cheek was another distraction. As Caylee told her, "Even a little change is often enough to draw attention away from the rest of your face." The use of canned tanning spray made her skin darker than normal, almost leathery.

The bigger problem for their little covert rescue team was creating the job openings at the Supermax. Caylee solved that issue. Four of the guards had a habit on Thursday nights of frequenting a bar in Florence, Colorado. She 'arranged' for them to have an auto accident that had tragically killed all four of the occupants of the car. Charli knew that Caylee had help from Travis for the act. As much as she was curious about how they had pulled it off, she also knew enough not to ask for the details. *There are certain things I don't want to know about how Caylee does her job.*

Caylee met her immediate boss, Captain Drew Harrison, who seemed cordial enough as he took her on her first walk-through of the prison. Unfortunately, it was proving to be as formidable as the rest of the team had thought. She drank in every detail, noting things like the make and model of door locks and the nuances of security access on the computer system.

Each unit was a two-story structure ringed with solitary cells. The prisoners were locked up 23 hours a day. Their showers had timers to limit their use. Cameras covered every possible angle, leaving them with virtually no privacy. The inner courts between the units had steel poles erected as camera mounts, and to prevent helicopter landings, much to her chagrin. Dana looked at the roofs of the units, but they had challenges as well. With sloped surfaces to prevent the thick Colorado snow buildup, the roofs also had antennae on them.

When they were brought out of their cells, they were taken to a large cage carpeted in AstroTurf where they were allowed to walk around. She had seen Joaquín "El Chapo" Guzmán, former leader of a Mexican drug cartel during his time in the cage. Captain Harrison was proud of the caliber of prisoners they had under their control. "We have the worst of the worst. Oddly enough we have a lot of bombers here. You've got Ted Kaczynski, the Unabomber, Tsarnaev, the prick that bombed the Boston Marathon, and Eric Rudolph, the Olympic Park bomber," he said as he walked her between units. "Kaczynski is a genius, but keeps to himself. Most of these guys are dumb as rocks. They didn't get caught by being the brightest kids in the class," he said chuckling. "The difference is the folks in Unit J."

"What's Unit J?"

"Politicals, folks that the FedGov doesn't want to see the light of day," he replied. "We've got a Senator in there, a pair of Governors, a former Fox News White House correspondent … anyone that they don't want to get a chance to speak to visitors. They bury them here, lock them up isolated from the rest of the world."

That is probably where Raul is. "How do they adapt to the isolation?"

"Unit J is different," Harrison said as a stiff cold wind hit the two of them, penetrating her own new, thick uniform coat. "We let them comingle for a few hours a day, even eat together when we decide to let them. The other prisoners get TV, but no news from the outside world. With the folks in J, we let them see the news. The warden thinks it's a form a punishment for them. You know, they used to be on the news. Now they see the world going on without them … that kind of thing."

"That makes sense," she said as they reached the unit he was leading her to. "It must really upset them."

Harrison shrugged as he slid his passcard on the lock and keyed in his code—one that Dana saw him punch in, and she committed it to memory. She wore a body camera on the job which also would capture his password, but at the end of every shift, she had to pull the SIM card out and dump it to the NSFCloud. She had prepared for that by bringing a corrupted duplicate SIM card that she would switch with it. It would appear that the camera was faulty. He opened the heavy metal door for her as he continued to talk. "Most of them are pretty quiet. One of them is going to face a People's Tribunal soon. I just got the notice yesterday. They want to get through with the assassin's Tribunals first; then he's up."

"Who's that?"

"Raul Lopez, you know, public enemy number one … the terrorist."

"He's here?"

"Yeah," he said, entering the code for the interior door. Dana noted the pair of cameras that covered the room. "They sent him to us to prevent anyone from doing something stupid, like trying to break him out."

Dana did not show a bit of reaction to his words. "From what I see, the designers of this place have thought of everything. Nobody is getting out."

He ushered her into the warmth of the access corridor where he took off his coat and hung it up. She did the same. "It's part of what makes this job so interesting. You are guarding the most high profile prisoners in the country in a place where it's impossible for them to get out," Harrison said with pride, hiking up his utility belt from his slight stomach that tried to force it down.

As Dana followed him, she was worried that he might just be right

... this place has so many layers of security; it's like an onion. When you peel back one layer, there are dozens of more under it.

Pembroke, New Hampshire

The New Hampshire National Guard had abandoned their training center in Pembroke when the Newmerica forces had invaded the state. From what Su-Hui saw, it was a smart move. If they had tried to hold the campus-like base, it would have forced a straight up fight with the invading forces. Instead they had moved to the countryside, waiting, biding time for the right moment to strike. From what little Su-Hui knew, part of General Griffiths' strategy was not to concentrate their force. It was something that the enemy wanted, and for now at least, he was denying them that.

The training center had been taken over by Connecticut and New York National Guard units and turned into their base of operations. Su-Hui noted a subtle irony; they were concentrating their force in the exact spot where the resistance had refused to do so. From Pembroke, they would launch daily patrols all across New Hampshire. Convoys of armored vehicles and troops would drive through the towns, making their presence known. Some were ambushed; some were the victims of IEDs, and others were left unmolested. The randomness made them edgy, nervous, fatigued ... *exactly how we want our enemies to be.*

Today was going to be different. The SOL and loyal New Hampshire National Guard were going to strike in the one place that the enemy felt safe: Pembroke. The base was surrounded by razor wire-topped fencing and armed patrols worked a well-worn, plowed path inside the fence line, constantly on watch for the enemy. The Connecticut and New York armored vehicles were lined up on what had been the parade field, in neat rows, each awaiting their turn on patrol.

Leading an assault on the base was less about wiping out the defenders and more about making them aware they were not safe there, forcing them to defend their base and thus reducing the number of patrols. General Griffiths himself had come to Lisbon to ask for the Sons of Liberty to assist in the attack. 'We don't need a big body count. We just need to rattle them. Snow and paranoia are our best allies.'

The attack was to consist of three components. First, some demolition experts from the National Guard were going to plant explosives under several of the vehicles that were on patrol. They would be shuttling explosives into the base that could then be remote detonated—making the attack seem bigger than it was. Su-Hui didn't know when they planned to set off the explosives, but was assured it would be done to sow the most confusion.

The next attack would come from machine-gun-armed snowmobiles engaging the perimeter defenders. His friend and driver Trudy was going to be part of that attack. This was to be a diversion from the real assault at the other end of the base. Ski troops would cut the fence and attack the barracks. This was where he figured in the plan. His machine gun was posted on a small hill, mostly buried by snow, just outside the base. He was to provide suppression fire on the barracks, hitting the upper floors to keep the defenders pinned and afraid. Randy Birdsell assured him they would leave plenty of little surprises behind for the defenders. There was something in the jovial way he told that to Su-Hui that made him wonder what his SOL comrade had planned.

When they reviewed the plan of the attack, Su-Hui had a few moments where his experience in the Army came through. He pointed out the surrounding terrain and how the snow would muffle their sounds, allowing them to get in close. He had also recommended some changes to the machine gun mounts on the snowmobiles to prevent anyone from accidentally hitting their driver, wedges that made sure the gunner couldn't shoot straight down when firing forward. When they reviewed the plan, they loved his suggestion of the snowmobiles going in single file to make it hard for the enemy to determine how many of them were used in the attack. Randy and the New Hampshire National Guard troops working with them complimented him on his observations.

The attack force would not only hit the barracks, but they would use Molotov cocktails to hit the trucks and other vehicles. The intent was to make the entire assault last less than 20 minutes, enough to do damage and force them to start calling in their patrols to defend the facility. Of course, by the time they arrived, the attackers would flee into the countryside, leaving nothing but chaos and mayhem behind.

There was more to the plan. The New Hampshire National Guard had positioned some of their armored fighting vehicles in the town of

Belmont. After the attackers unleashed their assault, they would flee to Belmont, hoping that the Newmerica forces would pursue. If they did, they would face something they had not seen since invading the state, an actual stand-up battle with the National Guard.

Su-Hui was assisted by a young private from the National Guard, Mark Abernathy. They had done some shooting together on the range in Lisbon. He was young, almost the same age as his son Akio. Abernathy had wild blonde hair and was overly anxious, at least in Su-Hui's mind. *He craves the excitement of battle where I am content to do my part and get out alive.* A part of him admired Abernathy's enthusiasm for the cause, but at the same time it served as a reminder that he was more mature than his partner, in some ways vastly older. *I wish I had his energy at times, his zeal.*

Their position was only 25 yards from the perimeter. They had come in the middle of the night and had hallowed out the deep snow, digging down to the frozen ground. While the snow offered zero physical protection, if anyone fired at them, it did make their heat signatures almost invisible for anyone using infrared gear. He had meticulously dug out a firing hole, just big enough to give him visibility toward two of the barracks. Just beyond that, he saw the rows of vehicles. The rumble of engines told him that some patrols were coming and going through the main gate. From time to time he saw parka-wearing soldiers moving briskly between buildings, doing what they could to minimize their time in the cold. He could appreciate that. His feet felt like pins were sticking in them. *I wonder what this place looks like when all of the snow is gone?*

Abernathy checked his watch. "They said six … it's three minutes to that," he said.

"Relax. It will happen when it happens."

"What if the diversion group didn't make the hook up? What if they are behind schedule?"

Su-Hui looked over at the twenty-year old. "Patience, Mark." His voice rang like that of a seasoned combat veteran. The realization hit him. That's what he had become.

More time passed, far more than three minutes. He didn't check his watch out of concern it would only make his partner even more fidgety. Darkness had enveloped the white countryside, and a stiff wind tore at the pine tree boughs above them. *Maybe he is right; maybe something has gone wrong.*

Then he saw the brilliant crimson flare shoot into the sky over the base. *It's on!* From a distance came the sound of bursts of machine gun fire. Commotion stirred the base. Figures moved to the windows of the barracks and looked out. In the distance came muffled cries in the stark night. One long burst of machine gun fire rang out. *That has to be Trudy* ... he convinced himself, and that made him smile.

Glancing off to his left, he saw the infiltration team had skied up to the fence and were already crawling through; Their backpacks were loaded with death and destruction. The white sheets they wore tucked into their white winter gear made them difficult to spot.

"Now?" Abernathy asked.

Su-Hui shook his head. "We don't want to catch our own people in our field of fire," he said. "So we wait."

An explosion rang out, orange flames casting strange shadows between the buildings. It was hard to say if that was one of the hidden explosives, or if it was one planted by the assault teams. The main training building erupted with its own ball of fire, shattering glass in the distance. Another explosion shook the ground so hard that bits of snow dropped from their little carved igloo and onto both of them.

He wanted to fire, but waited until he saw the figures running back to the hole they had cut in the fence. "Now," he said, catching a grin on his partner's face as he prepared replacement ammo for when Su-Hui ran out.

The M249 made his shoulder ache as he stitched bullets along the third floor of the nearest barracks. Glass shattered and the bullets slammed into the bricks, pulverizing many as they hit. A light flickered out in several rooms. Pivoting hard, he aimed toward another barracks and fired a burst low into the second floor, and then back to another building in the distance. His tracers were arcing yellow in the night as he adjusted his aim, spraying the structure with controlled bursts.

The barrel heated up and began to melt the snow around the opening they had dug. A blur of figures, outlined by the orange flames of the vehicle park, emerged from one of the barracks, and he fired a long burst at them. Two enemies dropped quickly while the others dove for cover out of his line of sight.

"Reload," he commanded. Abernathy moved like a precision machine, getting him ready in a matter of a few steamy breaths. He fired again at the first barracks, blasting out windows. The cracks of gunfire came from everywhere at once as the base seemed to be rallying. Another pair of explosions went off, one sending a ball of crimson and orange flames and black smoke rolling some 100 feet into the air before dissolving into the night.

Su-Hui fired another burst at the second barracks ground floor, all but demolishing a side door and several windows. Flashes came from the upper floors, bursts of gunfire no doubt aimed at him. He responded with his own bursts, chiseling away at the brick exterior and into the rooms beyond.

A metallic thunk hit the ammo container, and Abernathy let out a slight moan. "Damn it, I think I'm hit!" Looking down he saw that a bullet had punched through the almost empty ammo container and had torn the Private's coat. He fired another burst, then turned to Mark. "How bad is it?"

The young man removed the coat with trembling fingers. His shirt sleeve was bloodied and wet from the wound. Mark pulled the sleeve back and it looked more like a nasty cut some four inches long on the lower part of his arm.

Su-Hui turned back and fired another short burst at the building where he had seen the flashes of gunfire. "That's not bad. It's just a light wound. Get your coat on; we need to pull out."

As he carried the heavy M249 out of the back of their little snow fort, he helped Mark stand. They made their way down the long hillside where a pickup truck was idling. He helped his partner into the extended cab; they hoisted the gun into the back, wrapping it in a tarp.

"I can't believe I got shot," Abernathy said, cradling his injured arm.

"You'll be fine," Su Hui assured him as he buckled his youthful partner in. "A few stitches and a little rest. Think of it as your red badge of courage."

"My what?" he asked as the truck turned a corner sharply and accelerated.

"You know, from the book about the Civil War."

Abernathy gave him a blank expression and Su-Hui shook his head in disbelief. *The problem with Americans is that they have a rich culture that few of them take advantage of.* When he came to live there as a refugee, he made a point of reading the great books of American history and the humanities. This wasn't the first time he had found an American youth who had not enjoyed all the arts had to offer.

"You will heal up quickly. It will hurt, but you were lucky. Trust me, I know." As the truck tore off toward Belmont in the blackness of the night, Su-Hui realized that something that should have shocked him just a few short months earlier was now something that he was strangely calm about. *Is this the new normal?*

CHAPTER 14

"Your personal pronoun defines your suffering."

The District

The Vice President-Elect sat alone in the gallery where the execution was going to take place. She convinced Daniel not to attend, that it might make him look oppressive. She had convinced the Chairman of the Ruling Council that people already viewed her as a hard ass, so she would attend in his stead. "Besides, there's no point in both of us witnessing this." *I convinced him that I was taking one for the team, when in reality, it makes him look weak. That is something I may be able to leverage sometime down the road.*

The gallows was painted white, almost making it blend in with the background walls of the room in the basement of the District Central Social Correction Facility. Every sound in the room echoed, making the room seem more ominous … if that was possible. In a basement room of the facility, it was necessary to dig out the floor and lower it to allow room for the gallows. That had delayed the execution for over two weeks as the room was reconfigured and updated for the executions. To her, it was worth the expense and time. *There are a number of others that will swing here before we are done, making this a worthwhile investment.*

The other witnesses to the execution were the members of the People's Tribunal who had passed judgment on the now former Senator. She had the TRC test the various ways that people reacted to the witnesses. The consensus from the test groups was that the witnesses should say nothing, and should look somber and mournful, despite the guilt of the man. She had rehearsed for several minutes, recording herself with her phone and reviewing her planned reaction. The other witnesses were prepped in advance as to how the cameras would capture the emotions, real or otherwise.

Three guards led in Lewis. His jumpsuit hung limp on his body; he had lost even more weight since the last time she had seen him. His cheeks were sunken, and his beard had spread to an uneven sea of stubble all over his face. She watched him being led in, and he was hesitant with his footing, making him look feeble. *We will need to edit that in the footage released to the public. I don't want anything that might generate sympathy for him. We are not executing an old man. We are executing the mastermind of a plot to kill the Ruling Council. The people need to see that, and not see him as being pathetic.*

He was taken up the small set of four stairs to the platform under the gallows. The wire was placed around his neck, tightened just enough so that it pressed into the sagging skin on his neck. The expression on his face was one of resolve, as if he had come to grips with his fate. Slowly his eyes drifted across the small gathering. When he locked gazes with her, his brow furrowed slightly, and the look of resolve morphed into one of defiance.

The Tribunal leader spoke up. "Earl Taft Lewis," he intoned loudly. "In the eyes of the people of this great nation, you have been pronounced guilty of plotting to overthrow the government and assassinate its leadership. The punishment that we Enforcers believe to be just is that you die. You are here to face that sentence, for all to see." He was reading it perfectly from the small index card that had been provided by her writers at the TRC.

Lewis stiffened at the words. "I have something I want to say before you string me up," he announced.

The Vice President-Elect had expected that move on his part. *That was part of your downfall; you were so predictable.* With a single nod to one of the guards, a gag was produced. She had considered a simple cloth one, but had instead insisted on a sex ball gag, black instead of red. The ratchet ball-size ball was thrust into his mouth, and the rubber headband was pulled on tight. Lewis struggled, twisting his head several times, but to little avail. His voice was hopelessly muffled by what he hoped was a humiliating gag.

Once more Lewis locked an icy gaze with her and she only smiled back.

The guards moved off the small platform. "You may execute the sentence," the Tribunal leader said. A lever was thrown, and the platform dropped from under him. His weight took him down, digging the wire deep into his flesh. A rivulet of blood stained the left side of his orange prison jumpsuit, and his Crocs fell on the floor as he twisted and squirmed. His face went red, then almost a purple color. Lewis let out a scream, muffled by the gag to sound something like a high-pitched whine. His legs, still shackled, kicked violently, then slowed; then one of them seemed to quake, twitching as the body spun slowly.

The Vice President-Elect was surprised at how exhilarating it was to watch. *He thought he could challenge me, take me down a notch or two. He never realized that was going to be his undoing.* It was somehow exciting for her to think that one of the last things Earl Lewis saw in his life was not his family or friends, but her, smiling at him as he dropped.

She pulled a handkerchief out of her small purse and dabbed the sweat on her brow. Knowing that one camera would be on her, she dipped her head and shook it slowly, as if she were struggling with the image she had seen. *That will play well with people who think I am heartless. They will see that I can be moved.*

"And we are clear," the producer called from the floor. The lighting in the room went up as the guards moved to Lewis's lifeless body and checked him for a pulse. She rose from her seat and started to file out of the gallery, when her phone vibrated. Picking it up, she glanced at the message.

"Caylee Leatrom spotted in California"

The façade of grief dissolved to one of joy. She had her people in the NSF monitoring for activity involving the woman that had killed her mother and brother … and now they got her. She scrolled through the report and spotted a name she had not expected—that of Deja Jordan. *I was right about her. She is wonderful!* Moving quickly, she got to her limo practically jogging so that she could place the call in private.

"Deja, this is the Vice President-Elect. I understand you ran a query that identified Caylee Leatrom—"

Salem, Virginia

Two days earlier, Grayson Steele had buried his only daughter Maddie. It had been a private ceremony; the Steeles had been living under false identities since the Fall, so inviting family and friends might attract unwanted attention from the authorities. The only outsider to attend was Frank Campbell, the private investigator who had helped them find her.

His wife had asked that her remains be cremated. Grayson had seen her body beforehand, not long after the NSF had confirmed who she was by DNA testing. Some of her was missing, and the investigators apologized for that, saying that animals sometimes took bones miles away. The skeletal form he saw on the stainless steel table was not Madison, not the Maddie he knew. It was just a body … her soul, well, that was elsewhere. That daughter was the one that drew her gun and fought back against those that were going to kill her. In his mind, he played out that scene repeatedly, remembering the area where he had discovered their bodies in every disgusting detail. In that moment he resolved to find the people responsible for murdering his daughter and the others, and to kill them.

He knew revenge was wrong, that it was like a cancer, consuming a part of him, but he no longer cared. Detective Schrank knew what he was thinking when he led him out of the medical examiner's office. "Mr. Steele, you need to let the law handle this." Grayson had only stared back at him. *They are not going to do anything—they already admitted that. These Social Enforcers are beyond the reach of the NSF. The Commonwealth Attorneys won't prosecute them. The whole system is corrupt. I have to do this myself.*

His son David had shed a few silent tears, whereas his wife sobbed over the closed coffin. Grayson remained stoic, rigid. He had shed his tears in a field in Broadway, Virginia. He held his wife and son close, almost painfully. As they finished, the family turned away from Maddie's remains. Frank Campbell made eye contact with him, and as his wife and son left, Grayson stayed behind.

"I didn't know you owned a suit," he said.

Frank looked at his sleeves and then back to him. "The job requires me to blend into a lot of places." He paused. "I'm sorry for your loss."

Grayson nodded once. His face felt heavy. As he lifted his head once more, he locked gazes with his friend. "I'm going to go after them."

Campbell nodded. "I thought you might."

"Someone has to be held accountable," he said. The lawyer in him screamed for some sort of justice, regardless of its form. "From what the NSF told me, they recovered twenty-two bodies out of that ravine. Some had been there for years. A few will never be identified. The monsters that did this have murdered over and over again. It was a game to them. Clarice was lucky. She and a few others managed to get out alive."

"She wasn't lucky," Frank said. "Your daughter made her escape happen. Madison saved her life."

"I'm doing this for Maddie."

"Are you? I've seen the look on your face and on the faces of other people. I'm not going to try to convince you that you're doing the wrong thing … I know that is a waste of time. All I ask is that you don't lie to yourself, Grayson. This is about vengeance and blood. Madison would not have wanted it. I never knew her, but I have met your wife, and she didn't raise a cold-blooded killer; neither did you. I need you to accept that this is something that *you* want."

Grayson stood more erect. Frank was right, and that hurt. It was easier to do this in Maddie's name. It somehow made it more palatable. The PI was correct though; this was about filling the hole in *his* life. "Damn it—you're right. This is about me. I need to do this. If I don't, they will kill again. The NSF isn't going to do anything about them. The whole legal system is broken. So yes Frank. This isn't about Maddie— it's about me setting things right."

The short private eye nodded. "Good. Most men can't own up to the bullshit they tell others. The fact you did means that you are still a human being, not a murderer. You still have a shred of decency in you. I don't help killers. I help good people who do the right thing." He reached into his suit jacket and pulled out a folded pack of paper, extending it to Grayson.

He opened the five pages and saw names, photocopies of faces, details like home towns. "What am I looking at?"

"Those are the *Grays*, the SE group on campus that is responsible for what happened to Maddie and the others. In the bodies that were identified, there were three members from their little club in with the others—shot and beaten from what they could tell from the bones."

"How did you get this?" he said, looking up from the papers to Frank.

"Detective Schrank," he said. "It's easy to lump all of the NSF together and say they are dysfunctional, but that's a mistake. He's a good cop; he's just trapped in an organization that is corrupt. I met with him, told him what I wanted, and he gave it to me … he said he'd treat it as a FOIA (Freedom of Information Act) request."

"If I go after them, he'll know it was me," he said cautiously.

"Probably. He's a father too Grayson. He can't appear to be helping you, but he will look the other way I think."

Grayson folded the pages and put them in his own suitcoat. "Thank you for this Frank. You didn't have to do it."

"Yes I did," he replied. "All it takes for bad people to do bad things is for good men to do nothing."

"I think you got that quote wrong, but I appreciate it."

Frank shrugged, then took a half-step closer to him. "Whatever you are going to do, you need to be sure you don't make a big enough mess that they are forced to come after you. You'll need some sort of accident or way to cover up what you're going to do. If you walk in on one of their meetings and shoot them up, the NSF will be forced to come after you."

His words were good consolation. "How in the hell am I going to do that?"

"You're a smart man," Frank said. "You'll figure something out. Just do me a favor."

"What's that?"

"Don't lose yourself in the hate."

"What do you mean?"

"You don't see it yet, but you will. It will come for you, the hate. Don't let it blind you, and don't let it consume you."

Newmerica Penitentiary, Administrative Maximum Facility Florence, Colorado

Deja's desk phone chirped for her attention, and she saw the number was from the District. "Hello," she said, wondering who would be reaching out to her.

"Deja, this is the Vice President-Elect. I understand you ran a query that identified Caylee Leatrom."

She sat up more rigid in her tiny little office in the prison. *The Vice President is calling me!* The excitement was more than she had expected when she had trudged through the frigid Colorado winter into the Supermax earlier. "Yes ma'am," she replied, gathering herself.

"How did you come by this?"

"The people in that image. They kidnapped Maria Lopez, Raul's sister, out of Social Quarantine in California. The images are blurry, but there was a high probability that one of those people is Caylee Leatrom." Her heart was pounding in her chest as her mind rushed with thoughts that her digging had attracted the attention of the Vice President-Elect. "I believe that she was the person that assisted Lopez in escaping Newmerica as well."

There was no response for several long seconds, to the point where she wondered if they had been cut off. She was about to ask, "Are you still there?" when the voice came back.

"It appears that you and I share the same obsession. You were looking for her, and I have been too." "I know she posted some documents on the Internet," Deja said. She knew it was unwise to go into the details—the woman on the other end of the phone was also the Secretary of the NSF.

"That was only part of the crimes this person has committed against the state," she said in a low tone.

She paused again, then continued. "What I am about to tell you has never been made public; nor can it be. Understood?"

"Of course."

"This woman killed my mother and brother," she said solemnly.

The words hit Deja hard. *No wonder she called. My God. This Leatrom woman is a murderer!* She considered for a moment how she would feel if someone had killed her mother. *What kind of a person would do such a thing?* "That—that's just terrible."

"She was one of our best agents," the Vice President-Elect said. "Then she turned traitor. I shouldn't be surprised that she is somehow involved with Raul Lopez. Evil people like them naturally attract each other."

"She was living with him when we took him into custody," Deja added.

There was a third pause from the Vice President-Elect. "Deja, you finding her is a stroke of luck, but I think it is more than that—it confirms everything I think about you. This Leatrom is a very dangerous person. When she worked in the NSF, she was the person we gave our most difficult assignments to. Her skills are remarkable. She is a killing machine though. You were fortunate enough to survive tangling with her."

Raul had said that this Caylee would kill her. Now she understood that his words were not a threat, but a warning. "Thank you."

"No, thank you. She will finally pay for what she did to me. You are giving us a fantastic opportunity."

"Ma'am?"

"Don't you see? Leatrom has some sort of connection to Lopez; otherwise why go after his sister? She is going to come for him. He's our leverage. She's going to come to you."

"This is the Supermax prison," Deja said. "No one can break out or in."

"*She* can," her voice said with complete confidence. "More importantly, she will try."

"She's not alone," Deja said. "There is at least this woman working with her. They also somehow overrode the cell tower and impersonated an SE commander to pull off the kidnapping. So there is someone else working with her as well."

"So they went to a lot of effort to get his sister. They must have assumed you would be using her for leverage against him."

"That's correct," Deja replied. She was starting to realize that Caylee Leatrom was even more dangerous. *She has a team of people working with her. She knew that if she simply came and rescued Raul, we would still have his sister to use against him. The VP is right; she is going to come for him.* In that moment, the security of the Supermax didn't seem nearly as impregnable as it had a few minutes earlier.

"That gives us an advantage. For months I have hoped to find her; now we know where she will come."

"We can use Lopez as bait."

"Exactly! I am going to send a pair of our best people, people with the same skill sets and training as Leatrom. I want you to work with them.

I want you to set a trap. When Caylee shows up, I want her apprehended. I would prefer to get her alive, but I am willing to be, shall I say, flexible on that point."

Deja understood completely. The Vice President-Elect had carefully avoided using the word 'operative' because officially, that program didn't exist. But the people she was sending were just like Caylee Leatrom, which meant she was sending in operatives. *People like Leatrom wouldn't go down without a fight. We will need the help.*

"I will do whatever is necessary," she said.

"I know you will Deja. We are bound by our secrets. You now know mine—that Caylee took my family from me. Secrets shared run deep as blood … you understand that, don't you?"

"Yes," she said, honored to have been so trusted.

"Good. If you assist in the capture of Leatrom, you will be an even greater hero to the people of Newmerica. You have proven again your gift at detective work. A simple promotion will not suffice. When this is over, you will sit on top of the SE organization. We need leaders like you, strong and smart women of color."

Deja felt the blush wash over her face. "I won't fail you. If she comes here, I will take her down myself."

"Excellent. I will have my people contact you when they arrive. Make sure that they get whatever they need. This is not just personal. It is a matter of national security."

"Thank you ma'am."

"No Deja, thank you." The line went dead.

Deja was in a tornado of thoughts. *She trusts me! Me … a nobody from Minneapolis. And now a real promotion, to a position of true power! All I have to do is capture this Caylee-person. It should be easy. She has no idea we will be waiting for her.*

As she calmed slightly, she thought more about the conversation that she just had. In the back of her mind, she knew the documents that Caylee posted had exposed the operative program. *Were they really lies?* She wondered why Caylee had killed the Vice President-Elect's mother and brother. *Why not simply kill her? She has the skills; the VP all but said that.* Deja also mulled over how anyone could consider breaking someone out of the Supermax. *There's no way in or out of here. That's why it exists, to hold people forever.*

As she settled back in her seat, the lumbar support pushed hard into her lower back; she suddenly wondered where the rescue attempt would come from, and how big the body count might be before it was over. *This isn't going to be a cakewalk, not by a long shot. Caylee has a team, and so will we. The only real advantage we have is that we know where they are coming, not when or how.*

The biggest advantage was more simple for her to digest. *I have Raul Lopez.*

CHAPTER 15

*"Guns, religion and racism are the greatest
killers in the history of humankind."*

Cañon City, Colorado

The townhome Travis had rented for the team was three stories
tall, giving them a great deal of privacy and a good family room
space to work in. The stiff cold winds whipping through Cañon
City made the older windows frost slightly around the edges. The local
mountains attracted skiers years ago, but after the Fall, many had been
forced to close as people were no longer able to afford such luxury
vacations. The rolling COVID lockdown mandates were the final nails
in the city's coffin. It had allowed them to rent the townhouse for almost
nothing. The owner was simply happy to have tenants ... no questions
asked.

At one time she might have thought of the downtown as quaint. Now
it was mostly empty. Unlike bigger cities, where the evidence of riots
and looting were visible, none of that violence came to Cañon City, at
least none that she had seen. It had suffered from the economic downturn
that had followed the coup. The Ruling Council blamed it all on their
usual scapegoats, the Traitor President or COVID. A lot of people simply
accepted those as the root causes. It was easier than acknowledging
that the overthrow of the government had been the driving force in the
economic downfall. *The majority of people simply believe what the
media and the government tell them.*

I am not like most people. Higher taxes cost jobs. Paying people's
unemployment at record levels encourages them not to work. Every

variant of COVID that was used to instill fear in people was simply another nail in the coffin of small businesses. There was no one cause that led to the economic downturn. There were hundreds of them, all linked to the coup and the FedGov.

In some respects, the townhouse reminded Caylee of the home she and Raul shared at Arnold Air Force Base, though with more voices. She remembered watching television with him on the well-worn couch, eating pizza, even laughing at times. It was the first time in years that she had allowed herself time to relax, unwind, and a part of her still yearned for it. She would never admit it out loud though … not even to these people, now her closest friends.

Charli, under the guise of Dana, had been in the prison for nearly two weeks. The intelligence that she had gathered was invaluable, if not daunting. All of them studied the bodycam footage that Charli had gathered, memorizing walkways and paths. She had been able to confirm that Raul was being held in Unit J, a cell block for political prisoners. While the cell affronted them more freedoms than the other inmates of the Supermax, there was no time when they were ever brought outside of the unit.

As they ate tacos that Andy had prepared, she wanted a plan. For her, there was a point where gathering intel became less useful. A plan would allow them to structure their thinking and to focus on specific challenges with the breakout. "So how do we operationalize all of this?" she asked, taking a bite out of a taco, narrowly catching some of the contents that tried to escape the back of the tortilla shell.

Travis spoke up. "Initially, my thought was to blow holes out of the facility; get him to a chopper we would land on the grounds outside the perimeter; get the whole team out. Having seen the wall structures in the videos, the defensive issues—I think we need to nuke that idea."

"Agreed," Charli said, poking at the salad she had put the taco meat on. "Even if I could disable the security systems, there are too many barriers between the unit and freedom."

Andy came in from the kitchen area and took a seat. "But we still have to disable the security system, right?"

"Yes," Charli said. "I know where the servers are. If I can get in there, we could destroy the servers. The control of the cameras will be toast, though most will stay on and continue to run on their local backup batteries. The key is that the monitoring room itself will likely go down too, so even if the cameras are running, no one will be able to see them. Of course, that means we need to be able to get into the server room, destroy the servers, and get out."

"I've been thinking about that," Travis said, pulling out a black Sharpie pen.

"A pen?" Andy asked.

"It's filled with plastic explosive, Semtex to be specific. "Easy to smuggle in. Every day, you bring a pen with you, leave it in your locker or desk."

"You brought that to the table?" Andy asked.

Everyone else chuckled. "Andy, it's perfectly safe until it is detonated," Travis assured him. "I even left in the tip so that you can use it for writing, just not a lot. It should pass any security check." He handed it to Charli who held it, uncapped it, and then recapped it. "It's heavier than a normal pen, but it will work," she said, handing it back.

"How much do we need?" Caylee asked.

"One should get me through the door to the server room; then it is a matter of blowing the room."

"I'll get to work on that. I'm still working on the detonator too."

"Good," Caylee said, reining in the conversation tactfully. "So we have the means to take down the security systems. The doors will go into automatic lock-mode, but the guards will be partially blinded. So where do we go from there?"

"I assume a tunnel is out of the question. If you can't go down, and you can't go out at the ground level, why not go up?" Andy offered.

For a moment, everyone looked at him, thinking about what he said. Caylee suddenly appreciated having Andy there for a great deal more than his cooking ability. *Sometimes it takes an amateur to see things we can overlook.* She then turned to Charli. "Can we land a chopper on the roof?"

Charli paused, her brow wrinkled in deep thought, her eyes narrowed. After a few moments of silence, she spoke up. "There are antennae on the roof, and poles mounted with cameras. They will interfere with the rotors."

Travis beamed. "If I can get some det cord, someone can wrap it around the bases of that stuff. One quick little detonation, and those things will go right over."

"What's det cord?" Andy asked.

"It's a flexible cable filled with explosives. You can wrap it around stuff; then set it off. It's a way to shape explosive charges," Travis replied. "Fun stuff to play with."

"I have no idea as to whether the roof can support the weight of a helicopter," Charli said. "And so far, I haven't seen the access to the roof."

"That can be addressed," Caylee said, focusing intently on the idea. "Assuming you can get to the roof, we should be able to take down any obstructions. If we bring in a helicopter, it will come under fire from the towers."

Charli nodded. "In orientation, they told me they have shoulder-launched anti-aircraft missiles in at least one of the towers. If a helicopter comes in, it will be susceptible to gun fire and possibly a missile or two."

Travis shifted in his chair, clearly getting excited by the possibilities of the plan. "We can arm the chopper. Before it lands, it can blast the towers first, then land on the roof for the extraction."

Caylee mentally processed the elements of the plan. "Raul and the rest of us don't have to get exposed trying to get him out of prison on the ground ... that's the big appeal. Going that route introduces too many variables that bump up the risk. Taking him up to the roof, we only have to worry about the guards that are in Unit J at the time of the breakout."

"There are a minimum of ten guards in any unit at any time," Charli said. "All armed. On top of that, the unit assignments rotate. If I am in position to disable the security systems, I'm not in Unit J to deal with the extraction."

"With a timer on the detonator, you can be," Travis said. "Pop the door lock with a small charge. Plant the explosives on the servers; then leave. You can get to the unit and be far away from the servers when they are taken out."

Charli nodded, taking another bite of her taco salad as Caylee pondered the outstanding issues. "We are left with the guards in the unit, any one of which can throw a wrench into our extraction."

"Assuming I get to Unit J before the automatic lockdown happens when the servers die, the odds are still roughly ten to one."

There has to be a way to take out all of the guards, something that will not raise a red flag and alert them that a breakout is coming. This was a complicated barrier to Raul's freedom because shooting and sheer firepower would not necessarily solve the issue. Incapacitating the guards all at the same relative time required creativity.

An idea came to the former operative, something subtle. "Talk to me about lunch," she asked Charli.

"Fairly simple. We eat before and around the prisoners meals in alternating shifts. We aren't allowed to bring any food in so as to prevent us from smuggling in any contraband."

"So your food is prepared on-site?"

"Technically, yes. Unlike most prisons, we don't use the prisoners in food prep—too risky given the people we have there. A kitchen staff prepares our meals. We go to a separate admin building and get 45 minutes to eat; then we rotate back to the units. The prisoners' food is brought to them."

"What are you thinking Caylee?" Travis asked.

"Poison," she said in a low tone. Andy's mouth slowly dropped open with the word, so she quickly clarified her idea. "We don't need anything lethal, but something that will incapacitate the guards. Chances are pretty good they all get some food and drink on their break. We somehow lace their food supply with something that takes a little while to activate. If they start dropping immediately, it will raise too many flags. We introduce a poison into their food that takes a short time to kick in, something that might make them think it is simply something bad in their food. While they are scrambling for the bathroom stalls, they won't make the connection that their illness is tied to a breakout. It might actually help us with the guard towers too, if they get the same food."

There was a long half-minute of silence before Charli shattered it. "It might just work. Figuring out how to introduce the poison will be tricky, but they do give us the month's menu in advance."

"We can taint the food before it even comes into the prison," Caylee said. "If we do it right, the guards will assume that they all have gotten explosive diarrhea from the outsourced kitchen staff. If nothing else, it limits the number of guards that are able to respond, and those that do may be struggling with symptoms of what they will assume is a stomach bug."

"This sounds like a plan that might actually work," Andy said.

"We will need to layer this; put up contingency plans," Travis said, the Navy Seal training showing itself. "There's a lot of moving parts to this. Something is bound to go to shit. And we may need to modify it. On the whole, it's a framework."

Caylee cracked a grin. "It's risky, but doable. A lot depends on timing, our air asset, and good luck. At the same time, having someone on the inside, it has a good chance of working." She took another bite of a taco. Her mind went to Raul. *I promised I would take care of you. And I will.*

Concord, New Hampshire

General Donaldson bent slightly to pin the Purple Heart medal on the pillow of the injured soldier. The woman was asleep. He had insisted on not rousing her for the act. She was one of the dozens of wounded and dead from the battles at Pembroke and Belmont three nights earlier. The corporal's face was bandaged and her legs were in casts. From what he had been told, her Bradley had been one of the first on the scene at Belmont, chasing the insurgents that had struck at the training facility in Pembroke. They had run into a perfectly staged ambush. *There was no way that I could have foreseen that happening.*

The officer in command at Pembroke, Major Henry Rhea, was already being charged with dereliction of duty for his failure to have a more robust defensive position. There had been calls from the government to hold someone accountable, and Donaldson was more than willing to serve up his subordinate. He knew that only some of the blame could be leveled at him. *After the attack where I was wounded, he should have had more troops on the perimeter—better defenses.* In the pit of his stomach, he knew that the attack still would have happened though. Pembroke was designed as a campus for training, not a forward fire base. *They wanted someone's head on a platter, and it wasn't going to be mine.*

His people had pursued the attackers all of the way to Belmont. *Where stage two of this clusterfuck unfolded.* The New Hampshire National

Guard had been hiding for the most part since the invasion—refusing to engage his forces in a straight-up battle. They had found the occasional tank or armored vehicle, but for the most part it was as if they had simply become part of the rolling hills and forests that made up the state.

There was no reason to expect them to sortie a squadron of armored vehicles the way they had at Belmont. When his lead vehicles arrived, they were wiped out quickly from a perfectly staged ambush. They hadn't even managed to signal the rest of the pursuit force about what they had run into. The fighting there lasted less than an hour, and while there were losses on both sides, there was no way the General could paint the situation as anything short of a defeat.

The Army Chief of Staff had called him personally, as had the commander of what was now referred to as Continental Army Command—a Newmerican designation. While they wanted to know what he needed in terms of support, the fact that they had called at all was a bad indication. *They aren't confident that I have this in-hand. No one in the Army calls when things are going right.*

None of this is my fault, he thought as he softly limped away from the wounded soldier and to the next bed where the soldier was awake. *There was no way that I could have known that the New Hampshire National Guard was going to show up in Belmont—they had been hiding for us for weeks.* As he bent down and pinned the medal on the next wounded warrior, he shook the young private's hand and thanked him.

He finished handing out medals and walked slowly out of the hospital ward. He hated hospitals, and this was no exception. It wasn't the slight sting of disinfectants lingering in the air or the dull wall colors; it was the thought that these were the places where people went to die. He remembered spending hours in one when his mother had slowly died of lung cancer some eight years ago. He had hated hospitals then, and now they only served as monuments to his defeats.

He had told his superiors that he needed more troops on the ground. He wanted satellite coverage, but that was proving impossible. The Pentagon was unwilling to give either side in the civil war access to their intelligence satellites. Besides, most of the satellites were trained on the Russians and the Chinese. He did get a commitment of several Predator drones though, which was a welcome sign of support.

Donaldson knew that the defeats he had weathered and the siege in Atlanta were working against him. They want quick results, but neither situation seemed to offer that. *Up here, I can't kill what I can't find. Down in Atlanta, the enemy is refusing to come at us—they are opting to starve us out.*

His new G2, Captain Andrea Burnside, approached him. "Sir, one of the prisoners that we captured is conscious now."

"Take me," he said, following her through the hospital. They arrived at a bed where an older man, in his 40s, was handcuffed to his gurney. At his side was an armed guard who snapped to attention as Donaldson entered the room. The prisoner was badly burned; his arms were wrapped in gauze and his graying hair was mostly gone; the top of his head was wrapped in bandages.

"This is Jackson Turley," Captain Burnside said. "He is from New Jersey."

"I am General Donaldson," he said, leaning over the injured man.

Turley's eyes narrowed. "I know who you are. We all do," he uttered through gritted teeth.

"Then you know what I am capable of."

Turley tried to shift, but it was obvious from the way he winced that any motion put him in pain. "You going to let me get better for the firing squad, or are you going to prop me up and shoot me right now?"

"Where are the Sons of Liberty?"

The man forced a chuckle, despite the agony. "We are everywhere. We operate in cells. By now even you know that. I don't know where everyone is; no one does."

"Where's your cell operating out of?"

"Fuck off," he spat back.

His words felt like a slap to the face. "I don't think you understand your situation Mr. Turley. You are an insurgent, rising up against the rightful government. You're a terrorist traitor that killed loyal troops on the ground. I'm not bound by rules and regulations when it comes to how I treat you."

"You've betrayed your word," Turley said. "The President of the United States is your Commander in Chief five years ago. If anyone's the traitor here, it's you."

Donaldson knew that he didn't have to respond to what the injured man said, but the words he spoke dug deep. "What I am doing is what is right for the people."

"Of what country?" Turley asked. "Newmerica? It's all a big lie. The military turned their backs on the last President when he called them in to defend Washington. I'm not a terrorist. I'm a patriot!" He paused, coughing for several seconds. Each jerk of his body clearly was causing him more pain.

"I want answers. Where did your cell operate out of?"

"Bite me."

Donaldson reached down to his burned arm, grasping the gauze tightly, and squeezed. Turley's body tensed as the ripples of pain shot through him. Sweat formed on the parts of his face that weren't bandaged and his skin went red. He moaned, loud, but struggling only made matters worse for him.

"Tell me what I want to know and this can come to an end."

Jackson Turley said nothing; he only stared intently at Donaldson, a glare of pure defiance. *These people are so misguided, so ignorant of what they are fighting for.* He squeezed the burned arm again, this time with both hands, much tighter. Turley growled as his jaw set. Donaldson held on for almost a minute, as if he were massaging the arm.

As he let go, he could see and hear the man on the gurney breathing fast and heavy, his pillow showing signs of sweat from where he had twisted. "Just tell me where your friends are, and this will stop. Otherwise I can have these bandages removed and we can rub a little salt on your burns." He paused for a moment and then added a little more pressure. "I will order you tortured to death if I have to. You are doing this to yourself. Just talk."

Donaldson turned his eyes to the burned legs. As he started to reach for them, Turley uttered a single word. "Stop."

"Where are they Mr. Turley?"

"I am a prisoner of war!" he fired back with another squeeze of his arm. Donaldson could feel a wetness oozing through the bandage, but he refused to loosen his grip.

"No, you are a domestic terrorist who has earned this pain." He gave another twist of his wrist, making Turley cry out. Tears ran down the proud man's cheeks.

The betrayal was almost as bad for Turley as the pain Donaldson had inflicted. It showed on his face. "Lisbon," he uttered, barely audible. "A few of the cells are in Lisbon."

General Donaldson smiled. "See, that wasn't so hard." Turning to Captain Burnside, he said. "Have him taken outside and form a firing squad."

"Sir?"

"You fucking bastard!" Turley called out from the bed.

"I'm not going to waste medical treatment on a terrorist."

"You said this would come to an end!" Turley said. "You lied!"

"It will come to an end, yours," he said casually, turning away from the man. *Now you know the price of questioning my honor.* "If it's any consolation, your death will ultimately save lives. Once we squash your cell, less of my forces will be sniped at or blown up by your misguided insurgency."

"Captain, I want you to gather information on Lisbon. I'm not going to rush our people into an ambush. Be discreet and quiet. This is only one of their bases, but when we go in, I want to give our forces the victory they deserve."

Captain Burnside saluted, saying, "Yes sir," and then left to make the necessary arrangements. As Donaldson started to walk out, Turley fired one more verbal volley. "You can't win," he called out. "We'll come for you eventually you asshole! We'll come for your family if we have to. You will pay for your treason!"

Donaldson ignored the cries as he left the room. *What Jackson Turley thinks doesn't matter. In just a few minutes, he will be dead. And in a few days, so will his traitorous comrades.*

Lisbon, New Hampshire

Su-Hui joined the huddle of members of the Sons of Liberty that centered around Randy Birdsell. The long-closed storefronts of the businesses on the main street of Lisbon were bustling with activity, which was a sign to Su-Hui that another operation was being planned. After the last mission, everyone was excited to be a part of the next attack on the Newmericans.

The attack in Pembroke and the ambush in Belmont had been big news. It was hard for the TRC to entirely cover it up, and the news that came out of the Southern White House about the attack labeled Su-Hui and the others as 'patriots of the highest order'. He liked the sound of that, despite the oddness of it all. *Newmerica was responsible for the fall of my homeland. I came here as a refugee, and now I am a patriot.* Life, it seemed, had taken him on a long and strange voyage to end up in New Hampshire. As bizarre as it seemed, there was only one thing he wished he could change … what had happened to his daughter, Ya-ting.

Randy climbed up on a chair so that his voice would carry. "I've just gotten back from a meeting with General Griffiths. We both agree that we need another big operation to stir the shitpot that General Donaldson is currently in." His words elicited a chuckle from the SOL members gathered around him.

Randy beamed at their happiness. "We need to remind Newmerica that this is not just about the fate of New Hampshire … this is about the entire country. Another attack outside of the state will force Donaldson to divert resources elsewhere and will send a little more fear into the surrounding states that this war can and will come to them."

There were murmurs and nods of agreement. "What's the target?" Valerie Turner asked.

"Waterbury, Vermont," Randy said. "The NSF state police headquarters there."

"That's a long ways from here," another voice, that of Cheryl Kramer, said.

"Around 70 miles one way, cross-country," Randy replied. "We will use our snowmobiles and a refueling operation, as well as some ski forces who will throw off any defenders with a little diversion in Montpelier. Our raiding force will not only hit the headquarters, but raid their armory there."

"I think we'll need more snowmobiles," Su-Hui stated. "We lost two on the Pembroke attack."

"We are already outfitting them," Randy said. "And we are going to make sure that the ones we have are up to the long trip."

Randy paused, giving the people a chance to process what he had just said. "I know this sounds complicated, but I assured the General that we are more than up to it. He didn't give me the details, but I got the impression that New York and Maine might be getting the same treatment from other cells.

"We have already humiliated Donaldson, several times in fact. He will be wanting some revenge, but we don't intend to give him that chance. If we move fast … strike hard … the invasion force is going to be pressured to regroup or even pull out. We owe it to the good people of New Hampshire to not only try this, but to pull it off."

Su-Hui was in agreement. In his short time in the Republic of China Army, he knew a bit about strategy. To him, it felt as if the two sides squaring off in New Hampshire were playing two different games. *The Newmericans are playing Go. They are trying to hold territory. We are playing chess, attempting to remove pieces from the board.* The difference of play was intriguing and deadly. *At some point they will figure out what game we are playing, and if we haven't crippled them by then, we will be facing a superior opponent.*

"Our diversionary force will stir things up in Montpelier. The NSF will send most of their force to protect the state capital, which will allow the *real* attack to take place at their headquarters." It seemed simple enough to Su-Hui, but he knew things could unravel quickly, especially in a mission that required coordinating and timing.

Randy went over the details, gathering input from the SOL members there. Su-Hui and Trudy would be going out again for the attack on the state police headquarters. For almost 2 hours the plans were reviewed, routes planned and contingencies rehearsed. When they finished, he retired down to the basement of the laundromat. He and Hachi had a small space where they slept. It was little more than a few tarps to separate them from the surrounding beds. The privacy was nearly non-existent, but they had learned over time to tune out the sounds from the others sleeping in the basement.

Two old tunnels led from the basement to the frigid Ammonoosuc River behind the building. From what he had been told, they had been used by bootleggers back during prohibition to smuggle liquor to the river where waiting rafts would take it to other communities. His and Hachi's room was next to one of the doors for the tunnels, which the SOL had converted into a makeshift armory and a possible emergency exit. Su-Hui liked being that close to a way out of the building, in case the Newmericans ever attacked.

He told her he would be leaving in two days, but offered her only scant details. He had come to understand that the more he told her, the more she worried. "Why always you? They always want you to go."

"I didn't go on the ambushes last week at all," he said. There had been two IED attacks on the Newmericans, and he had stayed behind.

"You know what I mean," Hachi pressed. "They send you on the dangerous missions."

"They are all dangerous," he said.

"Some more than others," she countered.

Su-Hui smiled. "I will be fine," he said, trying to convince her of it. "They have no idea what we are planning."

Hachi was unconvinced. He could read that on her face. "When you go out, I am left here alone. I don't sleep well knowing you are out there. I keep busy, cleaning, helping in the mess hall, but most of the time, I am left here to sit and wait."

Hearing the words from his beloved wife, he understood her worry over him. Su-Hui put his hand around her shoulders and pulled her close as he sat on the bed. "After this mission, I will ask Randy for some time off. Perhaps we can leave this place, relax a little."

"I think that is a good idea," she said, hugging him back.

"It's a date then," he said, kissing her on the cheek. "As soon as I get back."

CHAPTER 16

"Freedom is taking advantage of the security offered you."

Charlottesville, Virginia

Grayson Steele stared at the laptop screen in the darkness of the apartment, holding back his frustration. They had rented the small apartment in town, a few blocks from campus so that he could work to track down the Grays, the group responsible for the murder of his daughter. He had managed to identify several of the students from surveillance on campus, but following them to and from class had not given him any insights into the Grays. It had been both exhausting and frustrating.

The problem seemed to be rooted in the fact that the Grays were a secret society. The University of Virginia had always had a history of secretive societies on campus, rivaling Harvard and Yale for such institutions. Some UVAs dated back to the campus starting operations in 1825. Some, such as T.I.L.K.A. used 'mystic words' as a layer of security. All were, by their very nature, secret—with members closely protecting their membership. A few, like the Sons and Daughters of Liberty, had been disbanded after the Fall when patriotism and links to America's past had become equated to racism and hatred. There was video footage of Social Enforcers beating some of them and chasing the others off campus ... hailed as 'a move against racism'. *Young people killing and beating others just because they don't like their politics ... it is disgusting.*

The Grays were relative newcomers on campus, a dangerous and toxic blend of the historical secret society and student social enforcement. They had a simple gray flag that was waved during protests, something that would not offend anyone. While Grayson had a list of their members, he never seemed to even determine where the group met. Such a meeting would be the best time to implement any vengeance he might care to inflict.

David spoke up from behind him, startling him. "You won't find them this way," his son said, resting his hand on the back of the chair.

"What are you doing up?"

"Looking over your shoulder," his son responded in a low tone so his voice wouldn't carry to the bedroom. "You'll never find them this way. They aren't going to leave a digital footprint."

"David, you should go to bed," he urged.

"No. She wasn't just your daughter—she was my sister," he said flatly, as if all emotion had been drained from him.

"This is dangerous—what I'm planning."

"I know. And I'm going to help."

"You can't."

David crossed his arms. "I will. I'm not a kid any more. I'm seventeen, almost eighteen. We have been forced into hiding a big chunk of my life because of people like this. Worse, they killed my sister and are getting away with it. You can't find the Grays and when they meet because you stand out on campus like fly on a wedding cake. I can blend in."

David's point was something he had not considered. Grayson was in his early 40s and, like most people, he didn't like to think of himself as aging. *I probably looked like a lost professor wandering around campus, or worse, some sort of pedophile, stalking young coeds. He's right. I don't fit in there.* "David, these people are not some social group. They are mass murderers. I've already lost one child to them. I can't risk losing you."

"This is my fight too Dad," he said, his voice rising slightly as he spoke. It hit Grayson that this was the most emotion he had shown in weeks. *We have been so focused on finding Maddie and then finding her killers, that I didn't notice what this had done to him.*

"You're right," he conceded. "Maddie was your sister. They took her from you as well. But the risks are high."

"I know," he said firmly. "The reality is you can't do this alone. You've tried, but it hasn't gotten you anywhere. I know that the NSF has swept this under the rug. There's no one that will fight for Maddie other than us. The only way she will ever get justice is if we do it. Even if you do manage to locate them, you're one person. You don't stand a chance alone. I can help ... I have to." His voice was on the edge of pleading.

Grayson knew it was bad parenting. His wife would be upset too. At the same time, he understood how his son felt. It was the same emotions he felt—the desire to do something, to make sure that Maddie's death had not been in vain. As he looked back and looked up at his son, he saw not the young boy of his memories, but a young man ... one that had lived in secrecy and fear most of his mature life.

He wanted to say *no*, but he couldn't. Would Maddie want him to involve David? He knew she would. *I raised both of the kids to be independent.* They are both strong-willed, Maddie was a little more so than David, but they both were headstrong. Deep down, Grayson knew that if he told David, 'no,' he was going to do it anyway—that was clear in his defiant stance.

"Alright David," he finally said in a firm but low tone of voice so as not to wake his wife. "There's some rules. We work together on this—I don't want you taking action without my knowledge. Understood?"

David nodded. "Understood."

"So what's your thinking on how to find these Grays?"

David leaned back slightly. "You won't find anything by following them during the day on campus. Groups like this, they meet late at night or on the weekends. That's part of how they stay secret. I say we pick one or two of the names and focus on them. I will need to befriend one or more of them. They need to bring us into their confidence. Sooner or later they will lead us to where they meet."

As much as Grayson wanted to shoot holes in the idea, it made sense. *David won't say it; he's right; I have been a fool trying to follow them in broad daylight.* "Okay. Once we track down where and when they meet, we will need to figure out how to deal with them." He avoided using the word, 'kill,' but it was implied.

"I have some ideas on that too," David said.

Grayson looked up at his son with new appreciation and respect.

In that moment, he knew he and his wife had raised their children right and had done so in a nation that wanted to ship them off to some camp or see them dead. His wife would balk at the idea, but eventually come around to him using David. Most importantly, Maddie would want him involved … she'd want me to take his help.

Stone Mountain, Georgia

"The Chief of Staff on Tac One," the communications officer said from his seat in the back of the Bradley mobile HQ.

This can't be good. Since he had begun the campaign, he had been sending the President reports of his progress, but Jack Desmond had been true to his word. He had not interfered or micromanaged him. He had contacted him a few times for short briefings, merely asking questions. This wasn't one of those scheduled calls, which might spell trouble for Trip.

For the last few days, he had been personally reviewing the Stone Mountain region as a potential battlefield if he managed to lure out the Newmerican forces. The ground was good. It favored his deployment of artillery and use of armored vehicles. A part of him wanted to evacuate the locals as his troops dug in, but he didn't want to signal his preparations to Atlanta if they could be avoided.

"Jack," he said as he switched to the first channel.

"Trip," came back Desmond's voice. "I hate to interrupt you, but a new situation has just popped up."

"Go on."

"Yesterday, three counties in Texas proclaimed secession from America and are calling themselves the Republic of Texas. We've heard rumbles about it for some time, but it seemed to be just a few loud voices. Well, we sent in the state police to assert our authority, and they opened up on them with missiles and machine guns. Groups of armed citizens seized the county and state government offices with little opposition. We're not sure if that is a sign that the population supports them, or if they were simply caught off guard and are waiting to see how all of this plays out. They have declared a no-fly zone and are enforcing it."

"Enforcing it how?"

"Surface-to-God-damn-air-missiles!" Jack spat back.

Damn it! Trip was from Texas and understood the yearning to be a separate country. It was a matter of deep pride in the state that they had once been their own nation before joining the United States, and a number of people felt they would be better off doing so. His mind danced with the threat it might pose. *The timing of all of this couldn't be worse, which smacks of outside influence.* "You said they had missiles?"

"Yes," Desmond replied.

"Which counties?"

There was a pause for a moment, and then his voice came back. "Wilbarger, Ochiltree, and Dallam, so far. All up in the north part of the state. We've kept it out of the press, but chances are the TRC will be running with the story soon. The President is going to make a statement to get in front of this saying it's a few malcontents and that we seek to end this situation peacefully. In reality, it's a bit of a standoff right now."

Trip's mind was processing the situation from a military perspective. "Sir, there are no armories in those counties."

"Go on."

"So, where in the hell did they get surface-to-air missiles and machine guns?"

"Trip, I assure you, I have no idea."

Reager paused, leaning back in the seat. *It's damned peculiar for them to pull this stunt right now. And where did they get that kind of firepower?* Some groups, like Texit, had been advocating for Texas to become a sovereign nation for some time—not through open rebellion—but by ballots and conscious decision. This didn't feel like their handiwork, not unless they had a dramatic change of strategy. *They certainly have never advocated violence.*

"What do you need from me?" Trip finally asked.

"You're from Texas. These are your people. Sooner or later I'd like you to meet with them. We need to diffuse this situation. We can't have Texas rise up as a nation state."

"I'm a bit tied up at the moment," Trip conceded. "We got word from some of our SOL people that the Newmericans may be nibbling on the bait that I dangled in front of them. New Hampshire is going to be escalating their operations as well. The timing of this sucks … which makes me think it may be deliberate."

"Understood. Until you resolve Atlanta, it is still your top priority. At the same time, we need a show of force, but not a major confrontation— just a sign that we take this seriously."

"We have the diversionary task force we sent into Missouri. We just pulled them back. We can get them on trains and get them to deploy on friendly ground, something visible."

"Good," Jack said, clearly relieved at the words Trip had given him. "I fear you're going to need to get hands-on with them before this is over."

"In the meantime, there's something that you can do."

"Go ahead."

"There's no arsenals in those counties. If they really do have missiles and heavy machine guns, they got them from somewhere. If you can do some digging into that, it may help."

Desmond didn't respond for a moment. "You think they have help?"

"There's something fishy in this. Texans love to talk independence, but it's not reached this point in a while. It doesn't feel right to me. And with that firepower, they have to be getting it from somewhere."

"You're thinking Newmerica."

"That or our enemies abroad, or both," Trip acknowledged. "Someone is spurring them on."

"Let me get some of our intelligence people to poke at that *and* where they are with finances."

"Follow the money."

"Good call General."

"In the meantime, I will cut orders in the next hour to get our task force to move out. Tell the President that he will get a show of force."

"Thank you Trip," Jack said, "I couldn't ask for more. If I learn anything else, I'll let you know."

"Roger that," he said, cutting off the line.

Trip reached for his thermal cup and took a sip of coffee from it. *Someone is messing with us. I'll be damned if I solve this Atlanta issue only to lose part of Texas in the bargain.*

Philadelphia, Pennsylvania

The Federal Philadelphia Prison was an ugly building, a stark, tall, block-wide structure that towered up some nine stories. Normally, officials of her status did not come to such places, but the Vice President-Elect wanted to savor this visit with an old comrade.

The Bureau of Prisons fell under her prevue as the Secretary of the NSF. So that she would enjoy some privacy, she ordered the rest of the cell block moved, so that she could visit her former ally with a degree of privacy. She could have ordered her transferred to the District, but this was more fun, more humiliating. *She'll hate me seeing her here, as a prisoner, behind bars. It will make our time together all the better.*

The Vice President-Elect had a great deal to be thankful for. She had gotten word that her investment in a Texas revolt was finally starting to bear fruit. There was no real care if the little rebellion against America was successful or not; the fact that they had to deal with it was enough. *Besides, it will play well on the net and with the new media. People will start to doubt if America under the Pretender President can hold out. Doubt can be a powerful comrade in arms if applied properly.*

Daniel had agreed with her plan but tried to give himself some plausible deniability with the operation. "Go and handle it—I would prefer not to be updated on it." She knew the game; it was one she had played hundreds of times before. If the uprising was successful, he could claim he was in the loop and approved it. If it failed horribly, he would dodge the responsibility and try to put her head on the chopping block. *I'm not the fool everyone played me for when I first came to Congress. I know exactly what they will try if this falls apart.*

Daniel was struggling with decisions that were squarely his anyway. The siege of Atlanta was on the verge of being a humanitarian and military disaster. While her TRC staff had done an admirable job of selling the public on the idea that the blame for the suffering was the work of the Pretender President and Bloodbath Reager, polls told her that the belief in the story was waning. *They are moving past who is to blame and focusing on the disaster ... exactly what we don't want them to do.*

New Hampshire was yet another debacle. The Battle of Belmont had been a defeat, despite the fact that the media had claimed it was a stunning Newmerican victory. The reality of dead soldiers starting to come back to their homes was something that could not be obscured by simple media and Internet manipulation. *We need to begin the process of determining whose going to be held responsible for this. Daniel will certainly dodge the blame, push it down. So it's really a matter of finding the right head for the chopping block and waiting until the next failure.*

As the two guards led her down the cell block, she noted the chipped paint on the bars and walls, and the aroma, the smell of sweat, made her wince slightly as she walked in her Christian Louboutin pumps on a floor that she knew would need to be scrubbed from their soles. It was a fitting place for the prisoner, a place she had earned.

She came in front of the cell and dismissed the guards. The woman sat on the edge of her bunk. Her once perfectly styled hair was now cut short; *probably by a blind barber from the looks of it.* She wore dull gray prison scrubs with dirty orange Crocs on her feet. For a full minute, she didn't lift her head. The prisoner's head rose and her eyes widened when she saw the Vice President-Elect standing in front of her narrow cell door.

"You," Rebecca Clarke, the former Director of the Truth Reconciliation Committee, growled when she saw her. She slowly rose to her feet, putting her hands on the bars of the cell door. "I should have known that you would come here at some point. I suppose you're here to gloat."

She smiled back at her old colleague, knowing that her grin would cut like a knife. "Becky, you look simply awful."

"I'm doing just fine," she lied with a hint of bold pride. "So why are you here?"

"I take it you saw Earl Lewis's Tribunal," she said, countering pride with her own vanity.

"I saw enough of it," she replied. "Enough to know that you faked the evidence against him … and me."

"I have no idea what you are talking about," she said casually. She almost believed it herself. "The bombing of the Capitol could have very well killed me. I was merely a victim in this entire nasty business."

"You have never been a *real* victim Alex," she snarled back. "Oh, you've wrapped yourself in that cloak from time to time. You whipped up tears when it played well for the camera. You even dropped all of the right words to pretend to be a victim. Even I will concede that. But you have never truly been a victim. You've just worn that label when it was convenient for you."

She ignored Becky's assessment. "I came down here today to tell you that your Tribunal will be starting soon."

"You came all of the way down here to tell me that?" Becky said in disbelief. "How touching."

"You can knock off the bitterness Becky," she said. "And yes, I did come down here. Some of it was to see you, to see how far you've fallen. I'd be lying to say that I don't find it enjoyable. I wish I'd brought my phone in … I'd love to have a photo of you in those prison Crocs."

"Maybe one day you'll get a pair of your own."

"Doubtful," she said. "Very shortly I will be sworn in as the Vice President. You, on the other hand, will be facing a very difficult proposition. You saw the execution of Lewis, so you know what is inevitably waiting for you."

"The piano wire was a nice touch, very Third-Reichish of you," Becky slapped her with a nasty comparison. "I bet you loved watching him twitch up there."

"I hated it," she lied back. "I have come to realize that I would hate to see you like that, struggling for air, the wire cutting into your skin like that. You've always had wonderful skin—you know. I was actually jealous of it."

She paused for a moment. Then the tone of her voice dropped an octave. "We've known each other since the Liberation. Watching the Senator die, well, that was justice. In fairness, I barely knew him. But you and I have been there ever since the start, ever since the murder of Congress and the Senate."

The mention of that night seemed to give Becky some pause. For a few moments she said nothing. "We both have blood on our hands. Mine is old and dry—yours is still fresh. But you still haven't said why you are really here."

Still defiant—I almost admire that. "Becky, you've seen the evidence that we chose to release during the Lewis Tribunal. Sadly, for you, there's more. If it is put out, everyone out there that had any doubts about your involvement in the assassination attempt will see you as an active participant."

Becky didn't respond; she merely scowled back at her.

"Anyways, Daniel and I spoke about it. We are both concerned about you—"

With those words Becky laughed. "I bet."

The Vice President-Elect continued as if the interruption had never occurred. "He pointed out that you have been with us from the start. You played an important role in the Liberation and the Great Reformation. Even though you were led into this plot to kill us, you still have a long history with us, unlike Earl Lewis. He suggested that I offer you an alternative to what Lewis faced."

"An alternative?"

"A full confession from you, admitting that you were dragged into this plot by the Pretender President and his people. Naming names of course would allow you a better fate. I will provide you a list of suggested guilty parties to make it easy for you. I could arrange for the Tribunal to simply lock you up for the rest of your life. If they do push for death, well, there are ways to die like lethal injection that would be far less painful and humiliating."

Becky nodded, drinking in the words. "You know that I am innocent. I know that I'm innocent. You wouldn't make this offer if it wasn't of benefit to you. I'm willing to bet that showing video of an old man strangling to death didn't play well with the people."

She's sharp, still on her game. So much the better. "Why this offer is being made to you is none of your concern. The offer is there. If I were you, I'd confess. You saw that execution—that's what's waiting for you. It's a messy way to die, unable to get air, choking to death, the wire cutting into your skin." Her words were slow, hanging in the air between them like the tolling of a bell.

"I don't want to die like that," she said. "But not enough to help you and Daniel. Not enough to lie and confess to something I didn't do."

"Your guilt has already been established."

"You mean fabricated," Becky snapped back.

The Vice President-Elect crossed her arms and forced a smile to her face, something that Becky could not refute. "I tried to help you, and you've refused. You will have time to think it over before the Tribunal meets. Given your skill at crafting words, I'm sure you can create a confession that meets our needs and spares the government any embarrassment. If not, well then," she said, taking a step closer to the cell door. "I will see you swing."

CHAPTER 17

"Prisons are racist."

Newmerica Penitentiary, Administrative Maximum Facility
Florence, Colorado

Deja Jordan didn't recognize the two guards that walked up to her. One was a tall male, muscular but thin. His female companion was shorter than Deja, of Asian heritage, with fair skin, a thick neck and the chest of a body builder. "Ms. Jordan," the male said, "We need to talk."

She ushered them into a nearby empty break room used by the guards. "What can I do for you?"

"We are with the NSF," the male said. "We're here because there's a high probability of Caylee Leatrom attempting to penetrate this facility. I'm Dominic Gant and this is Rita Zhang."

They didn't extend their hands; nor did Deja. "I was told by the VP that she would be sending people."

"So we were told," Rita said. "We will be routinely working in Unit J."

"Is there anything I need to do?"

"We are discreetly informing select guards posted to Lopez's unit about who we are. We have, shall I say, a unique set of skills. If something does go down, we will be taking point on it. All we ask is that you go about your normal routine, but if something happens, follow our lead and orders." Dominic said.

"Are two of you going to be enough?" Deja asked.

They looked at each other; then looked back to her. "More than enough," Rita assured her.

I wish I had your confidence—it would help me sleep at night. "Is there anything I should be on the lookout for?"

Dominic nodded. "Anything out of the normal pattern. Keep your eyes on Lopez since he's the target of any penetration that is attempted."

"I meet with him almost daily," she said.

"Has he shown any signs recently that he may have had contact with Leatrom?" Dominic asked.

"Signs?"

"You know, is he suddenly happier, perhaps a bit more confident?"

"No. Why?"

Rita weighed in. "If she is coming here to get him out, she may get word to him, to make sure that he's prepared. We want to be on the lookout for that."

"No, I haven't noticed any change in him."

"Good. Leatrom is good, *very* good. She is an expert at tradecraft. So she can disguise herself to get in here. Keep your eyes peeled for anyone that is behaving out of the ordinary in even the slightest way. Any strangers, regardless of how they appear, should be reported. If you see *anything*, pass it on to us."

Shit! It never dawned on Deja that Leatrom might simply walk into the prison disguised as someone else. *These operatives are dangerous people; they don't think or act like the rest of us.* The nightmares she had about Caylee Leatrom coming for her had not subsided. Now that these operatives were here, the nightmares were bound to increase. Ripples of paranoia ran up and down her spine as she listened to them. "How will she get him out of here?" Deja asked. "This place is more than a normal prison. It's impossible to overcome all of the security Lopez has around him."

Rita responded for the pair. "In our line of work, we don't believe in the impossible."

"Damn," she said out loud. "Sorry, I mean, it feels like we should have more security."

"Introducing a new number of guards or layers of protection won't stop her," Dominic said. "If anything, it gives her something she might be able to exploit. This facility's pattern has been effective, so we don't want to change it. What we have working for us right now is that she doesn't know we are on to her. It's our intent to exploit that."

Will that be enough? Deja didn't have to wonder how Leatrom would react because she had seen her before in Ohio. She was an artistic killer, moving with such speed and skill that she was a literal killing machine. While Dominic and Rita were operatives as well, she wondered if they were up to facing Caylee.

One thing was for sure: Her nightmares were only going to increase with their arrival at the prison.

Waterbury, Vermont

The headquarters of the NSF state police was an immense structure, three stories tall, surrounded by massive snow banks and thick pines. The roof of the structure was spiked with antennae and dishes, no doubt to coordinate the Vermont State Police. The parking lot and walkways were clear, and they were clearly unguarded. Su-Hui understood that thinking. After all, it was some 60 plus miles away from any of the fighting. *They possess an aura of safety here. To them, the war is somewhere else, far away. They don't see themselves as a target because they are not military.* To him and the others, that didn't matter. They represented the authority of Newmerica. The NSF was a symbol of oppression to many, cloaked in a veil of security. *Whether they like it or not, tonight, they are a target.*

There had been a buzz of activity a half-hour earlier as the diversionary force opened up in nearby Montpelier. The rumble of distant explosions shook off of the hillsides and made some snow fall from pine boughs. A half-dozen vehicles tore out of the headquarters, heading to the Vermont state capital to aid in its defense.

Trudy kept the snowmobile off, along with the other attackers, waiting for the go-signal. One of the snowmobiles turned over, its engine purring, and the others followed suit. *This is it,* Su-Hui thought as he felt the throbbing of the snowmobile come to life under him. He swung the machine gun around and prepared to fire.

They didn't rush in; they didn't have to. Coming down the hill toward the parking lot, they split their formation, half going one way, half the other. They avoided the parking lot pavement, but stuck to the snow, coming up alongside the building.

"Now," Trudy barked, one hand cupping the earpiece where she was getting he orders out of.

Su-Hui opened fire, aiming first at the camera array above the main entrance and riddling the first floor windows with short, little bursts. One of the other snowmobiles fired a more sustained stream of bullets into the main lobby, shattering glass and sending sparks from ricochets into the early evening darkness.

A pair of the attackers dismounted and rushed toward the building. They struggled for several minutes to light their Molotov Cocktails leaving them dangerously exposed. Once the rag fuses were lit, one cocktail went into the main lobby of the structure, lighting it up brilliantly. The other went through one of the shattered windows, making the room erupt in orange flames.

A warning siren went off, and one machine gun riddled a visible speaker with a burst. Su-Hui aimed at the upper floor windows, shattering each one in rapid succession. The two comrades that had thrown the fire bombs went back and got several more, throwing them into the structure as well. Some were tossed through windows. Other were lobbed at the exterior of the building, lighting it up brilliantly.

Trudy reached up and tapped him on the left shin. "Second wave," she yelled, accelerating the snowmobile to a side entrance. Su-Hui fired a sustained burst into the door lock and handle mechanism, turning it into worthless metal in a matter of moments. Climbing down from his seat, he grabbed his AK-47 and headed to the door, accompanied by three more of the attackers. They threw back the door, weapons aimed, but there were no targets. The other attackers still on the outside were peppering the headquarters with more machine gun fire.

Entering the interior, his senses were alive with adrenaline and fear surging in his veins. He poked his head down the hall and saw a state police trooper running toward them in tactical gear. Su-Hui recoiled, dropped to his knees, then angled out again, firing at the man.

The NSF officer fired, but his aim was too high. Bits of cinderblock dust fell on Sui-Hui as he fired, hitting the man square in the chest. His body armor may have stopped the bullets penetration, but the kinetic energy could not be ignored. The force of the impacts knocked the man back, sending his helmet flying down the hall. Another one of the SOL darted out to him, firing a shot into the man's pistol hand as he lay on the green carpeted floor. It wasn't enough to kill him, but he wouldn't be firing a gun anytime soon.

There were sounds all around him, and echoes of distant gunfire were heard elsewhere inside and outside of the building. The taint of fired shots lingered as he approached the injured trooper that was moaning and trying to hold his hand that splattered blood everywhere. A haze hung in the air as Su-Hui moved forward, almost numb to what was going on around him.

They moved down the hall until they found an emergency evacuation map. It showed the layout of the building. One of the attackers surveyed it for a minute. Then Sui-Hui recognized him as Mark Abernathy, his green and black corporal's stripes were freshly sown on his winter coat. "Down the hall, first left, then first right," he ordered. The trio sprinted to the corner, angling around it for a quick glimpse. A makeshift barricade of a folding table had been hastily thrown in front of the armory, and two troopers were behind it. The moment they were exposed, the hallway erupted with gunfire. Su-Hui's ears already throbbed from the fire, but now the bullets were aimed at him.

Abernathy pulled a hand grenade out and made sure that everyone knew what he was planning. Silently pulling the pin, he tossed it around the corner, and there was another burst of gunfire. Suddenly the entire building rocked as the explosion went off, throwing bits of the table into the intersection past where Su-Hui squatted. Smoke rolled out, and the sprinkler system started spraying water everywhere as he jutted out, firing a long burst toward the doorway.

One of the troopers was already dead; his body was draped over the now decimated table/blockade. The other trooper held his hands up. The woman was short, pudgy, and had a drizzle of blood coming out of one nostril. "Don't shoot—I surrender!" she said, tossing her gun to the floor.

Abernathy rushed forward and grabbed her, tossing her face first onto the blasted and torn carpet. "Get in and grab explosives and the heavy stuff," he barked. Su-Hui shouldered his weapon and entered the vault-like armory. It wasn't as large as he had expected, but was packed with cases of ammunition, racks filled with automatic weapons, etc. He found a case of grenades, which was incredibly heavy. Somehow he managed to adjust it enough to wrap his small fingers under the box and hoist it out. Struggling with it, he made his way back into the hall where the injured state trooper had somehow managed to crawl and prop himself up against a wall, moaning in pain. "Who are you people?" he moaned.

"We're the good guys," Su-Hui replied as he passed the man and reached the brisk air of the outdoors.

The gunfire against the building was still coming from half of the snowmobiles. The bursts tore into the holes where the windows had been, savaging the inside. When he got to the snowmobile with the crate of grenades, Trudy looked at him with amazement. "That's too damn heavy. You gotta get rid of some of those, yah?" she said, her UP accent ringing loud. Glancing at her, he saw her offer a rare smile.

For a moment, Su-Hui was unsure what to do. Trudy sensed it and wrenched off the lid. The grenades were inside and she pulled one out, pulled the pin and threw it through a third story open window. A massive whomp came back a few moments later, showering the white snow with bits of debris.

Su-Hui took his cue from her, pulling a grenade himself. He threw it into a first story window, and it went off with a loud blast that billowed smoke from the hole, followed by a rush of orange and yellow flames that flared for a second, then disappeared.

He grabbed another and threw it at a second story window, but his aim was off and it hit the metallic sill. The grenade dropped and plunged into a snowbank. "Grenade!" Trudy howled as she dove for cover, with Su-Hui following her. They hit the snow and there was a muffled explosion; big chunks of snow rained on them.

His face was wet from the snow as he got up and saw the crater at the base of the building. Reaching for the grenades to throw another, Trudy grabbed his wrist and stopped him. "You've had your fun. I used to play softball. I'll get rid of a couple more; then we are out of here," she said smiling.

Private Abernathy came running out of the building in a full sprint, followed by another explosion deep in the structure. The roof of the building, some 20 yards down from Su-Hui's snowmobile, shot up on a pillar of fire and destruction, and rained bits of debris all around them in the snow. Flames roared from the damage lighting up the entire area with dancing shadows of light. Su-Hui checked his watch and barked out, "Time to roll people!" Instantly people started to move to their rides.

Su-Hui climbed aboard the rear machine gun mount and made sure he still had plenty of ammunition. As he reloaded, he noticed that after the last muffled explosion of a grenade in the headquarters, the sounds seemed to stop, other than the crackle of the fires that were now raging inside. Trudy used bungie cords to secure the grenades. It was a rush job, and he held the small crate in place with his feet as she fired up the snowmobile.

As they raced away, Su-Hui glanced back into the night while the wail of fire trucks grew closer. The building was bellowing smoke into the darkness, blotting out the stars as the flames lapped skyward. He was satisfied with what he saw—the destruction was utter and they had caught the NSF completely unaware.

It will be a long time before they consider tangling with us again ...

Lisbon, New Hampshire

General James Donaldson was poised some two miles from Lisbon, New Hampshire, but he could monitor the tiny town on nine flat screens in his command post. In the pre-dawn hours, it was almost hard to make out the town from where he was; there were so few dots of light coming from it. He had been told that the local economy had all but collapsed. There was supposed to be hardly anyone there. But there were people, around fifty right in the middle of downtown. At least that was what infrared readings said. That told him he was in the right place. *This is one of the Sons of Liberty's bases. We've caught them flat-footed.*

From above an unseen Predator Drone, he had a top-down view of the old brick buildings, covered in snow. Even in the complete darkness, the drone's live-feed was almost pristine, outlining all of the main structures. Plenty of heat signatures were coming from the buildings, showing people moving about the boarded up structures—all the proof he needed that this was indeed, one of the bases of the Sons of Liberty.

As much as Donaldson wanted prisoners to interrogate and parade on television as proof of a victory, he wanted the victory itself far more. This was going to be the day that he proved to everyone that had whispered behind his back that he was the General that could get the job done.

The naysayers will have to kiss my ass by the end of the day.

The attack on Lisbon was to be coordinated with a breakout from the siege of Atlanta. General Kotter had informed him that the enemy defenses to the east of the city were an empty shell, and that the American commander was concentrated to the south and north, protecting his command and control center in Alpharetta. Rather than starve to death, the bulk of the soldiers and SEs in Atlanta would break out of the siege and wheel north once they got on open ground. It was risky, but it was better than the slow starvation that loomed for the citizens that remained in the city.

Meanwhile, Donaldson himself would lead in the assault on Lisbon. Some of his officers had suggested a less brutal attack than he had planned. They worried about the civilians that might be in the combat zone. Donaldson was not burdened with such thoughts. "If they are there, they have been aiding the enemy. That makes them the enemy." He knew that the only way to shatter civilian support of the insurrection was to make a clear demonstration of the price of supporting that. *What we did in Gorham wasn't harsh enough—cutting off their power. These people thrive on being defiant. Going without electricity was an inconvenience at best. This will be a lesson they won't forget.*

"Sir, we are ready," Captain Andrea Burnside said from her seat in front of the monitors.

"Let 'em rip," he said with a hint of glee.

The Predator drone unleashed a 500 lb. bomb on the main street's largest structure. The explosion made Donaldson's chest throb as the bomb went off in the middle of the main street. The enormous blast lit up the night sky in the distance and devoured structures on both sides of the road. The debris hadn't finished falling when the artillery barrage started to rain down on Lisbon. Dozens of mortar and light artillery rounds tore into the red brick storefronts and white clapboard buildings that were poised along the Ammonoosuc River. Several cars that had been parked on the streets exploded into balls of fire rolling skyward. Two car alarms blared in the night, set off by the concussion of the blasts that rained down on the small town. They soon shut off as the vehicles were destroyed.

Donaldson wasn't rushing troops in where there might be IEDs or other booby traps. He was first taking advantage of all of the firepower at his disposal. Once the town was destroyed, he would send in squads at dawn to mop up. In the meantime he stared at the screens and remembered the last time he had unleashed such firepower …

Four Years Earlier …
Kirbyville, Arkansas

"Attention. This is Colonel James Donaldson, United States Army. You already know you are surrounded, but what you now need to know is that I have brought a company of armored fighting vehicles with me. By order of the Ruling Council, you are to lay down your arms and surrender."

There was a short pause. Then a voice came back over the hollow that separated the two hills. "Go fuck yourself you damned traitor!"

"You have women and children there. When we come, and we will, they will be injured or killed. Will you at least consider sending them out?"

There was a long pause, one that dragged on for at least three minutes. He tried to put himself in the minds of his opponents.

Looking down, he noticed that he was rubbing his left hand with his right. Once he noticed the gesture, he stopped, confused as to why he had been doing it in the first place.

Donaldson lowered the bull horn and shut it off. "Then we will have to do this the hard way."

The Sheriff stepped forward. "Let me go up there. They know me."

"You've had your chance Sheriff. Talking to them is a waste of time."

"Do you want dead women and children on the television tonight?" the Sheriff snapped.

"Are they hostages? Are they up there against their will?"

The Sheriff shook his head.

"Then they are just as guilty as the parents." Donaldson turned to the Lieutenant Colonel of the 10th Mountain Division. "You may begin your bombardment—artillery and mortars at this time. No one advances without my authorization."

The Lieutenant Colonel gave him a slow nod and began to bark out orders. The metallic 'thunk' of mortar tubes on the backside of the hill went off like a dull organ, followed moments later by the compound erupting in explosions. Some rounds hit the trees, splintering them. One cabin was directly hit; its roof blew into bits that showered the ground.

The artillery below joined the cavalcade of death; the massive, ground-shaking booms sent high explosive carnage at the compound. The explosions and smoke were so thick that Donaldson could barely make out anything on the hilltop. An underground propane tank was hit, sending a column of fire raging skyward. The ground throbbed under Colonel Donaldson as the barrage continued. He saw no need to stop it, not until he was sure that the gun nuts were dead or unable to respond.

For 45 minutes the artillery and mortars roared, churning the hills where the lawbreakers were dug in with a cratered vision of hell itself. He finally ordered the barrage to end. Slowly the smoke lifted, rising like a gray fog. The cabins looked like a jumble of Lincoln Logs, many in flames and all seemingly shattered. The standing tree trucks were jagged, and their limbs and bows were either blown up or still ablaze. The compound was obliterated.

"Send up the armored squadron," he said. "I will go with them."

The Bradleys slowly made their way forward. A few minutes later they were in the devastated landscape. Donaldson and a squad followed them. When they reached the area near the center of the compound, he saw the trenches they had dug. One trench held a blasted corpse. Missing its head and both arms, it was barely discernable as human. The camouflage pants on the body were pitted and smoking from shrapnel.

As he walked a few steps away from the horrific sight, he saw another blasted body, that of what he assumed was a teenaged boy. The blast had torn his intestines apart, and they are draped like a hose out of the foxhole he had been in; it was now a smoldering crater. The stench of his bowels, the stink of human shit, punctuated the smoke in the air and tugged at him. As he glanced down, he saw the paling face of the youth, his mouth open, his bright blue eyes staring blankly toward the sky.

His stomach pitched at the sight and he nearly doubled over, fighting the urge to vomit. It was a battle that he lost, and he ejected the contents of his own stomach, some of it splattering on his pant legs and boots. He wretched several times, rising, then wiping his face was his sleeve. One of the troops looked at him with a mix of pity and disgust, and his glare back at the man was enough to send him walking away. *I've never seen a dead body before, not in real life.* The image of the boy staring skyward burned itself into his memory. *They brought this on themselves.* He began to rub his left hand with his right, not bothering to stop the nervous habit. As he rose erect and looked away from the victim, he saw Daniel Evers of the ATF looking over at him as he carefully stepped over the debris from the attack. Evers made eye contact, and then shook his head in what was clear disgust. *You may hate me, but I was the only one with the courage to bring this standoff to an end.*

The Colonel was convinced that no one could have survived the barrage. As he approached one cabin, he saw several soldiers suddenly jump down into the debris that had been a basement. They struggled to move one of the heavy logs, a job that eventually required five troopers. As the logs were removed, a woman and a small girl came out. Both were filthy; the little girl was trembling. The soldiers slowly helped them out of the hole, and one called for a medic. How they had survived the barrage was beyond Donaldson's comprehension. It shouldn't have been possible.

He approached the adult female. Her hair was singed from fire, her face filled with stunned rage and bitterness. It was clear that her arm was broken; a bit of white bone poked through her skin. Cuts covered her face, and a stream of blood flowed from one of her ears onto her flannel shirt. "Help is on the way."

She spat at him, hitting his face. He wiped the spittle away, but could feel its slight chill in the air. "You bastard!" she wailed, struggling slightly against the soldiers that held her arms.

The little girl lunged at him as well, but he knocked her to the ground. "Sasha!" the older woman called, bending down to the child but unable to reach her because of the soldiers' grip on her. She moaned from the pain in her arm.

"Take them down and have them charged," he said to the soldiers who led the pair away. Donaldson turned and saw the Sheriff standing near him. "My God," the older law enforcement man said, putting his hands on hips and surveying the scene. "What have you done?"

"I enforced the law," the Colonel replied flatly, taking another wipe with his sleeve at the spit on his face. "If you had done your job earlier, none of this would have had to happen."

"Don't try and lay this clusterfuck at my doorstep," the Sheriff said defiantly. "I knew enough to not push good people too far. This is not about me. This is about your response. Look around you Colonel. You've killed women and children up here. And for what? To gather their guns? These people were not terrorists. They hadn't posed a threat to anyone. Most of the stuff they had was antiques, not weapons of war."

"This is a victory for the people. Guns kill people. They had plenty of opportunity to turn themselves in and avoid this. I didn't kill those kids; their parents did. If they had simply complied with the law and common sense, they'd be alive right now."

The Sheriff shook his head. "You keep telling yourself that Colonel," he said.

Lisbon, New Hampshire

General Donaldson lifted his head from the screens. The explosions in the early morning hours became too blurred and obscured from the blasts that were leveling the town. He wanted the town destroyed, erased from the map. Some of the explosions had shifted out from the epicenter of the town, and rubble rained down on the nearby homes and houses. As he moved to where he could get a line of sight on the town, he saw flames and smoke and explosions in the distance.

His mind, for a moment, went back to Kirbyville and the standoff he had brought to a conclusion there. *Sometimes brute force and firepower is the only thing that the enemy understands.* Four survivors had eventually been pulled from the rubble of that standoff—and the adults were all sent to prison or executed for their actions. *I'm not going to give the SOL the same consideration. The survivors will be shot. It's the best way to get across the message about the price of resisting.*

For several long minutes, he watched the explosions going off. One structure, a church, was on fire, and flames roared up the front of the building and the steeple. Watching the carnage unfold was oddly calming to him. *I should have done this earlier. If we knew where they were, I would have. They are terrorists, and the people that help them are just as guilty as the SOL.* He hated to admit it, but it felt good to watch the death he was raining down. *I have lost a lot of men and women to reach this point.* "Sir," Captain Burnside said, coming up next to him as another high explosive blast echoed into the darkness before the dawn. "We just got word … "

"What is it?"

"The SOL—they have hit the NSF headquarters in Waterbury. They've attacked Montpelier too." Her voice was that of stunned surprise with a dab of shock thrown in.

"That's impossible," he said. "We are in the middle of blowing them up here."

"The reports are preliminary, but the Governor of Vermont is already screaming."

"It has to be another cell, not this one. We got them," he said stabbing his finger down the slope of the hill to the explosions going off in the distance. "You saw them—they were in those buildings." A new fear hit him. What if Lisbon *wasn't* a base for the Sons of Liberty? *It has to be. We had a source* … Still, a wave of fear mixed with anger tore at the General. *This can't be another My Lai massacre. I won't be hung out to dry for slaughtering innocent people. I will put guns in the hands of their dead bodies before that happens.*

Another explosion tore at what little was left of Lisbon, the light from the blast catching the corner of his eyes. "Halt the bombardment," he ordered.

God damn it; why can't these terrorists just die!

CHAPTER 18

"There is no crisis or disaster that cannot be blamed on evil men and their twisted beliefs."

*Newmerica Penitentiary, Administrative Maximum Facility
Florence, Colorado*

Dana Bartlett made her way into Captain Harrison's office. For the last week she had been rotated into Unit J as a guard and had been able to get eyes-on with Raul Lopez. She had not tried to make contact with him; she knew that would be far too risky at this point, but confirming he was there was important.

She determined where the roof access was as well, but did not have the clearance to be able to go up and check it out for herself. Bit by bit she was filling in some of the gaps in their plan to break Lopez out. Dana had accumulated over a dozen Sharpie pens filled with explosives, not to mention two detonators that Travis had fashioned to look like innocent packs of cigarettes. The batteries for them had come from the guard's supply cabinet. Despite all of the external security, she had managed to get them past the metal detector thanks to some exceptional design on Travis's part and the use of 3D printed parts. *They don't have to look pretty; they just have to work ...* That was his mantra, and she had come to appreciate it.

She recognized some of the inmates in Unit J. A former Texas Senator that she had presumed long-dead was locked up there, a former Fox News Media figure who sulked in his cell rather than circulating. The others were less recognizable faces. Their files were all secured, unlike the others in the prison, preventing her from getting the whole picture as to who was being held there. In total, thirty-one prisoners were held in custody in Unit J, left to rot well out of the public eye.

Dana knew her role was intelligence gathering, and she did it so smoothly that few would have noticed. One regular guard, Dirk, took smoking breaks almost like clockwork—at 10:30 a.m. and 3:30 p.m. Carmen, another guard, always took off at 4:00 p.m. to call her son— often taking as long as half an hour—to make sure he got home from school safely. She even made notes about what the guards ate for lunch.

She had never been a technical geek, so a lot of her time on the computer was spent learning how to control doors and cameras. Travis had tried to give her some tips for, what she called "hacking," a word Travis said she was abusing. As it turned out, Andy was able to translate into plain English a lot of what Travis told her to do.

She had been called to Captain Harrison's office and presumed it was a routine discussion. Her senses went hot as she entered and saw that they were not alone. Two other guards were there, faces she had only recently seen in the Supermax prison—a tall man and a female who looked more like MMA fighters than a prison guard. "You sent for me sir?"

Harrison nodded. "This is Rita Zhang and Dominic Gant," he said. "I'm assigning them to Unit J with you."

She gave them both a single nod. "I've seen you around. You're new here."

Harrison spoke before the two of them could. "Dana, these two are … well … special agents of a sort, working directly for the Secretary of the NSF."

Rita interjected. "He's trying to avoid the word, 'operative,'" she said.

Operatives! Shit! She wondered for a moment if she had somehow failed, slipped up. There's two of them and Harrison. The odds weren't in her favor, but she quickly calculated her next move if they got aggressive. It took a great deal of restraint to not put her hand on her sidearm. "I thought there wasn't such a thing as an operative."

"Officially there's not," Dominic said. "Obviously what we are talking about is classified."

"Of course," she replied. *Why are operatives here? Has our plan been compromised?* Dana didn't relax internally, but kept up a casual pose for those in the room.

"We're here looking for this person," Rita said, holding up a grainy photo. It was of her, Charli, and Caylee, taken from what appeared to be the Social Quarantine camp where they had rescued Maria Lopez. The image was blurry, and thankfully, her own face was mostly obscured; what was visible, was wearing different prosthetics. Dana took the image in her hands and pretended to study it. "It doesn't look like anyone I've seen," she replied. "Who is she?"

"A rogue operative," Dominic replied. "Her name is Caylee Leatrom, though she may be going by any number of different aliases. She's likely in disguise in this photo—her nose and chin may be different. Dangerous and operating beyond the law. We believe that she is going to try and extract a prisoner from Unit J—one Raul Lopez."

Dana nodded, taking a more intense look at the image, exactly what they would expect her to do. "We should move him to solitary," she said, speaking like a professional guard rather than one of Raul's rescuers.

Rita shook her head. "No. If we do that, we might be tipping her off that we are on to her. Lopez is important, but capturing her is much more important."

Dana handed back the photo. "So how would she get in here? I mean the guards are screened and this place is impenetrable."

"We don't know," Dominic replied. "No system, not even the security here, is perfect. Leatrom is trained to exploit weaknesses. If there's a way in, she'll find it."

"What about the woman she's with," Dana asked. She knew that the best way to throw off suspicion was to do the exact opposite of what people would expect. *If they haven't made the connection yet, they certainly wouldn't expect me to draw attention to it.*

Rita shook her head. "She's a missing NSF officer, name of Angel Frisosky. Have you seen her?"

Dana shook her head. "Sorry. But I'll keep my eyes open."

Captain Harrison stirred a little in his seat. "We are keeping this under tight wraps Dana. There's always the risk of someone working with Leatrom on the inside. You were just cleared during the hiring process, so we know that your background is airtight. I want you to work with these two; give them whatever access and support that they might need."

"Yes sir," she said, giving Rita a nod of espousal. Rita returned the gesture.

"They will be posing as new guards. Show them the ropes, and answer any questions they may have. Whatever they need, you bring it to me, and I will give it to you."

"Understood," she replied. "I guess we should begin with a tour of Unit J," she said. As they left the Captain's office, she considered her options. *Either they know I am working with Caylee and are playing me to get to her, or their story is genuine. This is something that I can leverage in either instance, as long as they don't grab me first.*

One thing was for sure. The escape of Raul Lopez just got a lot more complicated.

Cañon City, Colorado

Andy's second week at the Mixing Bowls in Pueblo, Colorado was an immersion into the world of disgusting. He understood why they had so many job openings once he started work there. Mixing Bowls was a commissary that provided food for large institutions, their largest client being the Supermax prison in nearby Florence. The smells were a constant assault on his ability to work. There were several times, especially when preparing the large cooking pots with barbeque, that he thought he would vomit at the sight of veins and other parts that were mixed in with the meat. His coworkers had laughed at his gagging, telling him that everyone went through it at first and that he would eventually get used to it. The sad part was that they had been right.

When he reached the townhouse that served as their temporary home, he almost immediately stripped off his clothes once inside the front door. His clothing picked up a number of food-related smells, none of which was appreciated by his housemates. Andy carried the clothing to the washing machine, poured on the detergent, and went to his room to pull on running pants and a T-shirt.

He entered the kitchen/dining area where the others were busy assembling sandwiches. "You want me to throw together one for you?" Charli asked.

Andy eyed the ham and salami and winced. "Pass."

"Something wrong?" she pressed.

"I have been working with food that is graded as F. I'm talking meat. Until I got this job, I didn't even know that there was a grading that went that low."

Travis chuckled as he smeared on the honey mustard. "Pretty gross stuff, eh?"

"It would be more humane to kill the prisoners rather than have them eat the stuff we prepare."

Caylee was chewing and when she finished, she hit him with a typically blunt question. "Are you confident yet that you can doctor the food for the guards?"

Andy nodded. "The prisoners get Grade F parts; the Guards get grade C. All kidding aside, their food is prepared separately because it is better … not great, just better. I do prep for the inmates first; then I work with a team of four on the guard's meals—lunch and dinner." There's a lot of time that I am alone—the guys that work there take a full hour for their own meal and go off-site. They don't like the place any more than I do. Our food is prepared in a separate part of the commissary kitchen and—given the slack management—I could have an hour or more alone with the food when we decided to *do it*."

Travis pulled out a mason jar and put it on the dining table. "I secured this, industrial strength bisacodyl. It's the active ingredient in laxatives. This stuff has a binding molecule with it, meaning the guards have an hour or two before it kicks in."

Andy glared at the clear liquid. "Can we please take that off the dining table?"

Travis grinned and moved the bottle to the counter as Charli spoke. "The guards go in three 45 minute shifts for lunch, one right after the other. That means that by 2:30 p.m. or so, they will all be incapacitated."

Travis had taken a bite while she was speaking and began to talk while he was still finishing chewing. "Andy, you can't get this stuff on you. They use a very tiny amount of this stuff in laxatives, diluted. My chemist buddy that got this for us says that if you get a drop of this on your skin, you are going to be in the same condition as the guards."

"Will it hold up to the cooking process?" Andy said. "Or do I put it on after the food is cooked?"

Travis finished his mouthful of food and swallowed. "After would be best."

"That's doable," Andy said, and he began to make his own sandwich.

"There's a wrinkle," Charli said. "I filled in the others already—but the NSF has slipped two operatives in Unit J."

"Shit," Andy said, flopping down into a chair. "I've seen what one operative can do," he said, shooting a glance over at Caylee. "The thought of two of them there is … well … horrible." He turned to Caylee. "No offense."

"None taken."

"Why are they there?" Andy asked.

Charli nodded over toward Caylee. "Her. They got a photo of Caylee and I from the camp. Fortunately they don't have a very clear image of me, but they were able to identify Caylee despite the makeup."

"So," Andy said, pausing for a moment. "They are there to trap her?"

Caylee responded to that question. "You go off and kill the Vice President-Elect's mom and brother, and apparently she takes it personally … go figure," she said with heavy sarcasm. "But to answer your question, yes, they are there to kill or capture me."

"How does that affect our plan?" Andy asked. A part of him wondered if this would put everything on hold, or force a dramatic change of plans.

"It changes nothing," Travis said as he cut his thick sub sandwich diagonally. "We planned on having you poison the food to incapacitate the guards. These two are posing as guards. They will be doubled over in pain like everyone else."

"Not quite," Caylee said.

"What does that mean?" Andy asked.

She eyed him carefully; then she turned to Travis. Andy watched the slow and deliberate turn of her head. "As soon as they see guards rushing to the bathroom, they will suspect that we are making a move."

"Why is that?" Andy probed.

"Because *I* would. "The guards may suspect that something is wrong. These two will definitely piece it together fast. They are hardwired to look for threats … I know."

"So we will have to deal with them," Charli stated.

Caylee shook her head. "Absolutely. If it were me, I would assume that anyone not curled up in a ball from pain is a threat. Charli, if they see you moving around, they will engage you." The casual way that Caylee spoke about someone shooting at Charli was something that Andy was just starting to get used to. *She is so blunt, it's oddly refreshing despite the implications.* Caylee was, as his father would say, *sangfroid.* There was a calmness about her that he admired. No matter what life seemed to throw at her, no matter what the risks, Caylee didn't lose composure.

"Not if I shoot first," Charli said.

"You may have to," Caylee replied in an almost bored tone of voice, as if murdering equaled drinking a bottle of water. "They will have to be fully negated fast, or the plan will be at risk."

Andy finished making his sandwich and then surveyed the room. "I don't want to sound like the guy that is worried about himself, but how do Travis and I get connected with you two," he said looking at Charli. "Caylee is coming in on the helicopter, and Charli is already there. Are we driving somewhere to rendezvous with you?"

Charli spoke up first. "The Supermax has a doctor and two nurses on staff. They eat with the guards. From what I have learned, if there is a major medical emergency, they rely on having local EMS to respond. You will come in posing as EMS. Chances are with the staff crippled in pain, they won't scrutinize you nearly as much. That means you and Travis are in the facility to provide additional support and firepower."

Andy turned to Travis. "You're going to steal an ambulance?"

Travis grinned. "All in a day's work my man."

He felt better, knowing that he would be in the prison with Charli, especially with the new knowledge that a pair of operatives were there. *I'm not sure how much help I can give, but being there makes me feel better. You have to take your victories where you can.*

Newmerica Penitentiary, Administrative Maximum Facility Florence, Colorado

For Raul Lopez, time had little meaning in prison. He could only really judge the time of day by when meals were served, when there was community time, and when Deja Jordan came to interrogate him. When he saw her enter Unit J, he mentally braced for the ordeal. Would it be physical intimidation, or would she threaten Maria? There was no way to know for sure which version of Deja would show up. When he saw her come into the unit, he rose to his feet and prepared for the long walk to the room used for interrogation.

She walked past his cell to Ted's, ordering the escorting guards to open it. They grabbed Ted and pulled him out. The older man didn't struggle, but the guards also didn't make it easy, manhandling him the same way they did Raul as they put him in wrist and leg shackles.

They never came for Ted before ... I wonder why? Ted had told him that he had not been interrogated in years. Raul moved to his door and watched as they led his friend away. Then Deja made eye contact with him, flashing a faint grin. In that moment, Raul realized that they were going to beat Ted as a way to get to him. *No ... that's not right! He hasn't done anything!* That didn't matter. He knew that. They had taken his mother and sister into custody to use as leverage against him. Now his mother was dead because of Social Enforcers like Deja. *It isn't right that Ted is going to suffer because of me!*

As the minutes dragged on, he found himself pacing in his cell. Feeling anxiety about what might be happening to Ted as a result of himself was worse—no different than the tension he felt when being led off by Deja for his own questioning. *Ted can't answer anything because I haven't told him anything. Why would they interrogate him?*

Slowly he understood. *They are doing it to get the reaction they are getting right now. I'm anxious, nervous, pacing. Deja thrives on that. It is her way of knowing that she is getting to me.* Raul remembered the cameras that were on him and the other inmates at all times. No doubt she was watching him right then, savoring his anxiety.

Drawing a long breath, he calmly went to his bunk and laid down, closing his eyes, faking being asleep. *Screw you Deja—you will get no satisfaction from me, not right now.*

It was two hours before the guards brought Ted back. His arm was in a sling, still cuffed to his free hand. His wild hair had been shaved bald. For what reason, Raul could not contemplate. He had a dark purple bruise on his left cheek, spreading up past his gray-ish beard onto his upper cheek. Ted spotted him as they took his leg shackles off and winked at him, which seemed to erase the bulk of the nervousness Raul had felt for his friend.

Deja paused at his cell door and stepped back, per the rules of the prison. "Your friend told us quite a bit Raul," she said, shooting him a smirk. "Talk to you tomorrow."

As she left, Raul whispered Ted's name. "Give me a few," the older man said. "We'll talk during our common time."

A few hours later, the guards opened the cell doors and announced the community time. Raul immediately went to Ted's cell. His bruise had grown to the point where his eye was slightly swollen as a result of the beating he had taken. "I'm sorry they did this to you," he said, helping Ted to his feet.

The older Senator cracked a grin. "I'm more used to being beaten up by the media or my former Senators, but this wasn't entirely new. When I first came here, they would sometimes take me out and hit me just for grins."

"What happened to your arm?"

He glanced down at the sling and his swollen hand. "Sprain. That Deja woman didn't pull her punches. She has serious anger management issues my friend."

"What did they ask you?"

"Not much," he said as they made their way to the staircase that led to the common area one floor below. "She asked me if you had ever mentioned someone named Carlee."

"Caylee."

"Right, Caylee," Ted said as he gingerly took the stairs down to the epoxied concrete floor. "It was hard to hear with a fist connecting with my face. She sure has a hard-on for that woman."

"She's afraid of her," Raul confided. "With good reason."

Ted smiled, forced, but present. "I hate to admit it, but I like the fact that someone in this administration is afraid. They have had years of inflicting fear and pain on others. The thought that one of them is worried, well, I like it."

That was something that Raul appreciated as well. "Caylee is a former operative," he said in a low tone, hoping that their microphones wouldn't pick up his voice. "She flipped against them." Ted held up a hand. "Don't tell me anything else," he said. "First off, they are listening. Second, if you tell me, they will beat the shit out of me to get it. The less I know the better. I'm a politician, but I don't like to lie, even to those assholes."

"She's using you," Raul said. "You're my only friend in his place—and she wanted to hurt you to hurt me."

The older man nodded. "It's an old game Raul," he said. "Tyrants love brute force. She couldn't break you, so she went for your family. When that didn't work, she came for me. It won't stop. ... she can't stop at this point. Even if you told them everything you knew, they would continue to apply pressure to you and those around you. They've had my family in Social Quarantine for a long time. Every now and then they show me photos of them, how they are wearing rags for clothing, how they have lost weight. It's not enough to break a man. It's not enough to humiliate a person. It's not enough to strip him of everything ... his family, friends, or his freedom. You have to hold such men down."

"Why is that?" Raul asked.

Ted smiled, if only a slight expression. "Because if you don't keep them under your heels, they will rise up against you. They will stand up and seek revenge."

"Why not just kill us?"

"Oh, they've done plenty of that. They like wrapping themselves in a cloak of civility. Killing your opposition clearly defines you as a tyrant, and they hate that label. The problem they face is that death is the ultimate way to remove your opponents. They will eventually resort to doing that, mark my words. It's the ultimate expression of power, taking lives."

"Doing what, mass killings?"

"Yes," Ted said. "It is an unstoppable proposition at this point. They have tried everything else and look at what happened. A man they thought they had killed has run for President, and, depending on what camp you are in, won. America, which they thought they had erased, is back once more. They thought they had secured victory, but in reality, the war they ignited is starting to turn against them.

"They will be forced to start killing their enemies, not just on the battlefield, but everywhere they find them—including here. They are afraid that the world will learn what they have done. The fear they have pushed down on others is starting to come back at them. They are worried that if the President down in Tennessee secures his position, they will be brought to justice. All of their dirty little secrets will be public … the world will see them as they really are. So yes, they will slaughter all of the opposition. They have to."

Raul felt numb for a minute. He had seen the insides of a Social Quarantine camp, and he had spent time with the tormented survivors. Raul knew that Caylee had been an operative, that she had killed people for Newmerica. Through all of that, there was a part of him that thought that the government was still run by human beings. He wanted to believe that there were good people still there who, eventually, would do the right thing.

It was all a lie—a lie he allowed himself to embrace. Ted's words made him ashamed of that.

They will slaughter thousands, tens of thousands, just to hold on to power. His mother had died at their hands. To Raul, her death was a horrific wound on his soul. Now he saw it in a different light. She wasn't just a victim, she was a statistic. Ted understand these people. *They will keep killing until they are killed.*

For a few moments, he thought of Caylee. *If you are out there, hurry up! It's just a matter of time before they get fed up with me and do to me what they did to my mother.*

CHAPTER 19

"Some people must be forced to see the values of diversity and inclusiveness."

Stone Mountain, Georgia

General Reager was almost regretting luring the defenders of Atlanta out of the city. He knew it would lead to slaughter and death. They had begun their push in the middle of the night—a composite force of SEs, National Guard, Army regulars that left their posts, and armed citizens. Their armored vehicles slammed into his forces with brutality and surprising efficiency. They pushed hard, hitting his faux line of defense, seeming to drive them into retreat.

Once free of the confines of the autonomous zone, they had surprised him by attempting to drive south, toward the airport. He had anticipated them coming north or west, either at his command and control center in Alpharetta, or toward Stone Mountain. Instead they were initially attempting to secure the airport ... no doubt to attempt to fly in reinforcements. *They caught me with my pants down—I hadn't thought they might try that.*

His solution to the unexpected threat had been one of brute force. Task Force Gleaming collided with the Newmericans in a pitched battle in the Gresham Hills neighborhood before they could reach the airport. The rolling hills and trees were perfect hunting ground for the M1 Abrams tanks. The Georgia National Guard forces made a pitched fight, but once the artillery began raining down on them, they fled, heading north and west. The cost for the battle of Gresham Hills had been high, but he finally had the enemy heading for the grounds where he hoped he could destroy them—Stone Mountain.

The roads leading to Stone Mountain had been cleared of his American forces. They were dug into the dense forested grounds of the vast park there. The prepared positions would protect his forces, but not entirely. This was not a skirmish. This was to be a battle. The rumble of the approaching vehicles marked it as such. Already he had the remains of Task Force Gleaming swinging in behind the enemy, cutting off any chance of them retreating back into Atlanta. *The siege ends here ...*

Trip wanted to be in a tank commander's seat, where he had spent his time in the Middle East. It wasn't that it was a safer position; it was merely the place where he felt most comfortable. Since the events in San Antonio, he had been a leader—hoisted up on a pedestal, both admired and hated by half of the fractured nation. The battle in Chicago had elevated him even further. Reager never sought out promotion and advancement; it seemed to come with the victories. He was a cavalry officer in his heart. Now he led armies instead of following his passions. *We all have our assigned duties ... and this one is mine.*

"Sir," the tactical officer called out from the back of the command Bradley where he sat. His voice shattered Trip's moment of calm. "They are engaging on the right flank, grid G3."

Trip leaned in on the display as the distant throbbing of exploding artillery got his attention. "Very good," was all he said. That grid was near the edge of Howell Lake near what had been Robert E. Lee Boulevard. The roadway had been renamed "Traitor's Way," after the Fall, a mark of bitterness that was hard to ignore. *They are going to skirt the lake because they believe it will protect their flank.* He was poised just off of what had been Stonewall Jackson Drive, now renamed, Sharpton Drive—which ran parallel to Traitor's Way, on the far eastern side of the lake. At only 1,000 feet across, Venable Lake eventually led into the much more expansive Stone Mountain Lake.

What Trip wanted to know was simple: Was this the main thrust of the Newmericans, or had they simply stumbled into his position? "Get me the strength of the enemy there," he asked the lieutenant working at the tactical station.

The officers talked over the comms channel for a minute, and Trip could feel the tension level rise in the back of the Bradley. The lieutenant wheeled around on his stool. "Sir, we are getting overrun. Our forces are redeploying to the south. I can't get an accurate count, but it has to be their main thrust."

Trip's jaw set slightly, and he rubbed his right hand back over the crew cut of the remaining hair on his head. *If they get out past Stone Mountain, they will get into the countryside, and we will have hell to pay to get them rounded up.* "Okay then, it's show time people," he said. "I want artillery brought down on them—have ground observers feed in their coordinates. Moderate rates of fire for now." Leaning forward he looked at the defensive positions. "Let the forces in grid G4 know they have incoming enemy."

A chorus of "Yes sirs" filled the air as he turned. "Comms, message to Colonel Paredes: Get his birds ready. Then get our ground air support up."

"Radar is picking up enemy air support scrambling from Virginia," his air support officer called out from her seat. "Six jets and they are coming in hot."

"Inform our CAP," he said, despite knowing she most likely already had. "Ground command, have our mobile forces pull out of their positions to the south and cut north, head for G4 and G5." His hope was clear—hit the enemy in the flank. While Howell and Venable Lakes would provide some blocking, there were paths around them that his forces could use to drive into the sides of the enemy's main advance.

Outside came the low whoof-whoof of the helicopters of the 36th Combat Aviation Brigade, Captain "Lariat" Paredes's Lakota and Blackhawk helicopters started to spin up in the clearing. Trip had held them back for much of the siege, keeping them hidden for a little aerial surprise. Apparently his opponent had done the same.

Trip moved to the front of the vehicle. "Terry, get us rolling. Head north to Traitor's Way. Then swing us east." *I need to see the battle to win the battle.*

Lisbon, New Hampshire

As sunrise came to Lisbon, General Donaldson got his first clear view from the hilltop. A thin gray haze of smoke clung to what was left of the town that he had shelled the night before. Two buildings were still ablaze, though their flames were now low. One structure was a church that was little more than an empty shell. Its roof was now crushing the smoking pews underneath. The snow, which had been dirty along the streets but stark white everywhere else, was pockmarked with craters and there were bits of black ash and debris from the blown structures everywhere.

The main street brick buildings, where he believed the Sons of Liberty had been operating from, were now festering piles of smoking debris, mounds of brick blasted everywhere. One building façade had been blown into the main street, making it all but *impassable*. The Dollar General near the epicenter of town had been gutted by explosions and fire and little remained of the building itself. Its parking lot was riddled with the burned and melted hulks of what had been cars and trucks. Large craters tore up the blacktop, scattering much of it into the surrounding snowbanks.

Lisbon was gone. Even the private homes and other businesses along the river had been blown up, per his orders. This was not a surgical strike; this was designed to be complete devastation. The SOL had been raiding and striking at will. If the reports he had gotten throughout the night were correct, they had destroyed the NSF HQ in Waterbury and had attacked the state capital building in Montpelier. In order to calm the Governor of Vermont, he had deployed three companies of troops into that state to try to find the raiders. *Sooner or later we will pin them down and finish them off—it really is just a matter of time.* The General wasn't sure if it was the same group that had been using Lisbon as a base, but to Donaldson it didn't matter. *I delivered a blow to them. This will crush their morale.*

This was the kind of victory he wanted, utter and devastating. *All I have to do now is bring in the media. They will film it and I will tell them the story of how this was a terrorist base. The Destruction of this town will serve as a reminder for the rest of the citizens of this damned state. If you harbor the enemy, this will happen to you too.* He savored the moment as the sun started to rise behind him. With no breeze, he could smell the aroma of what seemed to be burning garbage rising slowly out of the devastated town. He heard a dog in the distance, howling in pain. Out of all of the things he had seen, that sound bothered him the most.

Hopefully someone would get down there soon to put it out of its misery.

The communications officer moved beside him, holding a field walkie-talkie. "Sir, it's General Kotter," she said.

Donaldson took the walkie-talkie and toggled it on. "This is Donaldson."

"Sir, this is General Kotter. We have successfully broken out of the city."

More fantastic news! Donaldson beamed. "Have you secured the airport?"

"We could not," Kotter said. "The enemy launched a counterattack with heavy armor and rocket artillery support. We went to our contingency and have headed northwest, into Dekalb County. We are starting to engage the enemy at Stone Mountain, but anticipate breaking through and swinging north."

He had hated to abandon Atlanta, but the position had become untenable. *If we can defeat the American forces in the field, force them to fall back to Alabama, we can get the needed supplies to the city and reinforce it from the air.* Being freed from the shackles of the city had been the heart of his strategy for dealing with Bloodbath Reager. Once in the open country, the odds were going to be even.

If I can hand Reager a defeat on top of what we have done in Lisbon, it would cement his role leading the Newmerican military. I won't need the approval of the Joint Chiefs going forward—President Porter will name me as the Chairman. The thought of being in change of the military once America was finally defeated was something that Donaldson savored. *I will prove them all wrong about me. By the end of the day, they will know the kind of leader I really am!*

Stone Mountain, Georgia

General Reager stepped out of the back of the command Bradley just in time to see the helicopter battle begin over Stone Mountain Lake. Only a few helicopters and crews had joined either side in the civil war so far. Trip had held his back in the fighting for Atlanta, and apparently General Kotter had done the same thing. When he had ordered in Captain "Lariat" Paredes's attack choppers, it had forced his enemy to commit as well.

Paredes had managed to unleash some Hellfire missiles before the enemy arrived, blowing up the initial advance recon force of the Newmericans pushing into the vast park around Stone Mountain. Now Trip could see the helicopters banking and diving with such skill and grace that he didn't think their maneuvers were even possible. One of his Lakotas was hit, spinning wildly as the pilot tried to glide toward the blue waters of the lake. As it splashed hard and deep into the water, Paredes's Blackhawk gutted a gray and black Newmerican Hughes MD 500 Defender, which started to crash, then exploded on the way down, raining burning debris into the trees along the shore.

A Newmerican Lakota dove low, aiming for the entrenched American armor which all fired at. A shoulder-launched Stinger fired by a stalwart infantryman caught it almost head-on, turning the Lakota into a brilliant red and yellow ball of fire that crashed into the trees, lighting up part of the forest just beyond the American positions.

An AH-1Z Viper helicopter, painted in gray, with the current flag of Newmerica emblazoned on its narrow fuselage, unleashed its deadly rotary cannon on the American defensive positions. The tracer fire was so fast it looked like a yellow-crimson laser stabbing at the dug-in infantry, chewing up the ground some 300 yards from Trip's position. Its rockets roared out of their pylons, lighting up one hillside that overlooked the lakeshore. Trip cringed as he watched it bank around over the lake, obviously swinging wide for another pass. A trio of Stinger missiles snaked in the air after it. To the credit of the pilot, the Viper dodged one missile with some fancy last minute maneuvers—but the odds were against it. One missile went off on the right side, with the other taking out the tail rotor assembly. Bits and flaming pieces of the Viper rained down on the Newmerican forces as they reached the woods to the west of the lake. Trip pointed his right fist into his left palm with the hits. *Yes!*

The last Newmerican chopper, a Blackhawk, unleashed a pair of Hellfire missiles downward. At least one found its mark; the explosion of the vehicle made the ground throb around Trip, even though he couldn't see what had been struck.

The Blackhawk made a long arc just a few yards over the lake surface, rippling waves as it roared over the water, searching for another target. Paredes's Blackhawk unleashed its 12.7mm guns, raining bullets and a stream of yellow tracers downward into the craft from above. The rotor assembly of the Newmerican bird made a sickening metallic grinding sound as the rotors seemed to fly apart, flailing outward from the helicopter. The arc of its flight took it cockpit first into the water, flipping it end-over-end until it was upside down. It plunged deep into the water. There was no sign of the crew from where Trip stood.

Another concussion went off to the south, a massive explosion to his far flank. *I know that sound*—it was a 500 lb. bomb. A flashing memory of Afghanistan and calling in air support came rushing to the forefront of his mind. Squinting, he could barely make out the distant ball of flames rising skyward, igniting the trees all around it. *Apparently the combat fighter jets are having less luck than Lariat is having.*

He ducked back into the Bradley command post slamming the hatch behind him. "What's the word from above?" he asked.

His air tactical air control specialist, Lieutenant Balford, turned to him. "The situation is still evolving," he replied as he checked his radar.

"Evolving my ass," Trip said. "That bomb hit our rear area."

As if the pilots above heard him, another rumble went off at the far end of the lake where the advancing Newmerican forces were forming up. Bits of trucks and armored vehicles spiraled skyward on a rising ball of fire and rained down in the distance. *Damn, they are almost on top of us!*

The friendly Blackhawk helicopter unleashed another pair of Hellfires into the distance, the pair of missile explosions devastated another Newmerican armored force probing the lines. Trip hit the button to close the hatch on the Bradley. *I am no good to the fight if we get hit.* He called to the Bradley's driver: "Terry—get us rolling," he said, moving to the map display. "Head to Phase Line Roughrider." The armored vehicle lurched as the driver sped out.

Trip's eyes looked at the tactical display and tried to match what he had seen. The Newmericans were advancing the fight at his force and were giving a *good* fight. "Order all units from G5 to G10 back to Phase Line Roughrider. All other units, hold your positions and provide fire support." He was tossed to the left hard, almost to the point where he fell. Instead, he grabbed his seat and pulled himself into it. Outside of the vehicle, there was another explosion and the sound of bits of metal slamming into the side of the Bradley ... thankfully none of them punching through. *That was close ... too damn close.*

The battlefield was complicated; then again, they all were. Stone Mountain itself was to the west. Traitor's Way ran around the base of the mountain in the distance. Beyond the road, to the south and east was Stone Mountain Lake. Trip's position, as near as he could tell, was near the eastern shore, near the old Stone Mountain campground, now a rundown shell of its once pristine facilities. Phase Line Roughrider was to the north, a solid line of entrenchments that ran from the mountain to the lake's edge. It was an anchor line which Trip had just ordered. One that could not be walked over once fully manned.

Luring in the Newmericans along the western edge of the lake, he had essentially corked a bottle with the phase line. Their only way out was to either break through, or fall back over ground they had already taken. Reager had another force, Task Force Gleaming, that would come in behind them, hopefully in time. *I have no intention of letting them out of here into the countryside where they can fight some sort of guerilla war.*

Artillery rumbled in the distance as the Bradley seemed to accelerate. That was another sound he knew, fired rockets from a M142 High Mobility Artillery Rocket System raining down on the other side of the lake, or so he guessed. *Good! Pulverize them!*

"General, we are in position," Terry called back from the driver's seat. Popping the side hatch, Trip stepped out and saw the position of his command HQ. It was in a shallow hole of sorts, with a thick berm of felled trees covered with dirt providing additional protection. As he stepped out, the 25mm cannon barked off a stream of rounds to the south, no doubt at the advancing line of Newmericans.

Putting his binoculars to his eyes, the smoke made identifying the enemy difficult. There were several flashes from tank cannons, followed a few moments later by explosions off to his left. Bits of dirt and pieces of splintered trees rained down on him. Suddenly there was a roar overhead, running from his lines toward the enemy. An American jet dropped its bombs and peeled off as the explosions devoured a massive chunk of the forest in the process.

"General," Lieutenant Balford called out. "Spooky is above."

"Don't wait for me! Tear them a new asshole," Trip replied. Balford smiled and began to talk to the ground fire controllers. Not far from where the bombing run had taken place, the ground seemed to come alive, as if being plowed by some deadly invisible force. Up above, Trip caught a glimpse of the AC-130J Ghostrider, scrambled out of Hurlburt Field in Florida. The slower moving gunship had 105mm and 30mm cannons that purred as they rained death and destruction downward. The gunships were known for unleashing utter devastation, and were living up to that reputation. The explosions seemed to churn the very ground presumed by Trip to be the enemy's line of advance. Trees disintegrated and vehicles exploded to the south.

All along his own line, explosions went off, almost erratically, with no apparent pattern. Moving back into the Bradley, he leaned over to his communications officer, Second Lieutenant Dianne Holt. "Get me Colonel Kendrick," he said.

She nodded as he slid on his headset. "Tac two sir."

Switching to the channel, he calmly said "Chet," as he heard the ping of small arms gunfire hitting the turret above him. "Please tell me you are on the move."

"General we are about 20 minutes out," Kendrick said.

"Double-time it Chet," Trip urged. "I need you to take positions north of Venable Lake, preferably in our old positions."

"We're on our way sir, Kendrick out," was the response he got back.

More gunfire pinged and banged on the Bradley. The turret roared back to life, banging out 25mm rounds above him. Explosions rocked the armored vehicle on its tracks, near misses by high explosives. Outbound fire thundered overhead, close enough for him to hear the rush of shells heading at the enemy.

A part of Trip hoped that the SEs and the rebellious National Guard units would surrender. The SEs were not military but more like ad hoc militia units. The fact that they were still pressing the attack surprised him. "Can we get some air support?" Trip called loudly so that his voice could be heard over the thuds and booms of the battle all around them.

"Incoming," Lieutenant Balford said. "Close and dirty." To emphasize his point, he put his hands over his headphones and Trip did the same.

The Ghostrider opened up only 100 yards away, the rolling thunder of the incoming artillery rounds devouring everything they hit. The dull sounds of things hitting the Bradley continued for a minute or so from the steady stream of fire that rained down on the Newmericans. *Jesus— that* was *close!*

He glanced over at the tactical chart. "Are they still advancing?" he asked.

"No sir. They are holding their ground."

Trip didn't like the sound of that. Such battles could easily turn into fights of attrition. *I need to break them, send them fleeing into Task Force Gleaming. If they are unwilling to come at us ...*

"Signal all units, charge."

"Sir?"

"You heard me—rapid advance—everyone. Drive them back or overrun them."

The tactical officer barked out commands. The Bradley he was in roared to life again and started up the berm, the 25mm banging out shot after shot as it lurched forward.

Suddenly there was an explosion on the right side of the armored vehicle, this one more savage than before. The Bradley lurched hard, tipping to the left, finally crunching to a stop on its left side. Trip fell along with the rest of the command staff into a heap on the side hull which was now the floor. Sparks flew from some of the electronics, and his ears were ringing from the sound of blast that had knocked them over.

Disoriented, Reager struggled to get his bearings in the now dark Bradley. The only light came from the buckled side-hatch that had been near where he had been. His ass ached, and his head throbbed. Rubbing his head, he felt the stickiness that came from blood. *Damn it!* The interior lightly flickered, as if it were struggling to come back on. Moans from the officers tossed around in the interior mingled with the smell of ozone, burned wiring and spent ammunition.

Outside he heard the roar of an Abrams tank firing. He hoped it was one of theirs. *I have to get out of here. It can't end this way!*

Charlottesville, Virginia

The Virginian was the oldest bar in Charlottesville. It had a rustic feel to it, as if each grain of wood oozed with history. As David Steele entered, his nostrils were seduced almost immediately by the aroma of macaroni and cheese. The smell reminded him that he was hungry, and while the restaurant was known for its fare, he was not there for the food.

It had taken weeks to befriend Katrina Hoffman, one of the members of the Grays. Pretending to be a college student at the University of Virginia was easy; all it took was a sense of arrogance, some books, and the appropriate college branded attire. His father had rented him a tiny studio apartment off campus, and he had set it up to look like a dorm room. It was expensive, but provided the kind of camouflage he knew he would need if he were pretending to be a transfer student. A few old milk crates and boards to make shelves, a second-hand bed, a TV and a PlayStation ... along with the scattering of dirty dishes and unwashed clothes—the room looked like most dorm rooms he had seen when visiting his sister over her time at UVA.

He claimed his name was David Adair, a pre-law student studying history. Sitting in on classes with her helped round out the illusion that he was student. David flirted with her, asking her to join him for coffee. He had connected with Katrina by sprinkling their conversation with comments like, "We haven't gone far enough with these conservatives."

They met for dinner, and she had told David that he wasn't alone; several Social Enforcement groups were active against suspected conservatives on campus. Katrina said that she could help connect him, which he feigned appreciation for. She referred to the meeting as "just a few friends that think the way we do," and he knew he was prying open the door to get him to the Grays. David didn't appear eager to attend the private party, to the point where Katrina insisted that he attend.

As he made his way to the back room of the Virginian, she met him at the door, taking his arm and draping it around her slender waist. "I want you to meet these people—they think the way we do."

The room was filled with faces just like his—young, white students, all physically fit—mostly young men but several women as well, and a few somewhere in between who could identify as either sex. "This is David Adair," she said.

David gave the room a single nod and a forced smile. These were the people that had killed his sister, and he had to befriend them. It was the only way to get justice for Maddie and the others they had slaughtered.

Swallowing his emotions, he was introduced around the table, bumping elbows, shaking a few hands, and accepting an offer of a beer.

He was careful not to drink too much. He needed his senses clear. David knew what these people were capable of. The students made casual conversation, dropping obvious hooks in their talk to feel him out. "What do you think of the Pretender?" David fed them what they wanted to hear—hate, calls for violence, crafted lies that he knew they were expecting.

The most disturbing thing to him was how Katrina reacted to what he said. It was almost as if she were getting excited when he said that he wished he could get his hands on some conservative student. 'They wouldn't walk again, that's for sure,' he said. Katrina squirmed in her seat and clung to his arm even tighter with that phrase. The words burned in his mouth, each one a lie, but lies were necessary.

When they finished, he took Katrina back to his apartment and they made out. He couldn't deny that he liked feeling her up and down. Katrina was fantastic to look at, with long black hair and perky breasts that were like softballs in his hands, but that was just her body. She had made comments during the evening that the South needed to burn for turning its back on the Ruling Council. And from the way she said it, he knew it came from her black heart. He acted and behaved exactly how she expected. While she was hot, she was also evil, and he never fully forgot who she *really* was—the enemy.

Three days after the private party, she told him after class that he would be hearing from her friends soon. David was suspicious enough to make sure that the gun his father had given him was loaded and easy to get at. *If they have discovered who I am, they will try and do to me what they did to Maddie.*

Around 11:00 p.m. he heard shuffling outside of his door. A plain dark gray envelope had slid under his door, marked only with a large stamped letter 'G'. He opened it and saw the invitation, printed to look as if it were a ransom note, with letters taken from various media publications. "Initiation Invitation. You are cordially invited to a party with the Grays, one of the most prestigious societies at UVA." Under those words were the date and location.

This was it, a chance to have all of the Grays in one place. David called his father with the news. Finally, Maddie might get the justice she deserved.

Stone Mountain, Georgia

Trip pulled himself out of the toppled Bradley and was greeted by a wave of heat and the stink of burning wood in the air. He stumbled for a moment, his bones and muscles protesting the strain they had endured with the hit that had incapacitated the vehicle. Once on the side of the vehicle, he saw that the damage had crumpled much of the side armor, no doubt as a result of the explosion that had left a smoking crater next to the vehicle. The tread of the Bradley had been twisted and was off its drive bogie. *We were lucky. Another few feet, and we'd be dead.*

His ears were still ringing as he dropped down, followed by the rest of the command staff. Through the tones, the muffled roar of the battle seemed to be racing past their position, driving south. Lieutenant Holt, her helmet still off kilter, handed him a walkie-talkie. Reager moved down the berm where the battered Bradley lay; his knee joints protested as he moved toward the sounds of the battle.

The enemy was falling back. That was obvious as an Abrams tank roared past him off to the left. Its massive cannon fired on the move. Trip jogged to the edge of the blasted tree line. Many of the trees showed the signs of battle; some were blasted into splinters; others were pockmarked with smoldering bits of shrapnel that made the sap sizzle as he passed them.

When he reached the edge of the forest, he saw the infamous Stone Mountain carving. Before the Fall, it had been a tribute to the heroes of the Confederacy—featuring Robert E. Lee, Stonewall Jackson and Jefferson Davis on horseback. After the fall, the Governor of Georgia had deployed a unit of the National Guard to destroy the monument, claiming that the stone was racist. Trip remembered watching the artillery shell the carving on the flat face of Stone Mountain, blasting the edifices. Now, Trip saw the mountain through the miasma of the battle, and it struck him as if the mountain were watching the events unfold at its feet. Robert E. Lee's face was all but gone, replaced with two shell hits that had blackened the gray stone. Only a bit of his nose and brow remained to mark where it had once been. His arm holding his hat was oddly untouched by the barrage that had destroyed the monument. Stonewall Jackson's nose and eyes remained, but below that his face was gone. The upper portion of Jefferson Davis's head was missing; the slender cracks ran down his shell-marked body. They'd even put a small caliber shell into the neck of Traveller, Lee's horse.

Travis was no fan of the Confederacy, but destroying the monument made no sense to him. Stone Mountain had been a meeting place for the KKK, which he despised—but he didn't blame the mountain or the carving for their actions. Destroying the monument had changed nothing. If anything, it only served to make many southerners even angrier at the Ruling Council. A part of him wondered if that had been the plan all along—to rub the noses of people that didn't support the coup in their defeat. Now the remains of the stone carving stood as if it were a battered observer, casting judgment on a new civil war that was unfolding at its feet.

Trip switched to tactical two on the walkie-talkie. "Chet, this is Trip. I lost my ride. What's your situation?"

A crackle came through as his right ear cleared and he could hear the commander of Task Force Gleaming. "We are engaged, and they are falling back to the lake shore."

"Keep pressing them," Trip urged. "I'm on my way down there now."

An hour and a half later ...

There was still the occasional pop of gunfire, but most of it was ammunition cooking off from the fires that had been started by the battle, or the pops were from ammunition in the hot hulls of burning combat vehicles. Trip had walked past things he hadn't seen since Chicago, destroyed Abrams tanks. They had gone through the wars in the Middle East, and the Army had not lost one of the deadly tanks in battle. *It took fighting here in the Dis-United States for these magnificent beasts to be destroyed.* The irony was not lost on him.

The Newmericans had fought back viciously as they were pushed into a pocket on Stone Mountain Lake. Now over a thousand of the survivors stood, weaponless, many wounded, all wearing solemn faces of shame, anger, and exhaustion. Trip knew those faces well from his time overseas. Seeing his fellow Americans—even those that had fought against him—with those faces was something he realized he was going to have to get used to.

Colonel Kendrick led a General up to him, a man wearing filthy fatigues, smeared with black marks and mud, his jowls hanging low. *This is the enemy commander—the man that stood against me.* "General Kotter I presume," Trip said as the man stood before him.

"General Reager," he replied flatly.

"General," he said after an awkward moment of silence. "You and your forces will be taken into custody and processed according to the conventions of war that we both still respect. Your National Guardsmen will be held as prisoners of war. The civilians that fought alongside you will be held for criminal charges."

Kotter shifted on his feet slightly. "Criminal charges?"

"Yes. As they are not military personnel, they will be charged with domestic terrorism, sedition, armed insurrection and anything else the civilian authorities decide to throw at them."

"They fought beside us as militia," Kotter protested. "As such, they should be treated just like my personnel. In fact, I insist on it."

Trip flashed a fast smile. "It is *cute* that you think you are in a position to make demands General Kotter. You are not. You have been beaten on the field of battle."

"If they are found guilty of terrorism—"

"Yes," Trip cut him off. "They will face the death sentence."

"You can't be serious," he scoffed.

"I'm not known for my joking," Trip said back. "They have taken up arms against the legitimate government of the United States of America. That comes with a legal price tag attached to it."

"What constitutes the legitimate government is a matter of perspective," Kotter said, half under his breath.

"It is a matter of *fact*, sir. Georgia voted for the President in Tennessee. This little stunt of yours, this autonomous zone, was an act of defiance and insurrection that was not going to be tolerated. You may not think of the President as legitimate, but I assure you, the Ruling Council, in leading a *coup d'etat*, has no legal standing whatsoever. You backed the wrong horse, General. Accept your fate and take with you what little dignity you have left."

"I will never recognize the Pretender as the President!" he shot back.

"I don't care what you recognize," Trip said coldly in response. "You can't pretend gravity doesn't exist just because you don't like it. This is part of the problem you and your people have. You think that defiance alone makes your feelings somehow important. Your feelings are not facts; they are not reality; they are simply emotions. So you can sit and pout all you like about your fate and who you think is legally entitled to what … it no longer matters. This is the real world, General, not this fantasy-land the Ruling Council has forced on the people."

"Will my military people be paroled?"

Trip shook his head. "No sir. They will not. Why would I consider allowing your people a chance to take up arms against the legitimate government of the United States of America again? No sir, you and they will spend the duration of this conflict in custody as prisoners of war."

"You are a heartless man," Kotter said. "You are one of the few that live up to your reputation."

I am that and much more. "I'm the result of what happens when you push good people too far. I'm also doing my job," Trip snapped back. "I am honoring my oath to defend the Constitution of the United States. I am keeping my word to protect the nation from all enemies, foreign and domestic. Those were not words subject to interpretation; they were a commitment of my soul. It's a damned shame that you turned your back on them."

"You support a man that wants to take our nation back to its racist roots. He's a fascist."

Trip twisted his grin. "Your side has used the word 'fascist' so much and so inappropriately that it no longer has meaning. What you think of the man who won the election does not change the fact that he won."

"He cheated. Those voting sites—they were racist—designed to deprive people of the right to vote."

"They were necessary to ensure that no cheating took place," Trip said.

"Is that what you did in Chicago?" Kotter said angrily, his face getting redder as he spoke. "You slaughtered innocent protesters."

Reager shook his head in disbelief. "You can believe whatever lies the TRC served up regarding Chicago. I was there. Those 'innocent protesters' were armed and attacked us first, and they were backed up with the Illinois National Guard. You have been fed a steady diet of bullshit for years now General. Didn't it ever occur to you that it all might be a lie?"

Kotter became flustered with his rebuttal. Trip continued. "Well, you'll have plenty of time to think that over as a POW," Trip said, walking away from Kotter, leaving him standing there to contemplate the final shot of the battle—albeit a verbal one.

CHAPTER 20

"Nostalgia is dangerous because it makes you
yearn for a time when the nation was corrupt."

Lisbon, New Hampshire

Su-Hui Zhou saw the smoke rolling skyward in the brilliant mid-morning sun, and his heart sank. They had received word during their refueling in Vermont that Lisbon was under attack. Now, as they carefully made their way along the rolling wooded hills, the smoke seemed to confirm what they had heard. As the snowmobiles stopped below the crest of a low hill outside of town, he climbed down, struggling in the deep snow to get some sort of view. They had smelled the burning buildings nearly three miles away; the stench hung in the air.

As he looked at that absolute destruction, a knot formed in his stomach. *Hachi! Is she still alive? She has to be.* After all that had happened with Ya-ting, the thought that he might lose his wife was something that made him want to throw up. He wanted to rush in, but Trudy pulled him back. "We need to come in along the river, where the smoke is thickest." She pointed in the distance, and they could make out the forms of Newmerican infantry starting down a hill to the east of their position. *We have to get there before they do!*

He detached the machine gun and held it as an assault weapon. Trudy and a trio of others who had been on the raid made their way down to the icy banks of the Ammonoosuc River. He fell through a piece of the shore, filling his left boot with icy water, but Su-Hui ignored it. All that mattered was finding Hachi. She was the center of their family, the bonding agent that held them together through everything they had endured. The very concept that she might have died was something he could not process ... could not believe.

They moved low along the banks, coming up on the exit of the rum-running tunnels that had gone all of the way back to the now destroyed main street. He wanted to cough; the smoke was so thick, but he wanted to be sure that he didn't make unnecessary noise. When they came to the opening, Trudy, Abernathy, and another one of the harasser force helped him pry the old wooden door open.

As soon as the door opened, guns were aimed outward at Su-Hui and the others. Holding his hands in the air, the weapons finally lowered, and the people began to emerge. Smoke rolled out of the hole, followed by several humans, covered in soot and grime. They were dazed. The fourth person to emerge was Hachi. He grabbed her and held her tighter than he ever had before. The trio of spent bullet cartridges he wore around his neck dug into his chest, but he ignored them—all that mattered was that his wife was still alive. Her eyes were glazed over, as if she were dazed. She wept, as did Su-Hui. "You're alive!" he said as he squeezed her even harder.

"They bombed us ... " she said in a wavering voice.

"We need to get to safety," Trudy said, helping out the eighth and last person. "They are going to be looking for survivors." She grabbed their machine gun while Su-Hui helped his wife slowly backtrack through the snow. Three of the people were injured, one badly cut in the face, with no winter clothing. All were struggling to breathe, having been forced to hide in the tunnels, afraid to emerge.

He held her waist and elbow as they struggled back to where the snowmobiles were left. The fear he felt was something that stirred memories in him. *If anything had happened to her, I don't know what I would do.* That wasn't entirely true. He would get revenge on those that went for his family. It was a lesson he had learned the hard way with Ya-ting, their daughter. Images of her back in Indiana at the assisted care facility where she lived came rushing to the forefront of his mind. She had been catatonic since the attack, unable or unwilling to respond to the outside world. The same sense of fear and loss made him keep Hachi close to him. *Not again. Never again.*

Four years earlier ...
San Jose, California

When he reached the hospital room, Su-Hui was out of breath. Hachi had called him, said there was something wrong at the restaurant ... that Ya-ting was in the hospital. He had wondered what could have happened. Was it an accident with the stove or the fryer? As he saw his daughter in the bed, her eyes closed, her face bruised, her arm in a cast, he knew that it had not been a kitchen accident.

Hachi hugged him as he entered. "What happened?"

"They came—that Beckett and the other two," she said. it was then that he noticed the purple bruise on her forehead. They—they—attacked her."

Su-Hui's jaw set as he delicately cradled her face in his hands. "What do you mean?"

"She's been raped," Hachi said. "They have sedated her. I tried to stop them, but they hit me."

He wiped away the tears streaming down his wife's face as a ripple of fury rose in him. *They attacked my little girl!* Su-Hui wanted one thing. Blood. *All because I refused to hire that girl!*

"What about you?" he asked. "Are you alright?" He feared that she too may have been raped.

Hachi nodded, ever a pillar of strength. "They hurt me, but I will recover. Our focus needs to be Ya-ting. The doctors tried to get her to talk, but she won't—or she can't. When she is awake, she just stares."

Su-Hui moved beside her bed, his trembling fingers caressing his daughter's cheek. *They have defiled her ... those monsters. They must pay for this.* He was unsure what to do next, but he was sure that he had to do something. *These Regulators, these Social Enforcers—they have no right to do this.* Ya-ting was innocent, just a child. *They should have come for me, not her.*

"Are you alright?" he asked turning to Hachi, his voice wavering slightly.

She nodded, but could not say *yes* out loud. His own lower lip was trembling as the urge to get vengeance pulsated through every fiber of his being. There were no words he could say that would ease Hachi's pain. Ya-ting was such a delicate and sensitive young girl that he couldn't imagine what she had endured, but the images in his imagination were horrific. *This will scar her, deeply.*

"Where is Akio?"

"He is locking up the restaurant," she said. "She screamed when they attacked her. She called for us, but one of them held me down."

"They will pay for this," he said in a low tone in his native language. "I will kill them."

"No," she responded. "I cannot afford to lose you to them too." Fear framed each word that she spoke, demanding his attention.

"What kind of person does this to an innocent girl?" he said, heeding her words. *This is not the time or place for us to argue. This is a time for support.*

"They said *you* caused this," she sobbed.

"They had no right."

A flash of rare anger rose in Hachi's face. "These people have no morals. They let our nation die. They told us where we could live, and these men tried to make us hire people that were unqualified. Newmerica is not friendly to us. They hate us. They call us 'boat people' and treat criminals from other nations better than us simply because we were made refugees. Our precepts call for doing no harm to others. These people are nothing but harm."

Hachi was right. What made matters worse was that Newmerica inflicted such pain in the name of being benevolent. *They call people "Nazis" while they act just like Hitler's storm troopers. They are a mirror. Everything they claim they hate, that they claim is evil, is who they are. Their lies are their truths, which makes them dangerous.* "I cannot fix this nation, not now. Our priority is our family, as it must be. We will help Ya-ting recover from this." *When that is over, I will set myself on a path to fix this country.*

Two NSF officers walked in, one a sturdy young female with dishwater blonde hair trimmed short. The other was a young Hispanic male. The female came forward. "You're the Zhou's, correct?"

"I am Su-Hui. This is Hachi," he said, refusing to shed his manners despite his seething rage.

"I am Corporal Frisosky, NSF. I spoke to the doctors," she said in a soothing tone. "I am so sorry for this."

"Thank you," he said. From her tone, he knew she was being genuine in her choice of words. "You are the police—the men that did this, one was called Beckett. They were Social Enforcers. They called themselves the Regulators."

She nodded, taking notes on her small iPad. "I'm familiar with the group. Can you tell me what happened?"

Hachi nodded and spoke in fragmented sentences as she often did when upset, caught between the horror, the sorrow, and her use of English. She told the officer the details she had not given her husband—how the three men had beaten Ya-ting; then each had raped and sodomized her, one by one. Hachi had been forced to watch her daughter's assault, forced to endure her cries of anguish and pain. Su-Hui's face became statue-like; his facial muscles flexed with each word of his wife's description. He held her hand tight in his own, hoping and wishing that somehow he could drain the agony from her.

The officer was gentle, offering Hachi a tissue at one point, resting her hand on his wife's shoulder. *She understands and will help.* That was a surety in his mind. When Hachi finished, officer Frisosky hugged her as her partner, who had been taking notes, looked on.

Su-Hui followed the officers to the door. "You will arrest them, won't you?" he asked.

For a moment, it looked as if the officer might cry—her face was draped in sorrow. "It isn't that easy Mr. Zhou."

It is perfectly easy! Why would she say otherwise? "You know who did it. My wife told you. You know who these men are; you said so." *Go do your job!*

Frisosky hesitated. "It isn't that cut and dry. These are Social Enforcers."

"What does that matter?"

"In California, hell, in most states, the prosecutors refuse to press charges against them. I can arrest them, but once I do, the prosecutor's office will toss the charges, and they will be on the street in a matter of hours."

"They raped my little girl!" he said, louder than before.

She nodded. "They did. But since the Ruling Council took over, they have treated Social Enforcers as if they are above the law. The system works against law enforcement when it comes to them."

"This system is broken."

"It is," Frisosky conceded.

"If it is broken, I will take the law in my own hands," he proclaimed. "I was in the Army … I know how to shoot. I will find these animals and put them down."

The officer shook her head. "If you do that, you will end up in jail. You don't enjoy the same protection from prosecution that they do."

"What am I supposed to do? Nothing?" he asked loud enough that people in the hall could have heard him. He didn't care. This was not right. *I did not have my family escape Chinese occupation to have this happen to them. This can't be happening in America!* His hands quaked with anger the more he thought about Ya-ting.

Frisosky hesitated. "There are *ways* these things can get resolved. Give me a few days. Can you do that? Can you let me try and resolve this for you?"

Su-Hui wanted details as to what she was going to do, but the way she spoke—he knew that he was not likely to get them. *If there is something she can do, I should allow her to do it.* "I can," he said, feeling somewhat humiliated at having to take the stand of doing nothing.

"I have your word," she said, leaning in so that her partner could not hear them. "I will see justice done."

Su-Hui nodded, then turned to his wife's loving arms.

Two days later ...

Angel Frisosky sat in her car with the windows down, watching the bar parking lot just over two blocks away. She was clad in a black, light-suppressing bodysuit, which seemed like dramatic overkill, but it was her habit when she went out on such nights. She triple-checked the sights on rifle she had taken from the NSF evidence room. Angel had test fired it several times, making sure she had it sighted in for the range with the flash suppressor on. Such practice was necessary for shots she had to pull off.

She remembered the Zhous and clung to that memory as she aimed out her passenger side window, waiting for her prey. None of Newmerica was fair, but at least with this gesture, she could reset the scales of justice, if only a little bit. *I'm a long way from the Presidential Detail in the Secret Service.* She thought back to how her failure to save the life of the President the night of the Fall had driven her into hiding. Angel Frisosky was a made-up persona, one that Charli Kasinski wore as if it were a bodysuit.

Waiting, she saw Jazon Beckett and his two buddies swagger out of the bar, half drunk, laughing and joking. She knew which car was theirs, and she knew their path. She aimed at the last person in their line. Squeezing the trigger, the gun cracked and tugged hard into her arm as the man fell into the tailgate of a truck in the parking lot.

Beckett and the other man stood, dazed, confused about why their friend had fallen. Her next shot caught Beckett in the center of his chest—the impact throwing his body against their car. The remaining SE stood, bewildered, still not sure what was happening or what to do. He managed to start to bolt, running one step before she fired again, catching him in the head, exploding it onto a nearby Prius.

Justice has been delivered. Casually she lowered the rifle and drove away.

One day later ...

The door to Taste of Taiwan opened and Su-Hui saw Officer Frisosky enter. He came from behind the COVID barrier to talk to her. "Hello Mr. Zhou," she said. "How is your daughter?"

Su-Hui shook his head. "She is awake, but does not respond to us. She only stares at the ceiling. The doctors say it is a mental trauma, that she may be this way for a while. We are hopeful ... " he said, his voice trailing off. It was difficult to talk about Ya-ting. It was as if the attack had taken all of the cheeriness and energy from his little girl. Her vacant eyes simply looked skyward, and nothing he or Hachi said seemed to reach her.

"I'm sorry to hear that," Frisosky said. "I am here because yesterday someone shot the three men that attacked Ya-ting."

A part of him wanted to rejoice, but he could not find joy in her words, only a sense of satisfaction. "I did not know."

"Two are dead. The third will lose his leg."

"And this Beckett?"

"Dead," she confirmed.

Su-Hui nodded. "Then they got what they deserved."

Frisosky nodded. "I am here because my supervisor wanted me to interview you to see if you had an alibi and to make sure you did not have access to a rifle that could have been used in the crime—that sort of thing."

"I did not do this," Su-Hui said. "I wish I had, but I was true to my promise to you."

"I know," she said. "It is a formality."

"How do you know?"

"Hold out your hand," she said. He did so and she placed three brass spent rifle cartridges in it. He stared at the three casings in his hand and slowly understood. Frisosky had killed the two men and crippled the other. His mouth hung open with the realization of what she had done for him and his family.

"Justice prevails," she said, giving him a thin smile. And with those words, before he could respond, Officer Angel Frisosky walked out of his restaurant.

Wrapping his fingers around the brass shells, he clenched them tightly. Her gesture meant more to him than he could put into words *Justice does prevail! I owe this woman for what she did. When the time presents itself, I will do what she has done. I will fight against those that allowed the crimes against my daughter to happen. I will make sure that no other father must endure what I have.*

Lisbon, New Hampshire

General Donaldson walked near a blasted building at the edge of the battle zone that had been Lisbon. His leg still ached, but he had left his cane in the Humvee. In the snow it was impractical for support anyway. The general had been trying to get in contact with General Kotter in Atlanta for over an hour with no luck, so he decided to use his time to walk through Lisbon while he waited for a response. He knew that the breakout was partially successful. The fact that Kotter had not replied most likely meant that he was still in the middle of combat operations. *If we can secure a victory there, combined with the blow I delivered here, it will do a lot to reverse people's morale and their opinion of this conflict.*

As he came close to what had once been a three-story house, the sting of the smoke stung at his nostrils and the back of his mouth. The bombardment, by artillery, rockets, and mortars, had been devastating to the town. In his mind, it had been necessary. The people of New Hampshire seemed to be embracing the resistance everywhere. Daily he lost soldiers to IEDs or ambushes. His dead demanded that he take decisive action—and the destruction of Lisbon was just that. *It sends the right message—if you assist the enemy, your town will end up facing the same fate as this place—eradication.*

The haze of the smoke from the bombardment and the still burning fires seemed to cling to the blasted snow on the ground. As he moved around the house, he was impressed with the level of destruction he had ordered brought down on it. The house was gone, a smoking pile of rubble. Fragments of bricks were scattered everywhere from what had been part of the foundation. The light gray siding was twisted and tossed in every direction around him. Most fragments were little more than crumbled vinyl half-charred pieces. As he trudged through the melting snow, much of it now blackened with soot and bits of dirt and debris, he saw what appeared to be a pile of clothing lying in the snow.

As he walked close to it, he saw more of the form. It was not clothing, but a young woman. Her body was torn apart, no doubt by shrapnel from the bombardment. The snow around her was soaked in blood, and her legs were burned to the point where they were charred, right to the bones that he saw protruding.

Donaldson's head got light as he staggered back with his eyes locked on the woman. In her arms was a child—almost a pale blue, locked in her arms. It was missing an arm and was splattered with child's blood and that of its mother.

Memories of Kirbyville, Arkansas rushed to the General as he staggered back. Along with those memories came the retching of his stomach as it pitched. The taste of bile rose in his mouth, and he gagged.

"General?" the private near him asked, watching him bend over in the haze of the smoke.

"Not now," he managed. Looking off to his left was a hill topped with low pines. Bits of broken wood lay on the snow, half-melted into it. Donaldson didn't want the people in his command to see him throw up. He started for the hill to get out of their view. The steps he took were slogging, hard to make. The snow had somewhat melted from the attack, only to refreeze in the frigid New Hampshire air. It formed a thin, icy crust that he broke through with each step as he made his way to the hill. Pushing past the pines, he doubled over and emptied the contents of his stomach into the snow at his feet. Each convulsion of his stomach forced up more hot liquid and food. The smell of the vomit mixed with the garbage-like smell of the smoke, but Donaldson didn't care. At least he had not humiliated himself in front of his troops.

Breathing hard, he raised his head and noticed suddenly that he had an audience. Six snowmobiles were poised on the backside of the hill. People stood there, staring at him. Then he spotted the machine guns. *What the—shit! It's them! The SOL!*

He immediately tried to turn and run, but the deep snow threw off his center of gravity, and he couldn't lift his feet out of the deep snow in time to compensate. General Donaldson toppled over into the snow, next to where he had thrown up. In a panic, he thrust his hands down, trying to push off, but the deep snow made that all but impossible.

Somehow he wrenched his right boot free and started to stand.

Su-Hui and the other survivors had made their way back to the snowmobiles, carefully skirting the Newmerican infantry in the center of what had been downtown Lisbon. Trudy remounted the machine gun, and Su-Hui was about to help Hachi onto the cramped snowmobile when he saw a winter-camouflaged figure come through the pines just above their position. It was an older man. His gray hair showed on his short, cropped sideburns. General's stars were visible on his epaulettes.

The officer doubled over, throwing up as the Sons of Liberty harasser force stared at him in disbelief, stunned that someone had simply walked onto their position. For a moment, everyone froze in place. The officer spotted them, then fell in the snow. Su-Hui stepped forward a half-step, and then reached down for the pistol that he wore as a sidearm. *I have to kill him before he calls for help.* With the survivors there, the resistance group was not prepared to fight another pitched battle. Instinctively he wanted to protect Hachi.

There was a tug at his side, and he reached for his pistol but was greeted instead by an empty holster. Off to his side, he heard three shots crack off. The pistol shots didn't echo at all; it was as if the trees and thick snow absorbed the sound. The officer dropped as quickly as he had started to rise, a spray of crimson mist from the bullet hits splattering the snow around him. Slumping down, his face seemed to crunch in agony.

Su-Hui turned to see who the shooter was, and he saw his wife, Hachi, holding his gun. Her hands were trembling as she kept aiming at the man she had shot. Gently Su-Hu reached up and carefully removed the pistol from her hands.

"We need to go now," he said calmly to her.

She looked at him and nodded, her body trembling with the rush of adrenaline. Helping her onto the seat of the snowmobile, the rest of the force started their engines and left Lisbon behind them.

General James J. Donaldson heard the snowmobiles start just above the roaring in his ears. The frigid snow stung on the side of his face as he lay there. He tried to call out for help, but instead coughed up blood. When he tried to shift his right arm to move, a ripple of pain hit him, like a hot poker being stabbed into his body.

I've been shot—badly. The coppery taste of blood mixed with the remnants of bile in his mouth, meaning he must have been hit in a lung which he knew was bad news. The more he tried to get air, the more he found himself struggling. His exhaled breath left little wisps of moisture in the air. He moved his legs, but that only seemed to make him feel light-headed. His vision began to tunnel into darkness, and with that came panic.

This can't happen ... not now. I won! Trying once more to move only forced the tunneling to increase. A wave of vertigo tore at him. He felt hands come down on him, voices that were muffled saying, "General! Where are you hit?" As much as he tried to open his mouth to respond, it was as if his body was acting in defiance of his orders.

"Help ... " he managed, followed by another thick red cough.

CHAPTER 21

*"Social Quarantine is the protection of
people from their bad ideals."*

Charlottesville, Virginia

Grayson Steele calmed his nerves by pausing and drawing a long, deep breath. The thin wisp of smoke rose from the soldering iron while he finished connecting the detonator to the last of the pipe bombs. As he finished, he carefully put the iron in its wire stand and unplugged it. Crossing his arms, he leaned back and looked at the results of his week's work.

The four bombs were each about a foot and a half long. The pipes were lined with small nails, bits of glass, BBs, and anything else he found that might inflict damage on their targets. He had originally started calling them 'victims,' but changed his mental wording. These were the people that planned the death of Maddie and five other innocent people simply because they didn't agree with their politics. *They are not victims. They are targets. They are not people. They are serial killers.*

Getting the explosives for the bombs had been easier than he thought. His family had changed their identities several times since going into hiding. Using those IDs, he posed as a farmer wanting to blow up tree stumps. Forging the ATF license for explosives, a simple document for using dynamite, it was pathetically easy. *The FedGov is so focused on rounding up guns; they overlook the obvious.*

Two big, plastic cans of tannerite gave the bombs a little extra 'umph'. He was limited to the quantities he could purchase, but by going to different sources, no one was required to check to see how much he had recently purchased. That was one of the weaknesses of the FedGov—

their bureaucracy was so onerous, so burdensome, that it failed to work. *Like every other socialist government, the more they imposed controls, the more the controls could be circumvented.*

Building the bombs had proven easy. While the TRC and Big Tech worked hard to make sure that the old US Flag or copies of the Constitution were immediately taken down from the Internet when they surfaced, they did remarkably little to hide bomb making instructions. He even purchased an Army field manual about IEDs from AbeBooks which showed how such devices were manufactured and deployed against the Army.

He had made a test bomb, and he and David had taken it to an empty farm field far outside of the city to test it. Using the phone as a detonator—the bomb had proven devastating. A part of him felt like a little kid, setting off fireworks. It was hard to suppress the grin after it went off, even though the smile was tempered by the thought that it was being built to kill people. From what he researched, one bomb in a room would likely be enough to kill everyone there. Two would be overkill, but would ensure no survivors. The fact that he had four meant they could not only kill the victims, but ensure that first responders would not get into the building to see what they did right away since the structure would be destroyed.

Plotting the demise of the Grays had been a strange bonding experience for David. His son had done a remarkable job of infiltrating the group. He was bullet-focused in his efforts, attaching himself to one of the females who brought him into their circle. He had never taken drama in high school, but he was proving to be a great actor. *He's only seventeen, but he has been through so much, with us living under different identities. He is more mature than any typical seventeen-year-old.* David didn't know that his father had shadowed his activities, watching him from afar. *I lost one child to these monsters. I won't risk losing David too.* So far they seemed to have been fooled by his stories that he hated conservatives and wanted to see them suffer if not die. *The hate he tells them. It is what they want to hear. They are addicted to hate as if it were meth. It gives them a rush, a feeling of power.*

The bombs on the tiny, round dining table in David's apartment were more than the product of hours of tedious and dangerous work.

They would save lives. The Grays were going to keep on killing students they didn't like. He put a blanket over them and settled in on the couch, waiting for his son to return from the classes he was sitting in on.

The knock that came to the door of the tiny apartment was a surprise. The apartment was nothing more than a front, a tool so that David could appear to be a typical student. What if it is the police? Grayson's heart pounded. He silently moved to the kitchen area and grabbed the gun there. Then he made his way to the door.

Looking out the peephole, he saw Frank Campbell standing outside. He let out a ragged sigh, and then unlocked the door, stuffing the gun into the pocket of his jeans.

Frank was dressed in a hoodie with a bit of flannel shirt poking through the top where it wasn't fully zipped. The hoodie had seen better days; there were a few holes in it, a dot of paint here and there, and a faded look to it. He came in with a smile and a hearty handshake.

"Frank," Grayson said warmly. "How did you find me?"

His face seemed to speak on its own, saying 'really?' "I'm a PI. So I found your wife and she told me where you were."

"What brings you by?"

"I'm here to be the voice of reason, if that's possible. Everyone needs a conscience," Frank said.

"What do you mean?"

"Come on Grayson," he said. "You asked me for a copy of an ATF permit for explosives. It doesn't take much of a detective to figure out what you are planning."

Of course he knows. "I don't know what to say."

Frank paused, glancing over at the table where the blanket covered the bombs. He could see the soldering iron and wire and the bits of wire still on the table top that were not covered. Then he turned back to Grayson. "Don't get nervous," he said. "I'm not going to try and talk you out of doing this. I just want to make sure you fully understand what you are doing."

"I think I have a pretty good idea. I'm getting these assholes back for what they did to my daughter. I'm making sure that they don't ever do this again to anyone."

"This is more than that, and you know it," Frank countered.

"What do you mean?"

"You were a State Legislator. When the Fall happened, you went into hiding, took a new identity. You were on the run from going to Social Quarantine. That was totally understandable. If you do this, you and your family will be hunted by the NSF. Social Enforcers are above the law, but you aren't. Sooner or later someone will piece this together." He gestured to the table. "They will call you a terrorist, a mass murderer if they figure out what you're planning. We're talking prison, or worse."

Grayson soaked up his words and said nothing for a few beats of his heart. Frank was right about the implications. At the same time, Grayson *had* already thought through the implications. "They won't find us Frank. We will disappear, like we did before. We will hide in plain sight, blend in. We've talked it over. This has to be done. We would be allowing these fuckers to continue to drag kids out into some cornfield and kill them. The cost of not doing this is my soul. I have to do this, not just for Maddie, but to save other families from going through what we have."

Frank nodded and pursed his lips with Grayson's words. "Alright then," he said with a deep resolved tone in his voice. "Tell me your plan and how I can help."

The next evening …

It was a warmer evening than most early January days in Virginia, with temperatures getting into the low 50s. The campus seemed far more active on the warmer days, with students willing to spend time outside. It was a hint of spring, one that he and others savored. As darkness began to settle in, so did a hint of the winter chill starting to return. The good days were rare … both weather-wise and emotionally. *They will be better soon.*

"Aren't you excited? Katrina asked. While she clung to his side, she led David Steele off-campus.

"You make it sound like I'm being made in the mob, like in *Goodfellas*," he chided back. Katrina had told him that he would make a perfect member of the Grays. She was excited because it meant they would spend more time together. She had said so. When he felt guilty for what was about to come, he thought about his sister and found it tempered any hesitation in him.

"What is *Goodfellas*?"

"Seriously, you never saw that movie?" David relied.

"No," she said, not shaking her smile.

"It's about the life of a mobster," he said as they turned a corner. "He gets sucked into their lifestyle." *He eventually turns on his fellow mobsters,* he thought, keeping that part to himself.

Katrina was a nice girl; she had a fantastic body. Her perkiness and charm were undeniable. The only real flaw he saw in her was her belief that anyone that didn't think the way she did, needed to be 'eradicated'. That was the word she used, and the way she said it—slow, firm—told him that she was not just mouthing the word. She meant it.

Her parents lived in Northern Virginia and had been vocal activists before the Fall, trying to infiltrate schools with critical race theory as part of the curriculum. Once Congress had been killed and the Ruling Council had come to power, they had benefited dramatically—landing senior positions in the Department of Education; or as his father called it, the 'Department of Indoctrination'. Katrina was proud of her parents' success and bragged about the power they wielded. "When I'm done with college, I'm assured a management position in the FedGov."

David understood how the system worked. People were dependent on the FedGov supplementing their income. The system of Reparations allowed individuals to report on each other to make more money. People in the FedGov got jobs for their friends and family further cementing their control and authority. His parents had raised him to have a healthy distrust of the government, where Katrina saw it as the center of her future.

"Who? What should I expect?" he asked. "I mean, this isn't like some fraternity hazing thing is it?"

"It's not that bad," she said. "I've already vouched for you. They will just ask you some questions. We need to make sure you are the right character for the Grays."

That made him concerned, but he didn't let it show. After ten minutes, they arrived at a stately white Victorian house with a massive porch. Katrina led him inside, and he saw a bench filled with backpacks. A few hung from pegs on a coatrack mounted on the wall. Carefully, he raised his to the rack and hung it; then he took off his coat and draped it over the pack. Pausing for a moment, he texted his father's burner phone and address.

Katrina introduced him to several of the members, mostly those he had already met. They shook his hand firmly; one female who no doubt identified as a male, gave him a big hug. Someone put a beer in his hand. He took only a small sip, and then set the cup down. *I don't want to dull my senses, not tonight.*

They huddled in what had probably been the living room of the house when it was first built. The wood floor was dark, antique, and polished. One of the members who identified himself as Jay spoke to him at length. "You know what we are about, right?"

David nodded. "I think so."

"Katrina has spoken for you, but you need to know what we do."

"You get rid of the problems on campus," he said tactfully.

Jay beamed. "Perfect response. Most people say the wrong thing; they use words like murder. We don't kill *people*. Conservatives aren't people—they're a cancer. They're extremists, a threat to democracy. We get rid of a disease that could corrupt the campus … students that taint our society. If we don't deal with these people, remove them from the equation, they will only cause trouble down the road."

"It's community service," quipped Katrina.

"It's like what's going on in New Hampshire," David said.

"Exactly!" Jay added. "A bunch of racists up there, refusing to accept the inevitable. They are killing good people with their terror attacks. That's what happens if you purge the people that support that kind of shit."

It took a lot for David to put on the face that Jay and the others expected. "I'm surprised more student groups don't go up there. You know—to kick some ass."

Jay beamed at his words. "Oh, don't worry. A lot of student SE groups are planning just that. Those racist assholes won't know what hit them if we ever get into the fight."

David's eyes darted around the room. Only a few of the Grays might pose an actual threat. Words and bullying tactics would not hold up in a real military fight. Even he knew that. Jay and the others clung to bravado which would not help them when someone was shooting back.

Maddie fought back. And because of her, a few of their number died. "I hope you feel I fit in with you," he said.

Jay nodded, taking a long sip of his Solo cup of beer. "You seem like Gray material," he said, and then ushered him over to the fireplace. On the old oak mantle was a placard, propped up against the wall. There was a list of names on it, with no title. "These are the people that we have taken care of," Jay said nodding at the list. "Their deaths ensured that no one would be influenced by their corrupt thinking."

David did not reply. Instead he leaned in and looked at the four columns of the list. The fact that the font was small, was only a testimony as to how many the Grays had killed. He made a point of reading each name, slowly, letting them burn in his memory. Near the bottom was Madison Steele. A chill rose on his spine, and his face felt like it was tingling—the shame and loss tearing at him. *They have made a monument of her with this. They celebrate her death. She isn't even a person. She's a statistic, another bad person they saved the world from.* It made what was going to follow easier for David.

When he turned to face Jay, the other student looked puzzled. "Are you alright David? Your face is all red."

He nodded, embarrassed that the veneer of being one of them was fading at the sight of his sister's name. "I'm okay," he said. "I got my COVID booster yesterday for the upsilon variant. The boosters always make me get a little fever."

Jay drew another sip of his beer. "Everyone is here. We'll get started with the ceremony in a little while."

David glanced at the door. "Why don't I go outside for a few minutes—you know, the night air might help."

"Sure," Jay said. "Take ten."

As he headed for the door, Katrina stopped him. "Hey, you okay?"

"Just a booster reaction," he said. "I'm going outside for a few."

"Oh, I'll go with you."

David waved his hand between them. "Just give me a few minutes alone," he said.

Katrina nodded in response. Her face had a look of concern. She cared about him; David understood that. He had misled her from the very start, just as she and the other Grays had done with Maddie. Snaking his way through the packed room, he went to the coat rack and reached for his jacket. Hanging on the wall peg was his backpack and its deadly contents. Sliding the jacket on and zipping it up, he stepped outside onto the large porch. His nose immediately picked up a hint of gasoline in the air, which was strangely reassuring.

His father emerged from the hedge. "David," he whispered. Moving down next to his father, he saw the empty gasoline containers. "Are they all there?"

David nodded.

"Alright, Frank is done on the back porch. We need to leave."

David didn't talk as they casually walked the half-block to the car. Frank Campbell was there waiting for them. "I take it we are all set?" he asked. David's father gave him a nod as he got in the car. The hint of gasoline fumes followed the two older men.

Grayson pulled out his burner phone and fidgeted with the numbers; then he stopped with his thumb poised over the dial button. "They will never again take the life of an innocent person," he said slowly.

"For Maddie," David said.

"For Maddie," Grayson replied, and pressed the button.

The blast was loud, even given their distance from the house. David knew it would be devastating with the backpack hanging at almost head level. The explosive force in the enclosed room should have killed everyone. If it didn't, the shrapnel would ensure that there were no survivors. He saw the railing from the front porch blast out across the street, one piece impaling itself into the windshield of a new Jeep-Zazz that was parked across from the Grays' headquarters.

Flames roared through the debris, fueled by the gasoline that his father and Mr. Campbell had spread just prior to the explosion. The house's first floor was obliterated in an instant, with the other two stories crashing downward into the carnage. The house next door, closer to where they were parked, caught on fire as well, the flames lapping up into the early evening darkness.

David thought about Katrina for a moment. Chances are she did not suffer … none of them did. The death that she received was swift. She did not get any of the terror that Maddie and Clarice had experienced, marched out into a farm field knowing they were about to be killed.

These all died swiftly, a complete surprise.

The next time I won't make that mistake. These people need to know what is happening, just like Maddie did.

CHAPTER 22

"Diversity equals prosperity."

Newmerica Penitentiary, Administrative Maximum Facility
Florence, Colorado

Deja Jordan spent her morning monitoring the videos of Raul interacting with Ted for the last few days. Where some would have thought that beating an old man might not have been prudent or useful, she rather enjoyed it. Ted was a former Senator from Texas, easily still one of the most racist places in the country. The world thought he was dead anyway. Most of the Senate had been killed the night of the Liberation. Each punch she gave to him had come with some satisfaction—retribution for centuries of oppression that her people had suffered.

While Raul spoke at length with Ted, he never seemed to say much that helped her get closer to Caylee Leatrom. If anything, his words always left a chill with her—one that tore at her in nightmares. "She's afraid of her, with good reason," Raul had whispered to Ted. She paused that segment, playing it over several times. *Am I afraid of her? Is that why she keeps me up at night?* Tearing at Caylee were memories of Raul's shotgun blast at the bridge that crossed the Ohio River and the memory of her systematically taking out the SE team she was with. *That fucker is right. I am afraid of her? Why?*

Deja had been worried about Caylee before she had even learned her identity. Now things were worse. This was an operative, a professional agent that killed as part of their job. Raul had told her once that Caylee would come for him and kill her, and that was now truer than ever. *It's*

319

her grace in the way she acts. She's like a ninja, so fluid, so effective.

The afternoon would come, and she had scheduled time with Raul again. Her interrogation coaches had told her that she was to threaten to do more harm to Ted if he didn't cooperate. "He's not afraid of you hurting him. You've done that. He's more worried about his sister and his friend. Use Ted to pry him open." They may have been right, but she somehow doubted that it would shake Raul. She had threatened to hurt his sister, but that was impossible now. *If I can't show him images of her battered and beaten, I can't rattle him. Ted had become the latest of the last resorts with Raul.* His Tribunal would be coming soon, and with it, his execution. The thought of him taking his secrets to his grave would mean that he won and she had lost—something that Deja could not tolerate.

At 11:30 a.m. she paused what was on her screen. It was time for the first shift lunch for the guards and administrative staff. She headed off to the private cafeteria where they ate. *Hopefully this afternoon, he will finally do the right thing and name names.*

Colorado Springs, Colorado

Caylee liked the helicopter pilot that Travis had enlisted for their operation. Faust Kidder was a former Army Ranger helicopter pilot with three combat tours under his belt before getting a wound that had taken his left eye. The word was he could fly and had flown just about everything that could be put in the air. He wore a patch with a glitter target sight on it, which was both ridiculous and oddly cool in her mind.

The helicopter he had secured was a big Huey. Faust had it repainted to look like an emergency airlift chopper—bright red, yellow, and white, complete with the fake name of an air service on the side, "Mortis Emergency Airlift Services." She got the joke almost instantly, dipping into the Latin class she had taken in high school. Mortis was the stiffness one got with death. That alone earned points for Faust who had a dark sense of humor.

Under her winter coat, she wore a prison guard uniform. Once on the roof, she wanted to blend in as much as possible when she went to secure Raul. The uniform was uncomfortable but necessary camouflage.

The knowledge that there were two operatives in the prison was personal to her. They were there to kill or capture her, plain and simple. She didn't like that thought. Neither of them were operatives she had met before, so she didn't know their skills or capabilities. The assumption that she went with was that they were as good if not better than her. Even if Andy's poisoning of the food was successful, they would try to fulfill their mission and take her down. She knew that because that was exactly what she would do.

Her mind shifted to Deja Jordan, the woman that had apprehended Raul. *She broke into our home and took him. She chose to make this very personal.* Deja had broken Caylee's promise to Raul, that she would keep him safe. Jordan had been in magazines, on TV, and on the net. She was the new darling child of Social Enforcement, and the TRC had packaged her perfectly for the public. Taking her down was going to be more than satisfying for Caylee; it was going to be retribution.

The chopper was armed with a custom, side mount machine gun. She would be manning in when they came to land on Unit J's roof to extract Raul. The M249 could be hooked up in the mount at the last minute, so all watching the chopper flying by would simply assume they were on their way to an accident or transporting a patient.

She got in as he started the main rotor spinning. It whipped the ice cold air as she shut the door, her eyes stinging slightly from the blast the blades generated. Caylee slid on the headset and mic, so she could communicate with Faust. She checked her watch. It was coming up on mid-afternoon. Assuming Andy had poisoned the food for the guards and staff, they were already going to start showing symptoms. Sweats, extreme cramps, vomiting, diarrhea. It would hit them hard and fast. From what Travis had indicated, the cramping alone would leave most of them doubled over in agony for hours.

"You all buttoned up back there, pretty lady?" he asked.

"Locked and loaded. Just make sure you bring my side around, so I can take out that guard tower." Charli had identified the guard tower with the anti-air defenses, which was their primary objective. While the guards might be incapacitated, she knew they couldn't assume that.

"No problem-o," Faust said as the helicopter roared to life all around her.

Hang on Raul—I'm on my way ...

Newmerica Penitentiary, Administrative Maximum Facility Florence, Colorado

At lunch, guard Dana Bartlett didn't eat. When someone asked what was wrong, she had replied that her stomach had been bothering her. It was a good cover given what was starting to unfold now that the poison was kicking in with the other personnel that had eaten earlier. It began with some stomach distress, then a hot sweat. She saw it with Captain Harrison wiping the beads of sweat from his extensive brow. A few guards rushed to the restrooms, one running fast, the other seeming to pucker her ass cheeks together as she waddled quickly to the bathrooms. Within a matter of minutes, all the guards began to run for the bathrooms. Some came up short. She saw one leave a drizzle of diarrhea behind him as he ran, and streaks appeared on the pristine floor.

Dana pretended she was feeling it as well, but not as badly as the others. Captain Harrison threw up in the wastebasket of the main security control room; the warm, wet stench of his vomit almost made her throw up as well. Taking one of the vacant seats, she nonchalantly pulled three Sharpies from her pocket and put them in the desk drawer, along with a pack of what appeared to be cigarettes, using Scotch tape to hold them together. She double-checked to make sure the cigarettes/detonator was the one rigged for remote detonation. The last thing she wanted was for the bomb to go off early and lock them all in the prison. Once she was convinced, she made sure the Sharpies were secured on top of the detonator and slowly closed the drawer.

"Something is wrong," he said as a breath fought back another heave.

"It must be food poisoning," she offered.

He nodded. "Are you okay?"

She feigned some discomfort, but gave him a nod. "I'm not as bad as you."

"We are going to need help," he said, throwing up again in the wastebasket. "I called the medical floor—they are down with this too."

"Let me call for EMS," she said. Harrison nodded.

She did not dial the number he thought; instead her call was answered by Travis. "What's the word?" he said.

"This is Florence ADMAX (Administrative Maximum Facility). We have an emergency situation. Please send EMS immediately," she said.

"On our way Charli," Travis replied.

"They are coming sir," she said.

"Can you get around?" Harrison asked.

Dana nodded. "I must have dodged the worst of it so far."

"Good," he moaned, clearly fighting back the urge to throw up again. "Take my badge. My PIN is 9966. I need you to go and check the facility. When you get back, we'll need to lock this place down and call for help."

She took his ID badge and nodded, having already committed his PIN to memory from her bodycam footage. It was a formality. She already had a plan for circumventing access to the facilities she had identified. It was helpful that Harrison was playing into her hand so well. "Shouldn't I go and let the medics in?"

"Go," he said, trying to stand, but hunched over from the stomach cramps. "Do a sweep; see who is still free; then get the facility locked down." Harrison stumbled out, heading for the bathroom. Because of the look on his face, she actually felt pity for him.

Her first stop was the server room for the prison. Once inside the room, she placed six of the Sharpie pens between two of the big, black computers, taping them to one of the servers. With a clenching of her fist, per Travis's instruction, she crushed the cigarette package which combined the chemicals inside, starting the sequence to set them off. With a little effort, she wedged the pack of cigarettes-camouflaged detonator inside on top of the Sharpies.

Closing the door she started back down the hall. A loud bang went off in the server room behind her, and then a flash of red appeared as the fire alarms went off. A whooping sound filled the air. Dana held back her grin. The explosion would give them two advantages—the cameras could no longer be controlled; they would be frozen in position. It wasn't enough to lock down the prison – not yet. Secondly, the fire alarm automatically would summon fire and rescue units to the prison. *A little chaos will give us the cover we might need.*

Dana's next stop was down the hall to the guards' locker room. She could hear the groans and hot splashes coming from the bathroom as she gathered up what she had smuggled in. The det cord had been the hardest material to bring in. She had sewn most of it into her uniform pants legs and had pulled it free. Travis had rigged a detonator that would work with one of the rooftop lights to provide the necessary charge.

Jogging down the long hallway from the central command center, she reached the guards who controlled the main gate access. One was curled up on the floor, clutching his stomach in agony. The other was in the bathroom, groaning loudly between wet splashes in the toilet. *Geez Andy, how much of that stuff did you use?* "We've got an ambulance incoming," she said, glancing at the cameras and seeing Travis and Andy approaching. "I'm letting them in." She used Harrison's card and PIN to activate the main gate. The big chain-link fence automatically opened, and the vehicle came in.

"Close up behind me," she said to the guard on the floor who was struggling to get on his hands and knees. He nodded that he understood as she left the room. *I need to get them inside. Caylee will be here in a few minutes.*

Ten minutes later ...

Deja sat on the toilet in the guards' bathroom and felt as if all of her internal organs were attempting to get out of her rectum at the same instant. Everything was liquid at this point of her illness, and just trying to sit up made her stomach muscles ache in protest. She eyed the toilet paper roll, but knew deep down that she was nowhere near done with her ordeal. As if to confirm it, in the next stall she heard another guard moaning followed by what sounded like someone dumping a bucket of water into the toilet bowl.

She saw the sweat drip from her nose down onto her pants as she hunched over. *We must have had something bad in the food. That's the only thing that makes sense.* Outside the stall, she heard someone vomit in the sink, groaning madly, then saying, "Oh God—make this stop!"

As she sat there, another wave of cramps swelled up within her. Her mind was torn between the pain and the humiliating feeling of getting sick and a new thought. *If we are all down sick, who's watching the facility?*

What if this isn't simply food poisoning? Her mind went to one place—Raul Lopez. It made sense. If someone was going to break out Raul, they would have to deal with the guards first. This had to be a breakout. *They are coming for Raul!*

As she exhausted another squirt into the toilet, she began to unwind a massive handful of toilet paper. *I have to get to him. That's where she will come.*

Three minutes later ...

Dana met with Travis and Andy as their ambulance pulled up, both perfectly attired in their EMS uniforms. They unloaded a rolling gurney and followed her lead. She took them out of the main facility and into the open yard where the wind had picked up. The air made her eyes ache, but Dana ignored it, leading them down the shoveled sidewalks, around Unit B, then out toward Unit J.

She badged them in, whispering in a low tone. "So far the guards are incapacitated," she said. Leading them into the unit, they carried the gurney up the steel staircase and led them to a cell. She manually overrode the lock with Harrison's badge. It opened and a young man stood back from the cell door as if he were nervous and stunned by their appearance.

"Raul Lopez," she stated.

"Yes."

"We're here to get you out."

He eyed them suspiciously, not moving. Andy spoke up. "We're friends of Caylee's."

Just mentioning her name made him smile.

Dana turned to her counterparts. "I have to clear the roof. Get him ready to move." She bolted out of the cell. Her next mission was to clear the roof of antennae so that the helicopter could land.

She had given herself access to the system and swiped her card and entered her PIN. She used her pocket note pad of paper to wedge the door open. Dana then went up the last utility set of stairs to the roof. Taking the stairs three at a time, she reached the roof door in less than a half-minute. It was difficult to force open, but she managed and was hit instantly with a gust of icy wind. Stepping out onto the small landing, she saw the slightly sloped roof and the antenna.

She reached into her coat and pulled out the det cord that Travis had procured. Travis had given her a simple detonator. All she had to do was remove one of the rooftop emergency light bulbs and jam it in the socket.

Uncoiling the material, she realized that Travis had given her far too much cord, but she was thankful. She removed the light bulb that flashed on and off, and started to step out on the landing to wrap the cord around the base of each antenna.

Four minutes later ...

Andy watched the big, open bay of Unit J as Travis tried to explain the basics of their plan to Raul. He was talking about someone named Ted; Andy only caught bits and pieces of their conversation as he spotted another guard moving to the door of the access staircase. It was a stocky female, more muscles than anything else. Her uniform shirt was wet and stained, no doubt from vomit and a vain attempt to clean it. She was focused, not on them, but on Dana.

Oh shit ...

It had to be one of the operatives. During all of their late night planning sessions, the rule Caylee had made clear was that someone had to be with Raul at all times. Period. No exceptions. He was tempted to point out to Travis what was happening, but there simply wasn't time.

Andy took off, heading for the staircase himself.

Two minutes later ...

Dana had just finished wrapping the last antenna with the det cord and was about to plug in the detonator when the door flew open, and she saw Rita Zhang holding a pistol on her. "Hold it right there," she called out as the wind tore at her. Rita took a step forward while Dana slowly and carefully rose to her feet.

Dana backed away from where she had been kneeling, and Rita moved into the same spot, just past the excess coils of the det cord that lay on the snow-blown gravel of the roof landing. "You—this is all you!" Rita said. "What are you doing up here?

"Redecorating," Dana replied, stepping back.

"You're working with Leatrom," she said. Her face was turning beet red either from the frigid blowing air or from the poison in her system. Either way, Dana didn't care.

"Where's your partner?"

"Don't you worry about him," Rita said, wincing in agony. She started to double over, but caught herself before Dana could make a move.

"Lay flat on the ground and I won't put a bullet in your head."

It was then that Dana evaporated in the wind—replaced by Charli Kasinski. The change was caused by Andy stepping slowly and quietly through the door to the stairs on the landing. He didn't have a gun and so far, Rita hadn't noticed him. No doubt the wind was masking any noise he made. She wanted to wave him off, to say something, but to do so would only alert the operative that stood between them.

He's going to get both of us killed!

Ten seconds later ...

Oh shit! Andy saw Charli with her hands in the air, and the operative with her back to him, gun aimed at the woman he loved. *This is an operative—just like Caylee. If I screw this up, I'm as good as dead, and so is Charli.* That knowledge allowed him to summon the calm he needed to act.

At his feet were several loops of det cord. *If I can get this around her neck, it might just give us a chance.* Bending down slowly, he picked it up. Charli was looking at the operative, deliberately not at him.

He lifted the loops of explosive cable and then brought them down around the neck of the operative, twisting them tight.

For an instant, he thought it might work, that he might choke her. The gun lowered and Charli darted toward the two of them as he started to ride the operative like a wild bucking bronco. The guard turned hard one way, then snapped back throwing him off his balance. He held on, hoping that Chari would spring at her, but he couldn't see her in the commotion.

Twisting the det cord tighter, the operative grabbed the cord with one hand; with the other, she aimed the gun over her shoulder and fired. The explosive crack of the gun so close to his own head panicked Andy. The bullet just missed his leg. His footing slipped, and he dropped down onto the gravel roof landing.

She whipped around to see who had dared attack her, leveling the pistol right between his eyes. *Oh fuck!*

Out of the corner of his eyes he saw Charli jam the detonator into the light socket. There was a bang from the blasting cap, enough to make the operative start to turn, unsure of the new threat. A millisecond later, just as she started her turn, the det chord erupted with the sound of a shotgun going off. The shockwave hit him hard, knocking him back slightly and making his chest throb.

The cable had been around the throat of the operative. Her neck was gone with the blast. The concussion threw her body down to the ground and sent her head onto the small pad on the roof where Andy stood. A mist of blood splattered his pants and coat. The antennae were gone as well, toppled over in the wind. For a moment, Andy simply stood there as the wind whipped the smoke off of the roof.

Then he saw Charli. She came over to him and hugged him. Andy was so stunned, he could barely move, but he slowly returned the gesture. "That was brilliant," she said.

Andy nodded back nervously. "I had no idea it would be so loud," he said, noticing for the first time that he was shaking.

Charli kissed him quickly. "Come on tiger. We've got to secure the package. Our ride is on the way."

Four minutes later ...

Deja struggled to walk because the stomach cramps were so strong. Her body was screaming to lay on the floor and curl up in a ball, but she ignored the urge. She made her way to the armory where she fumbled with the shotgun, dropping some of the shells on the floor as she loaded the weapon. If Leatrom was here, she was not taking any chances. Deja planned on shooting first.

The blare of the fire alarms only added to her feeling of tension. This has to be a distraction of some sort. We're all incapacitated. As much as she wanted to tune them out, she couldn't. If anything, they were a reminder that something was unfolding ... something she had to stop.

Once in the hallway, she felt her bowels begin another assault. There was a bathroom down only 20 feet away, but to her it seemed as if it was miles from her.

Fuck it. She let it go. A warm wetness filled her pants and ran down her right leg. The stench of excrement was instant, but she ignored it. All that mattered was getting to Raul. If Leatrom was in the building, that was where she would be.

One minute later ...

Faust Kidder made a wide swing over the prison in the helicopter. "Time to make some music," he said. Caylee slid open the side hatch and mounted the M249, preparing the weapon to fire. As he made the arc toward the roof of Unit J, a blast of machine gun fire came from the guard tower before she could even get it in her sights. Tracers lit the sky, hitting the helicopter and punching through the thin metal sides all around her.

Faust, to his credit, spun hard to bring her side of the chopper to bear on the tower. Caylee opened up on the tower. The first bullets missed, but she quickly adjusted, opening up full automatic on the tower. Glass shattered under the assault, and some of the spray of her rounds went low, tearing into the tower. The shooting from the position ceased almost instantly.

The helicopter seemed to start to vibrate, then waver. "Uh oh," Faust's voice came over the headset. "We've got problems."

"Talk to me."

"She's fighting me—we are losing hydraulic fluid."

"Get me over the roof," she ordered, and the helicopter dipped slightly, as if it were fighting the pilot.

"I don't think you understand," Faust said. "In five minutes this bird is toast. I've got to make a landing."

Caylee's mind was used to making big decisions quickly. "Make a low and slow pass on the roof. Then get your ass out of here."

"Coming up in 10 seconds," Faust said. "Good luck. Tell Travis I'm sorry," he said.

The edge of the roof came into view, some twelve feet below her, just over the antennea. Caylee jumped without a thought of hesitation. She hit the sloped portion of the roof that was covered with snow, and for a moment thought she might simply roll off of the roof. Clamoring for a grip, she punched her hands down and found the peak of the structure, grabbing hard. The helicopter roared on past her, black smoke trailing behind it as Faust headed for flat ground somewhere far from the prison.

She didn't wait to see the landing, but instead used her hands to grapple her way across the sloped roof to the flat landing area. When she set foot there, she saw a headless body, its neck burned and blown apart, splattered on the snow-covered roof. Three yards away lay the head of the operative that belonged to the body. Blood spray was everywhere on the disturbed snow. The open eyes of the severed head stared off into nothingness.

Well, there's something you don't see every day ...

Raul looked at the trio of rescuers and was still not entirely convinced. *Maybe they want to frame me, make it look like I was escaping.* The faces were not familiar: a prison guard and two EMS workers. *If Deja is playing some stunt, I am not going to fall for it.*

"I'm not going without Ted, and I want to see Caylee before I do anything," he demanded, crossing his arms.

"Look kid," the heavily muscled man in an EMS uniform said. "We need to get you to the roof ASAP."

Suddenly a figure appeared wearing a winter coat. He looked at her with stunned disbelief. "Caylee!" he said. There was a temptation to move to her and hug her, but Raul kept it in check.

"I told you I'd make sure you were safe," she said, giving him a rare grin. She then turned to the burly man. "We have a problem. The helicopter was hit and Faust is making a crash landing."

The big man nodded. "Fallback time. The ambulance is in the north parking lot near the entrance."

"Ted needs to come with us," Raul stated for Caylee's attention.

She eyed him for a moment, "Alright then." Turning to the female guard, she said "Get this Ted out."

It was at that moment that the gunshots started. Five fast shots from the commons area—two ricocheting off of the cells next to him. He dove for cover.

Caylee went flat as well, though the burly male moaned as a blood spot formed on his EMS uniform's left shoulder. "Fuck," he groaned. "I'm hit."

"How bad Travis?" the female guard asked.

"I'll live," he said as another trio of shots echoed throughout Unit J, pinging ricochets off of the concrete walls. "Does anyone have a bead on that asshole?"

Caylee slithered along the floor of the landing outside of the cells as she spoke. "Charli, go to the left. I've got the right."

The other EMS male lay behind the gurney. "I'm staying right here."

There was a long period of silence as Caylee and Charli moved, spreading out. Raul lay flat against his closed cell door. When they were some 50 feet apart, Caylee nodded to Charli who slowly stuck her head over the edge of the platform.

A moment later she jerked back as shots hit the concrete where her head had been. Charli pointed down. "Under you, ten to the left," she whispered, brushing the shattered concrete dust out of her hair.

Caylee coiled up, back against the cell doors, and then launched herself over the rail. One hand grabbed it, swinging her in a tight arc as she leapt over the edge to the floor below. Charli moved down a foot and came out with her gun aimed, firing a shot down as well, the sound bouncing everywhere around them.

Raul didn't hesitate; he ran for the stairs to join Caylee. *I'm not letting her fight my battle without me.*

The guard's face was known to her thanks to Charli's smuggled bodycam footage—it was Dominic Gant—NSF operative. She was hunched over. His face was so wet with sweat that it soaked his guard's uniform collar. The moment he saw her, his gun was instantly in motion, sweeping toward her. Caylee's was already out.

The shot from above, no doubt from Charli, made him jerk, throwing off his shot at Caylee. She was far less distracted, squeezing the trigger and compensating for his move, her landing, and at least two other variables that her brain adjusted for.

Her bullet hit his right arm inside of the elbow, forcing him to drop his pistol and whip about from the kinetic impact of the shot. This was an operative. She could not afford him another chance. Dominic dove for the pistol he had dropped with his left hand. Caylee stopped, held her breath, and squeezed the trigger again two times.

Both bullets hit him in the chest. The operative fell, face forward, onto the concrete. He lay on top of his pistol, blood oozing a river from under him onto the floor. Raul appeared at the stairs, but she managed to keep her focus on Dominic.

In three brisk steps, she stood over him and fired a round into the back of his head, splattering blood and gray matter all over the floor. She then put a fresh magazine in her gun. Raul looked at her and said nothing as if he was not surprised at all. "Professional courtesy," she said. "We are all clear down here," she called up. "Let's get moving."

Andy and Charli carried down the gurney while another prisoner, Ted, helped Travis down. "Travis, get on the gurney."

"I can walk," he said.

"I know," she countered. "Lay there; have your gun ready. We'll throw a blanket over you. They won't be expecting a bleeding EMS driver to fire."

He nodded and lay down. Caylee turned to Ted, who she recognized from his time in the Senate. "I thought you were dead," she said.

"There are days I feel that way," he said flashing a smirk.

She nodded at the dead operative on the floor. "Pull off his clothing and put it on." Ted stared at her, confused. "He's covered in blood."

"If we encounter any other guards, they'll know it is a breakout. We brought a uniform for Raul." She nodded to Andy who pulled the folded clothes from the gurney. "I can't explain a prisoner helping us. A guard, even one with some blood on him ... well that might buy us some time."

Ted nodded and Caylee asked Andy to help him as Raul stripped off his orange jumpsuit. Charli helped Travis wrap his wound, and Caylee kept her eyes on the door. Up above her, the other prisoners of Unit J all moved to their cell doors and watched in stunned amazement.

The uniform that Ted wore was wet with blood and a size too big, but it was passable. She had correctly guessed Raul's clothing size, and he looked every bit the part of a guard, except for the orange prison Crocs.

Caylee took the gun from the dead operative and handed it to Ted. "You know how to use one of these?"

He grinned a smile that she remembered seeing on television a half decade or more ago. "I'm from Texas," he said proudly, tucking the gun in his pocket.

"Alright," she said to the group in a low tone. "We move and move fast. We get in the ambulance and then Charli will blow the security system. By now," she said glancing at the red flashing fire alarm lights, "fire and EMS are probably on-scene. Just pretend you know what you are doing and keep moving."

There were nods all around. The group started to the exterior door. Things had already gone wrong. Their primary plan of using the helicopter was trashed, and while the operatives were negated, Travis had been wounded. Her mind went over all of the possible risk points, but there were more than she could mentally calculate. *We are still a long way from getting out of here.*

Deja leaned against the wall as she stumbled down the hall. She needed it for support. Her body was wet from sweat and her own excrement. Her legs quivered with each protesting step. It was as if her physical being was fighting her. While she tried to mentally tune out the blare of the fire alarm, she couldn't.

She came up on the main hallway junction and stopped. *If they are coming from Unit J, they have to pass here.* Chambering a round in the shotgun, she held it tight, still leaning on the wall for support. Her stomach cramps made her hunch over slightly despite her will.

Her plan was simple. She would shoot the moment she saw them, kill Raul and that bitch Leatrom. Then cut them in half with the shotgun. *I can't afford a shootout with an operative.* A fireman came around the corner and she hesitated. He rushed up to her. "Are you okay?"

"Do I fucking look okay?" she snapped back.

"We are on the scene now," he assured her. "Let me get you a stretcher."

"No!" she roared at him. "Take care of the others. I'm waiting for someone!"

Caylee saw the fireman round the corner and heard bits of their conversation between the wails of the fire alarm. The last bit, "I'm waiting for someone!" was a female voice, loud and anguished. He came back heading toward them. "What happened here?" he asked, staring at the blood on Ted's uniform.

"He fell, got cut. We've got this," Caylee said in an authoritative tone. The fireman nodded and moved past them, deeper into the complex.

As they approached the intersection, she held her hand up for them to stop. They did. She moved next to Charli and whispered, "Someone around the corner."

"So I heard. How do you want to play it?"

Caylee's mind raced. "You and Andy take Travis across. There's nothing out of the ordinary with that. Once you get on the other side, signal me if there is trouble. The rest of you," she said softly, turning to Raul and Ted. "Hang here with me."

Charli nodded and they rolled across the intersection with the gurney between them. "Hold it!" the voice called from around the corner. "Let me see his face." Andy reached down and uncovered Travis's face for the person. "Alright, move on," the ragged voice said.

Once on the other side, Charli stopped. She held up her index finger for *one*. With a chopping motion, she indicated that the person was on the same side of the corridor as Caylee. She then motioned as if she were holding a shotgun, chambering a round, and pulling the trigger. Charli then mirrored the hunched over stance of the woman.

Great—a shotgun. Shotguns were indiscriminate murder machines. They had no friends, especially when fired indoors. Even a moron could hit someone with a shotgun in a tight corridor. The shot pattern in that corridor will be brutal. *We are on both sides of the hall, which gives us an advantage.* Looking over at Charli, Caylee made a hooking gesture meaning to *go around the corner.* She then made a shooting gesture, with the number one—*fire one shot at her.*

Charli nodded and moved to the edge of the corridor, as did Caylee. She lowered her stance seeing that Charli was coming in high. Holding up three fingers, she counted down as Charli watched.

With the precision of a highly trained Secret Service agent, Charli angled around the corner and fired. As she pulled back, the shotgun roared, making Caylee's left ear pop and ring as she came around the corner and fired two rounds at the woman that was huddled against her side of the hall. One shot missed, but the other one hit her, knocking her back. She still clung to the shotgun in her outstretched hand. Bits of ceiling tile, caught by the shotgun's blast, rained down in the hallway as Caylee took very precise aim at her target's right hand holding the shotgun and fired again. Blood squirted as the bullet hit between her index and ring finger, they drove out through her wriest. The black woman recoiled her empty hand wailing in pain. *She won't be pulling the trigger with that hand.*

Quickly darting forward, her gun still aimed, she closed on the guard. Then she saw the face and could not help but smile. "Ms. Jordan," she said formally. *I have been waiting to meet you.*

The woman reeked of feces, and there was a slick trail of excrement from where she had come down the hallway. Her right hand was shattered by the bullet, and she had taken another in her knee. Bits of bone poked through from a nearly severed index finger and her wrist, the white of the bone shimmer under the florescent lights. Caylee kicked the shotgun down the corridor, keeping her own pistol on Deja Jordan.

Deja's eyes narrowed as she looked up. "You."

"That's right," Caylee said. "Me."

Raul came up next to Caylee followed closely by Ted. "Give me the gun Caylee," he said. "I'll do it."

Caylee didn't respond for a moment. *I should, but I can do better than a quick death.* Raul, do you trust me?"

"Of course."

She lowered her weapon. Raul reacted instantly. "Aren't you going to kill her?"

Caylee squatted so that she was face to face with Deja Jordan, studying the pain she was fighting. "No. Killing her is easy at this point. I speak from experience. I know she hurt you, but if you kill her, she's free. She needs to suffer with the consequence of her failure."

"Fucking do it!" Deja demanded in a growl through clenched teeth. "Go ahead, shoot me!"

Caylee shook her head and grinned. *Her humiliation at losing is so great, she wants the easy out.* "Not today Ms. Jordan. Not today. One, you want me to. Two, you work for people that expect and demand positive outcomes. You have failed. The people that pull your strings hate failures, and they destroy those that make them look bad. No, the best revenge on you is to let you live."

Raul was stunned and Caylee gave him a slow glance. After a moment of silence, he nodded. "It doesn't seem right."

Ted spoke up. "Trust her," he said. "They will destroy her for letting us get away. You are better than this…better than her."

"Ted is right," she assured him. Leaning forward she got right in Deja's face. "I know who you are Ms. Jordan. They made you a hero of the cause. Now you are their failure. They will ruin you for making them look bad. You'll be tempted to set that right. But know this. I read that interview with your mother in Minneapolis. If you come after any of us, I want you to know that she will die … slowly … painfully. Do you understand?"

The mention of Deja's mother shattered the anger and pain that wracked her face. Her mask of defiance was replaced with that of a little girl who was afraid. "No … "

"Good, you understand." Caylee rose to her feet. "Let's move out."

Raul paused for a moment, and she turned to watch him. Extending his foot, he put it on the knee that had been shot and pushed down, grinding his Croc hard into the wound. Deja wailed in agony, blood still drizzling from her blasted hand. He did it for two full seconds and then turned to Caylee.

"That was for *my* mother," he said. He spit on Deja, and the wet projectile hit above her left eye.

When they reached the ambulance, the fire department was carrying in hoses and stretchers. Guards lay along the entrance to the administrative facility, some covered in their own vomit, all twisted in pain. Andy tried to ignore them. His heart was still pounding in his head as they hoisted Travis into the back of their stolen ambulance and closed the door.

Police cars were coming in as well. No doubt a local panic was caused by reports of shots being fired and the entire prison staff being incapacitated.

Charli slid into the driver's seat, and he sat next to her. As they cleared the main gate, she turned on the sirens and pulled out her phone. She dialed a number, and then sped away. Andy understood, having committed the plan to memory. In the prison's main control room, her call set off the last bomb. With the control room taken out, the system would automatically lock down the Supermax.

"I can't believe we got away," Andy said, noticing his fingers still trembling.

"We're not out of this yet," Charli replied, turning onto State Road 67.

"I won't feel safe until we are back in Tennessee." She accelerated the ambulance as they passed several police cars from Pueblo's sheriff's department, rushing toward the prison.

"That stunt you pulled on the roof," she said. "You could have gotten yourself killed."

He nodded his concession to her point. "I couldn't let anything happen to you."

Charli smiled back. "We blew the head off of an operative!" she said with a morbid chuckle.

"Yeah," Andy said, adjusting himself in the seat. "That was pretty awful … and cool."

A voice from the open panel behind them rang out. It was Travis. "Hey you lovebirds, save it for later. I got shot back here."

For a brief moment, everyone in the ambulance laughed.

Raul leaned over Travis as Charli worked on wrapping his wound. He made eye contact with Caylee and looked at her face, smiling. "I knew you would come for me. I told Deja that."

"We're friends," she replied. "Most of mine are here, in this ambulance with us."

"They killed my mother. They have my sister still."

She shook her head and smiled proudly. "No they don't. We got Maria out of California a while ago. She's in Tennessee waiting for you."

He wanted to cry. Deja had lied to him, telling him that she was still a prisoner. Suddenly he wished he hadn't listened to Caylee, that he had shot her there in the hall. Wiping the tears from his face, he felt Ted pat him on the shoulder, a gesture of reassurance. "I thought I'd lost her."

"We aren't like them Raul," Caylee said. "They like painting themselves as the good guys, but they never would have been willing to even try what we did. I know. I worked for them. Bringing you back—it sends a message to the world—it defines our differences with Newmerica. It will give people hope."

"She's right," Ted said. "Hope is their enemy. They are masters of smothering it, but in the end, hope always prevails."

There, in the back of the ambulance, Raul realized it was more than hope. Memories of Father Ryan came back as he spoke about the struggles the church had faced with the Newmerica regime. "Not just faith. It is a matter of faith. I had faith in Caylee. I knew she would come. They don't just hate hope; they hate faith."

"Well," Caylee said. "They can't take that from you either."

EPILOGUE

"Your vote is important only if you use it correctly."

Atlanta, Georgia

Trip stood in front of the Atlanta State Capitol as the bulldozers plowed the remnants of the autonomous zone into a pile of worthless debris. The crude plywood structure and sandbag positions were surrounded by litter and refuse. The stench was a mix of garbage, urine, and feces. The occupiers had not bothered to even bag their trash. On the steps leading up to the capitol, he saw crude comments spray painted on the once stately stone. "Fuck America!" "Death to the Pretendor!" The last one made him shake his head. *They didn't even bother to spell it right.*

His trusted aide, Captain Judy Mercury moved up beside him. "We won, but the cost was high."

Reager nodded. "The cost would have been higher to leave them in control of Atlanta. It would have inspired them to pull this stunt elsewhere. I'm willing to bet that the holdouts in St. Louis are already starting to question whether it is worth it."

"I saw the intel reports on Iowa."

Trip nodded glumly. The Illinois National Guard had pushed across the border and were fighting the Iowa defenders around Davenport. *No doubt they are trying to secure the Rock Island arsenal in the Mississippi.* He had plans for dealing with this new front, but he'd have to tap fresh troops. *Razorback is proving to be complex and costly.* "They are trying to distract us there. I intend to make them pay for their arrogance," was all he was willing to reveal on the matter.

"Have you seen the Atlanta casualty reports?"

He nodded. *High—too damn high.* "You can't run a race without breaking a sweat," he said grimly as a front-end loader scooped a heap of garbage off of the street and put it in the back of a dump truck that the Army had commandeered. After a few moments of thought, he added, "The new Congress once they are sworn in will likely haul me in front of them, demand answers, question every decision I made."

"Maybe not," Captain Mercury replied.

"Oh, they will," he assured her. "It is the nature of politicians. We may be on the same side, but that doesn't make me exempt from their oversight and meddling. They are all armchair generals. I'm used to civilians questioning how I provide them their freedom." *That doesn't mean I like it. I merely am used to it.*

"It's going to take some time to refit some of our units," she said.

"We don't have a lot of time on our hands, so work fast."

"Are we going somewhere?"

Trip nodded to her. "Home."

"So the reports about a Texas succession are true."

"I sure as hell wish they weren't," he sighed. "The whole thing stinks worse than this place does." *I wonder if the leaders of this uprising are being played ... or do they know they are being used and don't care?*

"I'd hate to have to fire on fellow Texans," Mercury replied.

"So would I," he replied. "But that is the nature of civil wars. We don't get to choose who we are up against. We simply have a duty."

"At least we have New Hampshire still in the mix."

Yes ... at least we still have New Hampshire ...

Colebrook, New Hampshire

The survivors of the assault on Lisbon and the harassers had taken a long and twisted route to reach the town of Colebrook. A Sons of Liberty cell from Kentucky had been operating out of the tiny town since the start of The Defiance, as it was now being referred to by even the TRC-backed media. They operated out of what had been a sporting goods store located on the Daniel Webster Highway. The store had closed during one of the recessions. The loading docks allowed them to bring the snowmobiles indoors. They had lost one to mechanical problems on the way there. Inside, the locals brought food, changes of clothing, anything the freedom fighters might need.

Su-Hui and Hachi were greeted by a grandmother who led them to an inflatable mattress that was screened off from the others. "It's not much, but you all look like you can use some sleep." They thanked the nameless woman and Su-Hui lowered himself onto the mattress, bouncing slightly as he landed.

"You need to get out of those clothes," his wife insisted. "You stink."

He nodded, doing a quick check of his armpit and finding nothing offensive. It was far easier to respond to her request than to debate it. A shower had been set up in the warehouse portion of the building, and he took his time waiting to use it. The warm water helped clear his mind and ease the ache of some of his muscles. As he stood there, the steam rising around him, he remembered Hachi shooting the officer that had stumbled upon them. *I could have lost her in that bombardment.* As it was, her hearing in one ear was still not back to normal, and she claimed to hear a high pitched hissing. Su-Hui toyed with sending her back to Indiana, but he knew she would not go. *This is for Ya-ting.* His hand drifted to the three bullet casings he wore around his neck as an affirmation of his commitment.

Su-Hui put on some of the clothing that the locals had provided when they arrived, and they went back to their tiny private space. *I'm getting used to wearing flannel shirts.* The clean shirt they left for him was easily a size or two too big, but he didn't care. *It makes me look rugged.*

Trudy came by, carefully sticking her head through the hanging sheet walls. "Knock, knock."

"Come in," he said. Hachi greeted her as well. Trudy had changed too, and for the first time, he noticed the bags under her eyes. *When was the last time either of us got sleep?*

"I thought you should know," she began. "Randy didn't make it out. I talked to the survivors and none of them saw him."

Su-Hui lowered his head for a moment. "Also, on the news, they are broadcasting that the leader of the occupation, General Donaldson, was killed at Lisbon. I saw the photo. I think it was the guy that Hachi shot."

Su-Hui looked at his wife whose mouth hung slightly open in shock. *The universe seeks balance. Did we trade Randy for the General that Hachi shot? It is not a trade I desire, but rather one that the world demands.*

"I didn't know … " Hachi said.

"It's okay. Word is out it was you. You're something of a hero of the cause now. That bastard was the one that shot those people at the State House, General Donaldson. The Ruling Council is making him out to be some sort of hero, but we all know the truth. He was a brutal ass-fucker."

Hachi blushed at Trudy's language, but Su-Hui was used to it. "There's more. Those of us that came through this talked it over a few minutes ago. With Randy being gone, we need someone that is level-headed to take his place. We need a person that doesn't panic under pressure, who can help coordinate the cells and the National Guard. A level head that doesn't upset people."

"I agree," Su-Hui said. "Randy was good at thinking, good at working with people."

"He was," Trudy said slowly. "And we know you will be good at it too."

Her words seemed to hang in the air between them as he processed them. "I—I am not worthy of such an honor. Surely there are others."

"There are. The difference is they want the job. Everyone likes you. You're mature and, frankly, you aren't from America. In some respects, you love this place more than some people that were born here. The National Guard officers agreed as well, not that they really got a vote," she said, smirking.

Su-Hui looked to Hachi who only nodded silently in agreement. He turned his head back to Trudy, summoning his thoughts carefully. "I will not let you down."

She smiled. "I know you won't. The good news is that the job doesn't require you to throw grenades either."

Su-Hui laughed for a moment, remembering his bungle at the NSF headquarters. *I did not ask for this, but I will not ignore the will of those who chose me. I owe it to this country to set it on the right path.* Hachi seemed to be reading his mind. She reached out and took his hand firmly, squeezing it.

Salem, Virginia

Grayson Steele stood in front of the small stone marker with Maddie's name on it. A light misting fell, not quite rain, heavier than a fog. The dampness meant nothing to him as he stood there, staring downward. The happier times was what he wanted to focus on. The holidays they had spent together when she was a child, family vacations, her infectious laughter. As much as he tried to focus on those things, he could not.

Everything had changed with the Fall. He had led his family into hiding. Maddie had almost graduated college. But the specter of the Fall was there, stalking the family's every step. The people that had killed her didn't even know her. They had taken her life because she didn't think or believe the way they wanted.

We paid them back though. The bombing was initially attributed to a gas leak. For a few days, he hoped that might suffice, but the investigators found evidence of the bombs. Just the day before, they had issued a report that the Grays may have had the bombs in the house, and they had prematurely detonated. Why a campus group would have bombs was never fully explained; the TRC was like that—tossing out facts that didn't make sense, but were accepted by most people. In all, some eighteen members of the SE group were killed. *It was pathetic, how they had memorials for them on campus with students crying and holding up banners. These were killers!* No one had held a memorial for the people the Grays had killed. *No one mourns for Maddie other than us.*

He was so lost in his thoughts that he didn't hear David step up next to him. Grayson put his hand on David's shoulder. "I hope this gives her some rest."

David looked at the grave marker, then shook his head. "I don't think so Dad."

"What do you mean?"

"The campus system that allowed the Grays to be there still exists. The culture of hate on the campuses is what led to Maddie's death. You saw them on TV, all upset over the Grays' deaths. Others will step up and take the place of them. We cut out the tumor, but we haven't treated the cancer."

His son's words didn't seem like they came from a seventeen-year-old. David was much more mature. *He didn't have a choice. He had to be.* "So what are you thinking David?"

"We have to set this right. To do that, and we need to go after the professors and administrators that made this possible. We have to take down the system of indoctrinating students and turning them into socialist thugs."

"Do you have a plan?"

David shook his head. "No. I only know that this isn't the end—it's just the beginning."

Grayson said nothing, soaking in his son's words. *He's right. We treated the symptom, but we haven't cured the patient.* "Alright," he said calmly. "We'll need a plan though."

David cracked a thin smile. "For Maddie."

"For Maddie."

The District

Tess Ditka played the video on the large screen in the office of the Vice President-Elect. The memorial tribute to General Donaldson was well produced; she had to admit that. Making Donaldson into a hero who sacrificed himself for the nation was the most polish anyone had ever put on a turd, in her opinion, but it worked. *It's far better than he deserved.*

Of course much of the story was embellished. Instead of having him shot while he was throwing up, he was instead personally leading a charge which led his forces into an ambush. "Against overwhelming odds, despite the chance to withdraw, he heroically made his last stand in Lisbon." The soldiers actually present would know enough to not go public with the real version of events. They would be raining on the parade of Newmerica's latest hero.

"Can we make him a little whiter, and put on some weight?" the Vice President-Elect asked.

"Of course we can," Tess responded.

"I want subtext of this to be seen as a failure of another white male. I don't want that in print, but I want people to associate failure with who he was, rather than what he was fighting for." It was a mantra that her predecessor in the TRC, Becky, had mastered. *Never let a good crisis go to waste. His death can serve as a battle cry for more diversity. Whoever we pick to carry on this war needs to be a person of color, a woman, or some other minority group. That will send the right message, especially when they hand us victory.*

"Excellent idea madam," Tess replied.

"I'd like less coverage about New Hampshire," she said. "The only things the networks need to report on is war crimes and cowardly attacks by these insurgents and our killing them. That will buy us some time until we have a new commander in the field there." A part of her thought that Donaldson had the right idea with the destruction of Lisbon, but it was far too small an example. The bodies of some sixteen SOL terrorists had been found in the rubble, and over eighty-five civilians. She had Tess simply combine the numbers and count them all as insurgents. *If they were harboring the Sons of Liberty, that makes them terrorists.*

"And the coverage of the fall of Atlanta?"

"Talk to the networks. They are spending too much time on it. As far as the rest of the world knows, our brave forces broke out of the siege and are now roaming the countryside, still fighting on. Have them run an investigative series into the war crimes of this Bloodbath Reager. Make him the focus rather than what happened. Have them highlight the racist past of Stone Mountain and paint Reager fighting there as corrupt and racially motivated. Splash up some KKK images in the background every time we talk about Stone Mountain. We need to turn this defeat into a win, and we do that by telling people the right story."

It all sounded good to say out loud, but she knew the truth. General Kotter's surrender had been smothered by the TRC, but from the American news networks, footage had made it to the net, if only for a short time. Broadcasts of Newmerican forces in POW camps were damning. Worse, the Americans had sent snail mail notices to local newspapers and families telling them of the local boys and girls that were now POWs. Despite efforts, word about the Battle of Stone Mountain was getting out.

Matters were more complicated by the rescue of Raul Lopez from the Supermax prison—*by no less than Caylee Leatrom herself!* When the Vice President-Elect had heard about that, she had gone into a rage, throwing things in her office, breaking objects on her shelf. Lopez's Tribunal was to be a capstone event for the citizens, bringing a dangerous terrorist to justice. Now he was free again.

It cost me two operatives—with nothing to show for it. The TRC had played up the People's Tribunal for Lopez so much that all they could do was say nothing. Given enough time, people would move on. Oh, a few would ask questions as to what happened to him—but over time, she had learned, people simply moved to the next hot topic or crisis. Keeping people distracted was a key to holding on to power, and the Ruling Council was masterful at it.

Lopez's rescue had ruined Deja Jordan in the VP's mind. She was recovering in a hospital, but had let Leatrom slip through her fingers. Jordan was badly hurt in the attack, but that wasn't something that the Vice President-Elect thought they could leverage. It was best to bury her along with the Lopez story. *She failed not just me, but the whole nation. It's a shame. She had such potential. Now all she represents is an ugly fiasco.* Maybe the disappointment or her injuries would motivate her to go and kill Leatrom or Lopez? For the time being, however, Deja needed to go home in disgrace. *We will cut off her mother's reparations and take away her house—that might motivate her. She needs to comprehend the price of disappointment. Let her think over just how badly she's failed, and maybe she will find a way to return to our graces.*

Tess left her office, and Alex settled back into her big leather chair. The setbacks of the last few days would all change when she and Daniel were sworn into office. *We will have a new Congress, a loyal one. We will throw out the old Constitution once and for all and put in place a new set of laws that is not antiquated or subject to interpretation. Then we will take back the states that have rebelled and sided with the Pretender President.* She knew deep down that her mother would be so proud of her, that she was showing herself for what she really was, a strong woman of color.

And I will be one heartbeat away from the Presidency ...

Colorado Springs, Colorado

Deja tried to adjust herself in the hospital bed, but every move made her arm ache. She eyed her wrist, held up by wires, with pins screwed into her hands, and secretly wished the surgeons would just amputate it. The doctors told her it would heal, but she would never have full use of her right hand. Just looking at it seemed to make it pulsate with pain.

Her knee throbbed as well. The doctors had given up on repairing it; she was slated to be given an artificial replacement once her hand healed up enough for her to do the physical therapy required with a new knee. They had done enough repairs on it to tide her over, but walking was out of the question. She was facing weeks of surgery, recovery and hard work. Even then, the doctors told her, she would not be the person she was before.

I had her—both Leatrom and Lopez! She was angry at their getting away … angry with herself. In her silent moments in the hospital room, she fumed at Lopez's escape. The only thought that took the edge off of her failure was that two operatives had been killed. Anyone thinking that Leatrom was easy to apprehend … Deja could point to their deaths as evidence that she was anything but easy. Even that was not enough to mask the shame that Deja felt.

When she saw Lopez standing over her with the power of life and death, he had spared her. In her mind, that had been as devastating as being shot. *I would have killed him, without hesitation.* He spared her though, and it hit her hard. *What have I become? I was never a killer before. I tortured that kid and a part of me enjoyed it. My NSF handlers got me to beat up an old man, just to get Raul to talk. I used his mother and sister to try and break him.* None of these were things she could imagine herself doing even a year ago. *They made me into someone I'm not.* She felt indignity over the things she had done. *I need to get back to who I was before.*

She had tried to call the Vice President-Elect to report what had happened, but her call wasn't taken. That was a message all on its own. *I'm no longer the darling child. I've fallen from grace.* Shame, humiliation, and failure were her entire world.

I never asked for the fame that came with bringing in Lopez. Why does losing it hurt so much? As she lay there, fighting the throbs of pain, all Deja wanted was to go home and see her mother. *I need to find myself. I let them make me someone I wasn't. I was seduced by the fame. Now I need to find my old self.*

The Southern White House
Nashville, Tennessee

Raul was ushered into the conference room by a man named Jack and saw his friends that had rescued him. They were all his friends now. It wasn't just the rescue. It was the fact they had come for him in the first place—risking their lives for him. Smiles, even from Caylee, were what greeted him. Another face he saw was that of his sister, Maria. He rushed forward, grabbing her and holding her close. She cried and so did he. He held onto her as if she were all that he had left in life. Time seemed to come to a stop. She had grown since he had last seen her, but none of that mattered. She was alive.

"I don't believe it," he said, finally pulling back enough to see her face, soaking up every detail.

"I was going to say the same thing," she said, wiping away her tears.

Raul looked to the other people in the room … his new family. "I can't thank you enough—"

Caylee cut him off. "You've told us Raul."

"Only a thousand times," Charli said.

"I could stand to hear a little more," Travis said, with a wry smirk on his face, his arm in a sling from his wound.

"You have to admit, this wasn't bad for our first prison break," Andy added with a bit of pride.

Jack, the man that had escorted him to the reunion was smiling broadly. "Raul, you'll be happy to know that the President is going to issue you a pardon later this week—right before he's sworn in for his second term."

"I—I don't know what to say."

"You don't have to say anything," Charli said as Andy moved to her side. "That's the best part. You're free."

"So that's it?"

"Not quite," Jack said. "You just took a dump on the traitors in the District with what you did at Valley Forge. Breaking you out of the Supermax! That rubbed their nose in it. These people don't just walk away. They aren't likely to take this laying down. The one thing we've learned from the progressives is that they escalate, even when they should back down."

"Mr. Desmond," Caylee said. "Your sense of timing leaves much to be desired." She then turned to Raul. "Don't worry about what Jack said. You'll have plenty of protection." He knew by the way she said it that she would be close.

Jack spoke up again. "You've all provided us a much needed public relations coup. The information you got us about the activities of the SEs in California was big enough, but freeing Raul—the hero of Valley Forge, well, that makes great press. I'd like to arrange some interviews. This is a public relations coup."

"I just want to spend some time with Maria." Raul said.

"Jack, let the kid unwind," Charli said.

"Yeah," Andy piled on. "At least let him have a few days."

"Alright," Jack replied, holding his hands up. "You all can take a little downtime. But understand this. A storm is going on out there. While we took Atlanta, New Hampshire is still up in the air. Illinois troops are pushing into Iowa, and now I've got a bunch of Texas crazies trying to form their own country."

"What's your point?" Travis asked.

"This fight is far from over," Jack said.

Raul ignored his words and once more hugged his sister. *My fight, at least for a few days, is done.*

Andy shattered the moment of silence. "I remember Winton Churchill saying that this wasn't the beginning of the end. It was the end of the beginning."

Jack crossed his arms and swayed back slightly. "Churchill wasn't fighting a civil war. We are. We've had some victories, but they've come at a cost. The Newmericans are changing their strategy. They are starting to simply kill off the people in camps. Like all revolutionary movements, they become far more oppressive than the people they overthrew."

Charli spoke up. "We can't give them breathing room. We have to keep going at them."

Caylee shifted in her seat and stood. "Let's get Raul some downtime while we figure out the best way to hurt them."

There were nods around the room, and Raul himself joined them. *I owe it to everyone that has helped me on this journey ... we have to fight on.*

A Sneak Peek at the Next Blue Dawn novel

No Greater Tyranny

PROLOGUE

"If it is not for the betterment of all, it is not for the betterment of one."

Five Years Earlier ...
Ann Arbor, Michigan

Dr. Weber Liu watched the television in his modest home and could not help but smile. The White House was ablaze as rioters swarmed over the security fence, looting the icon of America. The camera cut to protesters swarming the inside of the Capitol as well, tearing down portraits, toppling statues, smashing anything of value.

He had known that these 'peaceful protests' were going to be different. One ANTIFA leader, Daniel Porter, was coordinating the ANTIFA groups and students—something that had not been done up to that point. Also the students that left from the University of Michigan, where he was an instructor, were taking real weapons—homemade mortars and rockets.

He felt a swell of pride at watching the American capital city descend into chaos.

For twelve years he had been a professor at the University of Michigan. While technically he taught social equity classes, the reality was that he was energizing the students for violence. When he taught, he wove a narrative of the corruption of the United States, how it was built on the exploitation of many minority people. He extolled the long criminal history of capitalism. It was a story that the students were more than open to hearing about. Their high school teachers had done their job well, convincing their impressionable minds that America was decadent and needed to be 'reset'. All that Weber Liu did was confirm what they had already been taught.

Liu loved his own backstory so much that he almost believed it himself. A refugee from Chinese oppression, he claimed to come to America with nothing. Despite the prevalent racism, he had saved enough money to go to college and eventually earn his doctorate in philosophy, securing himself a teaching position at a prestigious university. Liu told the tale as him being oppressed at every turn, yet somehow prevailing. He could speak freely about the horrors of America's systemic racism because he claimed he endured and overcame it. It gave him an aura of credibility that he knew resonated with the students who never suspected that it was all a lie.

As he leaned back in his easy chair, watching the flames from burning federal buildings lap up into the smoke-filled skies over Washington DC, Liu knew that the nation was at a tipping point. Many would claim that they saw it coming, but few could claim, as he did, that they had influenced it. It wasn't just the instruction of the students ... it was far more. Weber Liu led a network of Chinese, who, like himself, worked for the Ministry of State Security.

During the last two elections, their activities had been simply to ramp up tensions between the various factions in the United States. They had done it by planting thousands of memes that twisted facts and were aimed at escalating tensions and hate. Liu had been an advocate of backing the more progressive elements of the American government, so he attacked them the most, infuriating them more—making them appear as victims.

Race had been easy to prey upon. Police shootings, whether warranted or not, were twisted by his network of agents into being racially motivated. The defunding the police movement had been supported by his tiny Army of social media posters, using thousands of accounts to make sure that certain hot topics trended on Twitter.

Painting the sitting US President as a tool of the Russians had been easy as well. His cyber team had planted bogus reports, fake emails, and even played with the bank account transfers to make it appear that the Russians were indeed corrupting the President. For Liu and his Chinese handlers, it was a win-win, smearing the other two superpowers and pitting them against each other.

Liu had provided the students going to the riots in DC with money for riot gear. He contributed substantial amounts to their funds for banners, signs, baseball bats, Kevlar—whatever they needed. Discreet cash inducements to other local universities helped them go from peaceful protesters to armed rioters. No one questioned where the money came from. The students didn't care. And because it was cash, there was no paper trail that could link it to him. Money could purchase American influence, especially with the young who did not see the hypocrisy of his benevolence. *It is pitiful that these students are so easily manipulated. We have been able to convince them that capitalism, which enabled them to go to college, is evil. We have enabled them to go to their capital and destroy it. The west is as weak as we have always believed. They are so ignorant. They believe this is all their doing—that it was their idea. They have played into our hands perfectly.*

He had long argued that the way to take America down was to do it from the inside. After his successes in the 2016 election, the Ministry of State Security gave him additional resources, a cyber-attack team, additional social media response personnel, etc. He assumed that his efforts were not isolated. Liu assumed that his nation was a driving factor for the social equality initiatives in the military and in business. The push for businesses to create Diversity and Inclusiveness officers and teams was something that his government backed. *They will only sow more seeds of division, further dividing up America into furious little factions.*

Tonight was the apogee of a political arc. *From this point forward, things will never be the same for the United States.* There was no way that the President of the United States would come through this uprising alive. This was a *coup d'etat* of the highest order. America would be replaced by something else, something new, something that he and his people could manipulate and control.

His phone chirped, and he saw the number. The professor had been expecting this call on his encrypted, private call phone and seeing the number only made him grin more. "Hello," he said picking it up.

"You are no doubt watching the television," the female voice of his handler, Chun Koh, stated. She was a professor at Berkeley and only spoke to him when necessary. She, like he and others in the network of cells, was working hard to undermine the United States from within.

"I am."

"Things have escalated faster than most anticipated."

"Not me," he said, doing what he could to avoid saying, 'I told you so.'

"No, not you. You saw this before most. It appears you were correct about their military."

Liu had sent up a detailed report saying that if a coup had occurred, the American military would sideline itself rather than take sides. "I only applied logic to the situation."

"You have mapped this out quite well. As such, you recognize that this is a rare opportunity, one we must exploit."

"Agreed," Liu replied. "There will be a few weeks of chaos before the new order settles in."

"Our friends will want to know the best way for us to take advantage of this situation."

"I have several thoughts on the matter," he said politely. *More than a few.* "There will be a push for unity. This is only a greater opportunity to keep these people divided. A divided America is a crippled America."

"On this, we are agreed," Koh replied. "Assemble your ideas. I will arrange a secured conference call to review them. In the meantime, I offer you the appreciation of a grateful nation." She hung up before he could even respond.

On the television, he caught a glimpse of a group of young people setting fire to the American flag. He thought for a moment of the old proverb, "May you live in interesting times." *The interesting times are upon us right now ...*

Made in United States
North Haven, CT
24 April 2023

35815343R00193